Maiden of Dawn

Amelia Black

Amelia Black

ISBN-13: 979-8-9902123-0-5

For Rylie

1

The new dawn broke against the horizon like a hen's egg. Maeve crushed herbs beneath her stone pestle and sighed. Her fingers ached, and yet she shouldn't—*couldn't*—stop. Her neighbor Clarissa needed the remedy, and Maeve was responsible for providing it as the solitary priestess of Juno within Ferne. *Later, I will tend to the garden and clean those mushrooms I picked yesterday. I should check on Bertha and see how Lenora is feeling.* She watched the flame of a yellow candle lit for Juno. One candle lit at dawn, one at midday, and the final at dusk. According to her mother, these practices, alongside lifelong devotion and study, allowed Juno's magic to flow through her order.

She turned the page of her weathered novel propped on her desk before her cramped fingers continued their arduous motions. Maeve had mastered the art of solitude during her mother's absence. She hadn't mastered the art of stillness. *At least the story makes for fine company.* Her companions, a group of pirates, were about to unlock an ancient sealed tomb.

A fist slammed against her door. Maeve startled.

"Priestess Maeve!" She recognized the voice. *Clarissa? She shouldn't need the herbal tea yet.* Her heart pounded into her sore fingertips.

"Come quickly. It's Archie. He's broken his arm."

The damp air filled her lungs with moist heat. *Archie?* She snuffed out Juno's candle.

She followed Clarissa's gray-blonde bun and kept pace with her hurried strides. A group of villagers circled Archie before one of the livestock barns. Their faces crumpled in relief at Maeve's arrival.

She dropped to her knees in front of Archie. His snotty, tear-stained face shone beneath the mercurial morning light. Archie's bone protruded through his dark skin—*a clean break.*

"You can – you can fix it?" he cried before his voice broke off into a wail.

"I can, Archie. Yes." Maeve's tone reflected her calm confidence.

She would call upon Juno's power to heal this. Her dedication was stalwart, and her goddess never rejected her call. Maeve gingerly placed her hands above the wound as Archie's mother, Lena, gripped his shoulders and kissed the top of his head.

Juno's magic glowed radiantly beneath her palms and illuminated the slick, glistening blood around the perforation, the bone pink and jagged at the break. The golden magic swirled around his arm. Maeve's forehead beaded with sweat and glistened down her temple like burning morning dew. *I must be strong for Archie.* Her lips moved soundlessly in prayer as Juno's light sank into Archie's skin. The bone slid backward as if she were reversing time. Maeve's fingertips trembled. She pressed her lips together. *I trust that Juno will not let this child suffer. She will heal him.*

In agonizing slowness, the bone disappeared beneath Archie's skin. Juno's magic unraveled like a spool inside her chest. A wet trickle of blood slid from her nostril and dripped from her cupid's bow. A minor discomfort but nothing to be alarmed by. Her nose often bled when healing a severe injury.

His blood congealed. The scab crusted over until the skin was as pink as a baby chick covered the wound. Maeve retracted her shaking hands with an unsteady breath.

"Lady Maeve!" Clarissa caught Maeve's arm before she toppled over. "You've healed him completely."

Maeve swiped the blood from her upper lip.

"Not me, Clarissa. Our gracious goddess Juno healed him. I am merely her conduit."

"Take it easy for the next few days," she advised him and Lena, "to be safe."

"Of course."

"Thank you, Maeve," Archie said softly.

Maeve gently pinched his ruddy cheek and smiled. It was always better to smile through the pain. Her people didn't need to know she felt like her rib cage had been cracked open and its contents spooned out. She would make tea when she returned home. *My mother –* Maeve's empty chest squeezed – *used to drink hot tea after healing.* Maeve wiped her sweaty palms on her beige shirt.

Her quiet stone and wood cabin once housed herself, her mother, and her grandmother. Mostly, she didn't mind it. The space was hers; her village was filled with people she cared about and some she had helped bring into the world. Maeve was needed here. When she was younger, she had toyed with extravagant fascinations about the world outside their tiny village. She imagined herself tending to princes and princesses, traveling with merchants, and seeing marvelous sights of tall towers and endless deserts. But after her mother left, her fanciful dreams wilted like flowers in a vase.

Their village tended to livestock and crops and traded with the northern town of Silvercliff. Maeve, as healer and matriarch of Ferne, couldn't leave. Ferne was her home and her responsibility. She cared for livestock and the land, healing sick trees and plants or guiding a cow through a difficult birth. She had a purpose here. A reason to wake up at dawn and stay up late, ensuring she had remedies for fevers, stomach aches, and blisters. She couldn't use Juno's magic for everything. She would wind up drained and risk passing out. Her mother warned her against pushing past her bodily limits. *I can't heal anymore today. My connection to Juno isn't strong enough.* She could try meditating and asking Juno for more help, but that was a selfish idea. *I'll check on him in a few hours and ensure he's not climbing into barns again.*

"Maeve." Bertha, whose cottage sat squat next to hers, waved from her doorstep.

"Morning." Maeve leaned against the wooden fence. "How's the little one?"

The blonde-haired Lenora wobbled and meandered like a baby fawn in the grass. *She looks more and more like her mother every day.* Maeve remembered when Lenora was born. She helped ease Bertha through the pain of labor with Juno's magic and herbal poultices. It had been her first experience helping someone through childbirth without the help of her mother. Maeve remembered the moment with pride and longing for her family.

"She's teething." Bertha sighed and rested one arm below her swollen midsection. "And the babe is kicking up a storm."

"I'll bring something for her tonight." She smiled. "And something for you, too."

Bertha's round face lit up. "You're a blessing."

An unlit lantern swung near the upper hinge of Maeve's front door, and a prickling, uncertain feeling crawled across her skin. She listened closely to the leaves rustle overhead. A tremor vibrated beneath her feet.

A stampede of hooves barreled down the dirt street. Maeve scowled at the unfamiliar riders, their horses, and shiny armor. *They aren't merchants and traders from Silvercliff.* A man in a black helmet with two curling ram-like horns swung down from his steed and barked orders at the laborers mending a fence. One strong breeze might knock her sideways, but Maeve rolled up her sleeves and cornered her exhaustion into the back of her mind.

"Hail, travelers," she yelled as other riders scattered around the town in a deliberate, controlled formation.

"What news?" She walked with her chin held high and smiled pleasantly.

"Summons from our noble King Marcus Hagken, Lord of the Golden Coast and rightful crown to the Gilded Kingdom." The soldier in horned helm said with a grim line to his soured mouth. "All able-bodied individuals in this region are conscripted into his most righteous army."

Maeve glanced at the men surrounding her. Their hands rested upon the hilts of their swords.

"We're a simple farming village. We're not warriors or soldiers. If you need food, we can provide a little, but it's a tad early in the season." Maeve said, "My memory could be faulty, sir, but King Hagken doesn't have authority over this region.

"I believe he was deposed — seven or eight years ago? Ferne falls under the protection of General Fenris."

The rebellion and insurgence weren't as fresh in her mind, but she recalled her relief and gratitude when the fighting remained within the capital walls and hadn't bled into their peaceful town.

"King Hagken was *wrongfully* deposed. He is now requesting aid from his loyal people to return the throne to him."

Maeve looked at the villagers around her, her friends and neighbors, to their worried and skeptical faces.

"I'm sorry, sir, but we have no soldiers here."

"Do you speak for this village and its people?"

"I do."

"You are choosing to ignore the summons of your king." His gray eyes narrowed.

Maeve resisted the urge to call him out. Hagken wasn't her or anyone's king. Their modest homestead fell under the protection of Fenris, the war general from the now independent Lupine Forests, who fought alongside Hagken before betraying him and usurping the capital, Pyrite, and throne. However, she couldn't see how her people would aid in the fight or why they should. Neither the king nor the general paid much care to their little village. They paid their taxes and carried on with their lives, unconcerned with the political machinations and intrigue of the courts.

"You say you fall under the protection of General Fenris. Does he have men stationed here? A town militia?"

Maeve shook her head. It made her dizzy. She swallowed back the rise of bile in her throat. The soldier smiled razor-thin and terrible. *Oh no.* Maeve realized with a quiet dawning horror her mistake. The soldiers dismounted and grabbed her neighbors. The one nearest to Maeve tried to snatch her, but she slipped from his grip and ran. Many tried to fight, but their pitchforks and shovels were nothing compared to polished steel. People were knocked to the ground and kicked into submission. The village erupted into a panicked frenzy like a spooked stallion.

Bertha screamed high and shrill. Maeve bolted into a limping run toward her.

"What are you doing?!" she yelled. Her hands couldn't find purchase on the slick, cold metal of the stranger's gauntlet when she attempted to pull his arms off Bertha. Bertha screeched for Lenora who was being carried into an enclosed wooden cart. Maeve's heart stuffed inside her throat. Children and women were being dragged into wooden carts driven by two muscular black horses.

"Leave her be," Maeve yelled, "she's pregnant. Get away from her."

"If she calms down, then I'll let her go." The stranger shoved and tried to push Maeve's hands away.

"I'm calm. I am!" Bertha cried, snot and tears dripping from her face, her wide blue eyes searching for Lenora.

"I've already said we have nothing to offer in this conflict. What do you want?" Maeve demanded as the horrible and terrifying screams of friends and neighbors filled her skull. *Gods above. There is nothing I can do to stop them.*

"We're following orders," he replied gruffly. His meaty, cold hand locked around the bend of her elbow. "Now you'll come with me."

Maeve shoved fruitlessly. Her limbs were wet noodles. She dug her boots into the dirt and scrambled for purchase to wrench her arm free. The man ignored her. He ignored her questions. He ignored her actions.

Her chest slammed into the hay-covered floor of the cart. Maeve gasped and looked into nearly a dozen women's shivering, scared faces. She clambered to her knees, and her heart ran like a frightened rabbit inside her chest. Someone wailed.

"Stay put," the man said, his voice colder than ice across her skin. "Runaways will be killed."

Maeve got to her feet, numb, and realized everyone's eyes were upon her. They looked to her for guidance. Yet, she was as lost as anyone else. They were deer, and these men were wolves. *What chance could we possibly have against them?* Even if she could call on Juno's power, her magic was never to be used for violence, and part of her feared what would happen if these men knew what she could do.

She swallowed hard against her dry throat.

"I'll speak to them," she said with feigned confidence. "And I'll get to the bottom of this."

"They said they'll kill us," Bertha whispered while clutching her wailing daughter to her chest.

Maeve eyed the sword on the belt of one of two men standing near the cart. She didn't want to test whether or not these men were telling the truth. She witnessed the violence they were willing to foster. She doubted the lives of some random farmers would weigh heavily on their conscience. She touched her necklace, a gift from her mother, and rubbed her thumb across the face of the medallion.

Maeve inched near the door and said, "Excuse me?"

"Quiet." The man elbowed the cart, and several women gasped, the echo of their wet breath stuck to Maeve's eardrums.

"The man from earlier, the one with the black helm. I need to see him."

"No. He's busy. And we need to get this lot to Hollyhock."

Maeve's brow furrowed. *All the oldest maps have Hollyhock written upon them.* Hollyhock was a castle of myth and legend. The champion of goddess Theadora, Ul'gaar, was tasked with building a castle that could outlive even the gods. He built Hollyhock. As if to test Ul'gaar's craftsmanship, there was a great storm nearly two thousand years ago. It was the pinnacle of storms filled with mythology and old wives' tales. It erased cities and dragged them unforgiving into the dark depths. It flooded rivers and eroded centuries of farmland and agriculture. It carved off chunks of Estoria like a butcher slicing tender meat from bone. Hollyhock survived, and legends say Ul'gaar's spirit wandered the halls.

"That place is abandoned," she said. *And it's haunted if the tales are to be believed.*

The man snorted. The other man shook his head with a pitying look in her direction. Maeve clenched her fists. She was no fool. She might not be well-traveled, but her community wasn't disconnected from the outside world. She released a controlled exhale and unclenched her fists. *Anger serves no purpose. Ever.* She was meant to be the face of serenity and empathy. She was a priestess of Juno before all else.

"I'd like to speak to the person in charge."

"And I'd like a horse that can fly." The man shrugged and glared at her with unbridled venom. She looked back at the concerned, wary, and heartbroken faces of the women with her. *I need to do something.* She held the wooden bars encircling the cart.

"One question, please. That's all I ask. I promise I won't speak again until we reach Hollyhock castle." It sounded reasonable and fair, in her opinion. She combed her mind for the most appropriate and urgent question. Her first concern was of the children separated from their families and weeping inside a cart several feet away. *What will the older children's fate be? Will they be harmed? So-called King Hagken couldn't be so cruel as to harm innocent children.* The little ones were here with their mothers, which was a small mercy. Archie, whom she healed a few moments ago, stared out from the wooden bars of his transport with a forlorn and resigned expression as if he had an idea of his fate before the dice were thrown.

The soldier spat onto the ground.

"No." He patted the blade at his hip.

"Let it be, Maeve." Bertha touched her shoulder. "We'll know soon enough."

"Barely," she muttered, "Hollyhock is a fortnight away."

"I know." Bertha stroked Lenora's flaxen head. "But what else can we do?

Maeve flexed her fingers against the bars. She could try to do something. The question remained if it would be worth it or not. She was outnumbered. *Even if I could break free, what would I do? How would I defeat them?* Juno's magic lived within her and was tied to the art of healing, growth, and light, not war and violence.

They corralled her village into several carts. She was leaving the only home she'd ever known in the dust with an anxious feeling roiling inside her stomach. She leaned forward, body swaying as the cart rumbled down the road and touched her forehead to the bars. Her anxiety smoldered. It burned up her throat and left her tongue heavy with ash.

Once they arrived in Hollyhock, she would have answers.

* * *

They stopped every night to tend to the horses and let groups bound together at the wrists stretch their legs. The possible threat of execution loomed over their heads. Occasionally, someone would be beaten, though Maeve couldn't surmise why. Was it a tactic to flex their muscles and showcase their brutal strength and control? Maeve couldn't discreetly heal the men since they were contained in a separate cart from the women and children, but she healed those trapped with her.

They clustered in a protective circle, and Maeve knelt at the center. She called to Juno's magic and lessened the pain of their bruises, healed their bloody backs, and tended to dislocated fingers. She was careful. She didn't heal the injuries completely. She was afraid Hagken's soldiers would notice her abilities and separate her from her people. She lifted the linen of Willow's shirt to reveal her pale skin lacerated with thin, sharp, and bloody lines. Willow said they whipped her for taking too long to relieve herself. Maeve clenched her jaw. *She's fourteen*, Maeve thought, and her frustration hardened into a pit in her throat.

Willow wept into her palms as Maeve summoned Juno's magic. She eased the inflammation and coaxed the blood to congeal and scab. *I wish I could do more. I know Juno's granted me enough power to do more.* She gently pulled Willow's shirt down and hoped it wouldn't cause suspicion in the morning.

Shara knelt in front of Maeve. Her dark, wrinkled skin folded over her cheeks and lined her mouth like tree bark. Her white hair frazzled around her face in a short, messy halo. She turned her jaw to Maeve and pointed with a knobby finger to the bruise. Shara was one of their eldest in the village. Her wisdom and knowledge in the art of child birthing had brought Maeve into the world. *They harm our children, our elders...*

"They have no morals, no compassion," Maeve muttered. She kept an iron leash around her anger as it burned inside her stomach. According to Maeve's mother, it wasn't proper to use Juno's magic when she was upset. The light flared beneath her fingertips and burned brighter than Maeve intended.

"Hey! What's going on in there?" A soldier slammed his forearm into the side of the cage. Willow startled and broke the circle of protection around Maeve and Shara. His face soured like old milk, and Maeve's body stiffened. *Will he punish Shara again? Or me?* She would take the brunt of his scorn and violence if it meant keeping Shara safe.

"Open this one up. Now!"

Everyone scuttled away from the door. Maeve remained kneeling. The stench of sweat and fear was thick in her nostrils. She looked up at the soldier and hoped her defiance didn't show on her face. He dropped on one knee to her level and peered at her with suspicion and distaste. Her lip quivered. *He won't kill me, will he? They said they'd kill us only if we ran away.*

"What were you doing?"

"Nothing."

He smiled slowly and satisfied as if she were a lover who had whispered the sweetest nothing into his ear.

"Hm? Nothing. Then you won't mind coming to speak with our lieutenant." He rose to his feet and ordered two soldiers to bind her wrists and bring her to Lieutenant Duskryn. Shara clutched her shoulder with a weathered, soft hand.

"Be brave, Lady Maeve," she whispered before they hauled her away.

2

They brought her to a single large canvas tent. It held a cot and a desk with candles that painted the walls with flickering warmth. A man stood straight with his hands clasped behind him. His blonde hair fell flat and sweaty against his head. His gray eyes regarded Maeve as if she were a pathetic dog dragging mud into his austere tent.

"We caught her doing something, sir. It was—it was—some light."

No emotion crossed his features. Not suspicion, confusion, or distaste. She looked upon a black, silent lake without understanding its contents or depths. His angular face gave him the impression of something predatory. Her eyes glanced at the black-horned helmet on his desk. *This is the man in charge, the one who stole us from our homes on the orders of a single, deposed king.*

"Leave us," the lieutenant said curtly.

He poured two cups of water and offered one to Maeve. She took the clay cup between her rope-bound hands but didn't drink. If she navigated this interaction like the pirates in her storybooks, she might be able to barter for the release of her people. She could send the elders, like Shara, Old Ed, and Clarissa, back home or to Silvercliff. *Shara has family in Silvercliff.* The question remained as to how a woman in her eighties and another in her fifties would journey the road alone without supplies. She would need to iron out those details.

"I am Lieutenant Calom Duskryn." He sipped his water while peering at Maeve over the clay-baked rim. "I figure we may as well be on a first-name basis for this conversation, yes?"

He stepped closer, towering a few inches above, and leaned in to look at her face. Maeve stared at a spot beyond his shoulder. Her lips trembled and she pressed them together. She would be useless to Shara or Clarissa if she broke down in terror. *Juno, please give me strength.*

"Ah, yes..." he drawled, "I remember. You claimed to be the spokesperson for the little hovel."

Her gaze met his. "I am."

"And I may call you?" His breath wafted against her nose, floral and sweet. Around his collar, she noted his chafed and peeling skin from a sunburn on the juncture of his neck. The sight of it calmed her. He was human, and Juno's powerful light could humble him.

"Maeve Thewynn."

"Excellent." Calom, straight-backed and proper, said, "A lovely name."

"Thank you?" Maeve said slowly.

"The man who brought you said he saw a light. He claimed you were doing something. Would you care to elaborate, Maeve?"

"I don't know. I was looking at Shara's injury."

"Looking at it?" His silver eyes narrowed thoughtfully. "Do you have training?"

"A little."

She decided to dole the information out slowly. She didn't know if he'd become violent, though the threat of it exhaled coldly on the back of her neck. If she gave information piece by piece, she might be able to entice him enough to garner a negotiation for the release and protection of their elders. Perhaps she could appeal to his pragmatism and convince him it wouldn't be helpful to the king to have elderly folk in his army. During the bi-annual frost crown, Shara could hardly get out of bed because the cold affected her joints.

"I see." He pressed his lips into a stern line. "This may take longer than I expected."

He stalked over to the front flap of his tent, muttered to the guard standing post, and returned to Maeve. The flap was tossed roughly aside a moment later, and a woman stormed into the tent. She ignored Maeve and jabbed her finger into Calom's chest.

"I'm not your lackey!" she snapped. She wore a dark green riding vest, a leather book holster holding two books strapped beneath her armpits, and a pair of muddy boots at knee height. Maeve took an involuntary step backward. She didn't know the intricate power dynamics within this retinue of soldiers. However, this outburst was...odd. It bordered on disrespectful. *Does she rank higher than Lieutenant Duskryn?*

"You can't call me because your tea got cold or whatever," the woman said.

"I have never done such a thing." Calom sniffed and gestured toward Maeve. "I have a guest and need your help, Cara."

Cara's white-blonde braid whipped behind her and she narrowed her green eyes at Maeve. As Calom and Cara faced her, Maeve couldn't help but notice the similarity in their features. They had the same nose and heavy-set brow, but Calom's face was narrower than Cara's. They were likely siblings, which explained some of their interaction, although Maeve couldn't work out how it could be helpful. If anything, it made this whole ordeal confusing. How could Calom order the execution and beatings of her people when he had a family? Was he genuinely heartless? And if he was—then could she find an ally in Cara? The questions performed useless somersaults in her head.

"Fine." Cara reached under her right armpit and unlatched one of the books. "What do you need?"

Maeve sensed magic when Cara opened the plain, leather-bound journal. *A mage!* She never met a mage before. They kept to the cities of Everdawn, Pyrite, and Amethneas. She often pictured heavy robes and old, wizened faces with long, flowing white beards when she imagined them like the pictures in stories. Cara dressed like a forest ranger with dusty riding clothes and fingerless gloves. Her face carried a few lines around her mouth, but Maeve guessed she wasn't much older than herself. A mix of trepidation and anticipation churned through her stomach. *How will she perform magic? How will her magic look different from Juno's?* Maeve's understanding of mages was rudimentary at best. She knew they used materials and books, unlike Maeve, who devoted her life to Juno and was granted divine power like a conduit through her mortal body.

"Hogsworth said he saw a light. I need to confirm it." Calom looked around and said, "And a few chairs if you can manage it."

Cara slammed the book shut between her palms. "Chairs?"

"Yes." He rubbed his chin. "I suppose we could conduct this whole ordeal while standing, but it would get tedious."

"You want me to use the arcane magic I've spent years studying so I can conjure you up some chairs?" she spat the final word like it tasted foul.

"Nothing fancy; I assure you even a few stools will do."

Cara pinched the bridge of her nose and released a hissing sigh through clenched teeth. She opened her book, and her fingertip ran across the page. She muttered to herself, looking at Maeve, then to her untouched clay cup.

"May I use that?"

Maeve's tongue was frozen to the roof of her mouth. She nodded.

"I need this as well." Cara plucked an errant piece of straw from Maeve's hair. Maeve jerked away from her touch. A prickle of pain radiated from her scalp. Between Cara's fingers, two long, dark strands of Maeve's hair dangled from the piece of hay. *Ow.* Cara dropped the grass and Maeve's hair into the water. *What is she doing?*

"I'll ask a few preemptive questions while she's busy." Calom stood behind his sister with a smug grin. "You mentioned a familiarity with injuries. Who taught you?"

"My mother."

"Fascinating. Was she a herbalist?"

"Er..." Maeve couldn't stop glancing at Cara. She placed the cup on the ground and traced her glowing fingertips in the air while muttering low incantations—a spell in a language Maeve didn't understand. An angular, vaguely square shape shifted in purple light and materialized above the cup.

"She wasn't a herbalist," Maeve said. This was partially true. Maeve's mother studied herbs and understood their medicinal properties. Many priestesses of Juno were required to have at least a rudimentary grasp of healing herbs, as they couldn't rely on Juno's power for everything. "The only one we knew of lived in Silvercliff."

"How odd. No herbalists in a town so healthy." Calom riffled through some of his papers. "Let's see...I should have a report on Ferne...somewhere."

Maeve swallowed. Had she misspoken? Should she have lied and told Calom her mother was an herbalist? She needed to figure out how to angle a release of their elderly.

"Perhaps we can trade information." she offered, "I can tell you about—"

The clay cup shattered. Maeve recoiled. The shards of clay remained suspended in mid-air, surrounded by light and tiny water globes.

Whoah! A swirling, violet mist obscured her irises and illuminated her sclera with a soft, lilac hue. The clay stretched, malleable once more, and then contorted into a misshapen low stool. A spiraling geometric shape hovered above the wet dirt and pulled itself upward, flexing and building like clay until a second stool appeared beside the first. Cara dropped her hand with an annoyed look toward Calom. She looked fine. No nosebleeds. Not even a trickle of sweat on her pale face. Maeve burned with questions. *How does it work? Who does she call upon to gather her magic? Did she call upon Thorduun, our genderless deity of knowledge and magic? Or does all of her magic live inside her book? And if she was without it, then was she powerless?* A sudden curiosity overtook her—an eagerness to learn about Cara.

"Does this please you, O' Great Lieutenant?"

He wasn't looking at Cara. He freed a sheaf of paper and held it up like a prize.

"Here it is. A little dated, but that's what you get for having intel from nearly a decade ago."

Cara sat on the dirt-made stool, which miraculously held steady and crossed her ankle over her knee. "By all means, continue with your bookkeeping. It's not like we have other things to do."

Maeve smiled. Cara had a nice sense of humor. Perhaps this wouldn't be so terrible. Calom was reasonable and non-violent. *They will listen to me.* She could trust them.

"Did you cast the other spell?"

Her smile dropped. *What other spell?* The glyphs faded into clay and dirt. *How many spells can Cara cast at once?* Cara gave a pointed look upward. Maeve's limbs numbed. *What is that?* Above her head, an intricate dark glyph hovered and shimmered in the air. She thought of the cup shattering.

"What's that?"

"Have a seat, Maeve," Calom said.

Maeve sank into the chair without thinking. She blinked, and her confusion deepened but was swiftly pushed aside by a gentler feeling of gratitude. Her legs were getting tired. Calom's hospitality was a welcome change. *What?* She thought of standing up, but the thought was pushed from her mind with a quick nudge. *Why would I want to get up?* This chair was comfortable. Cara was a powerful mage, and she should do her best to please her. *What is going on?* Maeve shot a quick, panicked look at the glyph again. *What is it doing to me?*

"Don't worry, Maeve. It's not going to harm you." He circled his desk with the paper between his hands. "Now, tell me, who is Cait Theywnn?"

The answer fell out of her mouth, "She's my mother."

"According to our old reports, she was a Priestess of Juno. Is this correct?"

"Yes." Her eyes widened.

"Are you also a Priestess of Juno?"

The blood drained from her cheeks. She weighed the consequence of telling the truth against her sluggish and foggy mind.

I must tell them the truth. They're my friends. They want to help me. She thought of Shara, Clarissa, and the others. She needed to protect them. She needed to send them to Silvercliff before the soldiers reached Hollyhock. Maeve glanced furtively at Cara, who looked bored, her book secured underneath her arm once more.

"I..." She tested the lie against her teeth. It wouldn't release. Her words clung to her throat, refusing to pass over her vocal cords. She stared at her boots with pressure building in her temples. She shouldn't lie to them. But she needed to keep her people safe, too. Her emotions pulled, lulling her, reminding her of how kind and thoughtful Calom was. He would reward her for telling the truth.

His shadow loomed over her. He cupped her chin and lifted her face to his. His silver eyes carried flecks of blue around the pupils. They reminded Maeve of flashes of lightning during a storm.

"It's alright, Maeve. I'm not going to hurt you. I want to know what happened...I'm merely looking out for those under my care, the same as you."

Yes, yes, of course. We're the same. Her anxious thoughts were placated. She was proud of her connection to Juno and her faith. Calom would see this. He would understand they both carried duties and responsibilities.

"Yes," she breathed. The pressure on her skull from trying to hold back information released, "I am a priestess of Juno."

"You know, I'm a man of the sunlit path," he said almost warmly. "Although the Musana Solstice is celebrated differently in the south." He dropped his hand from her jaw.

"He says that because he likes dancing." Cara smirked.

"I don't deny it," he said, shrugging, "Maeve, do you like dancing?"

She frowned. *Is this a serious question?* The truth burbled to her lips without conscious prompting.

"I don't know. I've never been dancing."

His gray eyes brightened. "Once we reach Hollyhock, you'll owe me a dance."

Maeve blinked. *A dance?* His trail of questioning discombobulated her. Nothing made sense. Weren't they talking about something else? Her knee bounced. A sense of urgency pressed against her chest. Maeve tried to locate its root and understand, but it was like trying to hold smoke. Her lips twitched upward into a smile even though he wasn't looking at her. She didn't know how to dance, but she could learn.

Cara groaned and snapped her fingers. "Time is of the essence, brother."

"Yes, yes, of course." He cleared his throat. "What happened before Hogsworth discovered you? What were you doing?"

"I was healing Shara...she had a bruise..." Maeve explained. It was as if her mouth and mind were detached, and her gaze was trapped within the lightning storm of Calom's.

"She's one of our elders. She shouldn't be here. I wouldn't heal it completely because I knew it would cause suspicion."

The siblings shared a look.

"She's beyond a luminary," Cara said, "Hagken will want to know of this."

The Luminaries were apprentices to Juno's order. They lacked the divine connection to Juno and couldn't access her healing magic.

"Of course." Calom folded his sinewy arms across his chest. "Maeve, will you heal for me during your time here?"

Her gut clenched. Why wouldn't she want to heal for him? *No. No! He's not a good person. He's captured your people.* She wrestled against the cottony, warm thoughts and feelings swirling inside her veins. Her hands curled into fists and trembled. An internal war careened in her skull–the cognitive dissonance of wanting to help while knowing he wasn't a good person and understanding she was under a spell.

"Release the spell, Cara."

The magic popped like a blister. Maeve exhaled raggedly. The following sensation was a pure, hazy numbness. She blinked at Calom and wished she could feel anything, even burning embarrassment, but her emotions remained neutral. She touched Juno's magic within her solar plexus, and the warmth responded to her call. Whatever Cara had done didn't corrupt her tie to Juno but messed with her emotions. She had been as malleable as those clay cups, eager to please and willing to provide any truths Calom wanted to pull from her.

"Apologizes for the uncouth tactic," he said. Cara snorted.

"I generally don't have Cara use that spell. It's technically outlawed, according to General Fenris. However, our king wholeheartedly supports so-called unethical magic and says we shouldn't shy away from the full breadth of our abilities."

Cara stood. "That's my cue to leave." She punched Calom's shoulder. "The spell will wear off soon, priestess," she said before leaving.

Maeve watched her go in equal parts muted horror and fascination. It was no wonder the spell was banned. The harm it could do. It held the power to topple empires. *How can such magic exist? How can the gods allow it?*

"Back to business then. Maeve, will you do me the honor of healing my men should we ever suffer any grievous injuries?"

"Do I have a choice?"

"You do." He sat in Cara's chair, his posture impeccable, and slicked his long fingers through his hair. "One option is less painful than the other. If you agree to care for my men, then I will make an order to halt all beatings. This includes flogging and dragging folk by their hair.

"If you refuse, I will be forced to convince you."

She licked her lips. She didn't want to know what he would do if she said no. He offered a false choice. There was only one choice she could make.

"I'd be willing to help you, but there's something I'd like in return."

A single pale eyebrow raised. "The protection and safety of your people isn't enough?"

"I want the villagers of Ferne returned home. I'll stay. I'll serve in Hagken's army or remain with you. But, please, let them go."

She could feel her emotions returning like they were swimming upstream. She knew it was a tall order, but how many priestesses did King Hagken have? There were likely few, if any. Juno's priestesses either lived in Everdawn or Pyrite among the prominent temples. Her family's presence in Ferne existed because her priestess grandmother left Pyrite and moved there. It wasn't typical for a divine healer to live among the farmers and laborers.

"I am afraid I cannot. I am bound to the orders of my king." He shook his head. "But, you've found me in a pleasant mood. Aim lower."

"Release Shara, Clarissa, Ed, and the other elders. They cannot fight." Her throat prickled. "Send them to Silvercliff. They'll be safe there..." Her tone thickened in desperation. She resorted to begging but couldn't think of any other way to convince Calom. "I'm sure you could spare a few horses or soldiers to escort them."

"Silvercliff is in the opposite direction."

"They have family there."

"Is that so?"

Maeve nodded. Calom rubbed his chin. He glanced from the ground and met Maeve's eyes with an intense, focused expression.

"If I do this, you'll willingly tend to our injuries? At least until we reach Hollyhock."

"I will. You have my word."

Calom returned to his desk and poised a pen over a blank paper. "Give me the names and descriptions of these people—Shara and the rest of them—I'll write the order."

Her heart beat erratically in her chest. She didn't appreciate his methods of gaining information from her. However, it was a price she would pay a thousand times over if it meant she could save them. First, the elders, then she might convince him to release the children and their mothers. She assumed they had a little over a week before reaching Hollyhock. She would need to be clever. Calom finished writing his list and told Maeve to wait while he spoke to someone outside.

Maeve let her shoulders slump forward in relief. *I did it. Shara, Clarissa, Old Ed—they'll be safe in Silvercliff. They'll be away from any fighting.* She relished the victory with a tiny smile. Her head perked at the abrupt sound of shouting voices.

Calom returned, and Maeve jumped to her feet. She recognized the voices.

"What's happening?"

"What you asked for."

She went to leave the tent, but Calom caught her shoulders in an unyielding grip. His thumb and forefinger pinched the juncture where her neck met her shoulder, and a jolt of pain ricocheted down her spine. Her knees buckled. Calom held her upright.

"Relax, Maeve, I am a man of my word. I've released Shara, Clarissa, and the old grumpy one. Ted, was it?"

"What do you mean you've released them? It's the middle of the night."

"It is." He smiled thinly. "You didn't specify when they should travel to Silvercliff. I thought it best if they start now."

"They can't travel in the dark."

He forced Maeve into her stool, and his storm-gray eyes narrowed into slits.

"They will be escorted to Silvercliff with some of my finest men. Once they arrive, their families will be interviewed. We can't have anyone sowing the seeds of rebellion, can we? If I receive favorable reports, then they'll remain in Silvercliff. And if not...well..." Calom sighed and clicked his tongue. "You already know what happens to traitors of the crown, don't you?"

"They're not rebels or traitors. They're people. They're ordinary."

"Not everyone needs divine powers to spark a revolution. In my experience, ordinary people are the dangerous ones."

He released her shoulders and knelt before her. *He looks like a knight from the stories my grandmother used to read. But he lacks their kindness and honor.* His grip readjusted to her sore, rope-bound wrists.

"Now, be a good healer and fix this burn on my neck, will you?" he phrased it as a question, but Maeve recognized it for what it was— an order.

She twisted her hands outward and toward his neck. He held her ropes by hooking a thumb between the gap of her wrists. His firm grip kept Maeve's direct touch away from his throat. *Does he fear I might strangle him? What a ridiculous thought. I would* never. Maeve closed her eyes. She couldn't bear to look at him after everything she endured. She should've trusted her instincts. *No one who follows King*

Hagken is a trustworthy or compassionate person.

* * *

Calom used Juno's power for frivolous annoyances. She tended to his sore throat in the morning even though it could've been solved with water. He watched her with those calm, silver eyes as if he expected her to do or say something to reveal her secret inner rebellion. She healed tension headaches, sunburns, and bug bites. He refused to let her gather ingredients to make salves or tinctures to heal these minor issues. She called upon Juno, and Juno always answered no matter how benign and non-life threatening the injuries were.

Sometimes, Maeve wished Juno wouldn't answer so she could avoid being Calom's healer for the day. She'd tamper down on the thought as soon as it came unbidden to the front of her mind. She never wanted to endure a life without Juno's power flowing through her.

Her respite was in the evenings when he sent her under guard to aid the horses. She calmed their nerves and soothed their hulking muscles. She loved touching their silken coats and feeling their power and strength beneath her palms. The horses made for pleasant company compared to Calom and his unnerving, quicksilver gaze. She would pet their snouts and smile as they sniffed and nibbled at her fingers.

She listened to the sounds of the camp. Most of Calom's men were cordial to each other, but some sharpened their words in barbs and didn't land like friendly blows. Maeve tried find Cara Cara. Yet, it was as if she vanished into the smoke of the campfires. She patted the side of the horse's neck with a flowing surge of Juno's essence to heal some of its exhaustion.

She used Juno's magic day in and day out, which ground her

magical reserves to a nub. Maeve couldn't heal a splinter when she returned to their caged transport even if she wanted to. Her head ached with the echoes of children crying. She comforted as she could with quiet hymns and hopeful words. The soldiers didn't speak to them except for orders or to complain about their slowness. Calom upheld his end of the bargain. The beatings ceased. She hoped Shara and the others made it safely to Silvercliff. Her people were receptive when Maeve explained why the elders left and what Maeve must give to ensure their safety. However, Maeve noticed their wary and heartbroken glances even in their graciousness. As if they viewed her actions as a betrayal.

Their morale unraveled.

They huddled together, and Maeve summoned a small light between her palms. She cautiously glanced over their heads and confirmed that no guards were watching. The soldiers knew of her magic, but she was apprehensive when using it around them. She insisted to Calom that she would join Marcus Hagken if it meant Ferne's safety. She needed to prepare herself and her people.

"Should anything happen to me, know I will return to you. No matter the cost." She inhaled through her nostrils. "And Juno will guide us through this darkness."

Her mother left years ago. Maeve wouldn't leave her community and friends like her mother had. Cait went on a holy pilgrimage to across Estoria. She acted in service to Juno. But on these cold, dark roads through the forest with the sounds of quiet weeping around her, Maeve couldn't help but wonder why her mother never returned or sent a letter. Maeve twisted her fingers around the orb of light. *Have faith.* It was what got her through these lonely years. Maeve trusted and believed Juno would someday give her a sign. She looked for symbolism in each golden ray of light through the ancient canopies, in each new birth, in every flower blooming after frost. And although her mother never returned, Maeve hoped they would meet again. Her people needed the same faith now. They needed to trust Juno and Theadora, the goddess of justice, to deliver reparation for their suffering.

"What will we do in the meantime if you are gone?"

"Be cautious. Listen and speak to others if you can." Maeve bit her lip and tested the lie on her tongue. Her people needed hope. *They need a reason to keep going even if I'm not here to guide them.*

"Juno gave me a vision last night. I saw men in armor fighting amongst each other. I saw farmers, weavers, and butchers standing together against a great and terrible darkness."

There had been no such dream because Juno wasn't a goddess of premonition. *It's a necessary white lie.* Yet, she knew violence was on the horizon. She could feel it as succinctly as the cool breeze wafting through her dark hair. The people of Ferne needed to stay together.

"I believe Juno was trying to tell me we are stronger together. We can overcome anything as long as we walk in her light."

"Juno is asking us to fight?" Willow asked, appalled. Juno was a goddess of peace.

"No. Never. She's asking us to stay close and join with others who were forcefully brought into this conflict."

She glanced over their heads to check on the others huddled around campfires with furtive, uneasy expressions. *How many were ripped from their homes?* A soldier shook out their bedroll while cursing. *How many gardeners held a sword instead of a shovel? How many children lost their parents because King Hagken couldn't swallow his pride and ambition and let Fenris continue to rule the lands?* She couldn't look at the cart that contained Ferne's men.

"We're not the only people here who want to return to our

homes."

Maeve paid attention to the curt, scathing tones the soldiers threw at each other. She cared for the tired, salivating horses. King Hagken cobbled together his army. He gathered laborers and forced swords into their hands and fear into their hearts. Maeve wasn't well-versed in war, but she knew people, and this army was a tower of matchsticks.

"What if you don't return, Lady Maeve? What if they—" Bertha's eyes misted. "Kill you?"

Her light flickered out, and she blinked at their fearful faces in raw darkness and shadow.

"If this is when Janis collects my soul, I will find a way to bring everyone home, even if I must transcend death or weave the threads of fate myself."

Her words were said with a confidence she did not feel. *These soldiers won't kill me, will they?* Now that the idea was planted into her head, it began to take root, and she was thankful for the darkness to conceal her pinched brow and chewed bottom lip. Calom wouldn't let them. She interlaced her fingers together and squeezed so hard her knuckles cracked. She was far too valuable.

3

Hollyhock was a splotch of spires and steep walls on the horizon. The dark crimson and milky white towers reached skyward to the clouds. A flock of crows nested on the silver-tipped spires and screeched. This place was meant to be abandoned and haunted. Two gold banners hung from the ramparts. The crest depicted a black half-circle with an upward-facing arrow beneath it. *This must be King Hagken's crest,* she thought while frowning. Above the large oak gate was a carved motif of a hammer crossed by a pair of scales—*Theadora's symbol.* The cart rattled and swung as it ambled beneath the gates.

"How did they do all this?" Bertha muttered.

She glanced around the bustling camp. "I don't know."

The interior was filled with horses and marching soldiers. A blacksmith's hammer clanged like a resonant bell. More than one alchemist strode past, their protective, dark goggles hanging around their necks and belts laden with pouches and vials. Typically, alchemists remained in the southernmost part of Estoria outside the gilded kingdom. They often lived in the city of Amethneas, a region piously devoted to magical and alchemical study. It was easier to procure supplies and components where the weather was temperate and agreeable year-round. *Why would they come this far north?* Alchemists were expensive. Maeve met one once when she was young. Her grandmother bartered supplies with them, and Maeve thought they were pretentious and disagreeable.

The faces they passed gave them cursory looks. No one appeared concerned or appalled at a carriage full of dirty, downtrodden peasants carted through the courtyard.

"Halt!" the man driving the horses called. Maeve clutched Bertha's damp hand.

Maeve whispered, "It'll be okay."

She tried to take stock of her surroundings as they were pulled from the cart and brought toward the main keep. An impending sense of doom ran icy fingers down her spine. Lady Janis' watchful eye was upon her. Calom dropped from his horse; his pointed chin held high and silver armor reflecting the afternoon light.

"Lady Maeve." His eyes passed Bertha as if she were invisible. "I cannot wait to tell King Hagken about your...uniqueness. Am I right to presume your offer stands? You'll join us and become a beacon of light within our noble cause."

"I will join if all the people from Ferne are escorted back home."

Calom smiled. "I think you'll find my king most persuasive. Perhaps you can sleep on it."

A guard standing near the entrance clicked her tongue. "The shadow general returns, and they're empty-handed." She smiled without warmth. "Are we to assume your trip to the southern region went poorly?"

A person dressed in black leather armor stalked forward. They were cut sharp like obsidian with high cheekbones and narrowed eyes. Their dark curls were fasted in a low, short ponytail at the nape of their neck. They might've looked handsome if not for their look of contempt. They carried an air of aristocracy rivaling Calom's.

"Your assumptions may cost you your tongue," their voice was black silk. The guard who spoke paled and looked away. The shadow general was lean with none of the brute strength or brutality of the other guards. Their eyes, surrounded by shadows of dark makeup, darted from place to place as if they expected a sword through their back. The soldiers called them a 'General,' but a mocking note carried through their tones. Maeve clenched her jaw.

"I'll bring her," they said.

"I have it under control." Calom placed his hand on Maeve's shoulder, and she wanted to shake him off.

"Bring me where?" asked Maeve.

"Remind me, Lieutenant Duskryn, does your title outrank mine?" The dark-haired general smirked.

"You're pulling rank for a peasant girl?" Calom rolled his eyes. Maeve disliked Calom's tone and arrogance, but she hated that these two military officials spoke about her as if she wasn't there.

"You seem rather attached to her. Did you finally manage to make a friend?" They placed a hand over their heart in mock surprise. "I thought I'd never live to see the day! Someone should tell Cara immediately. She'll pop a blood vessel," they said, chuckling. "Though, I imagine she'd enjoy it."

"Fine. I *permit* you to escort *my* h–" He stopped himself. *Does he not want the general to know I'm a healer?* She couldn't blame him. The term 'shadow general' didn't conjure warm, fuzzy feelings. She suspected Calom kept the secret to himself to receive praise from the king. *Should I try to stay with Calom? Or go with the shadow general? Will they even let me choose?* She looked toward her friends and neighbors and offered them an encouraging smile.

The shadow general raised both eyebrows. "Your what?"

He cleared his throat. "My prisoner. However, it will be known that all these men and women"— he tilted his head toward the unloading carts —"I brought them here. Not you."

"Duskryn, I would never dream of stealing your praise."

Calom gave one last scathing glare to the general and left. The doors swung open. She wrinkled her nose. It was not the familiar scent of soil and animals. The air smelled raw and putrid. *An awful and cursed smell.* This place was metal, blood, and bone. *What would Theadora say if she saw it?*

"Ready to go inside?"

Maeve folded her arms. "We've been cooped up and traveling for days. My people are terrified. Is that all you're going to say?"

They shrugged. The constant traveling and terror had worn her patience thin.

"I'm not going anywhere until my people are cared for and someone answers my questions."

Their dark brown hair fell across their forehead as they inclined their head. "You can come unbound of your own volition, or I can tie you up. Your choice."

She gnashed on her tongue. *What is it with these people and their ropes? They have no civility whatsoever.*

"That's not a choice."

Their smile was slow and tauntingly sweet. "One is more fun for me."

She huffed. *Another tactic, perhaps.*

"Hollyhock is supposed to be abandoned. How is any of this possible?" She opened her arms at the efficient, active energy around her. "Calom keeps mentioning King Hagken, but he was removed years ago. He shouldn't be anywhere near the Gilded Kingdom. He shouldn't have an entire army."

"Why don't I show you?" They gestured toward the large birch doors of the inner keep. The last women were moved from the cart, and they milled around her like nervous fillies. She was getting tired of these people avoiding her questions.

"Fine," she bit the word out, and the dark-haired general smiled again.

The inner walls were white marble inlaid with blue. The dual banners hung by the doors stirred in the breeze. She noticed engravings covered the archway but couldn't parse their meaning. She guessed they were messages crafted by the champion Ul'gaar to honor Theadora.

The doors opened to reveal a large feasting hall. The dark cherry wood floors glistened beneath several silver candelabras. More soldiers stood at attention by the doors and windows, but servers moved to and fro carrying trays and pitchers. An expansive, fragrant feast was laid out on a long table. It was covered in roasted meats, steamed vegetables, and clear, damp pitchers of ale. People dressed finely, and others dressed as laborers sat around the table, and their conversation slowly quieted as the women entered the room with soldiers at their backs. The laborers at the table stared at them while the elegantly dressed barely looked up from their plates. The general who escorted her slipped toward the side of the room, and the shadows concealed half their face into darkness.

Maeve's stomach grumbled, and she rubbed her aching midsection.

"Wonderful," a man shouted from his bone-white chair, "my good people have returned with our honored guests."

Maeve couldn't see his features from this distance, but his voice reminded her of leeches squirming beneath the muck. Her companions' faces were a mix of awe, fear, and hope. *They hope for salvation and benevolence and kindness.* They hoped it had been Calom who was cruel and not the king he served.

But Maeve recalled Cara's dark spell. She thought of her neighbors beaten into the dirt and dragged and tossed like a sack of rice into a cart. If this man sanctioned these orders, there was no chance he was benevolent. They left a steel trap and found themselves at the slaughter. She inhaled through her nose. *You can do this, Maeve.* Hagken had no use for farmers and ranchers.

"Allow me to introduce myself." He stood from his throne. The gray streaks in his dark hair appeared sickly yellow in the flickering candlelight. A thin blade was strapped to the belt at his hip.

"I am King Marcus Hagken. I've governed Hollyhock for the past two years." He walked forward. "I've sent my men to each forgotten corner of my land to bring you into the fold." He clasped his hands. "To bring you into our triumphant new era."

Two years? She glanced at the wooden ceiling smudged with candle smoke. How could he build an army this large? It sounded impossible. No. It was impossible. *He must be lying. This must be a ruse of some kind—an illusion.*

"You're the king?" Bertha clutched Lenora to her chest. "Last we knew of it, General Fenris cared for these lands. No kings." Bertha's bravery didn't go unnoticed by Maeve. Although she wasn't the matriarch of Ferne, she spoke to this king as if they were equals. Maeve grasped Bertha's shoulder.

Hagken waved his hand dismissively. His fingers were adorned with rings. "General Fenris has done a poor job."

His dark eyes narrowed and scanned them as if he were weighing cattle to be sold at the market. The door hinges creaked loudly before Calom strode purposely forward. He knelt in front of Hagken. The feasting hall fell silent. Maeve's lungs shriveled. Hagken inclined his head in the barest of nods. Calom rose and whispered to his king. Calom's silver eyes cut like glass to Maeve. She wanted to duck further into the protective shell of her neighbors and friends, but couldn't. She was their matriarch. She was their protection. She promised to bring them back home. *Lady Juno...watch over us.* She would be as brave as Bertha.

She released her grip on Bertha's shoulder and took a step forward.

"I present Lady Priestess Maeve Theywnn," said Calom. A murmur of conversation erupted through the hall.

Hagken squeezed Calom's forearm, "Goddess be praised!" he muttered reverently, "thank you, Lieutenant." His tone reminded Maeve of a parent speaking to a child. *I was right.* Calom's lips twitched upward. *Calom wanted praise from Hagken and kept the truth from the shadow general to ensure he received it.*

Hagken said, "My men will see you fed and bathed. Lady Theywnn will remain here as my guest and as the spokesperson for the town of Ferne."

Maeve reached for Bertha, but she was pulled away. *I don't want to do this alone!* Everything shifted like a lit match being dropped into water. The guests returned to their meals with hushed tones. *They're not interested in us anymore.* She thought she might find an ally among the laborers, but they refused to make eye contact. Several guards remained at the door, but the shadow general had vanished. Hagken approached Maeve with a dawning look of wonder and curiosity.

"You are..." His brow furrowed, and the lines around his mouth softened as he reached toward her. Maeve side-stepped and avoided him.

"I'm sorry." He shook his head. "Where are my manners? You must be starving. Come and sit with me."

Her empty stomach clenched.

"I'm fine."

Hagken smiled, crinkling the corners of his dark eyes. "You lie as well as she did."

"You must have confused me with someone else."

"I don't," he said, his voice like a whip, "you've finally returned to me. I knew you would. I knew it. The old ritual worked."

"Respectfully." She sucked on her teeth. "We've never met."

In the darkness, someone tried to silence their chuckle. Hagken turned to pour a drink and fill an empty plate. Her treacherous stomach grumbled again.

"Not in this life, no." He sighed. Maeve ignored his rambling. She wouldn't indulge in this strange fantasy of his. She needed to focus on what mattered.

"Your men attacked my home. They hurt us. They kidnapped us."

"I'm sorry for that," he said softly, "but these things happen in times of war."

Maeve struggled to calm herself and keep her tone even, "We aren't in times of war. We were living peacefully on our own. We weren't bothering anyone."

He shook his head.

"It is a shame how ignorant you are." He offered her a full plate of bloody red meat with steaming rice and crispy green beans. Maeve scowled. She'd rather eat rotten apples or the dry rations from Calom's unit than accept his generosity.

His expression soured like curdled milk. He dropped the plate. It shattered at Maeve's feet.

"I've been at war for the past eight years," he said, "I've been pushed out of my home. I've lost my wife. It's through the grace of Oph—" he stopped himself. "By the grace of Juno–I mean–that we discovered this place and managed to rebuild my army. It is my duty as king to care for my subjects. I must protect you."

Maeve frowned at the strange slip of his tongue. *Odd.* This entire conversation was strange. *What god was he going to praise before he said Juno?*

"We don't need your protection."

"Oh, but you do. You have no clue of the storm on the horizon."

"I want my people returned to their homes."

"Their homes have no walls."

She glared at him. "We don't need walls!" Her frustration threatened to overwhelm her clarity. She forced air through her nostrils and refused to let her anger take root. *A priestess of Juno is never angry.*

"Come with me." He offered her his elbow, and Maeve took a pointed step backward. Curse this man, this so-called king, this man who ripped children from their mothers and sanctioned abuse toward her neighbors and friends. *I doubt Calom's promise of safety extends into the walls of Hollyhock. I'm on my own.*

"I can walk."

A pained look of longing crossed his face like the last harvests' leaves falling from a tree.

"You have her spirit," he said wistfully.

Maeve sensed eyes on her back as he led her from the feasting hall. A chorus of heavy, metallic footfalls echoed their steps several paces behind. *Are Calom and Cara around? Do they have rooms here?*

Where did they take Bertha and everyone else? Her heart squeezed. Hagken said they'd be fed and cared for, but she didn't trust him. The hallways were lined with oil portraits and colorful mosaic windows depicting Theadora's symbols: weighted scales, hammers, and eyes. The marbled walls flashed with opalescent color between cracks and rivets of stone, and a damp, musty smell surrounded her.

"I've had to employ alchemists for some of the repairs. Hollyhock is strong, but she needs help from time to time. Alchemy! It's a marvelous thing. Their company has been delightful these past few months."

"I didn't think alchemists traveled this far north. I thought they stayed in the cities or the warmer climates," said Maeve.

"They'll do anything for their rightful king." He scratched his bumpy, razor-burned jaw. He opened a door that revealed another high, vaulted ceiling with a roaring fireplace and a circular table covered in maps and parchment. Maeve checked behind her. A man and woman in armor stood at attention.

"This is the truth," Hagken said, running his fingertips across the map. "This is the world you've been blind to for years."

Maeve cautiously stepped closer, and her stomach wound into knots. The map showed the region of the Gilded Kingdom. She recognized Silvercliff, the fishing town north of her village. Someone marked Silvercliff with a red half-circle with an arrow beneath it. *That symbol matches the one on the ramparts.* Her lips pursed. Other cities and towns were marked with a blue wolf's head. Maeve blinked as if it would change the lines and markings before her.

"We'd know if our country was at war."

"You've lived in quiet, idyllic isolation, my dear."

She despised his condescending tone.

"I've been preparing for the past year." He smiled like a hungry wolf. "My mages have done excellent work keeping our location a secret."

How does he have enough coin to keep alchemists and mages in his employ? Maeve's heart leaped inside her chest. *Where did he come from?* She returned to the map.

"Where did you flee from?"

Hagken tapped on the capital city of Pyrite. Pyrite was north of Ferne and situated within a horseshoe-shaped bay. Pyrite was known as the busiest city in Estoria and the central hub for trading routes.

"Eight years ago, my crown was stolen. I was forced into hiding. I became a beggar, an outcast, and yet, like a firebird, I rose from the ashes a new man."

His eyes locked with hers across the table. A slick, slithering sensation crawled across her flesh.

"Together, we will restore our family name and return the gilded kingdom to its former glory. No longer will people look upon Pyrite and call it false gold. We will fashion it into the gem of the coast once more."

"You've mistaken me for someone else. I've got no interest in crowns or glory. I want to go home with my people alive and unharmed." Maeve pressed her palms onto the map.

"You are home."

He rang a bell by the fireplace, and two individuals dressed in robes of crimson with their faces veiled by black lace entered. *Are they mages?* Maeve didn't recognize their adornments, and they lacked spell books.

"Bring my lady to her chambers, see her fed and bathed and clothed."

"I'm not" —Maeve wrenched her arm out of their grip — "I'm not your lady!"

Hagken's smile was as stagnant as pond water.

"Get settled in, and I will answer every question."

He ignored every mention of Ferne. He ignored each time she claimed she wasn't whoever he had her confused with. He was utterly entrapped in his delusions. She struggled free of the grip of the veiled maidens.

"Where have you taken the others? I want to see my people."

He shook his head and clenched his fist, "I truly wish you did not make me do this, my dear." The gaps between his fingers glistened with black ooze. A thick, coiling miasma of oily blackness flooded the room and extinguished the candles. Maeve doubled over. She choked. She grabbed at her throat and clutched her necklace of Juno. Her head and heart pounded, eyes watering, while she stumbled for the door and met the cold, impassive marble wall. Her fingers scraped without purchase along the side. *The door had been right behind me.* She scrambled for Juno's light to burn away the pain, but her connection was weakened from her time traveling with Calom. *Goddess, don't let me die. Not here.*

She wheezed another weak, hacking inhale and slumped to the floor.

* * *

Her eyes opened to a ceiling painted like stalagmites and caverns. She rolled, head lolling off the side of the mattress, and dry-heaved. The muscles of her abdomen ached with the force of it as saliva coated her mouth and dripped from her lips. She squeezed her watery eyes shut and waited for it to pass. Her pitifully empty stomach grumbled with aching retribution, and a headache pounded between her eyebrows and at the base of her skull.

Like a newborn calf, Maeve sat upright and surveyed her new surroundings. The bedroom was lavishly decorated with midnight blacks and deep indigo. A fireplace at the other end of the room crackled merrily and cast the space in a warm, amber glow. A row of empty bookshelves lined the west-facing wall, and thick, cream curtains covered the windows. *This place might be more comfortable than the jail carts, but it is no less a cage.*

She recoiled in horror and discomfort when she looked down. A carnelian-colored dress pooled around her hips, and a pair of dainty, golden silk slippers covered her feet. Panic swelled, and she touched her throat. *Have they stolen my mother's necklace?* She sighed, relieved, and ran her thumb across the pendant.

Warily, Maeve climbed from the plush mattress. The door was locked. *No surprise.* She peered out the dark windows, and the courtyard's campfires greeted her like lonely red stars. Hagken knocked her out and had her cleaned up, dressed, and imprisoned. *Lovely. What a charmer.* She opened the drawer of an empty writing desk. Nothing.

Juno, be with me. She twisted her hands together. *What could he have done with the others? Are they safe?* Her anxiety gnawed with blunt teeth at her empty stomach. A dinner was laid on a tray beside a plush, navy armchair in front of the fireplace. She tore a chunk of dark-crusted bread from the plate and tossed it between her fingers, trying to decide if he'd starve her out or if the food was poisoned. Her stomach gurgled. Maeve, exhausted, hungry, and wound tight with fear, bit into it. She managed a few bites before tossing it into the fire. *Enough.* She spent the past two weeks being ignored, belittled, and used. It ended now.

She slammed her fists on the door. "Hello?" she yelled, "if you don't let me out this instant, I'll break the door down."

The sound of a bolt sliding free was music to her ears.

A melodic and taunting voice answered her, "I'm tempted to

keep it locked and watch you break it."

She didn't grace them with an answer. Instead, she slammed her fist against the wood.

"Fearsome." She heard the smile in their voice, and Maeve rolled her eyes.

"Open it."

Another bolt inched along as they spoke, "Calom was most eager to deliver you himself. Shall I fetch him?"

Maeve recoiled at the thought of Calom and Hagken in a room.

She said, "I dislike him."

The door opened to reveal the dark-haired and handsomely contemptuous face of the stranger from the courtyard. Their expression was benign, and shadows and swirls of dark makeup decorated their sharp blue eyes.

"It's a good thing he found himself preoccupied." They leaned against the doorframe and crossed their arms. "Same with the guards posted outside of your room."

"And that was your doing?"

"Somewhat." Their eyebrow cocked upward. "It's not my fault his sister has such a short fuse."

Despite their lean, muscular frame, they blocked the doorway from Maeve's exit. She shifted her weight. *What do they want from me? Why are they here?* Their eyes scanned Maeve's face.

"He's expecting you in his quarters."

She lifted her chin, feigning courage, "What are you? His messenger?"

That damn smirk. Again. She hated the way it dimpled their cheek.

"His heir." They gave her a languid, exaggerated bow. "Alistair, at your service."

Maeve stiffened. *Royalty and heir to that awful king?* She couldn't see any similarities in their features. Alistair's eyes were bright and sly compared to the dark, foreboding gaze of the king.

"Well," she huffed. "That explains your manners."

Alistair barked a laugh and tossed their dark curls.

"You're fun."

"Glad one of us is enjoying ourselves," she said acidly. "Are you going to tell me anything useful? Like where everyone else is?" Her mother's voice rang inside her head to control her emotions. 'Juno won't accept an angry priestess,' she had said, 'if you want to keep your connection with her, then you must always be calm and gracious.'

"Fret not, Maeve." They pushed away from the door frame. "They're safe."

"Forgive me if I don't believe you."

"The women of your village were brought to the bathhouses, given fresh clothes and hot meals, and put to work."

Something tight inside Maeve's chest was unwound.

"What do you mean 'put to work'?"

They offered her their elbow. "Walk with me, and I'll answer every question that beautiful head of yours comes up with."

She balked at them. *Why does everyone in this cursed place think I can't walk alone?* Alistair tilted their head, smirked, and dropped their arm. She fell into step and straightened her spine. She wouldn't be intimidated by Alistair or this drafty, old keep with its strange opalescent walls and cryptic etched carvings.

"Mending clothes, helping in the kitchen, caring for little ones, and others went to the barracks to join the fight."

Maeve scoffed.

Their eyes slid to her, calm as water. "You don't think he can win?"

"I doubt he'll join the frontline."

"True enough." They shrugged. "If he decides to fight, he'll likely remain somewhere safe with the protection of his mages and Calom."

"And you're fine with that?"

"There's little I can do in my position."

"You're his heir. Someone called you a general. You must have some authority."

"It would take a cosmic event to change my father's mind."

She flexed her fingers. Could she somehow negotiate the freedom of her people? What about the other citizens dragged into this war? Everything she witnessed spoke to luxury sharpened with cruelty. Perhaps the people serving him weren't treated unkindly, but where did that leave everyone else? Where did it leave *her*? He wanted something from her. She didn't know if she could use it to leverage for the safety of everyone else. A shallow pool of sweat prickled at the base of her spine, and the silken fabric of her dress stuck to her skin. She was a village healer. She dealt with broken bones, birthing babies, and sickness. She wasn't a diplomat.

Alistair stopped. Maeve mentally kicked herself for not paying attention to the turns they took to get here.

Alistair's blue eyes glimmered. "Until next time, Maeve."

"If I'm lucky, it'll be the last time we see each other."

Their smile widened, and they raised the back of their knuckles on the door. Maeve pushed her shoulders back and lifted her chin. Whatever happened next—she'd face it. She had no other choice.

4

The quarters of King Marcus Hagken were as elaborate and resplendent as Maeve expected. The room bloomed with saturated gold and gauzy, sparkling curtains that dripped like diamonds. Large, shiny bronze apparatuses balanced on tabletops, with books, rolled parchment, and variously sized rounded mirrors. A sickly, sweet smell permeated the air. Above the fireplace hung a portrait of a pale woman with narrowed blue eyes and a coy smile.

Hagken held vials of red liquid in each hand.

"Sleep well?"

"Clearly," she said with thinly veiled scorn. Hagken didn't comment on her tone. She glanced to her side, but Alistair was gone. Hagken's eyes were on her, so she couldn't look toward the long hallway and check for Alistair's retreating form. Her skin chilled, unrelated to the temperature of the room. They were alone. That or he had guards hiding beneath tapestries. Or, more likely, he assumed she wouldn't hurt him. She didn't like the idea of being alone with a temperamental king. But he named her an ambassador for Ferne. She would be their advocate and stomach the unpleasant burden of this meeting.

"Alistair told me you've recruited my townspeople," said Maeve. The words stuck to her tongue and teeth, for they both knew it wasn't the truth. He raided her home, stole her people, and coerced them into a war they shouldn't be fighting.

"Yes." Hagken set the vials into their holders. "If the gods are kind, this war will be over very soon, and they'll return to Ferne." His expression softened. "Orange is a lovely color on you. Your ladies-in-waiting chose well."

A tiny sliver of relief sliced through her heart. At least it had been women who dressed her. They were strangers loyal to King Hagken, but it hadn't been him—a small and barely palatable mercy.

"Would you like something to eat?" he asked.

"No, thank you. I ate in my room."

"Excellent."

Maeve crossed her arms. She wouldn't let him distract her or change the subject.

"The people of Ferne are not warriors."

Hagken ignored her. "I'd like to show you something."

The lines around his eyes crinkled when he smiled, but Maeve didn't feel any warmth. He wasn't handsome, even dressed in his splendid navy doublet and white breeches, with his salt-and-pepper hair slicked away from his face. It was a mask. A costume. She had seen the wolfish, hungry look in his eyes and the cruel twist of his lips. She knew in her heart what lay beneath the surface. *All the more reason to be brave.* She steeled her resolve. Even if she couldn't save everyone, she would save the people of Ferne. She would bring them home. Maeve circled the table and laced her fingers together, trying to embody a demure and pleasant nature, a mimicry of the princesses in her storybooks.

He smiled at the oil portrait above the fire. "Do you recognize her?"

"No." She squinted. "Who is she?"

"My good lady Maren Hagken. My late wife. Nearly a decade ago, she fell ill."

"Oh." Maeve bit her lip. "May Lady Janis rest her spirit."

"Do you see?" he asked urgently, gesturing to Maren's features. "She is you. You are her. You carry her spirit. You are her vessel."

He's speaking madness. Maeve's brow furrowed. A pale, slender, regal woman sat in a plush chair. Everything was different about her compared to Maeve. Maren had striking blue eyes, a square-shaped face and cleft chin, and long ringlets of brown hair. Even Maren's coy, enigmatic smile was unlike any expression Maeve could wear. Maeve's face and body were round and soft. Her skin was bronzed by years of sunlight. Her hair was ink-black and twice as long as Maren's. *We look nothing alike, and what does he mean by vessel?* No one could carry someone else's spirit. When someone took their final breath, their spirit belonged to Janis, the goddess of death, and they remained in her web of fate until they were reborn. Everyone knew that, even kings or would-be kings.

"You see it? Don't you?" His expression was wild and desperate. "The ritual said her spirit would return within a vessel of light! And here you are."

Ritual? Maeve didn't know of any rituals of Juno that involved combining spirits or halting death. *None of this makes sense. He said his wife died almost ten years ago. He's mad.* That was the logical answer.

"We can begin anew. The wretched child. That insolent whelp.

They'll never wear the crown so long as we rule together. I know you love them dearly, but they are a curse to my bloodline!" His face flushed, and spittle flew from his lips.

Maeve's eyes widened. His moods were worse than the changing of the tide. Her nails pressed half-moon circles into her knuckles as she clutched her hands together.

He took a breath. "I'm sorry. I'm sorry. They get under my skin."

"Alistair?"

Hagken scoffed at the name and waved it off as if it were a pestering gnat.

"I have something else to show you."

Regardless of her response, he'd drag her along. He pulled a ring of keys from his pocket. They varied in size and color. Some dainty and silver, others iron, and some iridescent. He unlocked a cabinet with two keys and opened a chest full of sparking, palm-sized gems and gold and silver jewelry.

Maeve's jaw dropped. The cabinet's contents alone would change every person's life within Ferne twice over, including herself. She watched Hagken warily as he carefully picked through the horde of treasure. She thought he was a beggar king living off the wealth of a distant family member. Now, it made sense as to how he could afford alchemists, mages, and blacksmiths. She wasn't well-versed in matters of war or finance, but alarm bells clanged inside her skull.

"How did you get all this?"

"My people love me."

Okay. Liar. She bit her tongue and held back the witty retort.

"Here it is."

He held out his palm. A small, pale orange stone flecked with gold and dark amber. Maeve recognized it from her books. It was sacred to Juno. The rare and elusive sunstone. She never thought in all her life she'd see one up close. An attuned sunstone could reverse death, heal blighted crops, or cure an entire populace of disease. It fractured and flickered in the glowing firelight and looked half-alive with the flames dancing across its surface.

"It'll be your wedding gift. We can set it into a crown or necklace." He reached beneath his collar, lifted his necklace from his throat, and a pale stone dangled from his fingertips. *Is that a moonstone?* The stone was sacred to Janis, Juno's sister. *Does Hagken realize what he has?*

"As you can see, I employ talented jewelers and blacksmiths."

Her mind stuttered to comprehend what was said and shown.

"Wedding?"

"Don't be daft," his condescending tone dug under her skin. His fingers closed around the sunstone, and he tucked away his moonstone necklace. "I explained everything earlier."

She withdrew. "I'm not carrying your dead wife's spirit. I'm not getting married!"

Hagken's expression went blank. "We must present a united front against our enemies."

"They're not my enemies!"

His face contorted, and he yelled, "Enough!"

A panicked, heart-pounding fear crawled up her throat. He would keep her here. He would lock her up. He would marry her, and she'd be trapped. She'd never see her friends again. She'd never walk along the rolling pastures of Ferne. She swallowed the saliva filling her mouth.

"Come, drink, and settle your nerves," he said, pulling Maeve to a table with a wine decanter. He poured her a glass without releasing her.

"I don't need a drink." Her mind whirled with ideas of how to escape. *This tower is too high to jump from.*

"Well, I do," he said sourly. He filled his glass twice, drained it, and drank a third. "I do not understand. I did the ritual." He muttered. "Perhaps your spirit is trapped within the vessel. Yes, yes, that could be it. I must release her spirit. My sweet Maren."

The door burst open. "My King!"

"What?" his voice was full of venom. He released her, and Maeve rubbed at the irritated flesh of her wrist.

"We were unable to capture Alistair." Calom shifted his weight.

"Say that once more, Duskryn."

"We couldn't—they're gone. I'm sorry."

"An entire retinue of trained guards couldn't capture and hold them?" His eyes bulged from his face. "An idiot who hardly reached their thirtieth name-day?" A frothy clear spittle bubbled at the corners of his lips.

Calom bowed his head. "I'm sorry–I'm sorry. We'll keep looking —I—you have my word, my King. I will find them."

"Useless!" Hagken threw his wine glass against the wall. Maeve covered her head with her hands as it shattered.

"I promise you, sire. I will do anything. I will–" Calom buckled over, capsizing beneath his weight, and caught himself on the wooden floor. King Hagken held his fist aloft toward Calom, and black ooze seeped between his fingers. The sickening wrongness of his magic permeated the air. It smelled of rot, wet clay, and infected corruption.

Maeve stared at Calom. His eyes went bloodshot, his mouth frothed, and his fingernails clawed desperately against the hardwood. A putrid vapor curled around his body. Hagken turned, storming across the room, shouting about the imbeciles and morons he had within his keep. He drank another glass of wine.

She didn't recall crossing the room. In one moment, she was beside the fire, and in the next, she was in front of Calom. She didn't like him. She actively disliked him. He was neither kind nor virtuous. And yet...Maeve crouched, her skirt pooling like liquid amber, and brought her fingertips together. *Juno, be with me.* Hagken wasn't watching. It was now or never.

Calom didn't deserve to die. All life was sacred. She would be a poor excuse for a priestess if she let him continue to convulse on the floor. Hagken shouldn't have the power to decide who lived and died simply because he was upset. It wasn't his call to make. That power belonged to Janis.

She touched her fingertips to Calom's flushed face. His storm-touched eyes rolled backward into his skull, and the sickness moved like oil beneath his skin. Maeve found the secret quiet and warm place inside her heart. It was wildflowers in full bloom, the sun at zenith's peak, and the shape of her mother's smile. A soft, radiant light emanated from her fingers, and Juno's magic chased the sickness from Calom's veins.

He hacked another rough, wet, bloody cough before he became quiet and still. Maeve opened her eyes to see him staring at her in awe. He likely suspected she would've let him die after everything he put her through. She pressed a finger to his lips and looked imploringly at him to not reveal what she had done. She didn't want to inspire more of Hagken's ire.

His misty gray eyes dropped to the floor. The wood was covered in thin scratch marks and gouges. Some were older than others. *How many clawed at the floor and died?* Her heart shriveled with cold anger. Her assumptions were correct. *Hagken is cruel to those who serve him.*

Calom rubbed his throat. "I'll sound the alarm, my King; we'll find them."

Hagken poured himself another glass of dark red wine.

"I don't need to tell you what will happen if you don't," he hissed without glancing at them.

Hagken said, "I'm sorry for this dreadful business. It seems the ritual will have to wait."

Oh no. How will I ever recover? Maeve toyed with the pendant at her neck. If the castle was on alert looking for Alistair, what were her chances of escape? Could she find everyone from Ferne and convince them to leave? She hardly understood the layout of this labyrinth. She chewed the inside of her cheek. *Hagken thinks I'm a vessel for Maren. He thinks I'm holding onto her spirit. I doubt he'll let me go.*

"Come and sit," he said, his voice distracted as he looked out the dark window.

I'm not a dog. Her upper lip curled with distaste.

"Why are your men trying to capture Alistair?"

"A stupid question," he sounded impatient, "Maren and I had no children together." Maeve's skin prickled with uneasiness. "Once her spirit is free from this vessel, we can change that. We can have a true heir."

Hagken whirled upon her.

"Imagine it!" he said, and the stink of wine wafted into her face, "an heir for my bloodline. A true son for my empire."

Her mind was sluggish to respond, and her heart faltered inside her chest.

"I thought Alistair was your child?"

"They were Maren's," Hagken snapped, "not mine. Through generosity and love, I kept them and raised them as my own." His face mottled with anger. "I will release Maren's spirit from your body, and all will be right. You will bow before me, Maeve. You will help me."

"No, I won't," Maeve's voice trembled.

He leaned in. The ever-present and rising panic bubbled inside her and fizzled across her skin. The prospect of escape narrowed and closed like a wire trap. Between her breasts, she focused on the heavy, warm weight of her charm. She wasn't a helpless child. She had power. She would escape this mad king no matter the cost. *Juno is with me. She's always with me.*

"You will." He bared his wine-stained teeth.

Her magic flowed through her veins and crackled across her skin like ember sparks. She shoved Hagken. One hand on his face and the other on his chest. Her palm erupted with hot, white light. Hagken shrieked as the flames caught his skin, and his flesh bubbled and peeled with sudden heat. A peek of white bone revealed itself between the flashes of firelight. He screamed, clawing at his burning face, and collapsed. His eyes rolled in his skull like a frightened horse.

The sunstone dropped from his hands and bounced against the scratched wood. Maeve snatched it and shoved it into her bodice. Her nostrils stung with the stench of burning flesh. She bolted for the door without looking back.

Alistair stood on the other side. A splatter of blood marred their cheek. Their makeup was smudged around their narrowed, bright eyes, and their curly hair was freed from its fastening and in wild disarray around their face. A wet, garnet-colored sheen glistened across their dark armor.

Their eyes roamed her face, clocked their father on the ground in agony, and they took a step backward to let her pass. Maeve picked up her skirts and ran with Alistair close behind.

"Good to see you're alive," they said with unnerving calm.

Her chest heaved with labored breath. Each hallway looked the same. The bells continued to toll, loud and ominous above her head and echoing through the marbled halls. Alistair followed her. But after the second dead-end, she glared at them.

"Are you going to help me?"

"Would you like help?"

She made a frustrated noise at the back of her throat.

"Agree to come with me, and I'll show you how to get out of here," they said.

They wiped their cheek with a gloved hand and smeared blood across their skin. Maeve tore her fingers through her sweaty dark hair. Her patience unraveled.

"Why does everyone in your forsaken family have to negotiate?"

Alistair shrugged one shoulder.

"Fine!" She threw her hands in the air. "Fine!"

A knife in her heart twisted. She didn't want to leave her people behind, but what other choice did she have? Her magic melted half the king's face off. It might have killed him. They would hunt her. They would imprison her. She couldn't help anyone locked inside Hollyhock's prison tower. Each toll of the bell struck a splinter of fear into her spine. They would discover the king at any moment. And they would know it was her. She tried to control her breathing and stay calm, but her body vibrated with tense, restless energy. Not even grasping her necklace brought her comfort. Alistair walked among the shadowed corridors with quiet confidence. More than once, they stopped her and flattened themselves against the wall as a group of guards or laborers ran past. It all went well until their luck ran out.

"You there!"

Alistair yanked her into an alcove, and her knees bumped into theirs in the confined space. Maeve bowed and prayed the guard would walk in the opposite direction. Alistair's breath stirred the wisps of hair at her temple. The clanking footsteps grew close.

"They've found us," she whispered. Her eyes lifted to see Alistair holding a small dagger by their chest. The bluish tint of moonlight cut sharp angles into their face. Their eyes narrowed, lethally cold and distant.

The guard's face came into view. His pale complexion was tinged green, and bloodshot storm-born eyes stared through her. *Calom.*

She snatched Alistair's wrist to stop their attack, and their strong pulse throbbed beneath her fingertips.

"Wait," she said to Alistair. Maeve swallowed and addressed Calom. "I can't stay here. You have a better idea of my fate if I do."

His jaw clenched. He touched the hilt of his sword at his hip. "I've got orders."

"His orders nearly killed you. I saved you. Please. Let us go."

His hand tightened around his sword. Calom wouldn't budge for bribery. She thought of their short time traveling together when Calom let slip a single piece of personal information.

"You told me you're a man of faith."

"What of it?"

"Then you know the teachings. You know the sacredness of life," she said, feeling like Estoria's largest hypocrite. She cut herself on the sharpness of Calom's eyes. "A follower of Juno wouldn't reject an honest payment of a life debt."

"Merciful thing, aren't you?" He sneered when he looked at Alistair. "Did they tell you how many they killed? The eastern wing is drenched in blood. A massacre."

Maeve placed her fingertips on Calom's bare knuckles wrapped around his pommel. After what happened, the tactile sensation of touching someone skin to skin made the hair on her arms lift. Her throat thickened with saliva. If appealing to his faith wouldn't work, she'd appeal to something else.

"I owe you a dance, Lieutenant Duskryn," her words came out raspy. She didn't know how to make her voice sound sultry or tempting. She was backed into a literal corner and desperate to escape with their lives intact. If he wanted her to beg, then she'd beg.

Calom chuckled.

"Do you think me so vain as to betray my King for a dance?" He rolled his eyes. "You surprise me, Lady Maeve. You're willing to throw your fate into the hands of the shadow general?"

"I'd rather my fate be with Alistair than the king," Maeve answered with false bravado.

Calom whispered low, "Stay, and I'll be the keeper of your fate."

Alistair twitched. "He's stalling."

Calom's grip adjusted under her palm. She threw herself at him to stop him from drawing his longsword. He stumbled, and Alistair's fist slammed into his jaw. His head lolled. He crumpled to the floor, and she winced. It wasn't the outcome she wanted, but at least Calom wasn't dead. *I don't want to kill anyone to escape this place. Not even him.*

"Sorry," she mouthed to him. Alistair's gloved fingers enclosed around hers. They pulled aside a tapestry of Theadora, pushing against the blue-veined marble wall, and the hidden door hissed as it swung inward. *Hollyhock is full of secrets.* Alistair shook dust from their hair, pressed their finger to their lips, and gestured for Maeve to follow.

Maeve clung to Alistair's hand as they guided her through the darkness. The air was stagnant. Their footfalls were flat against the dirt. In Estoria, underground burials were uncommon, but Maeve suspected a tomb would feel similar to this.

"I learned about these tunnels a few years ago," they said, quiet voice echoing. "Father preferred it if I remained out of sight. It also adds to the mystery and allure of the shadow general."

"I thought Hagken found Hollyhock two years ago."

"A lie. We lived here after he was dethroned. We spread rumors, and mages enchanted the castle to appear abandoned whenever we thought someone was getting nosy."

Maeve frowned. "That seems like a lot of work."

"My father is ambitious and petty. I imagine it delights him to live within the kingdom under General Fenris' nose and hide from his other enemies."

"Your father must have many of those."

They chuckled and said, "You have no idea."

"How long will they hunt us?"

"Depends," they replied, "did you kill him?"

Maeve's stomach rolled, queasy and uncertain, and she shook her head. The horrifying sight of flesh bubbling and blistering beneath her healing hand. She never used her powers like that before. Her hands were made to stitch wounds, to bring life into this world, and to heal the sick. She was raised by her family, following the goddess Juno, to honor all life's creatures. Like a rat trapped beneath the stone, she could feel tiny claws of shame scraping against the chambers of her heart. King Hagken wasn't a good man. He likely wasn't even a good king. But did he deserve it? She didn't know. A small part of her hoped he was dead, but if she killed him, then what did it mean for her? She chewed her lower lip.

Life and death overlapped one another. She was familiar with the pain and loss of illnesses and old age. It was how people in her community died. It was never violent or cruel. They passed from this life to the next, surrounded by family and friends with cloying, fragrant herbs clouding the air. Her mind flashed with the image of her neighbors being struck down by Hagken's men. *How am I any different? I'm not following orders. I'm in control.* Maeve shuddered.

"Maeve?"

"No." Her voice cracked like an egg, "I don't think I did."

"Then they'll hunt us until we're found."

The air stirred at their feet. Alistair muttered under their breath. The wall shimmered with light and faded into a transparent ghostly veil. The night sky opened like a vein of stars above them. The crescent moon smiled down at them, wicked and secretive. Alistair led her through the grassy hillside toward the forest at the edge of the property.

5

They crawled over dead logs and carpets of fallen leaves. Her breathing was shallow, terrified. They escaped Calom, but that didn't mean he betrayed his king. He promised Hagken he would find Alistair. *He once told me he was a man of his word.* Alistair froze like a fawn sensing a hunter. The forest emptied of sound.

"They haven't sent the hounds after us," Alistair whispered.

"That's a good thing, isn't it?"

She tugged on Alistair's gloved hand. The more distance and space she put between herself and Hollyhock, the better. She suspected Alistair was leading them north toward the independent lupine forests bordering Hollyhock. She would prefer to go east, towards Ferne, but perhaps she could loop around and use the forest to hide. Or she could keep pushing north, toward the hidden city of Lunesca, and find help among the rangers there—either way, she needed to keep moving.

"Not if they're sending something much worse."

A gust of wind blew against their backs. Maeve nearly toppled over, but Alistair's grip kept her upright. A thunderclap of noise broke through the silence as if several trees were blown away at once. Alistair crouched. Maeve's eyes strained to see anything in the absolute darkness.

There was a flash of indigo to their left, and Maeve winced at the burst of color. Through the thick, lush foliage, a shape appeared. It was skeletal with patches of rough, brown fur. Its bones were stark-white against the dark forest. It moved on four legs with pulsing, lilac flaring at the joints. Maeve's eyes widened. It was taller than a horse, and its massive skull was predatory with sharp, elongated canine teeth. The best comparison she could draw was the creature appeared to be bred between a wolf and a bear.

A flickering orange torchlight glowed beside it. The beast lifted its head and huffed. A pale-haired woman stepped around its hulking haunches and patted the beast affectionately on the snout.

"Good girl. They haven't gone too far, have they?" Her face turned toward the trees, and she raised her torch higher. Maeve's pulse throbbed in her neck, and her limbs stiffened. They had no chance of survival. Cara's powers were mostly unknown to her, and the beast could crush either of them with a single claw.

Alistair's breath tickled her cheek.

"Can you handle Cara? I'll distract her pet."

Maeve's stomach lurched. After what happened with the king, she wouldn't use Juno's power against Cara. *Juno won't forgive me.* Maeve could almost understand Cara's words in the nearly silent forest. The lilt and rhythm of her voice were an obvious clue to her spell casting, but Maeve had zero context for what the spell was. Another beast? Or something worse? It could be anything. She refused to let Alistair's hand go when they attempted to move away.

She said, "I can't."

"Of course you can. You handled Marcus fine."

"I don't want to!" She struggled to keep shrillness out of her voice. "If—I—we can find another way."

"There is no other way. We can't outrun it."

Another flash of color exploded from Cara's direction. Her hair drifted around her face like she was floating underwater and an arcane net interlocked with hexagon glyphs bubbled out from her hands.

"Yikes." Alistair drew their dagger. "Out of time. Go!"

They pulled Maeve to her feet and nearly wrenched her shoulder from its socket. Maeve stumbled through the thicket; every noise echoed like a death knell. A stampede of thunderous footfalls reverberated behind them. The net and the beast with Cara on its back advanced. Cara held one palm open in front of her to guide her spell.

"Keep running," Cara yelled, "she loves the chase!"

Alistair veered left. One of Maeve's slippers slid from her foot. They stopped suddenly near the exposed roots of a towering canopy tree, Alistair planted their feet and tossed their dagger. It spun beautifully in the air. The blade fizzled with arcane energy when it struck Cara's net and froze within the magical webbing. Cara twisted her torso, and the beast skidded to a sideways stop.

"Ah, my favorite looming shadow," she crooned. "I should've known you wouldn't go down without a little bloodshed." She drew the net toward her and plucked the dagger free.

"This is a pretty one," she said, "I assume you'd like it back?" Her tone was equal parts contemptuous and flirtatious. She slid the dagger into a leather fastening around her upper thigh.

"Come get it." Her knees kicked into the gigantic ribs of her beast. She stalked them deliberately and slowly. If not for the aura of light pulsing from the creature, Maeve wouldn't be able to see her.

Wait, that's it! Light! She wouldn't need to hurt Cara. Maeve called Juno's power. A moment of doubt surged and churned her stomach with bile. *What if Juno doesn't answer?* Divine magic blossomed beneath her skin. Her relief was sweet and immediate, but Maeve had no time to cherish it.

"Get ready to run," she said before a burst of light erupted in front of Cara. The beast screeched, grating and sharp. Cara reeled backward as her creature threw itself upward, its deadly paws swatting the air. The light burned for a few seconds. It was enough for Maeve to see some of the forest and grab Alistair's hand. They ran. The forest plunged into darkness. Her breath shook. Her mouth tasted like copper. She urged her feet forward, panicked but alive. The world blurred around her, and no thundering, trembling steps followed them.

Maeve waited until several long, tense minutes passed before risking her voice. She kept expecting Cara to emerge from the shadows with her creature made of pale bone and sharp teeth. She waited for howls to echo through the trees. Yet silence and shadow followed them.

"What was that?"

"The beast is necrotic. She calls it her bone chimera."

Maeve shivered. Necromancy was frowned upon in their religious faith and banned within the academies. No one openly practiced necromancy in Estoria. It was an insult to everything Juno stood for. It was a manipulation of life and death. She chastised herself for her earlier curiosity about Cara. *Calom said that Hagken allowed the practice of outlawed and shunned magic. I should've suspected Cara wasn't an average mage.* Cara Duskryn wasn't to be trusted or admired. Her brand of magic was insulting—an aberration.

"The other spell is a paralyzing effect. I've never seen her use it while moving." Alistair scratched their head. "We're lucky it didn't touch us."

The implication that Alistair worked with Cara weighed in Maeve's gut. *Cara will return to Hollyhock, and then what will she do? Will she punish the people of Ferne? Torture them for information?* A keen sense of guilt formed a boulder in her throat. First Hagken, then Cara. How many times would she abuse Juno's powers and justify it? Could this have been avoided if she stayed behind to protect her people? Her eyes ached.

"I need to go back to Ferne."

"No." They scoffed. "They'll look for you there."

"I need to get my things."

Alistair's eyes flashed gray in the moonlight.

"Be reasonable, Alistair. We need supplies if we want to survive more than one night."

"He might send Cara again."

"I have a plan."

They crawled through the brambles. Tiny, eager thorns snagged at her dress and caught in her dark hair. She tripped over roots and rocks, and Alistair's firm grip on her hand kept her from sprawling into the dirt. Alistair walked among the shadowy branches and thick-leaved trees with the same confidence they held within the keep.

"Can you see in the dark?" asked Maeve.

They laughed. "Do I look like a cat?"

"Well, I can't see." She snapped her fingers, and magic sparked along her wristbone in tiny, ember motes of light. A glowing radius pooled around their feet and shrank back the wood's shadows. *It should be enough to see and not draw attention.*

"How many tricks do you have up your sleeve?" A smirk toyed at the corner of their lush mouth.

"A few," Maeve said, wiping blood from her nose with her orange sleeve.

They led her over a stream to cover their scents. Ever so often, Alistair would stop and tilt their head, listening to the sounds of the forest and the fading howls of bloodhounds. The hem of her dress grew muddy with tiny snags in the fabric, and her feet throbbed. She notched her shoulders back and pushed onward.

"What's your plan?" Alistair asked.

"Hm?"

"What's your plan if we return to Ferne?"

She wasn't sure if she could trust them. Yes, they came to her aid, but she didn't know them. All she knew was their father despised them and issued an order for their capture. She didn't know their motivations. She thought they'd leave when the coast was clear, and she'd find her way back home.

"I thought we'd part ways before reaching Ferne."

"Eager to get rid of me, Maeve?"

She rolled her eyes. "Forgive me if I don't want to continue associating with the Hagken family."

Alistair rubbed the center of their chest. "Even without a blade, you know how to strike someone's heart."

"You'll live."

The stars winked at them, and exhaustion tugged her limbs. Alistair never made a sound. It was like walking beside a wraith. Her steps were clumsy and bumbling in comparison. She caught herself when she stumbled over a gnarled root.

Their cool gaze slid to her. "We can stop up ahead."

"How do you know?" Maeve wiped her dirty, raw palms on the front of her dress.

"I spent a lot of time in these woods."

"Hunting?" A child of Hagken would be good at hunting, she assumed.

"Foraging," they said, running their gloved fingers across a large, leafy plant. "I enjoy collecting herbs and mushrooms."

"Oh." Maeve's cheeks burned. "I see."

Her childhood was spent harvesting herbs and mushrooms and spending long hours learning to identify what was poisonous and what wasn't. When she was young, she would lie in the grass and fall asleep to the sound of her grandmother's voice droning alongside the flies and bumblebees. *Goddess, I wish my grandmother was alive.* She'd have some sage advice about how to deal with a tyrannical, mad king who believed she was a vessel for his dead wife. Or how to deal with dark-haired royalty with dangerous, knife-edged smiles.

* * *

In the silver moonlight, they came to rest at a caved-in house. It looked thoroughly abandoned, but Maeve's shoulders tightened toward her neck. This night wasn't going well. With their luck, they might stumble upon a sleeping bear. Alistair pushed the creaky door in. This house smelled of damp wood and animal hides. The roof's wooden beams had caved in, creating a treacherous maze of debris and dust. Whoever lived here left a long time ago.

Alistair found a candle stub on the mantle, though the matches alongside it were waterlogged and useless. "Can you light this?"

Maeve nodded. How much time would they have within this cabin? She wouldn't risk a fire. But the candle shouldn't be too obvious. A flickering flame sparked to life and cast a dozen shifting shadows in the small hunter's lodge. An animal howled in the darkness, and she thought of a solitary wolf searching for its pack. She rubbed her sternum. *Are Bertha and Lenora safe? Do the people in Hagken's army know how to care for a pregnant woman?* Alistair said the women were together. Maeve prayed that Bertha found a midwife or herbalist in the war camp.

"We should be alright here. We can catch our breath," they said, moving around the space with familiarity while Maeve shivered by the door.

"Is he going to track us all night?"

"Probably." Alistair shrugged. "Assuming he's coherent."

"You sound assured he's alive," she paused, weighing their tone, "more than that, you sound confident he'll survive the injuries."

"It'll take more than a single spell to kill him. Trust me, I know." Alistair leaned against one of the destroyed ceiling beams and ran a knife across a whetstone from their pocket. *Shhhick, shick.* Maeve's mind whirled with impossibilities.

"I've witnessed more than a handful of assassination attempts. He's developed a reputation for himself in being unkillable."

"He's immortal?" She frowned. Even in the Dawn Age, at the birth of Calorum, the only hero of myth to live beyond their mortal lifespan had been Lueltala, the first priestess of Juno.

"Not exactly. There's a magical force that keeps him here. I don't know what it is. He never told me."

Maeve scrubbed her hands over her face. *Eugh.* She flicked the mud and sweat from her fingers. Her toes were muddy, and her arches throbbed in tune with her pulse, punctuated by the sound of the knife on a whetstone. She summoned a tiny bit of Juno's power between her hands to heal herself and wiped the fresh moist sweat from her brow. The fear of being caught meant she needed to be sparse in using Juno's power.

Shick, shhhick. Their escape from Cara left her shaken. She didn't want to use Juno's power for violence. Juno's power was a gift. Maeve rubbed the charm on her necklace and yearned for her mother. *What would my mother have done?* If she were here, Maeve couldn't imagine her mother praising her for maiming Hagken and stunning Cara. Her eyes prickled. She rubbed away the tears with her knuckles and resolved to honor the sunlit path.

She searched the derelict cabin and brushed wispy cobwebs away from her face. The cot near the empty hearth contained a pile of wet, musky furs. A small clay token on hemp string hung from the bedpost. Maeve ran her thumb across the etched symbol. It depicted two crescent moons. A token of Janis. *Does she protect this cabin? Or did the prior occupant worship the goddess of night due to their secluded homestead?* Her musings drew quiet when Alistair crouched beside her, holding a wrapping of tanned animal hides.

"It won't be much, but it's better than those." They tilted their head toward Maeve's solitary, tattered silk slipper.

She wrapped her feet in the strips of hide and tied them using a leather cord. She ignored the musty, old smell as it tickled the back of her throat. At least the hide was more supple and softer than the flimsy slippers. She wiggled her toes. Alistair's generosity was surprising. They hadn't explained their intentions or communicated their plans, and she thought they would have fled to the far corners of Estoria. Yet they remained nearby and offered her this small comfort.

"Thank you," she said sincerely.

Alistair smirked. "Thank me when we make it out alive."

6

Maeve's mote of light extinguished when they stepped into the meadow. The canopy of trees opened to reveal a pocket of starlight and wispy clouds. Enormous, leafy foliage covered the trees' bases, and fireflies blinked around the dew-touched grass. Phosphorescent, glowing mushrooms sat squat like old toads, clustered into rings, and illuminated the clearing in an ethereal, dream-like luminescence.

"Close your mouth, Maeve; otherwise, a frog might hop inside," Alistair teased with a dimple-cheeked smile.

She snapped her jaw shut and flushed. The beauty of this place stunned her. They spent an hour in the abandoned cabin, then another moving through the dark forest with fear biting at her heels. This glade was her first breath of air after swimming underwater. It felt secluded, magical, and safe. The wide tree trunks gave the impression of walls protecting this meadow from the rest of the Calorum.

"Are all heirs so impolite?" she replied. Alistair chuckled from deep within their chest. They crouched near a large oak tree and yanked a burlap sack from under its old roots.

They asked, "Are all village girls impressed by nature?"

She knelt beside a ring of mushrooms. Their little caps were glossy, the stems milk-white. "They're glowing," she said. She never encountered mushrooms like mushrooms in all the foraging of her youth and adolescence. *Is it magic? Does this clearing have some connection to Janis or Thorduun?*

"They're poisonous."

Maeve withdrew her hand.

"Here," they said, tossing the sack to her. "It's better than what you have. I'm going to collect kindling for a fire."

Maeve peered within and discovered pieces of clothing rolled into tight balls. She doubted any of it would fit her, but she didn't want to wear this awful dress for the next few days. She mentally ticked another box into the column that read 'Alistair's generosity.' Even though they were fleeing through the dense forest and Maeve wasn't sure if they were headed north or east, Alistair was determined to make her journey comfortable. They found shelter, replaced Maeve's slippers, and offered her clothes. Her brow furrowed.

"Why do you have this here?"

"I was planning to run away and return home." They pushed their hair away from their face, their eyes lingering on hers momentarily. "Don't wander off."

She scoffed. "Why would I want to?"

Maeve had a moment to herself for the first time since she was stolen from her home. Numbly, she removed the dress and pulled on a pair of breeches. She rolled them at the ankles and tucked her loose-fitting shirt into the waistband. The sunstone fell from her bodice. Maeve pressed her lips to it in reverence and slipped it into her pocket. The crickets chirped and sang symphonies to one another. She was grateful for the solitude, but her loneliness, longing, and guilt demanded her attention.

She pressed her hands over her face as warm tears rolled down her cheeks, and her breath went staccato into hiccuped gasps. Her grief drowned the lively nighttime sounds of the wood. All her friends and neighbors were trapped and subject to the wrath of Hagken. She was supposed to look after them. It was her duty as the village healer and matriarch. She *abandoned* them. It would be her fault if anything happened to them after this. *What if he punished them? What if he* killed *them?* Her heart shattered among the luminescent mushrooms and winking endless starlight. She could go back. She could stumble through the forest and try to get them out. Maeve banished the thought as quickly as it came. A single priestess against the magic and might of an entire army? *Pure madness.*

Her regret washed into shame, denial, and fear, swirling like the wispy ash-colored clouds above. She needed to do something. She couldn't lie down among the grass and poison mushrooms and wait to rot. Her people needed her. She sniffled and wiped her snot away.

"Eugh." She wiped her sleeve onto the grass.

Her eyes tracked to where she saw Alistair disappear. Even two people against an army would fail. Besides, she didn't know if she could trust them. *What would they do if their stepfather was overthrown? Again.*

She interlaced her fingers and bowed her chin toward her chest. It wasn't proper to pray to Juno at this hour. Juno's prayers were for dawn and noon, while twilight and midnight were her sister's hours. However, Maeve's brain buzzed with questions and half-formulated plans and needed guidance. Her tears dried sticky on her cheeks.

"To sunlight and strength, we give our labor to the soil," she began, "and give our gratitude to the light, in service to the good of all and all that is bright." The repetition of prayer lulled her racing mind and frantic heart into a steady, thrumming calm. Juno's magic pulsed at the base of her knees, where they met the cool grass. The magic's golden threads slipped between her fingers and around the knobs of her spine. Even in devout prayer, she knew Juno wouldn't gift her more divine magic to use. Worriedly, Maeve squeezed her hands tighter. She would be lucky if Juno granted her any further magic after tonight. Although made in a moment of terror and desperation for survival, her actions were blasphemous.

She promised to wake up tomorrow and pray during Juno's hour. She would save her village, make amends for misusing Juno's power, and restore peace to the kingdom. Her responsibilities lay upon her shoulders like heavy, freshly fallen snow.

"Not interrupting, am I?" Alistair announced upon walking soundlessly into the glade, their arms laden with kindling. The leaves whispered overhead as if telling secrets to one another.

Maeve blinked. "No."

"Do you think you could use your"— they wiggled their fingers —"sparkly powers to get the fire started?" Maeve laughed awkwardly at Alistair's words.

The kindling crackled to life.

"Neat." They unclasped the band of daggers around their chest and unloaded various-sized blades from their person. She counted at least two blades hidden inside their boots. She watched from the corner of her eye as they peeled off their gloves. Their fingers were slender and long, and a flash of red smeared across their knuckles. They rolled their shoulders and unlaced the leather throngs of their dark, armored tunic.

"You're bleeding!" Maeve jolted as if she'd been dropped into an ice bath.

Alistair looked at their arm, exposed and bare to the firelight. An angry, dark red gash lined their bicep.

They poked near the wound and winced. "It's stopped bleeding."

"Let me see."

Their eyes met hers. They were striking, guarded, and flickering with the twisted, orange shapes of the fire.

"Why?"

Maeve rubbed her hands together. "I can heal it."

It would be the last act of magic she could do today. Even priestesses have their limits. She spent most of the day exhausted and starving or running for her life, and her weariness was settling into her bones.

"You're not going to burn me, are you?"

She set her lips in a firm line but quickly softened. They had no reason to trust her, just as she had little reason to trust them. They were thrown together by circumstance and survival. She extended an olive branch.

"No." She bowed her head. "If you prefer, I can search for herbs to make a poultice to ward off infection." She wished she had her herbal satchel from home.

Alistair grunted with discomfort as they awkwardly unfastened their armor and slid it from their muscled shoulders. Maeve cringed in sympathy when they winced. Alistair's warm tan skin was a smattering of old scars, some faint and nearly white, and others dark brown and razor thin. They marked their body like the lines of a map. Her attention snagged on two long, dark scars below each nipple. They were precise, as if done by a healer's hand. *That doesn't look like a scar from a fight.* She refocused and examined Alistair's injury. Their toned muscles flexed beneath her fingertips when she called to Juno.

"Do you get into a lot of fights?" she asked.

"Not really," Alistair said, "I try to avoid them." They glanced at a jagged mark near their wrist bone. "Some are from training; others were accidents, and a few were bad luck."

Her magic bubbled from the center of her chest and pooled with golden light in her palms. She covered the wound with her hands. The glow suffused their skin and sparkled with the goddess Juno's blessing. Maeve's forehead prickled with cool sweat as the energy pulsed through her. By the power of divine magic, the wound filled with light, mended and left behind a pink, raised scar. It reminded her painfully of Archie. She squeezed her eyes shut, not caring if Alistair noticed her grief, and blinked back her tears.

Alistair made a surprised sound in the back of their throat.

"Maeve..." their tone was different. They weren't mocking or haughty. They said her name as if it were a prayer on the night winds. A spotty blackness swirled behind her eyelids. Her reserve of power was practically empty. Maeve never pushed herself past her limits and didn't want to know what might happen if she ever did. She fell forward into their shoulder, powerless to stop exhaustion from claiming her.

* * *

Maeve woke to Alistair shaking her shoulder. The sky bloomed with light pink and gray. Her body ached, her stomach hollow, and her tongue stuck to the roof of her mouth. The events of the evening returned to her in fragments. The ghastly sight of skin burning, her body trembling with regret and shame and disgust. The sound of dogs howling, bells tolling, and fear clawing down her back.

"We should keep moving," Alistair said. Their voice wasn't urgent, but Maeve sensed the sudden passage of time like a rope around her neck. *How much closer is Hagken? Or did he give up during the night? Are the people of Ferne still alive?* A sharp, tight emotion caught inside her throat, and heat pricked behind her eyes, and Maeve pushed the tears back.

"I want to go home," she said.

"Tell me your plan."

She sat up and scrubbed her damp face. "How do I know I can trust you? How do I know this isn't an elaborate ruse, and you're still loyal to your father?" These questions plagued her last night and revealed themselves at Juno's hour.

Their eyes narrowed and then dropped to the sunlit pendant between her breasts. A flush of heat sprawled over her neck. She recalled collapsing into them, and the embarrassing heat tickled her jaw. She used the last of Juno's power to heal them and didn't regret it. But perhaps she should've given them a warning before knocking herself unconscious.

"You don't." Their lips tilted upward into a smirk. "Call it a leap of faith."

Maeve tucked her amulet beneath her shirt.

"I won't hesitate to burn you you if you betray me," she lied. She knew if it came down to it, she wouldn't be able to hurt them. The guilt of hurting Alistair's terrible father gnawed the back of her mind. It was a miracle she kept her divine connection. She didn't want to push her luck and lose Juno's favor. *I don't know who I would be without it.*

"I've seen what happens when someone gets on your bad side, and I'd like to keep my good looks. Thank you very much."

She rolled her eyes. "I'm sure all of Estoria would weep if

anything happened to your face."

"I can tell you're feeling better. Your plan?"

She could deny them and try to find her way. But she was in an unfamiliar forest with men and dogs and a wild necromancer hunting her. What were her odds of survival if she went alone? Her stomach grumbled.

"Breakfast first, please."

They split a rabbit caught within a snare. The hot flesh, dripping with fat, scalded her tongue, and charred bits dug into her molars. A family of orange butterflies fluttered overhead, and Maeve watched them dance while she collected her thoughts.

"We have a warding stone inside my cottage."

She licked the grease from her fingers. Alistair wordlessly passed her another piece of meat from their portion. She plucked it from their fingertips and bit back her smile. Another check in the generosity box. She was beginning to think Alistair enjoyed sharing. Their magnanimous nature was fascinating. They were called the shadow general among Hagken's army, but their kindness was at odds with that title.

"If I activate it, in theory, it should give us enough time to collect my supplies and flee," she said.

"Aren't those dangerous?"

"They can be. We never used it. Never needed to." The warding stone was her grandmother's. A gift from the priestesses she studied alongside in Everdawn. *If I were a sunseer with the gift of foresight, I would've used the stone when Calom and his men arrived.*

"So, you want to mess with an ancient, magical artifact you've never used before so you can collect your herbalist's bag?"

Maeve nodded. "Unless you have a better plan."

They wiped their fingers on their leather pants and pulled their gloves on.

"Not at the moment."

* * *

They remained within the forest, away from the roads. She was sure they double-backed more than once to confuse the trail and muddle their scents. Maeve clutched Alistair's hand in the darkness as they led her on silent feet. She no longer felt embarrassed about her stumbling steps. Alistair was her guide, and for the time being, she trusted they were taking her home. They made camp when the moon was high, and Maeve would collapse and rub her sore calves and blistered feet.

Usually, she'd be too tired to talk, but sometimes, she'd ask questions and discover new depths to Hagken's cruelty. Before becoming king, Marcus Hagken was an ambitious merchant, hoping to earn a place on the midsummer diplomatic council. One fateful night, after he had a seat among them, he poisoned the councils' drinks and laughed as they choked to death. He made himself ill to pander to the fabricated story that he survived a mass assassination. He dissolved the council and crowned himself king.

Many of the alchemists and mages within his employ were tied to him by blackmail, bribery, or threats of violence. Many, Alistair admitted, enjoyed they could conduct unethical experiments beneath Hagken. While other mages, besides Cara, practiced necromancy. Granted, necromancy wasn't illegal, but in her opinion, it should be. Her skin crawled in recollection of Cara's chimera.

In the capital city of Pyrite, King Hagken built his reputation through bribery, debts, and forgery. The betrayal of his war general brewed for years. Maeve considered her role in this war. He hunted her, but until her people were returned to Ferne, she wouldn't rest. She finished collecting dandelions and joined Alistair. She plucked the yellow heads of the dandelions and placed them on a flat stone. She sometimes worried the campfire would give them away, but Alistair assured her Hagken wouldn't send his scouts this far.

Scents of jasmine and honeysuckle touched the breeze. She crushed the dandelion heads with another stone. The silence between herself and Alistair was strangely comfortable and routine. The firewood crackled and launched an army of sparks into the air. She glanced and met Alistair's guarded expression. The firelight cut flickering shadows into their cheekbones and jaw, and her heart thumped loudly in her chest.

"Who do you pray to?" they asked while fastening their curly, dark hair in a low ponytail at the nape of their neck.

"Isn't it obvious? The goddess Juno," she said, touching the pendant dangling from her neck.

They broke her gaze, tossed grass into the fire, and brought their knees to their chest. She and Alistair had never discussed faith or organized religion before.

"Why are you asking? You don't strike me as a devout person."

"I'm not." Alistair smiled, and the dimple in their cheek deepened in the firelight. "My father, however, is."

Her stomach twisted at the idea of this cruel, terrible king praying to her benevolent, powerful goddess. Juno would never accept someone like him! She recalled the magic he used to incapacitate and sicken Calom. *How did he do it? Where does his power and magic come from? Is it necromancy like Cara? Or is it something darker and more sinister? He spoke of rituals, spirits, and vessels, but none of them sounded familiar to me.* She searched Alistair's expression for insight. But their attention returned to the flames, and their blue eyes hardened like frost.

Her hands stopped, and pollen stained her fingertips yellow.

"Who do kings pray to?" she asked softly.

They grimaced. "Nothing good."

7

When Ferne came into view on the dusky, rose-tinted horizon, Maeve's relief traveled from the tip of her sweaty head to her blistered, red toes. She would've wept if she had the energy for it. Her heart soon fractured down the middle, leaving pieces on the dirt road as she looked upon the vacant houses and fields. A few of the horses whinnied at their passing and stamped their hooves. Maeve spared a moment to press her palms against their muzzles and let them nip at her fingers. The air usually smelled of baked bread, fresh soil, manure, and smoked wood, but now it was as empty as the houses they passed.

"It doesn't feel real," she admitted.

"I'm sorry, Maeve."

Alistair stood a few paces away, their hands flexed into fists at their sides. She sighed and gathered the broken chunks of her heart. They could feel sympathy for her, but they were complicit in the violence. For all she knew, they took part in raids on other villages and helped their father. Alistair, despite their moments of kindness, remained a stranger. She couldn't comfortably call them an ally.

A chorus of dogs barked in the distance. Her mind emptied, and she limped to her cottage on throbbing, sore feet. For a moment, she was stunned by the familiarity and surprised by her overwhelming longing. The fragrant herbs, the idol of Juno beside the fireplace, Clarissa's unfinished remedy, and an arrangement of poultices and jars of salve scattered across her table. *This is my home.* The dogs howled. *And they took it from me.*

She spurred into action and yanked a palm-sized stone from the mantle. Its face was carved with a rune similar to a key.

Many years ago, her grandmother told her that all she needed to do to activate a warding stone was speak her prayer to it. Outside, the sky honeyed with dying, orange light, and the dogs howled and snapped their jaws.

"Juno, Lady of Light." She licked her dry lips. "I pray for safety. I pray for guidance. My home is surrounded by dogs and men who wish to harm me and–" She looked up to see Alistair and her heart skipped. "—Alistair, my companion."

She squeezed the stone. The men were shouting, though their words were barely audible. The light outside withered, and the last wisps of sunlight dripped beneath the horizon.

Maeve's lower lip trembled.

"Please. Please. We need a little time to flee. Please." *Juno should answer. Is the warding stone tied to the time of day?* Her grandmother never explained any finer details. *The prayer should work.*

Alistair moved toward her with a lethal, coiled grace.

"Yeah, this isn't working." They snatched the stone from her fingers.

"Hey!"

"We need a miracle to get out of here in one piece." Their throat bobbed as they swallowed and barked their order into the stone, "Give us one."

"Alistair," she hissed. *What are they thinking? You don't make demands to the divines. You speak to them with polite praise and gentle courtesy.* Alistair would get killed either by the gods or the men outside. She tensed, awaiting divine retribution.

The rune pulsed with silver light, and discordant, disembodied whispers filled the air. The first stars peeked through her window. Her village plummeted into darkness thick enough to have texture. Maeve was suddenly claustrophobic and afraid in her home's intimate, enclosed space. She waved her fingers in front of her face. Nothing. Not a shadowy outline or vague impression of movement.

Outside, dogs whimpered, and the pursuing men panicked. They called for torches and gravelight, an alchemical substance used in lanterns that emitted an eerie, greenish-blue glow.

"We have to hide," she whispered.

"And if they find us?"

Blinded, Maeve's fingers scrambled across the table until she grasped the handle of a peeling knife. She clutched it in her damp hand. *I don't want to hurt anyone.*

"Then..." She swallowed, mouth heavy and dry. "I won't hesitate."

The unnatural darkness shifted, and Alistair's breath wafted against her cheek.

"Stay quiet."

A whisper of movement, and the puff of their breath disappeared. Maeve groped through the darkness. She hoped her fingertips would touch the supple leather of Alistair's armor, but they met air. *Did they abandon me? Or are they hiding somewhere else?*

She maneuvered around the kitchen table, and her abandoned teacup jostled like a faint chime.

"The dogs!" someone shouted with terror in their voice, "someone's cut them loose."

The baying and barking of the dogs scattered across the village as the animals fled from the oppressive darkness. Maeve crept toward the window with one arm outstretched. It was disorienting to have her sight stolen from her. But she had the advantage of knowing the layout of her home.

A body thumped onto the dirt like a sack of potatoes with a wet, gurgling sound.

Their pursuer yelled, "What was that!?"

"Reveal yourself!" The blades scraped as they were released from their sheaths. Her hand trembled, and she desperately tried to inhale slowly through her nostrils. The men sounded too *close* to her home.

"The damn torches won't light."

"Use the gravelight, you fool."

"It's not working."

A scream was cut short and left gasping. Her heart kicked into her throat. Their swords whistled as they wildly cut through the air. Was Alistair out there? She pressed her face against the glass, although nothing could penetrate this magical darkness.

"Stay back wherever you are."

One by one, Maeve heard each body fall unceremoniously to the ground. Some gasped, their words clogged with blood, while others went down screaming and raging against the cold, sharp touch of Janis. Her heart pounded like a drum. *How many are left out there?* The darkness shifted like a roiling, living thing. It carried a pulse of its own.

She lifted the knife. The darkness ebbed. The moonlight cut through the windowpane and illuminated Alistair's sweat-glistening face, and the silver peeling knife poised near their throat.

They tilted their head, their smirk toying at the corner of their mouth, and their moon-touched eyes narrowed into slits.

"Looks like you hesitated."

Maeve pressed one hand to her chest and let the blade fall.

"You're lucky I did."

They shrugged languidly, their black armor shining wet with blood. "You would've healed me."

She shook her head in disbelief. Her magic was limited. A lethal strike could kill them, and no amount of fervent prayers to Juno would reverse it. She rubbed her palms and was eager to chase away the encroaching darkness and let the light flood in. Several orbs burst into existence and bounced through her cottage.

Maeve asked, "Why did the warding stone work for you and not me?"

"The rune on the surface belongs to Janis." They lifted a clay jar and shook it. "I rolled the dice and hoped for the best."

That explains why Juno didn't answer. It didn't explain why her grandmother never told her. *Maybe she didn't know.*

"Well, you weren't very nice about it," she said, crossing her arms.

Alistair plucked a dried herb hanging from the ceiling and sniffed it. "Who said you have to be nice to the gods?"

They don't understand worship at all. She clicked her tongue and left Alistair to their curious perusal of her cottage. She peeled the tattered, dirty wrappings from her aching feet and slid into her weathered, dark brown boots. Her comb struggled through the tangles in her dark hair, and she winced at the angry knots.

"I wasn't aware we came here for the sake of your vanity," they said while leaning against her door frame with their arms crossed.

She worked her fingers through her inky strands and wove them into a messy plait.

"Did you expect me to travel in borrowed clothes with no shoes?"

Their temple touched the worn, well-loved wood, and their dark, curly hair fell across their brow.

"I don't know what to expect from you."

Her brows pinched. Alistair grinned and sauntered away, a confident swagger and grace to their movements. It was as if they won some game that Maeve wasn't aware they were playing.

She searched the jars of herbs and transferred some into the leather pouch fastened to her hip. *Let's see, heimenta, blood-wormwood, caezinnia.* She drummed her fingers against the shelf while searching. *Nighthood could be helpful on the road to help us sleep, but I'll need to brew it.* Her herbal remedies were designed to be distilled into tinctures, teas, or salves. *I have to choose carefully. I won't be able to get more until we reach Pyrite.* Maeve noticed the unfinished remedy for Clarissa on the table and pointedly looked away. *She's safe in Silvercliff. I can't do anything else for her right now.*

Maeve's cottage had three rooms. The central room contained her desk, a vacant hearth, and a couch made of sheep hides and stuffed straw. Adjoining this was her bedroom and a small room for patients. She discovered Alistair lounging on the sofa as if they lived there. She unrolled a map at the table and gave them an expectant look. They sighed, a dagger point pressed into their thumb as they twirled it lightly against their skin.

"Another one of your dangerous plans?" Alistair asked.

"Yes."

"Very well." They got up. "Tell me."

She pointed to Pyrite and said, "I'm going to talk to General Fenris and reveal where your father is. I remember what Hagken's map looked like in the war room, and I'll tell Fenris everything."

Alistair's dark eyebrow lifted. "In exchange for what?"

She squared her shoulders. She thought of the bodies in the mud, people being dragged from their homes, soldiers being forced to fight, and the cruel wine-stained teeth of Hagken's smile.

"Justice."

They whistled. "You think General Fenris will give it to you?"

"If he wants to stop Hagken, then he will." She ground her teeth together. "I know I cannot rewrite time. So, I'm going to do the next best thing and force your father to surrender. I want him to answer for what he's done."

Her determination shaped steel in her bones. She would bring King Hagken to justice if it were her last mortal act. *Alistair said he's difficult to kill. That's fine. I don't want to kill Hagken. I want him to face justice for the pain he's caused.* Alistair's face brightened, and she was awestruck by their dimpled grin.

"Goddess, be praised. I love your optimism."

She couldn't tell if they meant it as an insult and decided it didn't matter. By morning, they would be gone. She would never think of them again unless it was to someday warn her future children about raven-haired fallen royalty with devilish smiles and strange acts of generosity.

"You're welcome to one of the horses in the stable." She rolled the map and secured it with a piece of twine. "I plan to leave at first light and suggest you do the same."

Their smile dimmed.

"Maeve, I'm coming with you."

"What?"

"To Pyrite."

"What?" Her mind lagged to keep pace. She thought they intended to part ways once they brought her to Ferne. She thought their paths, though intertwined for a time, were destined to separate. She was responsible for an entire village. She needed to save them. Her sense of obligation burned within her gut and urged her forward. *What does Alistair have? What burns inside of them?*

"I told you I was planning on running away and returning home to Pyrite, remember?"

"And after?" she asked with a furrowed brow.

"Ideally, I'll spend the rest of my days in lavish company, drinking wine, playing cards, and waiting for the next king to rise to power." They pressed their palm against the table and leaned into it. "If you succeed, and I get to see everything my father loves taken from him, that's merely a bonus."

She swallowed. A tentative trust blossomed through the fractured cracks inside her heart. For the past two weeks, Alistair remained beside her; they caught rabbits and scouted through the darkness. They collected kindling, and she lit the fires. They helped her search for beneficial herbs and fungi. They slew an entire band of trained, armored guards so she could have a chance to escape. After traveling with them, Maeve had no doubt Alistair could fare much easier alone. Yet, they stayed. If she agreed, then she would have their help when it came to setting up camp and keeping watch. It was the practical and sensible choice to say yes. The light she conjured gleamed against their raven shoulder-length hair and defined the hollow edges of their sharp cheeks. They regarded her with an easy, calm confidence.

She offered them her hand. "I suppose we're allies, then."

"What an unlikely pair we make." Alistair shrugged, loose-limbed and lanky, and curled their hand around her wrist. Unfamiliar, but following their lead, she copied their gesture and wrapped her fingers around their wrist. They stood, wrist-locked, clutching to one another, for several heartbeats. She could feel their pulse beneath her fingertips, and their blue eyes crinkled with amusement.

Maeve slowly released her grasp. "I'll make us something to eat."

"I'll see to the horses."

With a fluid movement of her hand, one of her lights followed Alistair out of the cottage and into the night. Her wrist tingled; she rubbed it and wondered what she had gotten herself into.

8

A month of traveling together passed like a half-remembered dream. They were early risers and traveled before Juno's light crested over the horizon. Alistair's company fluctuated from pleasant to brooding, depending on the weather. They sulked beneath their dark cloak whenever it rained. Yet, they would share their cloak with her. She'd find herself pressed shoulder to shoulder next to them, sharing warmth, a glowing ember of magic between her palms. Their evenings were quiet and undisturbed. Alistair guessed that Hagken wouldn't travel this close to Pyrite, but there wasn't a way to be certain. Despite Alistair's stalwart guard, Maeve's anxiety tightened around her ribs and gave her fretful dreams. The light of Juno on her back was a great comfort.

On sunny days, Alistair would tie their horse to Maeve's and scout ahead. They'd slip between the stark, tall shadows of the trees and disappear. In their absence, Maeve would try to connect to the sunstone. She'd whisper soft prayers and hymns to it. However, the stone remained silent, its magic trapped inside the golden-flecked surface.

Today, despite the feverish sunlight, Alistair remained beside her. Their chestnut mares whinnied and shook their manes as they descended the grassy hillside. Alistair patted the mare's neck affectionately and whispered sweet encouragement. Maeve smiled. *They've had a soft spot for the horses since we began.* The city glittered into view, and Maeve's breath caught. Her relief melted into awe.

The high-walled city was divided into sections, and at its center, three massive multi-colored spires reached into the sky. The rope bridges that connected the spires swung in the wind. Her stomach turned sour at the height. The tallest tower was sandstone, its windows shiny turquoise in the bright sunlight. The second was slate gray and rather drab in comparison. The third and shortest tower was a mottled dark green, and a canopy of lush leaves peaked from the open roof.

"Juno, Janis, and Theadora," Alistair said, naming the three matron goddesses of Estoria and the world of Calorum. "Those are their temples. Juno's is the one with the tree."

Beside the city, the teal ocean sparkled, and large, colorful merchant ships swayed at the docks. She had never seen so much water in her entire life. Maeve exhaled a breathy, astonished laugh.

Alistair's grin dimpled. "Wait until you see beyond the gates."

Above the gates, two dark blue banners were brought to life in the wind, and their surface showcased a silver wolf's head. *General Fenris' symbol.* According to Alistair, he hailed from the lupine forest in the west, where many Kaninne lived proudly and secretively among the trees.

Their horses followed a merchant caravan passing through a large, shimmering, magic-touched gate. They barely sanctioned a glance from the attending guards. Her neck twinged as she stared at the spires above and around the city. Pyrite was loud. It wasn't the peaceful sounds of Ferne with laughing children and clucking chickens. Nor was it the menacing, bustling noise of King Hagken's war camp. Pyrite had a flavor all its own. Boisterous and eager merchants shouted from their stalls decorated with rich silks and shiny baubles. Barefoot, filthy children ran through horses and dodged people with sharp eyes and sly grins. An incessant clanking rang throughout the narrow street—the sound of metal upon metal crunching, whirling, and grinding.

The buildings were stacked and mended together. They were connected by bridges over their heads and welded with machinery. She watched as two people stepped onto a platform, cogs spun, thick ropes pulled, and they were lifted onto the walkway bridge. She arched her neck to see what the second level beheld and discovered it was cluttered with tables and people drinking, eating, and a cacophony of live music jarring together.

Metal flashed on people's bodies. A missing arm replaced with copper and silver, pistons shifting like muscles, and ending in a pinching clamp. A pair of thick, bronze goggles rested on someone's head. A copper and amber-gold eye whizzed inside a scarred eye socket. There were flashes of gold within smiles, and thin, metallic apparatuses curved around ears.

"Out the way!" Someone shouted as they zoomed past in a wheeled chair with black smoke trailing behind them. Her horse huffed and stepped back, worried and spooked. She clutched the reins, calming her, and her eyes tingled from her lack of blinking.

She was dizzy, trying to soak in every detail. Magic sizzled in the air. It was in everything. Pyrite was more than a metropolis of stacked buildings, tall spires, and prosperous trade. It was a conglomeration of magic and artisans. The city pulsed with life and sound and color.

This is what the rest of the world is like. She thought with rich, abundant wonder. *This is how the world has changed.* She could bring some of Pyrite's knowledge home. But first, she would need to learn how some of the devices worked. Was it a foolish thought to hope she could return here once her business with King Hagken was settled? Her heart swelled with the dream.

"You're not going to fall off your horse, right?" Alistair called to her from over their shoulder.

She shook her head, "No."

Despite the rancorous noise of the city, Alistair's laugh filled her ears.

* * *

"Arriving through the copper gate is always like that. It leads into the merchants' walkway, the part of the city that never sleeps," Alistair explained after their horses were stabled, and they managed a quick breakfast of white fish and crackers at a nearby tavern. Maeve's tongue burned with the sharp, aromatic spices they cooked with. Truthfully, she loved it. Her heavy, burdened heart was lightened by the sights and sounds of Pyrite, even if it was temporary. She let Alistair lead her through the winding, cobbled streets while she stared at every passing marvel in childish wonder. An elderly dark-skinned man walked past them carrying a miniature white peacock on his shoulder. Two women, their hair blue and green, spoke in a language Maeve didn't understand or recognize with bright, engaged expressions. Their dusky cheekbones were dusted with glitter.

"The silver gate is near the docks. It's less chaotic, but the guards are hard to bribe and even harder to avoid. And there are routes into the city through the sewers, but considering our horses, I chose against it."

Her eyes followed the colorful strangers.

"What were they saying?"

"Who?"

"The women we walked by."

"If I had to guess, given the pouches and vials on their belt, they're likely part of the alchemist guild. They speak whatever alchemists speak."

She didn't recall the alchemist she met when she was young speaking anything other than Estorian. She risked appearing ignorant and asked the question on her tongue.

"Alchemists have a language?"

"They do." Alistair adjusted their dark leather gloves at the wrist. "Because the mages and alchemists hate each other, their guilds created their own language to protect their interests."

"Your father has mages and alchemists in his war party. They looked like they got along."

"War makes for interesting bedfellows." Alistair pantomimed between them. "Look at us! You're a damn paragon of Juno's virtue, and I'm the unwanted heir of a mad king."

"You're more than that, Alistair."

"That remains to be seen." They stopped at a charred and hollowed-out homestead. The smell of smoke clung to the air. Maeve's stomach threatened to revolt against her breakfast, with the memory of Hagken's skin burning beneath her palm. "We're here."

"Charming."

"Don't let her looks fool you," they said.

Alistair groped along the blackened door frame, seeking something. She rocked back on her heels. It was strange to be in a place so quiet after the hustle and bustle of the merchants' quarters.

This house was nestled beside others of similar or worse condition. A fire must've broken out on this street, forcing the residents to flee. And rather than repair the damage, it was left a graveyard full of black skeletons.

A low, vibrating hum trembled beneath her feet. She snapped her eyes to a grinning Alistair. A few feet past the threshold, a copper metallic trap door revealed itself and slid aside soundlessly. A woman with short, blonde hair popped out.

Her face split into a toothy grin.

"As I live and die by the sunshine! Alistair!" her voice was warm and sweet like honey. Her accent was rounder and fuller than Alistair's. Her amber eyes flickered toward Maeve, and suspicion clouded her features. Maeve waved awkwardly. *Alistair didn't mention we were meeting anyone.* She assumed they were taking her to a hideout or a sneaky rogue hidden city beneath the streets. Something like that, anyway. She quashed her disappointment.

"Friend of yours?"

"Near enough, Imogen."

"Alright," she said, shrugging, "come on down, then."

Maeve crawled down the ladder into a cool, sweet-smelling alcove. The room was the size of her bedroom back home. Imogen wore stained gray overalls with goggles hanging from her freckled neck. From the elbow down, her left arm was tarnished gold and filled with delicate, thin components built into the shape of finger bones and tendons. *It looks remarkable.* Maeve tried not to stare as Imogen hung a kettle over a stone pit illuminated with ghoulish gravelight. Gravelight never produced smoke and was particularly useful in homes lacking traditional fireplaces or cooking spits. However, it was expensive, so no one in Ferne used it. Imogen's metallic fingers clicked with each movement. Its construction held an elegance and raw complexity. *I wonder if she's studied the human body?*

Imogen asked, "What's your name?"

"Maeve."

"Maeve? That's pretty."

"Thank you..." She glanced at Alistair. They were fiddling with a ball-shaped, multi-level contraption on Imogen's table. Their tongue poked their lower lip as they twisted it between their hands. Maeve's cheeks burned. She averted her gaze. Each surface was cluttered by machinery, books, or loose parts. It reminded Maeve of her home. It was a little messy but well lived-in. A cloth hammock hung from the ceiling, crimson ivy crawled out from ceramic pots, and lanterns glowed with pale white light. Maeve peered through the dirty glass to see what it was. It didn't look like gravelight. The color wasn't green enough.

"Don't get too close, now." Imogen smiled a little. "It's a work in progress."

"What is it?"

She looked at Alistair, seeking some type of approval, and they tilted their head in the barest of nods.

"There's a flower that blooms at night during the height of frost crown. When treated properly, it glows for longer than gravelight does." Imogen jumped into an impassioned ramble about the various flowers that blossom during specific seasons, and Maeve's eyes widened. Her knowledge of fauna and foliage felt rudimentary in comparison to Imogen's. *She might know more than my grandmother.*

"How did you learn all of this?" asked Maeve. She maneuvered her body in the small space around Imogen's. Imogen lifted her bony shoulders toward her ears, and Maeve noticed the shiny raised flesh of a scar lining the base of her skull.

"I worked with the alchemists' guild for a time."

"And you left?" she guessed. Alistair chuckled. She met their gaze from across the table.

Alistair said, "They threw her out."

Imogen nodded.

"The alchemists love to experiment with transformation. They want to take dirt and turn it into gold." Her brown eyes rolled toward the low ceiling. "How boring. I started experiments pulling the essence out of things." She pointed a small wrench toward the hanging lanterns.

"That doesn't sound terrible."

Imogen's lips twisted. A flicker of shame and disgust crossed her freckled face.

"I could take scents from flowers and dilute them into perfume. I could take heat from the fire and bottle it. But it wasn't enough. It wasn't important enough!" Imogen huffed. "I tried to pull the sickness out of someone."

Maeve considered this. Juno's magic flowed through her veins without resistance. Yet, her magic had limits, and its tie to divinity didn't make it infallible. If a disease or sickness was too advanced or a body mortally wounded, then Juno's divine touch couldn't save them. *If someone removed sickness through a potion or tincture, it could change the world.*

"What happened?"

"They died." Imogen raked her fingers through her short blonde hair, leaving shiny black grease streaks behind.

The kettle whistled on the stove and ended their conversation. She poured tea into three misshapen clay cups. Maeve reached out to help her clear the scrap metal and glass, but Imogen brushed her seeking fingers away. She piled the various materials onto a cluttered shelf bolted into the wall.

"What brings you to Pyrite?" She sat cross-legged in her chair.

Alistair leaned back. "she's seeking General Fenris."

Maeve blew steam from her tea and took a cautious, slow sip. Imogen shook her head and swallowed her hot tea without a wince.

"He's not been in the city for weeks."

Maeve frowned. A worm of doubt crawled into her heart. *If General Fenris isn't here, who do I talk to about Hagken?*

"There's a reason Fenris never took the title of king and continues to call himself a general," Imogen said. "He loves the hunt. Last I knew, he was deep within the hematite mountains searching for Our Lady of Shadows."

Maeve sighed. She knew this myth. When Estoria was born, the hematite mountains bisected the west and east, and it was believed Janis and her underworld were deep within those mountains. People mined into the slate-gray stone for decades, and the goddess hadn't revealed herself to any of them. Maeve believed a scholar took the story literally, and Janis' myth was misconstrued into fact. It was fitting for the goddess of secrets to contain such mystery.

"Who is in charge of the city? Who can I talk to?"

Imogen laughed. "Plenty of people think they're in charge. The guilds and merchants more so than anyone. You'll need their sponsorship to get an audience with Fenris' council."

The walls closed around her. *I need allies and friends.* Maeve stared at her reflection in the dark tea. *I need people I can trust.* King Hagken's army was a behemoth of danger at her back. She needed to warn the citizens before the city was razed to the ground and stop the war before it started.

"Would anyone support Hagken if he returned?"

Imogen said, "The merchants support commerce, and the guilds support anyone who gives them the resources to continue their work."

Her shoulder slumped. She scrubbed a hand over her tired face. The guilds would open the gates for Hagken if their interests aligned. They wouldn't care about the villagers and innocents who died along the way: *a bloody and unnecessary war, all for the sake of one man's pride.*

"Aw." Imogen patted her back. "Cheer up, buttercup. Regardless of who is on the throne, much doesn't change around here."

"He raided and kidnapped my people," Maeve said softly, "I need an audience with Fenris' council so I can save them."

"You'd have better luck driving a knife into Hagken's heart and be done with it." Imogen poured herself another cup of tea.

"If only it were that easy," Alistair intoned.

"I'll reach out to my old friends and try to reach out to Alistair's, too," Imogen offered. "I'll see what I can learn. Maybe I can find a guild member willing to talk to you."

Maeve sighed, relieved. "Thank you."

"Don't thank me yet." She glanced at Alistair. "I don't do this for free."

Alistair placed a hand over their heart, mock-wounded. "In all our years of knowing each other, you think I'd come to you empty-handed?"

"You showed up at my doorstep with a pretty priestess and a distinct lack of coin in your pockets. What else am I supposed to assume?"

Maeve flushed. "How did you know I'm a priestess?"

Imogen didn't move her gaze from Alistair digging through their pockets, though her lips quirked into a smile.

"Magic casters smell different."

Maeve lifted the front of her shirt and gave a conspiratorial sniff when they weren't looking. A deep, earthly, and rich scent clung to her skin from the days of traveling. Alistair removed a pouch from their pocket and underhand tossed it to Imogen. She peered inside, and her smile brightened, glowing as vibrant as the lanterns.

She clicked her tongue. "Beautiful."

Using her metallic fingers, she plucked a dried, pale green mushroom from the pouch and held it aloft. Maeve recognized it as the poisonous, glowing mushrooms from the meadow. She had a gnawing, intuitive sense Imogen wouldn't be using these mushrooms for their unique, luminous light.

"I have some clients seeking this exact thing."

Alistair smirked. "I suspected as much."

"Alistair, I could kiss you!" She said with a playful wink. Alistair chuckled and glanced at Maeve. She swiftly hid her face behind her tea cup and scalded her tongue.

9

Imogen gave Alistair a list of safe places for the next few days. Fenris governed the city, but that didn't mean there weren't loyalists to Hagken sulking around. She didn't like being away from her people, but what choice did she have? Alistair said Hagken preferred to wait for 'auspicious celestial timing,' and Maeve hoped that wouldn't be anytime soon.

They ascended creaky, wooden steps to the second level of the merchants' walkway. While most of the commerce happened below, where the carts and horses passed beneath them, this level contained taverns, bars, and brothels. The scent of roasted meat and fragrant spices wafted through the noisy air.

"Stop touching your necklace," they said, their voice low as they craned their head down toward her ear. Their breath puffed against her cheek.

Maeve dropped her hand. "Why? It's a habit."

"Someone is bound to notice and steal it from your neck."

She shoved her hands into her pockets and rubbed her thumb

and forefinger across the warm sunstone. A purse could be cut from someone's belt, but someone couldn't steal jewelry without being noticed. She straightened her spine and thrust her chin forward.

"They couldn't."

"Oh, trust me." Their cheek dimpled and their eyes warmed with amusement. "They could."

"I'd see them," she said, "I'd stop them before they could run off with it."

Alistair stopped.

"Shall I give you a demonstration?"

She rolled her eyes. "You can't steal it from me, Alistair."

"That sounds like a challenge."

Maeve set her hands on her hips. "I'm not challenging you. I'm stating a fact: it's impossible for you to—whoa! Hey!" She stumbled as Alistair snatched her hand and pulled her, half-dragging, down the walkway.

"Trouble," they hissed.

Maeve checked behind them. A city guard stood in front of a boisterous tavern. She tried to match Alistair's urgent, long stride without falling onto her face. They yanked her into an alcove between an apothecary and an herbalist's shop bursting with green foliage. The scent of mulch and patchouli permeated the air, and an aching, sharp longing for home pierced her heart.

"Are you alright?" they asked, their voice uncharacteristically tender. The leather softness of their gloved hands brushed back her long hair and along her neck. Maeve's pulse skyrocketed, and her skin tingled with every delicate, passing stroke. The alcove barely fit them; their knees touched, and Alistair's chest brushed against hers with each inhalation and exhalation.

"I'm sorry for pulling you along," they whispered, "I panicked."

She hadn't known Alistair could panic. She peered at them from her lashes. Their high, sharp cheekbones were darkened and ruddy. However, she suspected it was because of running. *Alistair isn't affected by me in the same ways I'm affected by them.* She pushed her fanciful thoughts aside and jarred them alongside her other forgone dreams that died after her mother left Ferne.

"Why? I thought we were safe here."

"Generally, yes." They frowned. "But, some of the city guards could recognize me and would happily throw me into a cell for ransom."

"Isn't it more suspicious to run?"

Their fingertips slid along her collarbone, and all coherent thought evaporated. Alistair's pupils were blown wide, a blue crescent hardly visible. Maeve drowned in it. In them. Yet, rather than meet the sensation with fear, she met it with an eager sense of excitement. It had been so long since someone looked at her with hunger and desperation. This was nothing like holding hands with them in the dark forest or huddling under their cloak in the rain. She swallowed. *I'm with a dark and dangerous exile in a secluded alcove.* This must've been a warning her grandmother gave her at some point.

Their lips spread into a slow, sensual smirk.

"Oh." They exhaled. Their thumb grazed along her jawline. Her skin prickled at the contact. "This is the part where I say I told you so."

She blinked, frowned, and tried to rearrange their words in a way that made sense.

"What?"

Alistair held her necklace between their faces. Her flustered expression reflected in the shiny, golden surface. She snatched it, and a hot lick of shame burned down her face and across the nape of her neck. *Insufferable!* She stormed out of the alcove, and embarrassment burned her throat. *Of course they don't—of course, it was merely a game! A trick!* She wasn't an innocent, blushing maiden. Instead of engaging in Alistair's stupid little game, she should've kept her wits about her. Her fingers trembled as she re-tied her necklace and tucked the symbol of Juno underneath her shirt.

Alistair jogged to catch up to her. "It's a shame we didn't make it a wager. I suppose I'll have to settle for being proved right."

She set her jaw. Her expression was venomous.

She asked shortly, "Where are we going?"

It was better to focus on the task at hand than her silly feelings. Besides, it wouldn't help to be angry or petty toward Alistair. They weren't aware of the effect they had on her. Her stomach flipped. And they *clearly* didn't feel the same things she did.

"Old haunt of mine. It shouldn't be far now." They tucked their gloved hands into their pockets. She kept her eyes on the winding, wooden walkway and the dazzling, eager patrons and bards who scurried across the planks.

"I wasn't going to keep it. You know that, right? It'd probably burn my hand off if I tried."

She ignored them and released a slow breath. She wouldn't let her foolish embarrassment cloud her judgment. Nor would she let it muddle her connection to Juno.

"Besides, gold isn't my color. It's too flashy." They paused, then added quietly, "It suits you, though."

She quashed any thoughts about how her heart fluttered at the compliment. She looked to the sky-blessed towers. If they remained in the city for the next few days, visiting Juno's spire would be worthwhile. She would talk to other priestesses and gain insight or guidance. Right now, everything relied on Imogen finding access to one of the guilds. But she had potential allies in the temple. She doubted her fellow healers wanted a bloody civil war to break out across Estoria. Juno wasn't a war goddess or a battle maiden. Her domain ruled life and growth and war was the antithesis of life. *I'll find help within those dark green walls. I know I will.*

"Are you seriously giving me the silent treatment?"

"Not everything is about you, Alistair," she said, "I'm thinking."

"About?"

"My next steps."

They glanced at her boots. "You need to think about it? It's left foot, then right, and on and on again until you get where you're meant to be."

Maeve fought back a smile. "Shut up."

"As you wish."

* * *

The storefronts, taverns, and houses were a conglomeration of dark and light wood, their doorways carved with intrinsic motifs of fish chasing one another, crawling seaweed, or paneled by white scales and ribbed seashells. Their windows were mottled glass and shifted in red, green, blue, and white. Maeve ran her fingers across a silver wire wrapped around the support beams of the walkways.

"They light up," Alistair said after noticing her wide-eyed looks. "At night, this quarter is like a field of stars."

"Wow," Maeve exhaled. A nudge of guilt poked behind her belly button. She shouldn't be having thoughts about wanting to see it. She was in the city for one reason—to speak to the council and save her people and all the others affected by King Hagken. She wasn't a tourist and shouldn't waste her time ogling. Once her duties were fulfilled, she *might* be able to return to Pyrite.

The Willy-Nook Tavern tucked itself at the end of the walkway.

Its orange-tinted windows glowed warm from within. A painted sign depicting a sailor's ship capsizing due to an oversized octopus swung above the door. A symbol was carved above the door like a key with two teeth. It was identical to the rune on her warding stone back home. *Alistair said that the rune belonged to Janis. This tavern must be blessed by Her,* Maeve thought. Alistair rapped their knuckles against the door in a specific one-two pattern. It creaked open, and a wizened, old man blinked his sleepy brown eyes at them.

"I loved a woman who married the ocean. What's the cost for stealing her heart?" said the old man. Maeve squinted at the question. *Oh, I see. The tavern is blessed by Janis and run by a madman. How wonderful.*

"She'll stay with you but never love you," said Alistair.

"And so it is."

The door squeaked and opened to a quiet tavern. Nearly all its patrons were dressed in dark leather, carrying thin blades at their hips, and wearing hoods to conceal and shadow their faces. A curling miasma of smoke clung to the rafters, and dice clattered, hitting the tabletop, between muttered conversations and soft laughter. The patrons subtly glanced at them. She rubbed her thumb against the side of her hand and wished she could reach for her necklace. *This crowd could steal my pendant.* She begrudgingly appreciated Alistair's earlier lesson. However, she doubted these folk could coerce her into a shadowy booth or broom closet.

"We have to introduce ourselves to the Crone before we do anything else," Alistair whispered.

"Does she own this place?

"Something like that."

Alistair placed their palm on her lower back. A hunched, scraggly-haired woman sat alone in a booth in a dimly lit corner of the tavern. Her milky white eyes lifted from the weathered table when they approached.

"Hm." She sniffed the air. "We thought you were dead."

"I am very much alive. But, if you'd like to keep the rumor going, I won't object."

Her eyes swiveled onto Maeve. Despite her blindness, Maeve couldn't shake the feeling she was *seen*. Perhaps not on a physical level, but on a deeper, spiritual level. As if this lonely Crone could sense her essence. She thought of Imogen and her impressive lights imbued with the frost crown flowers.

"You brought a friend." She tilted her head, and her necklace, crafted from tiny bird bones and colorful beads, went *clack-clack-clack* around her neck. "She's sun-touched."

"I'm Maeve," she said. She didn't know if she was supposed to bow or kiss her hand. She decided to lean her head in a slight, respectful nod. "It's a pleasure to meet you."

The Crone pursed her wrinkled mouth.

"I am surrounded by dead trees—" She tapped her long nails on the table. "And dull company. Sit with me. I wish to hear of your travels and see the forest through your eyes again."

She looked to Alistair. *Surely, she means no harm.* They gestured for her to sit and gave her an encouraging smile. The Crone snapped her fingers, and two tankards of dark ale were brought over, the foam sloshing over the rim. Maeve wrinkled her nose and pushed the cup toward Alistair. *They can have as many cups as they like. That stuff tastes awful.*

"Your hand, child," the Crone said after Alistair sipped their ale.

Alistair scoffed. "I haven't been a child in many years."

The Crone made an unimpressed noise in the back of her throat.

"Until you've seen the rise and fall of kingdoms, the stars burn and cry for all your children's children. You are a child to me. Now, give me your hand, or you will not find a room here."

Alistair smiled again, and Maeve groaned internally at how her stomach fluttered. She hadn't completely forgiven Alistair for the stunt they pulled. Her anger and embarrassment may have dulled, but it didn't disappear. She would figure out how to repay them. *Maybe I could steal one of their precious and ostentatious daggers.* She noticed how they favored one with a pearl-inlaid hilt and often practiced twirling it between their gloved fingers when traveling.

They extended their arm across the table, palms facing up. "Very well."

The Crone took their palm and peeled the glove from their hand. Her eyes squinted, and she hunched deeper, her spine at a ninety-degree angle.

"Oh, beloved by the Dark Sister, aren't you?" Her smile contained four teeth. "Yes, yes, you've gained her admiration over the years. I see that." Her white eyes glistened. "I see a heavy crown on your head."

Alistair said, "Unlikely. I have no desire for the crown or its awful responsibilities."

The Crone either wasn't listening or didn't hear them. She touched their ring finger. Maeve leaned in to try and understand the faint lines crossing Alistair's palm.

"Your desire for freedom will require the love of an intoxicating maiden. Your story is written in the stars you were born under. And so it is." The Crone released them.

Alistair pulled their glove on, swallowed a gulp of ale, and wiped foam from their lips. The Crone's words rattled inside her skull. *The people in Hagken's army feared them.* If General Fenris and King Hagken weren't players on the board, would Alistair step onto the throne, or would they let a dogfight ensue? She couldn't tear her eyes away from Alistair. *Does this Crone speak truth and prophecy or merely possible outcomes?* Maeve believed the future was yours to craft. The goddess Janis wove the webs of fate and timing, but ultimately, any destiny could be made.

"I'd be a lousy ruler," they said, drawing Maeve away from her thoughts. "My father never wanted me as heir. He made me his spymaster and ensured his subjects would never trust me."

"Your mother never wanted to be queen," the Crone said. Her fingers toyed with a fragile bird bone on her necklace. "You must remember whose child you are. You are hers. Not his."

Alistair stood. "Excuse me." Their sharp tone cut their words into piercing, cold fragments. Maeve opened her mouth to—what? Stop them? Say something to comfort them? She was entirely out of her element. She pressed her lips together.

"They were born when Janis emptied the sky of her light," she said, "illumination comes slowly to them."

Maeve flexed her fingers beneath the table. A card table surged with rancorous hoots of delight and misery. The winner laughed and scooped a pile of gold and trinkets into their bag. Willy-Nook wasn't an ordinary tavern and inn. Did everyone have their palm read to rent a room? Or was it an arrangement for a select few? Maeve rubbed her damp palms together. *What secrets would the Crone find within the calluses and creases of my hands?*

"Do you need to read my palm?"

The Crone shook her head. "Alistair's gift was enough. Go. You are needed elsewhere." Her wrinkled mouth pursed. "You will receive three gifts. You will lose the first, cherish the second, and return the third."

Maeve sputtered, "W-what?"

That didn't make sense. She hadn't received any gifts. *Could she be talking about the sunstone?* It wasn't exactly a gift, considering she stole it from Hagken, but she couldn't leave an artifact of Juno in his possession. *I won't lose it. What is she talking about?*

The Crone pointed to the door Alistair stormed through. Maeve wanted to keep asking questions because the Crone's words left an unsatisfying taste in her mouth. She wanted insight. Not riddles. Maybe she should've expected as much from a place catering to rogues and gamblers. *This is an odd place to have Janis' symbol carved into the doorway.*

"I doubt I'm needed."

The Crone settled her chin in her palm. Her expression went soft, smoothing the wrinkles and brightening her cloudy eyes. "We all need each other. It is the burden of living."

Maeve tucked her hands into her pockets and thumbed the sunstone. *Does Alistair need me?* She chewed her lower lip. She could soothe burns, heal wounds, and bring children into the world. But she didn't know how to comfort Alistair. A sense of guilt took root at the base of her heart. She was raised never to turn away someone in need. If Alistair did need her, then who would she be if she ignored them? *At the very least, I will check on them and see if they're okay.*

"Will you be here when we return?"

The Crone sighed. Her breath rattled like old bones. "Perhaps."

* * *

Alistair pinched a piece of mint from a hanging plant, and their blue eyes widened when Maeve entered. They nibbled the leaf, turned away, and busied their hands with the rest of the dried spices on the shelf. Maeve stepped around the large, heavy barrels of ale, and the acidic smell of spilled beer saturated the room.

"You okay?"

"I always am." They raked their hands through their curly, dark hair.

Maeve bit her lip. Hesitated. They were somewhat close to allies, but they weren't friends. The uncertainty of their connection dug under her skin, and she didn't want to say the wrong thing.

"Did she hit a nerve?"

"I'll be fine." They spit pieces of chewed mint into their empty tankard.

"If you ask me I think she crossed a line," she said, nodding toward the door.

Alistair stepped into her space, toe-to-toe, and Maeve tilted her face. Their eyes met hers, and awareness prickled from her scalp to her spine. It was as if the spirit within her body came to life beneath their gaze. Their eyes reminded her of the cloudless, brilliant skies during high dawn over the fields of home.

"Maeve, when I stole your necklace, *I* crossed a line. I'm sorry. I wanted to prove a point and let my pride get the better of me."

They bowed, and their dark curls fell across their forehead. She stared. Her mouth opened, and no words came out. She hadn't expected an apology. She thought royalty born with golden spoons in their mouths weren't capable of the self-reflection necessary to admit fault.

Alistair shifted their weight, looking uneasy and uncomfortable.

"I'm sorry, Maeve. Even if our time together is short, I don't want bad blood between us." They smiled crookedly. "Dinner on me?"

She couldn't help but match their grin. Her silly attraction to them was set aside, and a sense of normalcy settled over her like a heavy quilted blanket. Their connection was tenuous, but she envisioned it like a seed planted in the soil. In time, through patience and sunlight, they could grow into allies and maybe even into friends.

"You're the one with the coin."

"Ah, yes..." They plucked another mint leaf and offered her one. "Being disgraced royalty with sticky fingers has its perks."

The tavern's tables opened up for cards and dice, and the conversations went from muted and secret to lively and clamorous. After sharing their story with the Crone, they ate spicy, aromatic, charred fish and rice together in a corner booth tucked into the shadows.

Alistair watched the patrons who entered, and she started to learn their nonverbal cues. A man with a vibrant red beard made Alistair's shoulders stiffen. *Trouble.* Twin femme-presenting individuals with inky, braided hair and dark skin made Alistair's lips twitch. *Also trouble?* She guessed but sensed it wasn't the 'get-yourself-killed' flavor of trouble. A burly, older gentleman wearing an emerald, tailored suit entered and Alistair's eyebrows raised.

"That right there," they said, pointing with their fork, "that's a walking carcass."

"What do you mean?" Maeve's pulse spiked. "He's going to die?"

"No." The candle flickering on their table kissed their angled jaw with fluttery, delicate shadows. "He'll be robbed and picked as clean as a carcass before the night's over and won't even realize it."

The stranger's red cheeks stretched into a genial smile. He clapped people on the back and shouldered his way into a card game. She couldn't hear his voice, but he made grand gestures and stroked his dark mustache whenever someone spoke to him. Maeve realized she wasn't the only one watching him.

"I'm sure he'll notice if someone takes his wristwatch."

"Care for a wager?" Alistair smirked.

"I don't have any money."

"We can wager something else."

She tilted her head. She wouldn't wager her necklace or sunstone. She doubted Alistair wanted her spare clothing, map, or healing poultices and herbs.

"Like what?" she asked. She recalled their moment in the alcove. *That had been a trick;* her cheeks warmed, *and Alistair doesn't see me in that light. We're sort of allies and nothing more.* Her experiences with romance and flirtation were few and far between. She shared bashful kisses in her adolescence, and her past romantic partners had left Ferne years ago. *But Alistair isn't interested in kissing me. Why am I bothering to entertain these thoughts?*

Their eyes crinkled when they smiled. "I want to see another one of your spells. I want to see something you've never used or shown anyone before."

Maeve pushed her rice around. Her magic came from within. Her intention and willpower shaped it. It was a creative, intuitive process. Her stomach rolled at the memory of Hagken's face, his skin bubbling pink and covered in pustules of blood and white blisters. She pushed her half-eaten plate away.

"I don't know if I can. It's not a parlor trick, Alistair. It's divine magic. It's a gift from Juno."

They sighed loudly like a petulant child. "Can you at least try?"

A gambling table erupted in laughter. She didn't want them to get arrested because of a silly wager. Maeve picked at the skin near her thumbnail. But she was curious. She doubted Alistair would drag the man into an alcove and charm their way into stealing the watch, although anything was possible. She wasn't an expert in their methods. *And it would be amusing to watch.*

"What if he catches you?"

"He won't." Alistair stole a bite of rice off her plate.

She squirmed in her seat as the battle of curiosity and sensibility warred within. "I really don't want to get thrown out."

"Priestess Maeve, have a little faith."

"I think you want an excuse to steal his watch."

Alistair's cheek dimpled. "Maybe."

They slid from the booth, and she lost them in the crowd of drunk patrons. She settled her chin between her hands, watching the card table and waiting for Alistair to appear. *This is less exciting than I hoped for.* Maeve yawned. The tavern carried on in drunken, merry bliss. The stranger stroked his sweaty mustache and joked with his fellow card players. *There's no possible way they can steal it. It's too crowded and loud.*

"Agh!" A shout louder than the rest. Her head whirled toward the bar. Two people were locked in a messy brawl. The bar stools nearby clattered to the sticky wooden floor. A third person jumped into the fray—though Maeve couldn't ascertain if they were trying to break it up or not. A few others cleared out, carrying their drinks carefully and laughing. Someone threw a clay cup against the wall, and the contents splattered across the dark wood.

"By the shadow, I'll throw the lot of you out," the barkeep yelled over the frantic chaos of limbs and profanity. Louder shouting and impressive, imaginative curses echoed his words. Maeve scanned the crowd, worried for Alistair. No luck.

The fight ended as swiftly as it began.

Alistair slipped into the seat before her with a self-assured, smug grin. "Hi, sunshine."

Maeve blinked. "Where were you?"

"At the table with our friend."

There's no way that was true. She watched the table like a hawk.

She would've seen them. Her brow furrowed as she tried to work out the logistics of the past several minutes.

"Did you get there before the fight?"

"Oh, no. No." They licked their lips. "I started the fight."

"You're going to need to tell me what happened."

"All it takes is a little distraction," they said. She wanted to shake the smug look off their face. She did. But a more profound, wilder part of her wanted to know more. They were impressive. Their skills were vastly different from anything or anyone she's ever met.

"By the time he notices his watch is gone, he'll be too drunk to remember when or where it happened. I doubt this is the first tavern he's visited tonight."

She squinted and fed the seed of doubt. *It couldn't have been easy, could it?* She held out her palm in askance.

"Let me see the watch."

Alistair bounced back up to their feet. "I'll show you upstairs."

The windowless room Alistair received from the Crone was cozy. A copper-plated vent was bolted into one of the walls and circulated warm air into the room from downstairs. The muffled noise from the tavern carried through the vents and floorboards. A single bed was tucked into the corner of the room. She wondered where Alistair would sleep. *Have they gotten a second room?* Their nights of sleeping in the wilds beneath trees and starlight weren't the same as sleeping beneath a roof together.

Alistair lifted the watch from their pocket, gleaming silver in the shadowy candlelight. Her eyebrows lifted. The conversation regarding their sleeping arrangement would have to wait. She carefully took it from their fingers, twirling it between her hands and inspecting it. It wasn't an illusion. It was solid and real. The face of the watch was pitch-black, and a white crescent gleamed beneath the thin layer of glass. It wasn't a watch to track the sun's progress across the sky. It tracked the phases of the moon.

"You distracted him and pulled it from his wrist?"

"That's the bare bones of it."

"Alistair...that's..." She pressed her lips together. They tilted forward, smirking, and waited for her begrudging compliment. "Incredible," she said, rolling her eyes.

She didn't want to give them the satisfaction, but she couldn't deny a job well done. Although, she hoped the patrons involved in the bar fight weren't injured. She dropped the watch back into their hand.

"Thank you." They beamed. "Now, have you thought of a spell to show me?"

Maeve sucked on her teeth, and a formless idea took shape inside the back of her mind. It might not work, but her magic came from a place of trust. She had to believe her willpower and Juno's divine connection would blend and manifest.

"I have."

She untied and pulled her necklace off.

"Take this and stand on the other side of the room."

Alistair reached out and delicately threaded the leather strap between their fingers—the sunburst pendant dangled from their wrist. Maeve relaxed and inhaled. Like a sacred wellspring, her magic crackled to life inside her diaphragm and fizzled beneath her skin. She called. It answered. *I never want to lose anything precious. I never want it to disappear.* Magic pulled at her sternum. It tugged on the hem of her shirtsleeves. *Please help me find my stolen and lost things. Guide me.* She held the image of her amulet in her mind.

A wispy, golden thread of light emanated from Maeve's chest. It crawled outward like thin tentacles, and their ends faded the further they traveled from her body, except for one. The thread of light traveled, seeking and curling across the room. Alistair's eyes widened as it approached. The light wrapped around their wrist and pulsed like a heartbeat.

"Wow," they exhaled; wonder and delight saturated their rough voice like honey. Maeve's amazement matched theirs. Her smile blossomed timid and proud.

"I've never done anything like this," she admitted. "I didn't think it was possible. Juno's blessing creates light and fire and heals people, but I never imagined I could..."

"Create something of your own?"

"Yeah," Maeve said softly. King Hagken's face burst before her, and the golden light flickered. "It's not hurting you, is it?" she asked with an underlying note of panic.

They shook their head. "It tickles a bit."

Maeve called the light back in sweet relief. It folded like the petals of a flower into her chest.

"Move your hair," Alistair said, holding her necklace.

There was a moment of stunned silence before she lifted the thick, dark waves from the nape of her neck and collected fistfuls at the base of her skull. She bit her lip as Alistair's quick fingers tied the leather strip. Her heart jumped at a brief, accidental touch of their gloved fingertips on her skin. The sun pendant settled between her breasts, and she let her hair fall. The way they made her feel was disorientating. She fluctuated between exasperation to admiration to simple, physical attraction. She knew it was foolish to entertain any ideas about Alistair and what their connection could hold. Their time together was limited. She shouldn't and wouldn't get her hopes up for a dark rogue who infuriated her as often as they entranced her. Her heart belonged to Ferne. Her role as matriarch and healer came before anything else. *Friendship is all I could ever hope for between us.*

"Thank you."

"Now, about the bed." They grinned as if reading her mind from earlier. "You don't need to worry. I have no intention of sleeping anywhere tonight. I'll be playing cards and listening to gossip until the sun rises.

"Really?"

She glanced at the bed. Her body sang with joy. It had been a long month of sleeping on grass and rocks. She wished for a hot bath, but a soft mattress was just as good.

"I might be a thief, Maeve, but I don't lie."

She smiled. "You're an honest thief?"

"Don't look so surprised. We all have our sacred codes." They tapped her nose with their forefinger, offered a charming smile, and slipped out of the room. Maeve giggled and pressed both hands to her hot, tingling cheeks.

"Stay on task, stay on task." She reminded herself. Imogen would track down magnanimous guild members, and Maeve would find allies to rally against King Hagken's return. She rubbed the slick and glossy surface of the sunstone across her palm. *Another task at hand.* She needed to attune to this stone. *Hopefully, other priestesses of Juno at the temple will have insight,* thought Maeve.

She didn't need to get trapped and flustered by Alistair's charm. Their companionship was temporary. Once Maeve met with the council, Alistair could find somewhere to hang out in the city and cause trouble for someone else. Their fates would untangle, and Maeve would return to Ferne and her life.

She sank into the feathered mattress and kicked off her boots. Maybe if she had the chance to revisit Pyrite after Ferne was saved, she'd find Alistair. They could get a drink at some seedy tavern like this one. Maeve sighed. *What am I doing? One thing at a time.* Maeve flopped onto the bed and stared at the wooden whorls of the ceiling beams. *There's no use in thinking of a future that doesn't even have a chance of happening yet.*

The rancorous laughter and merriment below pressed on the floorboards. She imagined people in the city spending their nights watching the sunrise. It was another world compared to her sleepy, peaceful village.

A threat of war on the horizon, a vengeful and scorned king, and a city without its general. *And I'm at the center of it.* Maeve lifted the sunstone and watched the flecks of gold shimmer. Whatever magic lived inside remained asleep.

"Someday, I'm going to need your help," she whispered, "and I hope you answer." She blew out the candle by the bedside and plunged herself into darkness.

10

Maeve pressed a hand to her heart as she absorbed the incredible splendor of Juno's spire. The magnificent mottled green tower shone beneath the sunlight, and a pair of large, imposing bolted brass doors stood before them. Embossed on the door was an intricate and impressive carving of Juno's light at dawn. Alistair whistled. She gathered her courage and tilted her chin high. This was her place, too. Her effigy to Juno at home might be small in comparison, but it was no less divine.

The air within was thick and warm with smoky incense. At the center, a sacred tree with its old, thick roots dug into the dirt floor. Its leafy branches burst from the spire's top like a crown. Magical orbs like her own drifted through the spaces in between branches and around tiny, sparkly, hand-made offerings. In front of the tree, a jade-carved statue of a robed faceless figure stood with its hands above its head, holding a golden-speckled sunburst between its palms. She approached slowly, and her fingertips grazed across her necklace tucked under her shirt.

She closed her eyes and let the steady thrum of life pulse around her. The rustle of leaves overhead and the slow, melodic humming of the luminaries filled her with an overwhelming sense of peace. All her fear and uncertainty ebbed away. When Maeve was a luminary in Ferne, one of her daily tasks had been to transcribe her grandmother's old notes. In Pyrite, many of the luminaries tended to their temple duties and guided citizens in prayer.

An ostentatiously dressed woman stepped barefoot over the tree roots. She reached above her head and hung a star-shaped paper ornament from one of the branches. Maeve watched her with longing.

"I dreamed of becoming a high matriarch," she whispered. It was a golden dream scattered like old leaves across the dead ground. *A child's dream.*

The dark-skinned woman wore orange and yellow ombré robes and an imposing golden acicular headpiece to signify her rank. Her lips moved in prayer with three thin yellow stripes painted from her lower lip to her chin. Her bare hands elegantly drifted across the candles, bringing the wicks to life with flame. The high matriarch was the highest authority of Juno within Pyrite. The ranks above her lived in Everdawn with the sequestered sunseers and the elected sunburst prioress.

Alistair asked, "Why?"

"My whole life has been dedicated to Juno." She dipped her fingers into a gilded bowl of sunflower oil at the base of Juno's statue. She missed this familiar nutty aroma. She applied a drop of oil to her forehead, the bridge of her nose, and her lips. *For clarity, for sacred breath, and prayer.* "It sounded like the right thing to do."

"And why didn't you?"

She sighed, a memory of gentle hands wiping away her tears, a memory of lips gone blue with death.

"My grandmother passed, and then my mother left Ferne on her pilgrimage," Maeve frowned. Her mother's absence ached like a bruised rib. *She'll come back someday once her work is done.*

Alistair's arm brushed against hers. "I'm sorry."

"It's alright. The village needed me. I stayed, laid the dream to rest, and found my purpose with them."

"Were you close to your family?"

"Yes." A wistful smile touched her lips. "They taught me everything I know."

"I wonder if we would've known each other." They toyed with a dried petal at the base of Juno's statue, which crumbled between their fingers. "If you came here sooner."

"A rogue like you? Would you have come to the temple and prayed?"

"If you led the prayers?" Their boyish and teasing smile brought brilliance to their light blue eyes. "I'd be here every day."

She flushed and sought an appropriate response, but the high matriarch approached them. She lifted her heavy, robed arm and traced a circle in the air with two fingers over each of their heads.

"In the light and brilliance of wild things, Juno blesses you."

Maeve bowed her head. She blinked back the prickling sensation of tears. The blessing given could only be offered through a high matriarch. *I can't believe it!* The words hummed through her body. *I never thought I would receive this blessing. I never imagined it would happen.*

"May her blessing shine through us all," Maeve whispered and was thankful to have remembered the appropriate response. "I've come to seek your advice. I'm priestess Maeve of Ferne. This is my companion, Alistair."

"Well met. I am High Matriarch Allustera." She gracefully sat onto the sprawling roots, and her dress spilled around her waist like liquid fire. "I will offer whatever wisdom I can."

Alistair took a step backward, and Maeve glanced at them, questioning.

"Go ahead. I'm gonna look around."

Allustera's headpiece glittered in the light when she tilted her head. "Be mindful of those in careful prayer." Around the temple were several individuals sitting on pillows with their spines straight and their faces tilted toward the light.

"Of course." Alistair gave a short bow toward Allustera.

In privacy and quiet solace, the lush, green light reflected off beams of sunlight and magic. It created an otherworldly painting of color. Maeve sat on the dirt while Allustera kept her position on the tree roots. She told her about the raid on her village, her guilt, her fear, the necromancers in Hagken's army, and her plan to speak with Fenris' council and uproot Hagken's rebellion before it began. However, despite her frank honesty, she couldn't admit she used Juno's gift to burn and maim the king. Her stomach turned, hoping it didn't play across her face.

Allustera steepled her fingers in front of her gray, kohl-smudged eyes.

"A great burden," she said after a moment of silence. "You said you feel alone. Yet, you arrived here with another. What is their part in all this?"

"They helped me escape. They..." Maeve was uncertain if she should reveal Alistair's connection to the king. "They have no love for Hagken. I don't know how long they'll stay with me, but I assume it's temporary. They wanted to travel to Pyrite."

Allustera nodded. "I see."

"Truthfully, Lady Allustera, I hoped I might ask for your aid."

She regarded Maeve with a cool, regal look. The sunlight glinted off the high points of her headpiece. "What would you have us do?"

"I..." she floundered. Her mind whirled with circular, echoing thoughts. "I don't know. I know I can't win alone. If King Hagken attempts to take the city, I guess I need to know you'd be against him."

"We are not fighters."

"That's not what I mean."

"If war came to our doors, would you ask us to turn away the wounded? The sick?"

"No, of course not." Maeve's palms pressed into her knees as she leaned forward. "You must have some authority within the city, right? You could stop him."

"I could no more stop the rain from falling than stop an ambitious man with an army at his back."

Maeve blinked away her frustrated tears.

"You can help me. I know you can."

"I have lived here for many years, Lady Maeve. Do you want to know what lies at the heart of this city? It's ambition. The guilds compete with each other. The lords fight over estates and land," she said. "The merchants bring their magnificent wares across the ocean and haggle for the best price. We have known years of peace, and we have known years of war. There is no preventing it.

"It is the cycle, the lifeblood, of this place."

Maeve shook her head, fierce. "I don't believe it."

"You cannot close your eyes to the world."

"I'm not! I'm saying there has to be a better way. A peaceful way." She clenched her hands into fists. Maeve reached into her pocket and held the sunstone. Allustera's expression remained composed. *My mother was the same. She was as unshakable as Juno's tree.* Maeve's heart ached. *I wish she were here. I'm sure she could convince Allustera to help.*

"Juno gave me a sign. King Hagken carried this within his hoard of gems and jewels."

She opened her palm. The sacred sunstone pulsated with quiet energy like a purring, sleeping cat. Maeve hoped being inside Juno's temple might spark the sunstone into action or fortify her connection to it. However, there was little difference within its magical aura. Allustera's grey eyes widened, then narrowed into thoughtful slits.

"This is an incredible stroke of luck, Lady Maeve." She leaned in and said, "Have you managed to attune to it?"

Maeve shook her head. The sunstone's magic remained inert despite her prayers.

"Very well." Allustera's hands twitched on her lap. "I never thought in my lifetime I'd see a sunstone. Many of us who trained in Everdawn believed it a myth or lost to the sands of time."

When Juno created Calorum and all the light within, it was said that a massive explosion scattered fragments of her power across the land. However, after the great storm, many assumed the stones were washed away and claimed by the sea. The sunstone was a direct link to Juno. If a priestess of the sunlit path dedicated themselves to the stone, the goddess would speak to them and grant them a boon for their service.

The boon extended beyond the laws of Calorum. It could give immortality or protect an entire civilization from a disease. The possibilities were endless. To have a sunstone was to carry and hold a piece of Juno herself.

"I can take this gift, Maeve, and study it further," Allustera offered with a thin smile. "It would be one less burden on your shoulders." She held her hand for the stone.

Maeve's brow furrowed thoughtfully. *Juno wanted me to find it. Why else would it have been with the king?* She doubted Hagken recognized the stone's power. Otherwise, he would've conscripted a priestess into his army and ordered them to take advantage of it. She thought of Allustera's cynical words about Pyrite and its heart of ambition. She wanted to trust High Matriarch Allustera due to their shared faith, but Maeve couldn't shake the feeling that this stone was tied to her destiny.

Although Allustera phrased her request as a kindness, Maeve's fingers protectively enclosed around the sunstone. Allustera's mouth tightened, but she didn't press further.

"I appreciate you've come to speak with me, Lady Maeve, and I hope our benevolent Juno reveals the answers you seek." A ray of sunlight reflected from her large, golden headpiece when she stood. "Pray on it, my child, and answers will come."

Maeve slumped. Hope turned to ash in her mouth. She looked listlessly around the temple, to the luminaries tending to the tree and citizens leaving offerings and bowing their heads. A gnawing frustration chewed at her gut. She believed she'd find answers here. She looked at the faceless statue of Juno. *I'd love a divine sign right about now.*

She closed her eyes and interlaced her fingers on her lap. The heavy incense smoke tickled her nostrils. She listened to the quiet chitters from animals climbing above and the soft rustle of leaves. She called her magic forward and let it settle in the center of her chest. *Anything, really. I'll take a bird call. I need to know my direction. I feel...*She swallowed. *I feel lost.* Maeve never felt more alone in this temple of her goddess, a place she should have loved and felt connected to. Her throat prickled. Her exhale shuddered, and she forced her mind into stillness and calm.

High Matriarch Allustera told her to pray.

Someone tapped her nose.

"Hello, sunshine." Alistair smiled when she opened her eyes. The light created a radiant aura around their dark curls, and Maeve's heart fluttered. "Do we have an army of fire-wielding priestesses to fight Hagken?"

She batted their hand away.

"No."

"No? Well, there are other temples." They bounced to their feet. "The day is young. We can knock on Theadora's door and throw some coins at the sailors. If the city is sieged, it'll be bad for business."

Maeve played with her necklace. "How much time do we think we have?"

"If Marcus knows General Fenris isn't here, then he'll take the city discreetly. We have a few weeks—perhaps a month—if we're lucky. Again, it all depends on the—" Alistair wiggled their fingers— "auspicious celestial timing," they said in a poor imitation of an old man's voice.

She let out an exasperated, tired sigh. "Shit."

Alistair's grin widened, and they slung an arm around her shoulders, speaking quietly into her ear, "My, my, Maeve, are you allowed to curse in such a sacred place?"

"*I* am." She nudged them. "You are not."

As they left, Alistair nudged her shoulder with their own.

"You ought to keep the stone close to your chest," Alistair said, "your matriarch friend looked ready to snatch it."

Maeve gasped. "She would do no such thing!"

Their dramatic, dark eye makeup glittered in the light. "You're right. The temples don't dirty their own hands. She'd send someone after you to snatch it."

"Not everyone is out to get us, Alistair."

"Everyone's out to get something from someone."

"You're paranoid."

Alistair snorted. "I'm a realist."

The tallest tower spire was Theadora's temple. It was sandstone with painted murals on the lower half depicting the story of Theadora's blindness. The myth varied from region to region within Estoria. In one myth, Theadora lost her sense of sight after praying to Juno in the citrine desert, and Juno granted her divinity. This mural showed Theadora building the underworld and then offering her eyes to Janis' ravens to ensure it remained a secret. Theadora was the goddess of justice, artisans, and merchants. Unsurprisingly, she was given the tallest spire given Pyrite's economy, but Maeve found it irritated her. *Juno should be given the tallest spire so it may reach the sky.* She bit the inside of her cheek and wondered if General Fenris would change the district after Hagken's threat was vanquished. Maeve pulled her attention from the mural and followed Alistair to the noticeboard by the door.

"What are you looking for?" she asked while scanning the postings. The board alerted potential visitors to arrest warrants for minor transgressions such as unpaid tabs within taverns, noise complaints, and a singular note about someone stealing someone else's tulip garden. Maeve gave a bemused grin to the noticeboard. *How does someone steal an entire garden?*

"Familiar names..." Alistair sounded distracted as their gloved fingertip ran across the pages. Maeve checked the board for Hagken, Cara, and Calom. She checked for Alistair, too, to be safe. *I don't see any warrants for them,* she frowned. *Does Fenris assume Hagken will never return?*

Nearby the board, Maeve's eyes caught a curling parchment with bold scarlet text. It had a colored print of an individual wearing crimson armor inlaid with bronze and holding their sword proudly aloft. The text said: 'Justiciars Needed! Serve Theadora with honor!' According to the notice, the justiciars leading service to the city and Theadora was to hunt down expensive bounties. However, they could be hired to mediate a business deal and act as protection and legal witnesses for both parties. Their station ranked above the city guards. A justiciar could arrest anyone, regardless of their title or employment, as long as they claimed probable cause. Maeve surmised that the justiciars maintained the peace, whereas the city guard maintained and organized the city's defenses. *Would they stop Hagken?* Maeve wondered, *or would they remain neutral as Allustera had?*

"Aha!"Alistair ripped the notice off. "Terrayn Brysk."

"Is she a friend of yours?"

"Nope." They beamed. "But she's an enemy of Hagken, which is close enough."

"Wait." Maeve glanced at the justiciar poster. "Is she a criminal?"

"Only gambling debts. We can go inside and pay them off and find out if she's in the city. Come on."

"Alistair, slow down." Maeve followed their long stride. "Does Terrayn have any connections to the guilds?" *Otherwise,* she thought, *I'm just adding another person who dislikes Hagken to my list of allies.*

Alistair held the door open for her. "She's part of the merchant guild."

The interior of the temple was set up similarly to Juno's. There were small pillows on the ground for meditation and several empty chairs. However, in place of a great tree, there was the four-armed statue of Theadora crafted from different materials. Her body was made of stone. On her back, two arms protruded from her shoulder blades. One was made of copper and held a pair of scales; the other was made of hematite—a glossy, grey stone—and held an open book. Her front arms were sculpted with sun-bleached wood and colorful blown glass. Her wooden hand held a hammer, and her glass hand offered an empty palm. Maeve. approached the statue to pay her respects, but Alistair gently took her elbow and led her to the side.

A handsome and sophisticated young man stood behind a desk. He wore a simple, gray jacket with a copper-plated pin of Theadora's scales over a ruffled white shirt. His cheeks were heavily powered with pink rouge, and a streak of dark kohl makeup circled his eyes.

He gave a deep bow when they approached. "Well met, my name is Ollie. How can I be of service today?" A familiar glyph was tattooed on the backs of each hand. Her chest clenched. It was nearly identical to the glyph she saw in Calom's tent. *Is Ollie a mage? Or is this somehow different?*

"I've come to settle a debt." Alistair slapped the notice onto the shiny gloss surface of Ollie's desk, and the clerk of Theadora smiled.

"I have a question," she said as Ollie sorted the papers at his desk. He nodded, and Maeve continued, "Why isn't there an arrest warrant for Marcus Hagken?"

Alistair coughed.

"General Fenris decreed Hagken should never step foot in the city again or face immediate imprisonment." Ollie said, "Every justiciar and city guard knows this command. We don't need to post notices for it." He stamped a wax seal of Theadora's symbol onto two envelopes and passed one to Alistair. Maeve's attention snagged on the tattooed glyphs again.

Alistair leaned their elbows onto the desk and tilted their chin toward a red envelope. "I can deliver it."

"That one is for Terrayn," he said, holding the envelope close to his chest, "it can only be delivered by a clerk of Theadora."

"We both know that isn't true," Alistair smirked. "Will she be in the city soon?" They shifted their gloved knuckles and flashed a platinum coin. Ollie's shoulders stiffened, and his eyes followed Alistair's hand. *Juno above! We're resorting to bribery.* Maeve pressed her fingertips to the middle of her forehead.

Ollie said, "If the winds are kind, then she should arrive tomorrow."

"Then we'll ensure the letter reaches her." Alistair extended their hand, and two platinum coins shone in their palm. "A donation to our blinded lady of justice."

Ollie swapped the envelope for the coins and smiled.

"Your generosity is witnessed," said Ollie.

Alistair held the door open for her, but Maeve stopped at the last moment and turned to Ollie.

"What do your tattoos signify?"

"Oh, these?" He twisted his hands. "My husband showed it to me." He smiled. "It's the glyph of the blinded eye. It symbolizes truth. I found it fitting given my occupation."

Once outside, she asked Alistair, "Is Ollie's husband a mage?"

Their eyebrows jumped in surprise, and she had her answer before they spoke.

"How'd you know?"

"I've seen the glyph before." Maeve clutched her necklace. "Cara used it..."

Alistair grimaced.

"I'm familiar."

11

An orange cat lounged atop a stack of wooden crates by the docks, watching them pass with impassive topaz eyes. The sharp brine and raw, stinking fish permeated the air. The seagulls perched on ship masts cried in euphoria whenever a fisherman tossed spare guts into the water. The churning, foamy water splashed against the dock, and she wiped her clammy palms on her shirt.

"Nervous?" Alistair tossed a glance over their shoulder.

"A little." Terrayn's connection to the merchant guild meant Maeve could gain an audience with Fenris' council. *After they hear my petition, they'll have to send forces to Hollyhock, and we can stop this war before it claims innocent lives.*

"Better to bargain with a devil than to try and make one with an honest man," Alistair said, "a quote from my stepfather. He believed morality and integrity a flaw."

Maeve balked, "How in Juno's name did he run an entire city?"

The deposed king must have had no shortage of enemies. *And*

Terrayn is among them. Maeve blocked the sunlight with her arm, and the ship's ropes swayed in the brackish wind. *Hagken claimed she brought a shipment of two-headed vipers to Pyrite. Her boat was seized and burned even though the vipers were never found.* Maeve sympathized with Terrayn. Her livelihood went up in smoke at the will of one charismatic man.

Alistair tossed their curls when they laughed. "Badly. You'd brand me a liar if I told you how many plots I thwarted."

"You must've known about General Fenris," she said. Alistair claimed to have a successful career as Hagken's spymaster.

"I did." They rolled their neck, languid and smooth. "I kept it to myself. The nice thing about being competent is no one double-checks your information. No one wanted to question the shadow general." They spun one of their daggers.

"Why did you stay afterward?"

"I enjoyed the comforts of my position, and I had freedom while the broken king conscripted his army."

"Conscripted is a rather polite way of putting it." The attack on her village stung like a wasp on her heart.

"I had nothing to do with the raids. I blackmailed landowners and paid off mercenaries."

"Alistair, you aren't blameless in this."

"Don't." They leveled her with a cold look. "You don't get to play high and mighty with me when you've never faced a difficult choice in your life."

"I'm—" she sputtered, "I'm saying—"

"You find me as cruel and irredeemable as my father and his war council?"

"No!"

She noted how they said 'father' instead of 'stepfather,'

intentionally tying themselves to Hagken in this argument, although no blood or love was shared between them.

"Everyone involved played a part. When Hagken goes to trial and faces Theodora's judgment...you may face judgment, too. You helped him. You stayed with him."

"I do love how your tone implies I had a choice," they said acidly. The orange cat leaped from its perch and darted past Maeve's legs.

"Did you not?"

Alistair sighed, their expression closed off like black curtains pulled over a stained-glass window.

"Marcus started training me when I was thirteen. I'd stay in the shadows, hide in rafters, under tables, and eavesdrop on meetings. He sent me out to make friends with urchins and orphans, relying on them to teach me what they knew and cutting his loss if I wound up dead because of a badly played con." They made a sweeping gesture toward themselves, all dark leather, buckles, and hidden lethality.

"This is all I know. That's all I am." They leaned their shoulder against a shipping crate. "Did anyone ask if you wanted to become a priestess? Or was it merely the expectation of those who raised you?"

Her mouth tightened. *If my mother never trained me, what would I have done?* She stared at the murky water below and imagined a different life. *Who would I be?* Her indoctrination into Juno's healing arts began when she was a child. She learned herbal remedies, woke at dawn to pray, and listened to the calls of songbirds and frogs. *If Juno wanted a different path for me, she wouldn't have given me the gift of her divine magic.* Although her family didn't give her a choice, Juno chose her, and Maeve honored her calling.

Maeve replied, "No one asked, no."

"Exactly." The sails and ropes snapped in the wind as a storm brewed on the horizon. "Did I have a choice? The simple answer is yes. I had a choice." Two sailors carrying rope over their shoulders walked between Maeve and Alistair. "And I chose to stay. I knew Marcus would try to kill me someday, but the rewards outweighed the risks."

Why stay and live on borrowed time? Alistair looked paranoid when she first met them. She couldn't imagine any amount of coin would be worth it. *Alistair is a talented thief. They could've left before the coup if they wanted to.*

"Alistair," she tried a gentler tone, "you could've stolen whatever you wanted and escaped."

"Not quite," they said, "information is the only currency in this world worth a damn. The longer I stayed, the more risks I took, the more information I had." They jutted their chin towards the ship. "Which is why I knew bribery would work on Ollie and why we know about this woman in the first place."

Terrayn's merchant vessel, *Solace*, had lovely cream sails embroidered with a blue and copper-scaled sky serpent. Alistair flashed the first envelope from Ollie, which awarded them access aboard the ship. Maeve's knees wobbled. She had no trouble on the planks of the docks because they were stable. This surface churned nausea in her stomach. Alistair offered their arm to steady her, but Maeve proudly waved them away. *We won't be on the ship long. I can survive it.* Alistair opened the main cabin door to the captain's quarters.

They shoved Maeve into the wall as a dagger spun through the air and landed with a 'thunk' into the doorframe. The light spilling from the doorway cut a sharp rectangle into an otherwise darkened space.

"Ease up, Terra!" Alistair bellowed. A faint smell of smoke

lingered from an extinguished candle. "I'm not here on anyone's orders." They held their arm across Maeve's chest, pinning her to the wall to try and protect her.

"Save your breath, shadow-slinger," she spat, "I've heard this routine before."

Alistair moved with fluid grace. They tossed a blade into the air, where it clashed with Terra's oncoming strike. The daggers clattered to the floor with a sharp tang.

"Alistair's telling the truth." Maeve raised her hands and reached for Juno's magic before everything escalated. Three pulsing orbs of light burst into existence. Terra stood nearly six feet tall, her black dreadlocks fashioned into a bun above her head. She carried a thin rapier at her hip and another two small, throwing daggers in her hands. She wore a loose-collared, flowing white shirt, high-waisted pants, and a dark blue sash low around her hips. Her septum was pierced with a thin gold hoop, and two golden studs adorned her nostrils.

"My name is Maeve. I'm a priestess of Juno, and I'd like to talk."

Terra's striking violet eyes narrowed. "I see. Your old man has a priestess working for him now, does he?"

"I don't work for him."

"She doesn't," Alistair drawled.

Terra's grip on her throwing dagger readjusted. Her eyes darted between Maeve and Alistair, and Maeve had the uneasy feeling that she was selecting a target.

"Try it." Alistair growled low, "I'll reach you before you strike her."

"Sounds like a challenge," she replied, "what proof do you have?"

Alistair lifted both hands, showing their lack of weapons, "I have a letter from the clerk Oliver in my pocket. We've paid your debts,

Terrayn."

"Have her get it." Terra pointed her dagger at Maeve.

Her lights bounced around the room, casting long shadows over the stacks of books and barrels of supplies. Alistair smirked and waggled their eyebrows when Maeve reached into the front pocket of their leather pants. *How can Alistair make jokes even when someone is threatening to toss a knife into their eye?*

"You're insufferable," she muttered, removing the wax-sealed red envelope. It was faintly crumpled, but otherwise, the seal was intact. She slowly walked to Terrayn with open palms, although Terrayn's gaze darted around the room to Maeve's summoned lights as if she expected them to explode and render her ship into ash and smoke. She seized the letter, opened it, and visibly relaxed.

"You aren't lying," she sounded surprised.

"Told you so," Alistair dropped their hands from the air.

"I'm not going to apologize for behaving rationally when a fucking assassin waltzes onto my ship," she said. She tucked her daggers into a drawer at her desk and looked at Maeve with a much friendlier expression. "However, I will apologize to you. I'm sorry for my stubbornness."

Maeve smiled. "Apology accepted. I don't know why someone—" she shot a pointed look to Alistair "—didn't think to knock first."

"I wasn't expecting hostility," they said, shrugging.

Terrayn rolled her eyes, sat behind her desk with her legs propped up, and started peeling an orange.

"Let's get to business. I've got people to meet within the city," she said.

The words rushed from Maeve's mouth, "I was hoping you might help us—well, me. I'm trying to reach Fenris' council and warn them about Hagken's army. Ideally, I'd like to rescue my people and free them. You see, Hagken means to call Pyrite to war."

Terrayn wiped the juice from her chin with the pad of her thumb.

"I'll be happy to be halfway to Amethneas by then."

Maeve's hope deflated.

"Do you know anyone who might be willing to listen?" She recalled Imogen's advice. "Maybe someone in charge at the guilds?"

"If you truly want to stop Marcus, then I'll offer you this." She nudged the dagger on her desk. Its silver hilt was shaped like two vipers intertwined. *A two-headed viper. How appropriate.* "Take the dagger and slit his throat with it."

Alistair lifted the dagger and smiled, but Maeve shook her head.

"I need allies, Terrayn, not weapons."

"Allies are weapons." She leaned back in her seat, gazing at the ceiling. "I suppose you could try and convince me. I don't usually bet on losing dogs, though."

I should have rehearsed the tale, Maeve thought. Terrayn collected her orange peels into a pile and toyed with a small golden hoop on her ear while Maeve told her story.

"I see." She lifted her inquisitive, violet eyes toward Maeve. "I'm assuming you want Alistair on the throne?"

Alistair inhaled sharply beside her.

"What? No." Maeve exclaimed, "I'm trying to avoid a war, not incite one. I want to stop King Hagken from destroying the city and save my people. I assume the people of Pyrite don't want Hagken to return, and Fenris' council should know what their citizens want."

Terrayn snorted and poured three glasses of amber liquor.

"General Fenris and his council don't care what the people want." Terrayn held a glass to her, and Maeve took it but didn't drink. "Besides, what makes you think they'll listen to you?"

"If I have the support of the people who hold power within the city. The priestesses, the guilds, then they will..." Maeve looked down. "They have to."

Terrayn knocked back her drink, and her golden rings glimmered beneath Maeve's summoned light. "You'd have better luck naming yourself a divine champion of Juno and claiming the throne."

Alistair took a slow, contemplative sip of their drink. "She'd make a better monarch than I would."

"All I want is for this to be resolved peacefully, save my people, and go home. Why is that so impossible for anyone to understand?" Her voice strained, and she tightened her grip around her glass.

"There's your problem. Men like General Fenris, Hagken, Gods —even some men and women in the merchant's guild—don't know peace. There is nothing but the space between every horrible strike. Tell me, do you think our city is peaceful?"

Maeve nodded.

"It's not," Terra said sternly. "Last year, the archmage was murdered. They blamed the alchemists, while the alchemists blamed the mages and said it must've been an inside contract. It took months for it to finally settle, and yes, people died, and we never found out who killed the archmage.

"Merchants sabotage their neighbors' stalls, and thieves roam the streets in daylight and dusk. All those wonderful inventions you've seen, all the magic, it has a price. I love this city, but it's full of bloodshed and trickery. We don't know any other way to live."

I can't lose this opportunity. Terrayn was her key to the merchant's guild. If she had their support, then the rest would fall into place. It *had* to. If she couldn't reach the council before Hagken arrived, the city needed to be prepared to defend itself. *I need people with power to protect them.*

"But...you don't want a war."

"Not particularly. Wars are tricky for business."

"Then what do you want?"

Terrayn stretched her muscular arms over her head. "I want to conduct my business. I want to make a lot of coin, retire, and marry a beautiful girl." She flashed a dangerous smile. "Oh, and I want to see Marcus burned to ash for what he did to my old ship."

Maeve set her glass on Terrayn's desk. She summoned every ounce of confidence and courage inside her heart.

"Get us an audience with the guild, and I promise you'll achieve your dream," she said, "I'll do whatever is necessary to uphold my end of the bargain."

Her determination might've wavered within the divine temple of Juno, but she wouldn't let this opportunity slip past. The merchants and sailors were the cornerstone of Pyrite's economy. If the city lacked coin and imports, everything would come to a grinding halt. Terrayn's violet eyes crinkled when she smiled.

"I like your attitude, Maeve," said Terrayn, "very few people would look me in the eye and make such a bold promise. You're either desperate or brave."

"I have one request." Maeve stepped to the side, and her fingertips brushed Alistair's arm. "You can't reveal you know who Alistair is or how they're connected to Hagken."

The tension in the room crackled like dry wood in a fire. Terrayn regarded her in quiet calculative interest, and the laughter faded from her eyes. A prickly sensation crawled over her scalp. *Terrayn can't read minds, can she?* All her stupid, fanciful thoughts about Alistair and their dimpled smile, slender fingers, and laughing blue eyes framed by dramatic makeup.

Terrayn reached across her desk. "You have my word."

Maeve grasped her calloused, rough palm between hers. "You have mine."

She scratched a note onto parchment, sealed it, and handed it to Maeve.

"This is your formal invitation to the merchant guild's next meeting. I'll warn you now"— she refilled her glass —"they're a hedonistic bunch of assholes. Appeal to their sense of vanity and pride, and you might have a chance."

"Thank you," she said sincerely. A blossom of hope flowered inside her chest. Finally, something good. She picked up her glass and drank as Terra had earlier. The robust and smoky flavor burned her tongue and smacked the back of her throat. Maeve coughed. Terra laughed uproariously, and Alistair patted Maeve's back.

"You should drink it slower," said Alistair.

She wheezed. "Thanks for telling me. You are so helpful."

"Yeah, that seals it," Terrayn said, "I do like you. Anyone who can take the piss outta Alistair is golden in my book." She winked, and Maeve's cheeks burned.

Before they left, Alistair tested the weight of Terra's dagger. "Can I keep this?"

"Only if you promise to put it to good use," she said.

Alistair grinned. Maeve tried not to think about Alistair's nonchalance when it came to killing. This altercation with Terrayn was a glimpse into their abilities. The scuffle at Ferne had been unseen and aided by divine darkness. Alistair didn't strike her as bloodthirsty or cruel, nor did Terrayn. Though, she couldn't be sure. *They could live a secret, murderous lifestyle in the evening while I sleep.* She clutched the envelope to her chest. *Allies are weapons.* She didn't want Alistair to become a weapon for her.

12

Alistair entered their shared room without a single teasing comment. Their lack of banter and confidence made Maeve worried something had gone wrong. *Are we being tossed from the inn? Are guards on their way? Did someone from Hagken's army find us?* Alistair sighed and sat in the lone chair by the copper vent, and the tense silence continued.

"Bad night at the card table?" she guessed from her folded perch on the bed, her hair tumbling around her shoulders in crowded, black curls. She worked her fingers through a stubborn knot.

"No." Alistair stretched their legs out. They tilted their head back to reveal the solid muscled column of their throat and sharp jawline. *If there were an emergency, then Alistair wouldn't be so calm about it,* she thought.

"Do you want to talk?"

"I had some business to take care of. This will be our last night here."

A flicker of nerves wound up Maeve's spine, and her shoulders bunched.

"Are we going to stay at another safe spot Imogen told us about?" Any place with a roof was better than sleeping in the alleys or being stuck outside the city.

"Nope." They crossed their ankles. "I cleaned up my old home. We'll go there in the morning."

"You have a house in Pyrite?" Her shoulders loosened. Hagken hadn't found them, and neither had opportunists looking to use Alistair for ransom. *We're safe for now.*

"My mother left it to me after she passed. I'm lucky to have lost her when I was an adult. Otherwise, Marcus would've happily burned the place to the ground to destroy what little remains of my father."

 "Do you miss him?" She curled her knees to her chest.

"Constantly," they admitted, "I was eleven when he died. He was passionate, loud, and well-read. He used to dance with my mother." They made a sweeping gesture. "All over the house, I'd hear the one-two step of their shoes from downstairs."

"He sounds kind."

"He was." They fell quiet and were lost in the recess of memory.

"I never knew my father," she said, her voice small as if this were shameful to admit. "He died when I was three."

Alistair turned their head toward her. "I'm sorry." Their eyes were dewy and soft. "Do you have any pictures of him?"

"No." She scrunched her nose and said, "Village girl, remember? We could hardly commission portraits."

Alistair dipped their chin. "Right, sorry."

"My mother told me I have his eyes."

"Wait." They joined her on the bed, and Maeve's heart quickened. "So when I look into your lovely eyes, it's like I'm looking at your dad?"

Maeve groaned and then laughed while covering her face. Alistair's sense of humor surprised her.

"You ruined the moment."

"And yet you're laughing!"Alistair nudged their shoulder against hers.

She was grateful they shook off their melancholy mood. While she twined her fingers through her hair into a plait, Alistair settled their chin against two fingers and watched her.

"I don't know how you do it."

"What? Braid hair?"

"No. I don't know how you keep going even though the odds are stacked against you."

Maeve pushed her shoulders back. "I don't have a choice."

"Of course you do. Get on a ship tomorrow and leave this behind. Or stay, work at Juno's temple, and establish yourself as a priestess in Pyrite."

"I can't."

Alistair frowned. "Why not?"

"I won't abandon them." She clutched her pendant. "I promised I'd come for them or die trying."

"Intense."

"They're like family to me." She paused. "They *are* family."

"What? All of them?"

The babies, the sick, the elderly, the healthy; she cared for all. She celebrated their victories and mourned their deaths. They were more than her flock of neighbors and friends. The promise she made was all she had in this new world of magic and bargains. She wouldn't leave them at the mercy of a mad and cruel false king. She would see everyone reunited and returned safely to their homes.

"Yes," she said evenly, "is that surprising?"

They regarded her with an unreadable expression.

"I think you're the last good, selfless person on Calorum." She couldn't tell if they were complimenting or mocking her.

* * *

They returned to the bustling merchant's quarter. A low buzz of conversation and machinery carried even in the early hour as gray mist reflected off the wet cobbled streets. The narrow and cramped pathways twisted through the streets like wandering streams. She spotted two men standing at a street corner. One held a blue fish by its tail, and he argued with a man who held a bigger yellow-tailed fish. Near their ankles, a little girl with sandy blonde hair fed pieces of raw fish to a scruffy cat. She smiled at the normalcy of the moment before Alistair tugged her away.

She needed to bring her people home, but the people in Pyrite had lives and families, too. She would keep that in mind when speaking to the people in charge. Fenris' council wanted their people safe, right?

Alistair stopped in front of a painted orange door. Its chipped paint exposed the underlying wood like bones. Many of Pyrite's doors and windows were engraved with fish, seaweed, or ships to signify its reliance on sea trade. This door, however, had a motif of salamanders engraved on its doorframe. Maeve touched the tail of a salamander near the doorknob.

"She missed our old home," Alistair said, sliding the key into the lock. "She carried it with her wherever she went."

"Where did you live?" She assumed Alistair lived their whole life in Pyrite.

"Everdawn."

Everdawn hugged the border of the citrine deserts. It was the last outpost of humanity before entering the mysterious rolling red dunes. Dawnbreak priory was in Everdawn and considered the apex of Juno's order. *I wonder what their life was like living there.* She joined Alistair in an open, airy chamber with gauzy white curtains separating the other rooms. Its walls were painted deep red, making the room feel like walking into someone's beating heart.

Two fine portraits were mounted above the staircases. She recognized Maren from her unfortunate time in Hagken's company. Maren had the same wry expression, her hands folded neatly in her lap and a gold necklace at her throat. Alistair's father had a radiant, dimpled smile, and laugh lines scored into his umber brown skin. No adornments, no flashy rings, or medallions decorated his body. Yet, an aura of charm and kindness emanated from the painting.

"That's him, I presume." She inclined her head toward the portrait.

"Vivindale Jas'dune." They smiled. "Follow me."

Maeve stopped to look at Maren's portrait as they climbed the stairs. She admired the brush strokes of the oil painting and lingered on Maren's necklace. It wasn't a golden chain like she suspected but a necklace of joined sunbursts and crystal teardrops. Her brow furrowed. *Did the sunstone belong to Maren? Was she a follower or a priestess of Juno? Alistair isn't forthcoming about their parents' stories, but I'm sure they would've mentioned it.*

"Did your mother study magic or follow the sunlit path?"

"She wasn't a mage or a priestess," they said, shrugging. "Her mother was in the midsummer council as a representative for Everdawn and had a relationship with Juno's temple. The southern region is—"

The floor wobbled, and a buzz hummed between her ears. *Alistair's grandmother was part of the midsummer council before Hagken took over.*

"—Devoted. I mean, I get it. There's life in the desert. It's no wonder people worship Juno so reverently in Everdawn, but they do it a bit differently." Their eyes brightened. "For starters, there's a lot more dancing."

"Wait!" Maeve grabbed their arm before they opened the door. "King Hagken—he—killed your grandmother?"

"Yes," Alistair said without inflection. They gently pulled their arm free of Maeve's stunned grasp. *How can Alistair act so nonchalantly in the face of such injustice? Hagken killed their grandmother.* If someone harmed her grandmother, she would be a walking shadow of grief and despair and unable to rest until justice was delivered.

A pair of floor-to-ceiling windows bathed the bedroom in

muted gray morning light. The light bled through hammocks of thin white and teal curtains, creating a dreamy blur. Her frown deepened, and her eyes caught on Alistair's hazy profile rather than the splendid, comfortable room before her.

"Alistair? Are you alright?"

They scrubbed a gloved hand over their face.

"Maeve." They swallowed. "I appreciate the concern. But it happened over a decade ago. Besides, I wasn't close to my grandmother like you were to yours." They spared her a sideways glance, and Maeve touched her pendant. *My mother gave me this, but it first belonged to my grandmother.*

"I'm sorry," she said, and the weight of the words burdened her tongue. They nodded, their eyes distant and scanning the room.

Built-in bookshelves cocooned the writing desk on the north-facing wall into a cozy nook. Judging by their titles, the books weren't storybooks as Maeve preferred but hulking texts on arithmetic, geometry, and Estorian politics. She plucked a jar of reddish dirt from the shelf and a few flecks of gold winked at her. She returned it next to a pair of black teardrop earrings made of shiny porous stone. *Another small piece of the citrine deserts.* A sketchbook lay open on the desk to reveal an unfinished drawing of a prickly, towering plant.

"My mother's." Alistair pointed to the small cursive 'M' in the corner. Maeve lifted the sketchbook into her arms and leafed through it. *They're impressive.* Maren sketched landscapes of the desert, this foreign place Maeve would never see, and it varied from rolling scarlet dunes to flat orange mesas. There were salamanders identical to the ones engraved on the front door. And there were several of a curly-haired baby. Maeve's heart swelled with warmth and then iced over at the cruel reality of this bedroom. Alistair lost their whole family. It wasn't fair King Hagken used his skills and influence to claw his way to the throne with blood-soaked hands.

"She stopped drawing somewhere between my father's death and her marriage to Marcus."

She closed the sketchbook with extreme gentleness.

"How could she marry someone like him? What happened?"

Maeve's mother taught her the importance of love and respect. Their worship of Juno was an act of love. Their work in the fields tilling the soil and planting seeds was an act of love. Everything Alistair showed her about Maren, all the precious pieces of their life, pointed to a thoughtful, intelligent, and loving woman.

"For that story, I'm going to need a drink." They opened a narrow door by the wardrobe. Maeve peered around their shoulder to see a narrow, dark staircase. Her magic responded to her call. It chased the chill of sadness, and a glowing orb illuminated beside Alistair's head.

"My father enjoyed eating late at night," they said fondly, "and they built the stairwell so he wouldn't wake me."

The stairs led into the quaint, modest kitchen. The asymmetrical clay tiles were arranged in turquoise, dark orange, and red. A cooking fireplace, surrounded by sandstone bricks, and a small table squeezed near the main window. Alistair rifled through the dust-covered storage rack of wine and swallowed in haggard and quick gulps from the bottle before sitting down.

Maeve folded her hands in her lap and studied them, her concern growing. A corded muscle in Alistair's neck strained, and their shoulders were a dark and tense line like the crest of twilight on the horizon. They removed a dagger from their sleeve.

"Marcus chipped away my mother's spirit," they said, carving a shape with their dagger into the etched rune-covered table.

"He put his best face forward, showered her with gifts and affection, and by the time he revealed his true nature...she couldn't leave." Their wrist shook with effort as they strained to make a 'C' shape. "He made her feel like she was nothing without him."

Their eyes glistened, and they hissed their exhalation through clenched teeth. Another shape gouged into the wood, and Maeve's heart softened in sympathy. *Hayken stole her art, her books, and this colorful and thoughtfully designed home from her.*

"It wasn't a full year after he crowned himself when she got sick. Whatever claimed her, be it grief or disease, it drained everything that Marcus didn't already take. It robbed her of her wit, her light, her laugh." They squeezed their eyes shut, and their dark plum eye makeup looked like a bruise.

"I used to beg her for the antidote because I was convinced she'd done it on purpose. I believed she saw death as her only option to escape him. I begged her to give me more time. I'd find another way for her freedom if she–" their breath trembled "— held on a little longer."

Maeve reached across the table and laid her hand on Alistair's wrist.

"Marcus refused to let the priestesses of Juno see her. He disliked the temple's power and didn't want to owe them any favors. And by the time he called for healers...it was too late." Their dagger clattered onto the etched table, and Alistair's forehand sank against their palm. "I loved her. I loved her, and all I could do was stand there and watch her spirit leave us. I couldn't help. I couldn't save her." A tear rolled down Alistair's cheek. "I should have saved her."

I wish Juno's light could soothe Alistair's guilt and grief. She squeezed their wrist and looked down. The table wasn't carved in runes or thieves' shorthand. It was a single name repeated over and over, *Marcus.*

13

The following days were blurred; An influx of travelers engorged Pyrite for the upcoming Pallanos equinox. Various yellow and white banners hung from windows and balconies, children painted murals on the upper walkways, and merchants sold flower crowns and dyed silk scarves. Maeve visited Juno's temple every morning to meditate. If Juno had answers for her, they had not yet come. High Matriarch Allustera didn't speak to her again, and Maeve hoped she hadn't accidentally insulted her.

Alistair brought her to a different restaurant for breakfast, and Pyrite's allure never failed to impress her. But she worried about convincing the merchants to support her cause—their invitation burning in her pocket.

"Here, sunshine. Try this." They set a teacup in front of her, and Maeve squinted. *It doesn't smell like tea.*

"What is it?"

Alistair stretched their legs out and placed their feet onto the chair beside Maeve. They cupped their mug between their hands, raised their eyebrows, and grinned. A group of children with ribbons streaming behind them ran past in a chorus of loud and joyous giggles. Maeve carefully drank, and a rich, nutty, and sweet flavor blossomed on her tongue.

"It's sweet." She smiled against the bronze rim.

"There's a few bakeries who have it. It's made from nuts imported from Amethneas," they explained, picking at their flaky pastry filled with blueberries. "Do you like it?"

She nodded. Alistair's cheeks dimpled when they smiled. *Beautiful.* Maeve's chest warmed, and she assumed it was the drink and not Alistair.

"Good." They broke a piece of pastry off for her. "Are you worried about the merchant guild?"

Her shoulders slid forward. "A bit," she said.

"Don't be. They'll love you."

Maeve sighed. She wished her mug held some of Alistair's bold, unwavering confidence.

"I know what will cheer you up. How about we take a walk to Thorduun's quarter?"

She swallowed the pastry sticking to her throat.

"And how are we going to do that?"

An arcane bubble separated Thorduun's quarter from the rest of the city. The barrier helped to contain the mages' and alchemists' guilds and living quarters. Alistair said it was a precaution enacted after 'the great burning' which had destroyed more than two dozen houses and killed countless citizens. The guilds didn't mind because the shield provided privacy for their secretive and protected rituals.

Alistair smiled. "Have a little faith in me, Maeve."

* * *

A pungent scent of sulfur hit the back of Maeve's throat, and she resisted the urge to gag. Alistair's supple, gloved hand remained clasped between hers, and their footsteps were confident along the slick and slimy stones beneath the city. *I can't believe these tunnels!* They functioned like a network of underground streets. The sewage system rushed by in frothy dark waves, and a rat skittered into a darkened corner. Her orb of light cast long shadows on the wet walls and flickered near Alistair's head; their dark hair gleamed orange beneath the magical light.

After several minutes of twisting corners and narrow pathways, they reached a metal ladder. Its rungs were slick with condensation. *I would've gotten lost if not for Alistair's guidance.* Alistair pushed the iron grate aside with a strained grunt. The sunlight stirred dust motes, and Maeve covered her nose with her shirt. Alistair waited near the exit while she climbed out.

Thorduun's quarter was unlike the Merchant's quarter or the burned district. Misty plumes of smoke clouded the air and congested at the apex of the arcane bubble. The houses were stacked precariously next to each other and on top of one another with ivory columns and painted windowsills and doors. The cobblestones glittered with copper flecks and more painted murals. Maeve arched her neck and spun in a circle, taking it all in.

Alistair slid their fingers between hers, and Maeve realized she didn't mind their touch. It was comforting to have the solid warmth of them nearby. The streets were crowded with individuals as vibrant as the buildings. The alchemists carried belts filled with pouches and vials, and their hair varied from bright pink to orange, sky blue, and neon green. With a flinch of sympathy, she noticed many carried burn wounds on their hands, necks, or faces. They strapped goggles to their heads, and some covered their faces with bandannas or scarves. She thought of Imogen's underground alcove. *They must've suffered burns from their experiments.*

The rest of the people on the street, she assumed, were mages. They dressed in breeches and shirts. They wore backpacks, carried scrolls, and strapped books beneath their underarms or secured around their waists. *I wonder if mages always have their books with them.* It sounded impractical. The mages shot contemptuous glares at the alchemists, and alchemists laughed behind their gloved hands at the mages. All it would take was a match before the whole place exploded.

And it did.

The ground shook with the impact and strength of it. She stumbled and gripped Alistair's wrist.

"Likely an experiment gone awry or a spell," Alistair explained calmly.

A metallic creature turned the corner and walked toward them. She squeezed Alistair's fingers again. Her throat went dry.

"What is that?" she hissed, trying not to draw attention, as the thing continued to stalk forward. Alistair grinned. The metal creature was humanoid-shaped. It towered at seven feet tall with bulky armored plates, pistons, and gears attached to its limbs. An undulating purple flame trapped within a dodecahedron swirled and pulsed at the center of its chest cavity.

"Hm." Alistair tilted their head. "You're not going to faint, are you?"

"No."

Maeve stiffened. *Is it alive? Is it magical? It* must *be magical.* There was no way it wasn't. But everything in Pyrite melded the two worlds: magic and theory, machinery and spells.

"It's got a few names. The mages call them elemental guardians, the alchemists call them sentinels, and thieves call them a nuisance." Alistair said, "It's the one project alchemists and mages agree to work on together."

The sentinel stomped past. Its heavy footfalls shook the ground, and its featureless face turned from side to side as if scanning the road for threats. She thought of Imogen again and wondered if she had built one of these.

"They're one of the city's best defenses," Alistair said.

"Wow." Maeve stared as the sentinel turned down the street. The rest of the citizens walked past unperturbed but gave it a wide berth. *How could anyone fight one of those? It could crush someone with one hand.* Her heart galloped. She grinned at Alistair.

"What are the odds they'd use those against Hagken?"

Alistair snorted.

"Slim. I said they're the city's best defense, but they hate letting them leave Thorduun's quarter."

"I'm sure if we talked to them..."

"Maeve." They squeezed her hand. "I know what you're thinking, but we need to take this one day at a time. Merchants first. They'll be more likely to listen if we have someone on our side besides Terrayn."

Maeve sighed. *Alistair knows this city better than I do.* She needed to be methodical.

She and Alistair walked hand-in-hand down the colorful street. Thorduun's quarter was contained to guild business, but Maeve noticed several taverns and herbalist stalls. The sage academy was a multi-tiered building of stone and thick, ivy-covered columns. At the front, near the door, was a red statue of Thorduun, the Patron of Magic and Knowledge. The robed figure was faceless and genderless, their arms extended upward, with a large, silver lightning bolt held between their hands.

"They've got the second-largest library in all of Estoria." Alistair frowned. "It rivals all the knowledge in Amethneas."

"Can we go inside?"

"Not without an invitation."

She bit her cheek. She thought about the small bookshelf inside her home containing hand-written notes from her family. Her mother taught her letters and measurements, as was expected for a priestess, but most of Ferne was illiterate.

At the base of Thorduun's statue, people offered dried flowers, folded notes, and coins. Maeve placed a silver coin at its feet. She bowed her head. She needed Thorduun's wisdom to know which choices were the right ones. She was out of her element, but it didn't mean she would fail. She couldn't fail. Her people needed her. She returned to Alistair, her smile soft around the edges.

"Where to next?"

"The alchemists are a tad more welcoming if you can offer them something interesting."

"And do you have something?"

"I do." Alistair's grin dimpled. "I won it in a card game last night."

Maeve bit her lip, guiltily eager to see what the alchemist had since the sage academy was barred from her. A sunburned woman cut into their path and shoved a flimsy, yellowed paper into Maeve's face.

"Have you seen my son, Gregor?" she asked. Her eyes were bloodshot.

"Uh." Maeve blinked at the rough sketch of a young man with a crooked nose. The woman shoved the poster closer to Maeve, and her hand trembled.

She said, "He has the same eyes as you."

Maeve shook her head. *Poor woman.* "I'm sorry."

The woman spun onto Alistair with a crazed, urgent look. "What about you? Have you seen him? Look closely."

Alistair said nothing.

"He's a mage. He didn't return home. Please, you must know something."

A group of alchemists walked by and quietly laughed. Her eyes shone with unshed tears. She whipped back to Maeve.

"My name is Neena. I'm a deckhand on the 'Sailor's Knot,' and Gregor is my only child. He's been with the academy for three moons now. He wanted to make a better life for us." Her chin wobbled.

Placing a gentle hand on Neena's arm, Maeve said, "I'm sorry I haven't seen him, but I will keep my eyes open. Okay?"

Neena looked barely placated, but she nodded and left Maeve and Alistair to ask another passerby. Maeve rubbed her palm against her tender heart. *It's a small comfort to know that the mothers of Ferne are with their children.* She could only imagine how Bertha would react if her daughter was missing.

"My heart breaks for her..." she whispered. "Do you think she'll find him?"

"Hm. Sounds like a question Lady Janis herself would have the answer to."

* * *

If someone combined all volatile cosmic reactions and each color in the rainbow and condensed them into a four-story building, they'd be left with the alchemists' guild hall. A chaotic mess of color and infrequent sounds. Its metal doors reminded Maeve of Imogen with all its gears, pistons, and delicate, wire-thin parts. The stone beneath her feet vibrated with a distant, deep explosion. Alistair smiled at the toad-faced, squat man sitting on the steps. Like other alchemists, he wore a bandoleer of pouches and fingerless gloves.

He pulled at his dark, singed beard. "I know your face."

"Ah." Alistair clicked their tongue. "Glad to see your eyes haven't failed you yet, Vox."

Vox guffawed. "Even if they did, I'd make new ones." His gray eyes scanned the courtyard before pinning Alistair with an outstretched hand. "You know the toll, old friend."

Alistair tossed him a silver coin, and Vox frowned. Alistair winked at her, and her nape prickled. She rubbed over the sensation. *Perhaps I'm getting a sunburn.*

Alistair said, "Flip it."

Vox's frown deepened, skeptical. The coin reflected the natural light in the air, and when it landed back in Vox's outstretched palm it had turned gold. *How?* Vox threw his head back and laughed. *What sort of magic accomplishes that?* Maeve thought incredulously.

"Where'd you find this, Ali?" Vox said, flipping the coin and returning it to silver.

"Card table."

"I'll be damned."

Vox stood, grunting, and removed a metallic tube from his shirt pocket. It slid into an impression in the door with a resounding *clunk.* The gears turned, clicking and shifting, a faint hum resonating through the metal before the doors swung open.

"Try not to touch anything explosive," he warned.

The central atrium led into a laboratory cluttered with long tables balancing glass vials, beakers, and burners. A cluster of tiny, metallic birds fluttered overhead, their wings buzzing, before they zipped through an open archway. Alchemists were either hunched over their work or rushing through the empty pockets of space with a determined purpose. A veil of smog coated the ceiling. An unfinished sentinel sat in the center of the room, and its chest lacked the glowing power source.

A hollow chime cut through the cavernous halls. Like clockwork, the alchemists moved from their stations, chatting, and several stopped upon seeing Alistair.

"Is it a trick of Janis, or does my eye see true?" a young woman said, her tanned face badly scarred and an eye patch over her left eye. Her opalescent hair piled on her head like a bird's nest.

"As if Janis would waste her tricks on you, friend," Alistair teased.

Maeve studied their interaction. Usually, Alistair played nice to pick someone's pocket or weasel information from them. However, talking to this alchemist, she couldn't shake the feeling they carried history. *First Imogen, now this one. How many alchemists does Alistair know?* The opal-haired woman introduced herself as Bismuth and smiled after Maeve mentioned she was a priestess.

"We never get divine types in here." She raised her eyebrows. "Allow me to show you around."

Bismuth brought them to an inner greenhouse—a nest of thick vines draped like dead snakes from hooks hanging off the glass ceiling. The tables were lined with clay pots filled with blooming flowers and short succulents. Maeve tugged her collar as the humidity sank into her skin. Bismuth lovingly caressed the petals of an orange and yellow-spotted flower.

"Magnificent, isn't it?" she said before clipping a stem. She held it aloft for Maeve to see.

"Oh? Um." Maeve blinked. "What does it do?"

I don't recognize it, but maybe Imogen would. She could learn from Imogen. *There's knowledge to be found in every corner of Pyrite.*

"It keeps you hidden in plain sight. You take one petal and rest it on your tongue. Don't swallow it, though." She returned her tiny scissors to her leather apron.

Alistair pointed to a spiked plant behind Bismuth and said, "And what's that?"

Bismuth turned to explain, and Maeve caught Alistair plucking a petal from the flower off Bismuth's worktable. *Alistair!* It disappeared between Alistair's deft, gloved fingers. *I can't bring them anywhere. They bribe clerks and steal from alchemists.* Maeve huffed. Her loyalty to Alistair and her desire not to get thrown out of the guild stopped her from saying anything. *I will encourage them to return the flower before we leave.*

"What brings you to Thorduun's quarter?" Bismuth asked.

"I'm giving Maeve a tour."

"Interesting." Bismuth dragged the word out and pinned Alistair with her gaze.

"Is this what you work on? Plants?" she asked. Imogen studied mushrooms. *Is it a common trend among alchemists?* Maeve wondered, *are they interested in combining the natural world with the unnatural?*

"This is a pet project," said Bismuth, "it soothes me. Most of my work is focused on defensive instruments."

"Like the sentinels?"

"Yes. Those are mine."

"How do they work?"

"D'you think I'd reveal all my secrets?" she said, looping her arm with Maeve's like they were old friends. "I'm a busy woman and don't give away anything for free."

Maeve studied Bismuth's profile. The art of bartering was a cornerstone of Pyrite's culture. If someone had information, they could bet it in a card game, although their opponents would need to trust it was accurate and worthwhile. If Maeve wanted answers, then she'd need to get creative.

"You said you don't get many priestesses here?"

"Mhm. They keep to their spires. Mostly."

"Then you've never seen our magic?"

The scars around Bismuth's mouth stretched when she smiled.

"Rarely and not in my lifetime," she admitted, "usually if any of us are sick, we tend to ourselves before calling upon a priestess to heal us."

"Maeve's incredible," Alistair interjected, "I've seen her perform miracles."

"I wouldn't say miracles," she said without conviction. What else could she call her magic? It was divine. It was a gift from Juno. It was nothing short of miraculous. She called to Juno. Her magic sizzled and popped at the center of her stomach. The foggy, humid air swirled and twisted. Her dazzling lights popped into existence. *It's as easy as breathing.*

"Marvelous!" Bismuth laughed, and the orb passed through her wiggling fingers. "You control them?"

"Yes."

The orbs danced, bobbing and weaving through the plants, and drifted to the roof.

"It was one of the first spells I ever learned," she said.

Bismuth scribbled in her notebook. The symbols were blocky and stacked on top of each other. *It's the secret language Alistair mentioned earlier.* Bismuth nodded before addressing Maeve and Alistair.

She said, "Imagine if the priestesses used their magic like this! We'd never need gravelight again."

"Well, we have limits," Maeve said, "eventually my body burns it up."

"Uh-huh."

"The priestesses have to conserve their energy; otherwise, they'd pass out," she clarified, feeling a kinship to her fellow priestesses. *We couldn't light an entire city.*

Bismuth rolled an eye.

"You're not from here, so I'll go easy on you. But, I assure you, they are not conserving anything in Juno's spire. They pray and hope to hear their goddesses' words."

"They provide a service to the city," Maeve said.

"So do we. We all provide something to the city, and that's why it's standing."

Maeve frowned. *She doesn't understand the priestesses.* Allustera's refusal to help against King Hagken had hurt Maeve's feelings, but Maeve understood Juno's order within Pyrite had their responsibilities. She would eventually convince them. Bismuth poked one of the orbs with her pen and observed it. For whatever divine reason, the lights didn't burn or produce heat. The divine magic that created them wasn't connected to the element of fire. *Unlike that spell, I used against Hagken.* Maeve dismissed her lights in a brief wave.

"Fantastic. Thank you for sharing it with me, Maeve."

She crossed her arms, stinging from Bismuth's earlier comments.

"Don't you have something to share with me?" she asked pointedly.

"Of course," Bismuth said. "That is the natural balance of life, is it not?"

She led them to a courtyard of splendor with tall grass hedges, wild plants, and a fountain gurgling with iridescent water.

"The sentinels are the perfect blend of magic and machine. We fortify the iron, you see, with a powder mined in the hematite mountains. It takes seven days to treat it, and very few blacksmiths even want to work with it. It's—" she cleared her throat, grimacing, "— it's harmful when inhaled. It'll burn your lungs. Once the armor is fortified, we send it to the academy for protective enchantments."

"What's at the center?"

"It's a pure elemental force." She bounced in place. "Sometimes the mages help us, but they're a bunch of assholes, so we usually wait for a storm. We harness, extract, and trap the lightning within those cubes."

"You trap lightning," Maeve repeated slowly.

"Don't look so shocked." Bismuth snickered, and Alistair groaned. "Excuse the pun. It's been a long day. But, yes, we trap it, and then it gives my sentinels life—or, more accurately — energy.

"There's some technical aspects to it, but that's the bare bones of the operation."

If Hagken attacks the city...these guardians could save lives. Alistair warned her to take it slow and work with the merchants before petitioning the alchemists. *But why wait?* A sense of urgency pulled at her gut. *I'm here now.*

"Does the guild send the guardians outside Thorduun's quarter?"

"Rarely." Bismuth's eye narrowed. "We need them here."

Alistair gave a pointed tug at Maeve's sleeve. She squeezed her hands into fists and kept her gaze locked on Bismuth.

"But if the threat were big enough, they would send them?"

"Perhaps. It'd be up to guild master Irryn."

Barter and trade is the life blood of Pyrite. Maeve swallowed. What could she offer to gain access to the guild master?

"I'd like to speak to them," Maeve said. "I could show you the healing magic we use." There was more to Juno's magic than dancing lights.

"Maeve..." Alistair's voice carried a note of warning.

"I suppose if you allowed me to study your magic and take some samples..."

"Samples?"

Bismuth plucked a glass vial from her apron's pocketed belt. "A bit of blood, a bit of saliva, and a few strands of hair ought to do."

"Is this necessary, Bizzy?" Alistair asked, "just to see Irryn?"

"Others have given more." She gestured a flippant hand to Maeve. "It is her choice, is it not?"

In the grand scheme of things, Bismuth wasn't asking for much. Who knew what her people were sacrificing while under Hagken's boot? She could part with some blood and hair.

"Alistair, it's fine." Maeve rolled up her sleeves. "I'm happy to help the guild if they can help me."

Bismuth laughed merrily. "Spoken like a true citizen of Pyrite. Come, I'll bring you to my other workstation."

14

Bismuth returned to the bustling station of workbenches in the central atrium and stroked the non-functional sentinel before settling on a stool. Maeve's heartbeat jumped at the sight of Bismuth's various sharp scientific instruments. She held something similar to a syringe, but a component was attached near the plunger. It was two inches in diameter, made of glass, with an a glyph etched upon the surface in an iridescent, shimmering color.

"What's that?"

"It's my signature," Bismuth said, "every alchemist has one. It's a way to protect our work. If someone tries to steal my sample, it'll be moot because the blood itself will be marked."

"My blood will belong to you?" Maeve said. A feeling of dread seeped into her bones. Maybe Alistair had been right to worry.

"The samples will. Your blood is your own." Bismuth smiled. "I promise."

She opened a medium-sized metallic box and twirled a pair of marked scissors in her hand.

"Left or right?"

Maeve stuck out her left arm. Bismuth used a piece of thin, black rubber to tourniquet Maeve's upper arm and her green-tinged veins bulged from the constriction in blood flow. Bismuth inserted the needle at the inner crook of Maeve's elbow. The bite stung. In well-practiced movements, Bismuth drew a single vial of blood, then prepared to dress the entry point with bandages. Maeve waved her off. Her right hand glowed with Juno's magic and healed the minor injury with little strain on her magical reserves.

"Marvelous," Bismuth crooned.

"Not too late to back out." Alistair placed their hand on Maeve's back.

"Do you have a better idea to meet Irryn?"

They sighed. "No."

"Now, I'm going to give you something to make you drool. It lasts a few minutes. Do your best to spit into the bowl, please."

She rapt her fingers against a pouch and offered Maeve yellow powder on a copper spoon. *Painless thus far.* Alistair draped a cloth over Maeve's lap.

"Thanks," she said, closing her mouth around the spoon.

It was horribly bitter, and Maeve gagged. Her saliva flooded her mouth once the powder dissolved. Bismuth provided her a shallow bowl, and Maeve sat, feeling a little foolish and unable to speak, as a waterfall of viscous yellow-tinged saliva trailed out of her mouth and down her chin. The few minutes Bismuth promised felt like an hour. Maeve reminded herself why she was doing this. She shoved her mortification to the back corner of her mind. A little blood and spit, and the guild master would speak with her. It wasn't a high price to pay. Bismuth carefully transferred the bowl's contents through a funnel into a marked glass vessel.

"Final offering. I'd like a strand or two of at least three inches," she said, passing Alistair the scissors. Maeve wiped her cottony mouth and met Alistair's curious yet guarded gaze.

"Would you like to do it? We could find a mirror." They spun the scissors around their index finger.

"It's fine. Cut a piece from the back."

Her black hair was long enough. Bismuth finished storing and securing her samples and smiled. It was the wide, impressed smile of someone proud of their work, and Maeve couldn't begin to guess what research Bismuth would conduct.

"Thank you so much, Maeve." Bismuth gestured plaintively to Alistair. "I'm afraid they'll have to wait outside Irryn's office."

Maeve frowned. "Why?"

"The deal was to provide samples for our research into divine magic, and I would bring you to meet Irryn. Alistair wasn't part of the deal."

"Do you want my hair and spit, too?" Alistair said with withering scorn.

"No. I do not." Her bright, sea-glass-colored eye narrowed shrewdly at Maeve. "If Alistair's company was something you desired, you should've included it in your request."

Maeve said, "I thought you two were friends."

Bismuth laughed. It sounded like someone scooped the mirth from her rib cage with a serrated knife.

"Friends? In this city? No, no, no, Maeve." A strand of her white hair came loose at her temple. "Alistair, what would you call us? Associates of the past?"

They shrugged and said, "Close enough."

Maeve reviewed their interactions through a different lens.

Alistair was at ease and comfortable with Bismuth. *Was I mistaken? Had it been an act? Did Alistair steal from Bismuth because there's no kinship between them?* She was stunned by the nonchalant and distant nature of the people she met. *Where is the loyalty or kindness?* They couldn't survive on self-interest alone. That would create a lonely and paranoid existence.

"It's alright, Maeve. I'm sure the guild master doesn't bite." Alistair smiled. A sensation not unlike regret began to crawl its way up her throat.

Bismuth took them to an alcove tucked beneath the stairwell. A tubed contraption built into the wall trembled with tiny vibrations. Bismuth approached it, removed her glove, and placed her palm against the glass. The machine clanked and exhaled a trail of steam through an attached vent. Bismuth's marker appeared on the wall opposite the alcove, and a wood panel slid aside to reveal a metal door.

Alistair leaned against the wall and crossed their arms. "Your security isn't as impressive as you think it is."

"Try and break in next time," said Bismuth, "and see what happens."

Maeve touched Alistair's shoulder in passing. She wished she could telepathically communicate to Alistair that she'd be okay. She would be savvier the next time she struck a deal with someone in Pyrite.

The guild master's room was sparse and shimmered in ghostly light. The guild master stood behind a meticulous workbench with a cautious expression on her fine-boned face. Her thin, dark eyebrows were naturally angled downward. She reminded Maeve of the scowling gargoyles she'd seen in picture stories. The room lacked sunlight or windows, but the vents overhead contained rows of gravelight. Irryn wore a sleeveless shirt revealing her impressively toned muscles, and her dark box braids transitioned into bright blue at the ends, decorated with colorful beads and pulled into a low ponytail.

She removed the round spectacles from her nose and squinted at Maeve.

"Explain." Her words were flat, though her voice was light and melodic.

"Maeve is a priestess of Juno, untethered to the temple here, and offered to assist in our research for a meeting with you."

"Interesting," Irryn said in a tone that implied it was not interesting at all, and she'd rather they left immediately.

Maeve took a quick step forward before she lost her nerve. "I need to speak to you about King Hagken."

Irryn said, "He's not a king."

"He calls himself king," Maeve replied, "he's built an army in Hollyhock to reclaim Pyrite."

Irryn flattened her palms against her metal workbench and leaned forward. A few vials rattled within their holders at the shift in pressure.

"How does this concern my guild?"

"It concerns everyone!" she exclaimed. Her cheeks flushed beneath the harsh, immovable gaze of Irryn. "If he takes Pyrite, who knows what will happen to your guild? He could burn it to the ground."

"Hagken would never dare to return to this city."

"Why not?" Maeve snapped, "because you are so well protected? Because you have a building full of mages who don't leave their halls and a few hundred town guards?"

Irryn ticked an eyebrow toward her braided hairline. Maeve's ears burned hot with shame. She never lost her composure. She was meant to remain calm and stalwart regardless of the circumstances. Her mother once said, '*Sunlight never wavers from its destined path.*'

Irryn said, "Thorduun's quarter is impenetrable."

Maeve chewed her tongue as tension rolled down her jaw and into her shoulders. It wasn't impenetrable, considering she and Alistair could crawl through the sewers to get here. However, she doubted Irryn wanted to hear that anecdote.

"What about everyone else?"

"What are you asking me?"

"For help," Maeve said, "your guardians could protect the rest of the city."

Irryn tossed her ponytail over her shoulder and laughed. Her smile was sharp, and her front canine teeth were gold-capped.

"Our sentinels do not leave the quarter," she said, "I appreciate the effort, though."

"What's your price?" Maeve asked. If Bismuth and Terra accepted deals, then there was a chance Irryn would, too.

Irryn regarded her coolly. "I'm afraid you have mistaken me for the peddlers at the docks selling fake pearls. The sentinels are not for sale."

"I don't want to buy them." Maeve said, "a loan, perhaps? Could you spare two or three?"

"For a ghost of a threat?"

"The threat is real, Irryn. I wouldn't be here otherwise."

Irryn's dark eyes narrowed and hardened around the edges. "I must return to my work, Lady Maeve."

She lifted a bone-white dagger from her workbench. She tested the point with her finger and hovered the blade over a blue flame until it blackened with soot. *What in Juno's name is she doing?* Maeve avoided Bismuth's outstretched hand. Irryn laid her off-hand flat on the workbench and lifted the dagger overhead. The intention was clear. She meant to maim herself for one of her experiments. Maeve reacted, and Juno's gift answered her call. Irryn's blade shot downward, and its blackened tip reflected off Maeve's shield of light. Its diamond shape hovered over Irryn's defenseless hand before vanishing. Her blade shifted like ash and smoke before reforming solid. Irryn's dark, angled brows raised in surprise. Maeve wiped the sweat from her brow with the back of her hand.

"The blade is designed to vanish when it comes into contact with physical matter," Irryn said.

Maeve sighed, relieved. "You could've mentioned that."

Irryn scoffed.

"Fascinating." Bismuth clutched her notes between her hands. "How many spells do you know, Maeve?"

Maeve didn't know how to answer. She summoned lights and healed the sick and injured if they weren't in mortal peril. This shield summoned over Irryn's defenseless hand was new. *It was reactive.*

"It's less knowing and more like a conversation. I ask Juno for help, and it manifests."

Bismuth scribbled onto her notes.

"Did you ask Juno to protect Irryn's hand?"

"Uh...no." She fiddled with her sunburst pendant. She hadn't asked. It wasn't the same as the tracing spell at the inn. "I suspected what Irryn was doing and wanted to stop it."

"Incredible," Bismuth whispered, and her face vanished behind her notebook. "It's entirely different from how the mages cast spells."

"Really?" Irryn stroked her chin. "As you might know, Maeve, Bismuth is researching magic. We understand pieces of it. There is power in symbols and elements of the natural world and limits—yes, limits to it all." She slid her glasses back on. "Our goal as alchemists is to eradicate those limits."

Maeve thought of the alchemists with scars and injuries and rebuilt pieces of themselves. *How can anyone achieve a sense of satisfaction in their work if they constantly pressure themselves into surpassing their limits?*

Irryn said, "Lady Maeve, if you stay the night, allowing Bismuth to complete further tests about your unique magic, then I would be persuaded to allow two sentinels to leave Thorduun's quarter."

"Only two?"

"There are two gates to enter the city. I doubt the false king will arrive by ship." Irryn smiled, and it softened her face when she wasn't mocking. "I will leave it to Bismuth and yourself to iron out the details while I arrange for the guardians to leave with you in the morning."

"Why can't I come back tomorrow?"

"It'll be easier if you stay. Besides, think of the good work you and Bismuth will be able to accomplish. You could change the world."

A sleepover at the alchemists' guild for the guarantee of two sentinels? Simple enough. However, she wasn't keen on offering more blood or hair to Bismuth, and she didn't know if any of it would be world-changing, but she owed it to the citizens of Ferne and Pyrite to try. Maeve approached Irryn and offered her hand. An alliance with the alchemists' guild would hopefully help with the merchants. *Who knew progress would smell like sulfur and charcoal and taste like bitter yellow chalk?*

"It's a deal."

Irryn pulled her glove off with her teeth and firmly shook Maeve's hand. Her skin was remarkably soft. Up close, flecks of silver were painted along Irryn's eyelashes.

"Set in stone, set in bone," Irryn said, "now, leave me to my work."

* * *

Maeve explained her deal to Alistair as they followed Bismuth through the wild kinetic space of the guild.

"Are you sure about this?" Alistair asked, "We could wait until we meet with Terra and the other merchants."

"I don't want to wait, Alistair. Hagken won't delay once he's ready to advance on the city. I have to do this. We'll receive two guardians to our cause."

They smirked. "I love it when you call it 'the cause.' It sounds dreadfully important."

"That's because it is." Maeve nudged her shoulder against Alistair's. "I'm fighting for Pyrite *and* Ferne."

Something uncoiled in the center of Maeve's chest beneath Alistair's pleasant smile. The coming days were less daunting when she knew she'd have at least one person on her side. Alistair knew the ins and outs of the city and its people. Although Alistair's vendetta against Hagken motivated their actions, Maeve was grateful for their continued support and altruism.

"Alistair, our visiting hours are over," said Bismuth.

Alistair placed a hand over their heart. "Such hospitality."

"I thought they were staying," Maeve said.

"You didn't ask Irryn." Bismuth shrugged half-heartedly. "And it's not my decision to make." Maeve mentally kicked herself. *I was so focused on the guardians that I forgot the smaller details. Goddess Theadora —please grant me the clarity of thought to negotiate better next time. Again.*

Vox twisted a wrench into a metal six-legged device on his lap and didn't bother to look at them.

"Don't worry, Maeve, I'll come here first light," Alistair said, "and we'll get breakfast."

"See you in the morning." Maeve smiled, and a twinge of nervousness fluttered inside her gut. She and Alistair hadn't parted since their meeting within Hollyhock. *They'll be fine.* Alistair pulled Maeve into a surprising embrace, and Maeve clutched the leather expanse of their back. *Perhaps they're as nervous as I am?*

"Don't let them push you around," they whispered, and their warm breath tickled her ear. "The alchemists are a tenacious bunch." *I wish they could stay.* Maeve's heart jumped.

Maeve said, "Lady Janis, watch over you."

Alistair's smirk reached their eyes and reminded Maeve of sunlight reflecting the ocean. They squeezed her arm before Vox opened the mechanical doors. Maeve stared at the exit with a strange longing pushing up through the dark soil of her heart. *They'll be okay. I'll see them in the morning.*

Bismuth said, "Come eat with us, Maeve, and we can discuss our plans for the evening."

"No more samples."

"I've got plenty of samples. I'm more interested in the practical uses of your magic."

"And I don't want anyone to get hurt."

Bismuth fiddled with her pen. "I'll do my best."

The dining hall fit four broad oak tables, and candelabras hung from the ceiling where two metal birds perched and chirped in odd tones. It was quieter here, but vibrations rumbled at her feet from the experiments conducted in the central atrium and below. Bismuth led Maeve beneath a balcony overlooking the hall. The kitchens were small for such a massive guild. Alchemists grabbed plates and bowls and filled them with food before returning to the dining hall or through another door in the back. Maeve assumed they were returning to their workstations. *This place is like a maze.* She filled her bowl with a creamy potato and fish stew and tucked two small loaves of dark bread under her arm.

Maeve sensed the glances of alchemists slipping from her face like oil. She smiled at them, but they looked away or turned their backs. When she and Bismuth sat down, Maeve couldn't shake the discomfort of being ignored. *Do they have something against outsiders?* She made stilted conversation with Bismuth until she could endure it no longer.

"Is it always like this?" she asked, "are alchemists always unfriendly?"

Perhaps her memory of the alchemist visiting Ferne had been correct. Alchemists were arrogant and standoffish. *Imogen was distrustful, too, when we met, but at least she warmed to me.* She hated to generalize, but the lack of courtesy made her scowl into her bowl.

"Don't take it personally, Lady Maeve." Bismuth dipped her bread into the broth. "New faces who aren't with the guild are treated with suspicion and dislike. It's the way it is, you know?"

"How does someone join your guild?"

"There's a fee to apply and a brief waiting period. Then they must show proof of a successful, independent experiment," she said. "The guild master reviews it, then their hypothesis is re-tested, and if a similar or identical result is produced—the applicant gains membership." Bismuth wiped her mouth.

"Do they know I'm here to help you?"

"Shh!" Bismuth waved her hands. "I'd prefer if no one knew anything about my research."

Maeve tried to piece together everything she learned about the alchemists. They had a hierarchy and protocols because Imogen wouldn't have been kicked out otherwise. They were methodical, obsessed with their work, and handled volatile components daily. *And Alistair warned me of their nature.* They were secretive and used custom markers for their research materials and notes. She couldn't understand how this organization functioned while using hyper-independent methods.

"Don't you have a team to help you?" She was Ferne's healer, but it never overwhelmed her. For a time, she had her family beside her, though Ferne's population never exceeded two hundred in her lifetime.

"No." Bismuth scoffed. "And I'd like to keep it that way."

How many other alchemists function as Bismuth does? Solitary and secret. And what about Imogen? Was she the only person working on her life-saving potion? Maeve pushed her spoon around inside her bowl. *I can't imagine the stress they're under.*

"Eat some bread. You'll need your strength." Bismuth broke the loaf between her fingers and shared half. Maeve looked at Bismuth with a strange pull to her heart, although Bismuth was immersed in coded conversation with a green-haired colleague. Maeve didn't bother to try to decipher it. Her face lit up the same way Imogen's had when Alistair gave her the poison mushrooms. *How can Pyrite change with the knowledge of Juno's magic? Could they re-establish Imogen's work? Could she be accepted into her guild again?* Maeve hid her yawn behind her fist. Many alchemists ate alone, but a few were in groups no larger than three. One alchemist sat in the far corner with a wide-brimmed hat and black reflective goggles on their face. *Is it lonely here?* She watched the alchemist lift the collar of their coat to hide their face further when they noticed Maeve glancing at them. *It feels lonely.* Once she was no longer distracted by the metallic birds or burning scents permeating the air, a thrum of emptiness vibrated through the chaos. *Will the merchants be the same?*

"Are you ready?" Bismuth asked.

Maeve collected her empty bowl and looked to the corner of the room where the shy alchemist sat. They were gone. *Well, Bismuth said they don't like strangers. They must've run off and returned to work.* She followed Bismuth into a workroom. It was as large as her old room at the Willy Nook Inn. The walls had bolted metal shelves containing empty glass bottles and small wooden crates. Her boots stuck against the tacky floor. She helped push the desks and chairs to the side. Bismuth wiped her hands on her leather apron, picked up her notebook, and smiled.

"Let's get started, shall we?"

Maeve sensed the reserves of Juno's power living inside her. It bubbled through her veins like liquid light. She recalled Irryn's words and Alistair's warning and clutched her sunburst amulet. *Irryn said I could negotiate the terms of our experiment.*

"We won't be able to do this all night," Maeve explained, "I'll need to rest eventually."

"Your magic is connected to your energy levels?"

"Yes."

"Fascinating." She made another note. "I will keep that in mind. Ready?"

Maeve squared her shoulders. "Yes."

Bismuth instructed Maeve to conjure her lights. She summoned them in different sizes and varied brightness until a sheen of sweat glistened across her skin. Bismuth measured the lights, captured them in jars, and tested them for flammability. And each test was followed by meticulous notes.

"Again." Bismuth poised her pen. Maeve inhaled and brought sunlight to life between her hands. *Is it frivolous to use Juno's power in this way? Or will I make the world a better place by sharing this knowledge?* A headache tightened around her skull like a winding vice. She ground her teeth and endured.

Bismuth allowed a short break for water and to use the washroom before she changed the direction of her experiments into Maeve's healing magic. At Maeve's request, Bismuth wasn't allowed to harm herself. As a compromise, Maeve executed superficial cuts on her own forearm. Every sharp bite of pain eventually grew numb as Maeve cut and healed herself over and over and over again. Her vision swam with black spots.

I don't think I can keep going. Maeve used Juno's magic to alleviate the pain in her skull, and her knees buckled. Bismuth caught her and lowered her gently to the floor. They sat together shoulder-to-shoulder, and Bismuth passed her a cup of water. A shiver ran through her sweat-covered body, and her headache pounded behind her eyes.

"I'm drained, Bismuth. Priestesses have limits. Juno gives us only so much." A familiar tickle of warmth in her upper nasal cavity forewarned a nosebleed.

"You don't have limits, Maeve," Bismuth urged, "smash the walls you've built around yourself. Keep going."

Alistair told me not to let them push me around.

"I need another break." She stared at her, but it was hard to focus when Bismuth's face doubled and blurred. *This will be the last healing magic I can do.* Her stomach cramped. *Juno, answer my call one last time. Please.* She folded her fingers over her bleeding arm. Bismuth's pen scratched along the parchment. She clung to the sound to keep her mind anchored in reality. Juno's magic glowed with ethereal light through the gaps in her fingers.

"One last experiment, Maeve." Bismuth said, "Irryn won't give you the guardians if we don't finish."

Her voice sounded far away, and her footsteps receded. Maeve slumped forward onto the ground. The floor smelled awful. She heaved. Her cheek pressed against the floor, and she blinked rapidly to clear the muddled swamp nest inside her skull. *I need to stay conscious. She's right. I have to see this through so I can have the guardians.* The door creaked like an old ship. Through her sweaty dark curls, someone's worn leather boots entered her field of vision. A wet cloth dropped onto her forehead.

"Here." Bismuth crouched and pushed a hoof-shaped gray mushroom into Maeve's hands. "Use your lights to ignite this tinder fungus."

I don't think I can. A sense of fear crawled across her spine like a spider. *I've never used Juno's gift to ignite anything this large.* Hagken's skin bubbled pink and blistered under her palm. *I can't. I'm too weak.* Her connection to Juno had never been this exhausted before.

"Go on, Maeve. A final test," she said.

Maeve squeezed her eyes shut. *For Ferne, Pyrite, Bertha, Lenora, Archie, and everyone I care for.* She cradled the rough shelf mushroom in her palms. *I have to do this.* Her head throbbed. A bubble of pressure popped within her ears. *Juno, one last light.* She called to the dwindling reserve of healing and light inside her chest. *One...last... light.* Her hands were cramped, and they convulsed around the fungi. And if there was light, Maeve didn't see it because her mind imploded and dragged her into oblivion.

15

Her neck twinged with pain when she awoke. She brought her hand to the swollen muscle and called to Juno with her eyes shut. The typical warmth that frothed within Maeve's sternum was absent. *Huh?* Her bones were lead weight lifted from the floor. The windowless room did not indicate how much time passed. However, Bismuth was sitting on her stool and taking notes. *I hope our experiment is finished...has Alistair arrived?*

"How are you feeling?" Bismuth asked.

"Like I've been thrown from a horse."

Maeve twisted the unfamiliar marbled bracelets adorning her wrists. They were lightweight, and their surface swirled with evergreen and jade. She fiddled with one to check for a clasp or latch. *Nothing.* She pushed the thin band toward her fingers but couldn't slide it over without dislocating her thumb. A sour pit hardened in her stomach. *They must've put these on me while I was unconscious.* Hagken's castle, a new dress, a bed that wasn't hers. Her skin crawled with revulsion. *Bismuth didn't ask beforehand.* She didn't want to compare the alchemist to Hagken and his allies, but how could she not? *Hagken knocked me unconscious. His men dragged us into carts. Calom nearly drained me of Juno's power for his comfort. Irryn said I could negotiate my terms, but these weren't part of the deal!* Her heart kicked inside her chest like a spooked stallion. Her breathing shallowed, and the room narrowed and condensed around her.

"Bismuth, what is this?" Her voice trembled. The dark stone gleamed in the low candlelight.

"Something new," Bismuth said, sounding distracted, "my working theory is that your power comes from your life force. It functions unlike the mages. Mages are required to use something of the natural world. Their magic needs an anchor. They combine that anchor with the appropriate glyph or rune and—I'm sorry, I'm rambling. Can you call your lights?"

Maeve forced air into her lungs. *Remember why you're here.* She thought of Bertha's kindly smile and Archie running past her cottage with his friends. *Pyrite, too. We're trying to save Pyrite.* Imogen came to the forefront of her mind, her oil-smudged face and warm, molten eyes. *This will be over soon; we will have our guardians, and Pyrite will be safer.*

Maeve called to Juno. She reached into the wellspring of golden, warm light and found it dark. A hollow echo reverberated inside her chest as if someone had cracked open her rib cage and spooned out her organs. *What in Juno's name?* Panicked, Maeve wiped her clammy hands on her trousers.

"The spell isn't working..." Her knees wobbled when she stood. "What are these?"

"Interesting. Let's try again without the dampeners."

She pressed her thumb near Maeve's wristband, and the bracelet hissed as it was unlatched.

"I wanted to see if we could neutralize your magic using these stones. They prevent mages from anchoring." Bismuth tucked the dampeners into her apron. "But your magic functions differently if my hypothesis is correct. Can you summon the lights now?"

"How would you know..." Maeve's words were slow. *The woman outside the guild. But, the guilds despise one another. Would they drop so low as to kidnap someone?* "Mages and alchemists don't work together."

"No, we don't." Bismuth looked up from her notebook and said, "Not willingly, anyway."

"You had something to do with that young mage Gregor, didn't you?" Maeve stammered. Her feelings of revulsion congealed into horror. *Terrayn mentioned the archmage was killed last year without resolution, but the alchemists wouldn't kidnap an innocent boy.* She stared at Bismuth's neutral expression.

"Directly? No." Bismuth snorted. "Don't look so appalled. We have to make sacrifices for the greater good, do we not?"

"His mother is looking for him." Her nails bit into the mounds of her palms.

"Sit down, Maeve. We have more tests to do."

"No. No." She shook her head. "You said it was the final test. I'm leaving."

"You are a goldmine of untapped potential, Maeve. We're not done." Bismuth's tone iced over.

Maeve's heart pulsed in her throat. She bolted to the door and ran down the hallway. Bismuth yelled after her. She called to Juno. *Juno, please help me. Find the boy. Find Gregor!* He had a crooked nose. Neena said his eyes were hazel like Maeve's. And yet, nothing happened. The spell she invented with Alistair didn't manifest when she called. *I'm exhausted, and my connection with Juno is too weak.* Maeve wove through the passing alchemists and ignored their confused looks. *It's fine. I'll find him without the spell. I won't hit another dead-end this time.*

She passed a door with two large, intersecting circles burned onto the wood and, shortly after that, noticed another with crisscrossed lines like a collapsed ladder. *Those are alchemist's marks.* She slowed and searched for the v-shaped mark belonging to Bismuth. She climbed a stairwell to the second level. Her hands trembled. *I haven't saved Ferne or stopped Hagken, but I can save him.* Her jaw clenched at every incorrect mark. *I won't leave without him.* A door at the end of the hallway stood out against the rest. She panicked at the idea of walking into a dead-end, but she urged herself onward. *I have to be brave like Bertha and confident like Alistair.* Bismuth's mark was inlaid into the door via thin copper wires.

She tried the latch. *Locked.* She slammed her shoulder into it. A sharp pain quaked down her side. The door shuddered, and the hinges creaked. She slammed her body again, and her sweaty fingers slipped from the iron latch as despair took root at the base of her throat. *I have to knock it down.* Her fists clenched. *I can't give up. I have to keep trying. I have to—*

"Maeve!" Bismuth's voice was getting closer.

She unlaced the leather pouch on her belt and dug through her meager healing supplies. She needed more time. An orange petal was nestled among the herbs like an offering. *Gods above and below.* She recalled Alistair's unexpected hug before they left. *They must've wanted to give me this without anyone noticing.* Maeve lifted the petal. A sense of trepidation danced in her veins. *It could be poison.* She rubbed her fingers into the petal's flesh. *But Bismuth said it keeps you hidden.*

Maeve shoved the petal into her mouth, and it stuck to her soft palate. Bismuth rounded the corner. Maeve froze. Bismuth looked right at her. *She'll drag me back to that room and lock the door. I can't be a prisoner again.* Bismuth scanned the hallway, and confusion and wrath contorted her features. She huffed and turned away, and Maeve released her held breath. *She didn't see me?*

Maeve discovered her body shimmered like heat rising from a hot stone. *I can't be seen for now.* She slid her hands across the wooden door. *I could melt the latch if I had access to Juno's power.* She rechecked her pouch, *but I must have something I can use.* Her fingers brushed against a brown five-pointed leaf. *Heimenta could work.* Typically, heimenta was mashed into a thick paste and applied to the lower back during childbirth or pregnancy. *I made some for Bertha when Lenora was born.* But when it was chewed, vigor and strength fueled the body akin to a reckless and wild mule. She spat the flower petal onto the floor and replaced it with a leaf of heimenta. The smoky flavor of the herb sang through her teeth.

She pressed herself against the door. This time, when she held the latch for leverage and struck her body into it, the pain in her shoulder barely registered. The wood groaned. She stepped back and pressed her boot beneath the latch. *A good kick. That's all I need.* She drove the heel of her other foot into the ground, and her veins pulsed like a thunderstorm. Emboldened by the heimenta, she kicked below the handle. Something *cracked.* Without a second thought, she barreled into the room.

A family of dust motes drifted through the shadowy air. From the hallway's light, the floor glistened with blackened, dried blood and pooled and congealed around a chair at the center of the room. Gregor's head lolled forward. Someone tied a rope around his wrists and torso. His fingers were flat on the arms of the chair and bound together in rust-colored bandages. His wrists were shackled by the familiar green dampeners Bismuth put on Maeve.

She clung to hope like a sailor shipwrecked in a storm. She pressed her fingers below his jaw. His skin was cool. His life force was empty. Hot, burning tears pricked Maeve's eyes. *I can still save him.* An edge of desperation cut through her heart. Maeve called to Juno with bated breath and an agonized hope. Her call to Juno echoed and echoed, but nothing called back. She cradled his ashen, waxy face. *I'm here, Gregor. I'm here.* She choked around a sob. *Your mother is looking for you.*

"Come on, please," Maeve whispered with difficulty. She pressed her thumb into the bracelet, and it hissed before unclasping. *He died for these?* She removed the dampeners and held Gregor's jaw. She needed to get him out of here and find Alistair before this went further sideways.

A shadow crossed over the light from the doorway, and Maeve spun in alarm.

An individual in a long, leather duster coat and wide-brimmed hat stood with their feet spaced apart. The light reflected off their goggles in a yellow-and-white flash. Her heart set a frantic, terrified, staccato rhythm in her chest. *They found me.* Soon, she'd suffer the same fate as this poor, innocent boy.

"Time to go, honey," the stranger said, their voice warm and bright. They smiled, and their coat flared behind them as they reached into their belt of alchemical supplies. Maeve tongued out the chewed-up herb from the inside of her cheek. *The heimenta can give me enough strength to overpower them. Knock them down. Run past.* The stranger tugged their dark goggles off, and Maeve's breath caught.

Imogen extended her hand and announced, "Let's not keep Alistair waiting."

"What about him?" *Gregor.* She couldn't save him. She was too late. Her heart squeezed. *I'll find a way to fix it.*

"No time." Imogen grabbed her hand. She ran, tugging Maeve along, and her metal hand clutched a vial of shiny, black liquid.

"There she is!" someone shouted.

Imogen jerked Maeve into a narrow corridor, and her big hat blew from her head. Maeve risked a glance behind them and discovered two alchemists were in pursuit. *How are we going to escape?!* The heimenta began to lose its rich, smoky flavor. *I can't keep going like this.* Her stomach roiled with nausea. She was grateful for Imogen's steadying, firm grip; otherwise, she would've tripped over her feet. Imogen stopped, and Maeve's shoulder was knocked into the corner. She scanned the hallway, but they were alone.

"Here we go." Imogen uncorked the bottle with her teeth and poured it onto the coals of a low-hanging brazier. The coals hissed. The embers shifted. The brazier sparked. The coals erupted into a shower of hot, orange flames, and Imogen protectively covered Maeve with her jacket. The volatile sparks ignited the wooden floorboards. They smoldered and blackened with heat, and Maeve blinked the smoke from her eyes.

"That should keep them busy along with the other ones downstairs," Imogen muttered. *Other ones? Imogen could burn the guild to the ground.* They hurried to the stairs. A cacophony of noise surrounded them. People were shouting. A monster of black smoke filled the air.

Alistair's voice cut through the chatter. "Return Maeve, I'll return Vox."

Alistair stood by the doorway with a knife to Vox's throat. Bismuth held her hands up in a placating gesture. *What is happening?* Maeve's head pounded in low agony. *All of this for me? For guardians? For a chance at peace?*

Bismuth said, "I told you. We don't know where she is. She ran off. It's a big guild hall with lots of rooms."

A group of alchemists surrounded Alistair but didn't move in. Three bodies were sprawled across the floor. Maeve blinked in dumbfounded realization. *That's why they aren't getting closer.* Imogen and Maeve descended the stairwell. A putrid, black smoke swallowed the ceiling, and dozens of alchemists fled the room carrying tonics and buckets of water to try to contain it.

"There she is."

"Is that Imogen?"

"Get them!"

Maeve yelped as someone grabbed the back of her head. Her clammy fingers slipped from Imogen's grasp; she screamed and tried to reach for Imogen. An alchemist tackled Imogen around her waist. *No! No!* Her chest tightened with panic. *Don't hurt her!* Maeve flailed. She kicked. Her foot slammed into a delicate apparatus on a worktable, and it ruptured into an explosive light.

The alchemist nearest to the table screamed. They blocked their eyes, and blood ran rivulets down their cheeks. The smell of copper and burning wood permeated the air. Maeve's stomach lurched. *What have I done? What am I capable of?* A swirl of bright spots clouded her vision, and she groped her face to confirm her eyeballs were attached and bloodless.

A flash of silver danced through the air, and Maeve stumbled as the grip on her hair released. Her scalp prickled. The alchemist slumped against the wall and didn't move. The hilt of Alistair's pearl dagger protruded from the alchemist's eye socket. Imogen grabbed her assailant's wrist and wrestled herself free with a sickening and grotesque crunch of bones beneath the metal. The alchemist howled and cradled their splintered flesh and shattered bones.

Alistair held their blade against Vox's throat, and their eyes darkened in an icy and callous rage. Maeve stumbled over a dead body; blood clung to the bottom of her shoe. A sweeping sense of vertigo pulled the floor out from under her. Her arms windmilled, but she caught herself on a workbench.

"C'mon, Maeve. Lean on me." Imogen pulled Maeve's arm over her bony shoulders.

"Our deal is off!" Bismuth shouted to her back. *No deal is worth this.* She sank into Imogen's side and allowed the alchemist to carry her to safety.

16

The knobs of Imogen's spine and arch of her shoulder blades pressed into Maeve's sternum. Her guilt shadowed her relief of escape. What had they done to Gregor? Maeve's tongue dried in her mouth. Alistair unlocked the door to their family home and stepped aside for Imogen and Maeve to enter.

"Are we – are we safe here?" Maeve asked, "They know you."

"They won't waste resources to search for us," Alistair said. "Besides, people knew me as Hagken's, and very few knew about my real father."

"Bismuth got what she wanted, yeah?" Imogen chimed in before carefully setting Maeve down.

"I guess so."

"Then we're safe," said Imogen, "it's a good thing Alistair is paranoid. They asked me to sneak into the guild before you arrived just in case things went sour."

Imogen's hand cradled Maeve's cheek, and her fingertips drew away smeared with blood. No matter how hard she tried, she couldn't shake the weight off her shoulders. *I knew Gregor was missing. I knew he could've been within the walls of the guild, but I chose not to investigate. I got swept up in the alchemists' allure.* White noise roared in her ears. This wasn't the same guilt that had shadowed her heart when she and Alistair had escaped Hollyhock. She tucked her blood-stained boot behind her ankle. Alistair watched her without moving. Something metal clattered to the floor in the nearby kitchen.

"You killed people to save me."

"I did," Alistair said without flinching.

"I don't want you to be a blade in the dark, Alistair," she whispered, "I don't want that. You're more than that."

Alistair closed the short distance between them. Maeve searched their face for regret and found gentle sympathy in their blue eyes.

"Oh, Maeve." They tucked her dark hair behind her ear, and she leaned into their touch. "There is a difference between killing under orders and killing to protect. I would do it again in a heartbeat."

She drew her lower lip between her teeth. A knot twisted in her throat, and she blinked back her tears. Once she wept, she wouldn't be able to stop. Alistair pulled her hands into theirs and brought them to their chest.

She said, "Who are we if we start justifying this? We're no better than Hagken or the alchemist's guild."

She spread her fingers across Alistair's chest. The leather was buttery beneath her palms, and their steady heartbeat resonated against her skin. Death was too steep a price to pay. Yet Maeve knew she wouldn't walk away from this. Ferne needed her, and she wouldn't abandon them. *At the end of this journey, will Juno forgive me?* Her chin wobbled. *Will I forgive myself?*

"If you're asking for a bloodless revolution." They bowed their head, and a curl fell across their forehead. "You will find yourself disappointed."

"What do we do?"

"We keep moving forward and meet with the merchants."Alistair covered her hands with theirs.

Maeve raised her voice, "That's not enough."

She pulled away and shouted for Imogen. She didn't want to be one of the people who walked forward and ignored the casualties. She was a healer. She wouldn't hide from an open wound. If they were going to do this, they would carve a different path. She wouldn't be like King Hagken and his ilk.

Imogen craned her neck around the corner.

"Do you think you could get a message to someone in the city near the guild?" asked Maeve.

"The guild we narrowly escaped from?"

Maeve nodded.

"Yeah, sure." She took a bite of the apple slice skewered onto the tip of her knife. "Give me an hour."

Maeve's head sank between her palms, and sour sweat and dried blood filled her nostrils. *Eugh.* The scent of blood reminded her of young Gregor. Juno's magic was limited. Every priestess knew this. They couldn't revive anyone from a fatal wound or advanced sickness. Juno gave life while her sister gave death. No one could stop Janis when she came to collect someone's spirit. It was natural. But Gregor's death wasn't. While Maeve was gawking at the alchemists' inventions, he suffered without salvation, his death cruel and unnecessary. She reached within to find Juno's light for comfort, but the terrifying emptiness greeted her instead. *I need to recover before I can connect with Juno.* She needed warmth, hot tea, a bath, or food. She lifted her head, and Alistair stared at her.

"I'm okay," she lied.

Alistair snorted. "Yeah, sure, and I'm the next high matriarch." They stroked the side of her face with the back of their knuckles, and her eyelashes fluttered. "What do you need?"

"A bath would be a good start."

"I'll get you a change of clothes from your bag," Alistair said.

Once upstairs in the washroom, Maeve tossed her sweaty, musky clothes to the sleek, brownstone floor alongside her bloodied boots. The copper tub was filled with steaming hot water, and Maeve submerged herself once it hit the brim. The scalding water sloshed over the sides. She held her breath underwater, bubbles tickling her nostrils, her hair floating around her face like the tentacles of a great, dark beast.

She broke the surface for air. Her gasping inhale resembled a sob. She thumped her head against the back lip of the tub. *What if I can't save anyone?* She asked herself. *What if all of this is in vain? Hopeless?* She blinked droplets away from her eyelashes and pressed her knuckles to her quivering mouth. Her usual comforting act of repeating Juno's scripture felt chafing and hollow. *What if everyone from Ferne is already dead? Sacrificed for an alchemist's experiment within Hagken's army,* She held the tub's edges and dunked underwater. In a rushing exhale, the bubbles of her cry buoyed around her face and nose. Her guilt and helplessness capsized her lungs like the hull of an old, decrepit ship. *I can't linger on failure.* She needed solutions, not imagined catastrophes.

Her mother would remind Maeve of the positives. When Maeve complained or whined as a child, her mother gently took her hand and pointed out all the beautiful things she had to be grateful for. She reemerged from the jasmine-scented water, and tears streamed down her face in tandem. She lifted her amulet and pressed her lips to the shiny surface.

"I have friends," she whispered, "I'm alive. I'm going to meet with the merchant guild soon." Once she met with the guild, she'd gain an audience with Fenris's council, and everyone would be saved without a meaningless war. By Juno as her witness, she would find a way to make this right. She would repent for Gregor's death and ensure it wasn't in vain. And she would return to her people before any lives were lost. Alistair said real change couldn't occur without bloodshed. She disagreed. For years, the midsummer council ruled Pyrite without senseless suffering. *How do you know?* A voice that sounded like Imogen whispered into the back of her mind. *You weren't here. The history books could be wrong or embellish the truth.* She pushed her hair out of her face. *Imogen or Alistair will know. I'll ask them.*

* * *

Alistair and Imogen were in the small, intimate kitchen. The largest window was made of mottled orange and yellow glass, and its light suffused the room in a golden hue. Imogen sat perched on a pale counter, her legs swinging back and forth. *She came for me.* Maeve's heart lifted. *She didn't need to, but she did. She went to the guild at Alistair's request and risked her life.*

"Feeling better?" asked Imogen.

"A little."

"Huzzah!" Imogen smiled, then winked. "You had us worried for a second."

"Sorry." Maeve took a piece of dried seaweed from the plate beside Imogen's thigh. "You both lived here when the midsummer council was around, right?"

Alistair said, "Imogen's lived here longest."

"Was it different? Peaceful?" Maeve imagined the magic and

invention of Pyrite flourishing like a well-loved garden without the influence of corrupt kings.

She said, "The council abandoned an entire neighborhood." Her brown eyes darkened.

"You mean the burned district?" Maeve asked.

"It used to be part of Thorduun's quarter. We called it Firefly Alley because mages and alchemists would work late into the night, and you'd see the lights in their windows, y'know, like fireflies." Her voice rasped like flint against stone. "It burned. And instead of fixing it, the council paid the mages to put an arcane shield around the guilds.

"Everyone was expected to move on, people who lost friends, colleagues." Imogen looked at Maeve and said, "Family."

Maeve clutched her pendant as a wave of sympathy crashed over her. *Did Imogen lose her family in the burning?* Maybe that's why Imogen chose to live within the burned district. It gave her privacy, and she could be closer to those she lost.

"Imogen, I'm sorry." She placed her hand on Imogen's knee, and Imogen's freckled cheeks flushed pink.

"To answer your question, it was different," she said, "the guilds didn't have as much influence. But there were still thieves and crime."

"Naturally," Alistair said over their shoulder.

Maeve removed her hand. That was enough talk of the past for now. *I don't want Imogen to reopen old wounds for the sake of my curiosity. The council might not have been perfect, but it would be better than now.*

"Can I ask you a question about the alchemist guild?"

"Ugh. I guess." Her face soured as she said it.

"Were they always"— she rubbed her hands together—"cruel?"

"Cruel?" Imogen frowned. "Depends on who you're working with, I suppose. Most alchemists try to make the world a better place."

"You said most alchemists want to turn lead into gold."

"Yeah, that's the elusive equation no one can solve." Imogen rolled her eyes. "But realistically, we had our secret passion projects and ordinary guild-sanctioned work. Like, someone would commission the guild to make a prosthetic eye that could see in the dark, or a ramp that could lower and raise in response to someone's voice."

Maeve perked up.

"What reason would someone have for commissioning this?" She pulled the bracelet from her pocket and explained Bismuth's definition. Imogen held the dampener up to the muted orange light and smirked.

"It's one of hers, that's for sure." The surface caught the light again, and Bismuth's marker flashed. "Clever bitch," said Imogen with gentle awe. Her thumb pressed into the smooth, seamless surface near the mark. The dampener hissed and split open like a cuff. Maeve's jaw dropped.

"How'd you know how to open it?"

"I know Bismuth's work."

Alistair said, "Knowing her work is a boring way of putting it."

"Shut up!" She playfully kicked Alistair's hip. They laughed, husky and warm, and stepped out of Imogen's range.

"Bismuth and I were together for a short time. She knows my old mark. The one I used when I was with the guild, and I know hers. I'm surprised she didn't change it."

Maeve digested this information. *Imogen and Bismuth?* She couldn't fathom it. Bismuth would dissect someone's stomach for answers, and Imogen wasn't as callous. *Imogen is capable of friendship. Bismuth isn't.*

"Anyway, back to the point," continued Imogen, "anyone who dislikes mages or priestesses would have reason to commission it. For all we know, it was Fenris himself to keep mage prisoners from escaping."

"I thought mages needed their spell books to cast," Maeve said, recalling her interactions with Cara.

"Common misconception," said Imogen.

"It's easier to cast with them on hand because their runes are written down," Alistair added, "but I've seen Cara cast blindfolded and gagged."

"Ohh," Imogen said and leaned in. "Why was she blindfolded?"

"Endurance drills. Hagken required them from his high-ranking officers to ensure we could withstand torture and eventually escape. As long as mages can move their fingers and have a bit of dirt underneath their nails, they can do something. And necromancers are even more dangerous..."

Maeve's blood turned cold at the memory of Cara's chimera and Gregor's bloodied, bandaged hands. *The alchemists must've broken his fingers as a precaution against his spell-casting.*

"Because necromancers use spirit in their spells?" Imogen guessed. Spirit classified anything within the body, such as blood, sweat, or tears.

"Exactly. A necromancer can cut their body and use their blood as the energetic power behind the spell." They ran their knife down the fish's spine from tail to head. "However, it's far more unpredictable. We're lucky Hagken has only one worthwhile necromancer in his army. The rest are nowhere near as capable as Cara."

"Okay." Maeve twisted her fingers together. "Is there any way of learning who commissioned the dampener?"

Imogen squinted at it. "Guild master Irryn keeps copies of commissions in her office." She glanced slyly at Alistair, and Maeve imagined the gears turning inside Imogen's mind.

"Maeve, what are you thinking?" Alistair said.

"Do you remember the mother outside the guild? I found her son, Gregor, covered in blood and wearing those dampeners." Maeve paced the kitchen. "We bring Gregor's mother, Neena, here. I'll tell her about Gregor and give her the dampener, along with a copy of the commission request, and she can bring the guild to justice for her son's death."

Alistair and Imogen shared a wary glance.

"I don't know, Maeve." Alistair's face flickered with shadow. "That seems..." They looked to Imogen to complete the sentence, and she shrugged with a mouthful of dried seaweed.

"If you're going to say impossible, I won't hear it." Maeve's cheeks burned. "Even without the commission, his mother can take the dampener to Theadora's temple. That's proof enough."

"Honestly, Maeve, I was going to say it's insensitive. His mother is better off not knowing the truth."

"No. She deserves to know what happened. Gregor deserves to be mourned and given a proper sending." Maeve's gaze darted to Imogen. "What do you think?"

"People die unmourned every day."

Maeve grimaced. "Imogen, that's cold."

"That's reality." She made a sandwich of pieces of seaweed and mushrooms. "Gregor won't be the last casualty in pursuing knowledge and progress."

"I'm sorry, Maeve, but I'm with Imogen. We can get a message to

Neena, but we shouldn't involve Theadora's justiciars."

"Bismuth killed someone." Maeve threw her hands in the air at their stubbornness. How could they overlook this glaring insult to Juno's pillars of faith? *Life is light, and light is sacred.*

"So did we," Alistair said, "you bring the justiciars into this, and each of us will pay the price. Some steeper than others."

If Neena went after the alchemist guild, a node of power and influence within Pyrite, there would be no escaping the justiciars' involvement. She deflated and stared listlessly at the crackling fire below the cooking pot. If Alistair and Imogen were imprisoned, Maeve would be forced to continue alone. And if she were imprisoned with them, there would be no hope for Pyrite before Hagken arrived. She doubted General Fenris would leave the hematite mountains to handle a lengthy trial and its punishments.

"That's it? We continue as normal?"

Imogen said, "I mean...if it's revenge you want, say the word, and I'm sure Alistair would remove Bismuth for you."

Alistair shook their head.

"I don't want revenge. I want justice!" Maeve's frustration bled into her tone.

"Are those not the same thing?" said Imogen, cocking a thin blonde eyebrow.

"Sunshine, we've had a storm's wrath of a morning, and it's not even midday." Alistair took her wrist between their fingers. "Get some rest, and we can talk about it later, alright?"

Maeve stared dumbfounded at them.

"We'll wake you when the soup is done." Imogen spewed seaweed crumbs into the air. How could they talk of rest and eat soup with blood drying on their clothes? They needed to act. They needed to find a way to repair the damage and fix their mistakes.

"Right." She pressed her lips together. "You're right. I should rest."

Her guilt pressed on her heart from all sides, hot and claustrophobic. She smiled weakly at her friends. They believed in her wild dream to save Pyrite and Ferne, but they didn't believe in this. Maeve climbed the steps and waited until Alistair and Imogen started talking before slipping into Maren's old room.

17

She opened Maren's wardrobe, and dried petals rained on the floor. If Alistair and Imogen refused to act, then she would act alone. She pulled a sage green cloak over her shoulders and braided her damp hair into a crown before hiding it beneath a wool cap. She checked within for Juno. No one answered her call. *It's okay,* she assured herself, *you're tired. You're tired.* Juno's magic would return. *The bath wasn't enough.* Imogen's loud voice carried through the empty, quiet spaces. *If I cross the kitchen, they'll see me.* She ducked back into the bedroom. The windows opened vertically in a limited range. *If I remove the screw on the latch, then the window should open further.* She snatched a letter opener from Maren's desk and twisted the latch until it unscrewed. She eyed the drop. *If I break something, then I'll be stuck here.* Maeve took a fortifying breath. *Let's hope nothing breaks then.*

She jumped.

Her ankle rolled on impact, and she caught the brunt of her fall with her hands. No one crossing the boardwalk granted her a glance. *I wonder how many people jump out of windows around here.* She tested her weight on her ankle. *Manageable.* She limped in the direction of Thorduun's quarter. A light rain painted the streets and houses in a blur of soft brown and glistening cobblestones. Two women wearing crimson and bronze armor turned the corner and spoke warmly to each other. *Justiciars.* Maeve pulled her hood up and averted her eyes when they passed. *The guild won't send justiciars after us, will they? No, no. They said the guild won't waste their resources.* She quickened her pace through the narrow alleyways that ran like veins between the houses. *I should find Neena as soon as possible.*

After several anxious minutes, Maeve found a metal grate laid into the stones. She hooked her fingers through the holes. Her spine and shoulders protested the weight of it. She squeezed her eyes shut, teeth-gnashing and strained. She lamented; *if only Juno were a goddess of strength instead of healing.* The wet metal dug into her flesh, and her boots scraped against the ground. The weight shifted. A pair of dark-gloved hands wrapped around the opposite section.

"You should've used the original one. Imogen coated it in a special oil that lightens in." They lifted the covering together.

She wiped her sweaty forehead with the back of her hand. "If I knew where it was, then I would've."

"I'll draw you a map," Alistair said, smirking.

She regarded them with admiration and caution stirring inside her chest.

"Did you change your mind?"

"Somewhat." They tilted their head to the side, rain glistening down the sharp planes of their face and catching on their long, dark eyelashes. "I think it's a bad idea, but if I'm going to wind up in a jail cell, it may as well be next to yours."

Maeve's chest warmed. It was strikingly similar to when she called to Juno's magic.

"And Imogen?"

"She's gone off to speak to Ollie. She thinks she can convince him to listen."

Maeve blinked rainwater from her eyes. Her gratitude ignited in her chest. Maeve gave Alistair a small, close-lipped smile before descending the ladder.

"You know..." Alistair began above her, "If it weren't for you, I'd be sleeping in a hammock somewhere near the ocean instead of crawling through the sewers. Again."

"Perhaps I'm a poor influence on you."

Alistair's laughter rasped across the wet stone. "Perhaps."

She reached into her healer's pouch and struck a match to illuminate their path. The flame was a poor substitute compared to Juno's globes of light, but she couldn't force herself to recover. *I've never depleted myself like this before, even when I was with Calom. Juno's light will return. I have to be patient.* The brown sewage and rainwater rushed alongside them. She followed the familiar shape of Alistair's lean back and dark curly hair. Alistair stopped and offered Maeve their hand to help her traverse over crumbling pieces of stone. She tightened her fingers around Alistair's and didn't let go after the path was clear. It felt safer to hold onto them.

"I'll hide us once we reach the quarter to be safe," Alistair said. "I doubt the alchemists will try and recapture you, but they might suspect you're trying to steal a sentinel."

"I wouldn't be able to move one unseen," Maeve said wrinkling her nose.

"Trivial details." They pushed the grate overhead and offered to help Maeve from the ladder. "Stay close and stay quiet," Alistair said while waving their hand languidly. The shadows on the ground drifted toward Maeve's feet and surrounded her body in a shifting, murky blanket of gray. *Alistair, the shadow general.*

"You can move them?" she whispered. The shadows clung to their bodies like liquid smoke. *It's similar to my powers with Juno and my manipulation of light.* "Why haven't you shown me this before?"

"I was waiting for the perfect moment to impress you." They winked. Maeve adjusted her hood to hide her suddenly warm face. The overcast sky aided their hidden trek toward the alchemist's guild hall. Alistair wove the shadows in swooping and delicate gestures. Her heart jumped whenever someone looked their way, but then their gaze would slip, and her nerves settled. Alistair stopped across the street from the guild and glanced around the bustling space of traveling alchemists and mages. The rainwater glistened across their furrowed brow.

"There's a tavern nearby." They pointed down the street. "Wait there."

"What're you going to do?"

"I'll get the message to Neena," they said, "you two can speak in private."

Maeve held her pendant and nodded. "Juno's light guide you."

"Janis, watch over you," they said, their blue eyes glittering with delight.

They kept their shadows close to Maeve when she walked to the tavern. Once she passed the threshold, the shadows vanished like dust being swept aside by a broom.

Maeve hunched her shoulders and sank into a stool at the bar. The arcane dampener lay heavy in her pocket. Her eyes darted around as paranoia gnawed with blunt teeth at her gut. *Is an alchemist hidden among the mages here? Will they recognize me? Will they care?* Her knee bounced. *At least Alistair is outside, and their shadows can keep them hidden.* The bartender refilled her ale, and the door opened. *Finally.*

Neena sat beside her and said, "I saw you and your friends fleeing the guild." Her dark brown cloak was soaked with rain, and Maeve waited for the bartender to leave before speaking.

"The guild intended to hold me prisoner."

Her thin mouth frowned. "I'm sorry."

"I found Gregor." Maeve cleared her throat and touched Juno's medallion.

Neena's red-rimmed eyes brightened with hope. Maeve squeezed her pendant, and its spokes stabbed into the fleshy bits of her palm.

"They were using him to study this mineral." She placed the unlocked dampener on the bar. "It blocks someone's magic or neutralizes it. Fenris found it within the hematite mountains."

"I see." Neena circled her fingertip around the rim. "Gregor died for this?"

How did she—? Maeve inhaled.

"I suspected as much," said Neena.

"Is this common? Mages or people going missing within the guilds?"

"People volunteer to aid the alchemists and mages all the time. Either because they need the coin or have nothing to lose. It's seen as a service to the city." Neena's eyes welled with tears. "My Gregor was different. He wasn't a volunteer. They took him when he was coming home from a tavern not unlike this one.

"I feared the worst, and now it's come true." She pressed her hands to her trembling lips, her eyes glassy in the flickering gravelight.

"I'm sorry," she said, grasping Neena's shoulder. Her words were brittle against the raw sorrow on Neena's face. "My friend is talking to a clerk at Theadora's temple for you." Maeve said, "Bring this to them, and you'll have justice."

Neena's grief was red and bloody, and Maeve's words sang like raindrops on dark metal.

"I do not have the coin to oppose the alchemists' guild," she said, "and nothing will soothe this beast inside my heart." She clenched her hand in front of her chest and sniffled her sunburned nose. "In Pyrite, we have a saying. Mourn the dead first but mourn the living longer." Fat tears rolled down her weathered cheeks. "They killed my son. My son."

Maeve bit her lip. *What can I say?* Neena folded into herself and wept with heaving and trembling sobs from the depths of her stomach. Maeve's practiced words about life, its sacredness, and the gentle passing to Janis' underworld were useless. They wouldn't soften the blow of this death, this injustice. She rubbed Neena's back. It was the little comfort she could provide.

"Keep this. I cannot bear to hold onto it." Neena returned the dampener to Maeve.

"Are you sure?"

"I am." She offered Maeve a watery smile. "Thank you for risking so much so that I may have a semblance of peace." Maeve caught the edge of Neena's cloak before she stood.

"Are you going to be okay?"

Neena shook her head and said, "Not today, no."

Her brow furrowed with concern. *What more can I offer? What more can I do for her?* She couldn't save her son. She needed to make amends. *What would I do if it was Bertha? Or any other parent from Ferne?* No answers came to her in the aftermath of Neena's grief.

She continued, "Don't worry, priestess. I will live to see the next dawn in spite of my broken heart." Maeve released her. Her fragile heart weighed heavy inside her chest, and she swallowed her breath. She watched Neena leave with a thousand apologies on her tongue.

18

Alistair used their shadow-weaving ability to guide Maeve out of Thorduun's quarter and through the twisting tunnels beneath the city. She was grateful Alistair stayed quiet. *Maybe they expected Neena's rejection.* She mulled over Neena's words until she could repeat them by rote. *Nothing will change.* That was the needle that dug into Maeve's chest and stitched regret onto her lungs. The alchemists' guild wouldn't suffer retribution for the pain and death they caused. *How can Pyrite stand tall with corruption at the root?*

Alistair's homestead was a welcomed sight. Maeve trailed her fingers across the salamander engravings on the entryway doorframe. *Alistair's mother carried her home with her wherever she went. Yet all I carry from my home is guilt. I haven't saved anyone from Ferne except the elders. I couldn't convince Neena to seek justice for her son.* Alistair leaned their shoulder against the wall. Their dark curls were plastered against their skull, and their smudged eyes trailed across her face.

"Coin for your thoughts?"

Maeve licked rainwater from her lips. "It's disheartening to run into obstacle after obstacle," she admitted, and all the outcomes stretched before her. "But we have time before Hagken reaches the city, and we can prepare for our meeting with the merchant guild."

Alistair unlocked the front door and said, "Your resolve is inspiring." Maeve's heart lifted. "You should visit my father's study. It's at the end of that hallway. I'm sure he had a book or two about Pyrite's merchant guild somewhere."

"Thank you." She followed the decorated hallway until she found Vivindale's study. Imogen sat at a cluttered desk with glass vials and leather pouches, and Maeve's smile widened. *It's nice to see she's keeping busy. Hopefully, her day has been more successful than mine.* Imogen didn't look up.

"It went well?" asked Imogen.

"I don't know." Maeve pulled a chair to sit beside her. "She said I gave her some peace, but she wouldn't do anything about Gregor's death."

"And that's disappointing?" She tilted her head.

"A little," Maeve said. "Did it ever bother you what the guild does?"

Imogen didn't respond. Her experiment completely entrapped her focus. Maeve tucked one knee to her chest and settled her chin on it. *I'll ask her again later.* Imogen's gloves were stained blue, and her round, tinted goggles perched on her freckled nose. She pinched her tongue between her teeth while pouring hot water through a funnel.

"How does it work?" Maeve asked after the fraught tension in Imogen's face softened.

"The pillars of alchemy are not unlike your pillars of faith," she said, "except ours are comprehension, distillment, and transmutation. Those are our gods, our guides."

She held the vial to the light, and mist rose from the top like frosted breath. Satisfied, she tucked it into a three-pronged holder and referred to her coded notes.

"It's practical and grounded. Everything has parts and pieces; we break and rebuild them. Sometimes, it's subtle, yeah? Other times, it's more complex."

She crushed a white, chalky stone beneath her metal thumb and lifted a tiny morsel with tweezers.

"But I've seen alchemists fuck up simple equations, so maybe there's some mystical element or an innate talent someone's born with or something. I dunno." She dropped the grain into the vial, which sizzled like fish meat in a pan of hot oil. An immediate charcoal scent ballooned the air, and the bubbles frothed and crawled upward.

"Oh, shit," Imogen said empathetically before she plopped a sloppy handful of maroon sand over the bubbling experiment. The dust neutralized the reaction, but a smoky taste lingered in the back of Maeve's throat.

"And here I was"—Imogen pushed her goggles to her forehead, and a fine layer of soot encircled her eyes— "hoping to impress you."

"You *are* impressive." Maeve smiled. "Regardless of your success."

She laughed. "Alistair is right. You are too kind." Her expression sobered. "I think my finest work is lost within the guild."

"Lost?"

"To enter the guild, you have to offer something worthwhile. I created this–" Imogen broke off and trilled her lips while checking her notes. "Medicine for severe headaches. It was a liquid you dropped into your eyes.

"I thought it was brilliant; the guild thought it was brilliant, but no one commissioned it. And now my notes are left to rot within the vault."

Maeve grimaced. She was grateful Juno's magic came from within and wasn't confined to bits of paper or raw materials.

Maeve asked, "Couldn't you make it again?"

"I could. But it belongs to the guild now," Imogen said, annoyed. "If I got caught selling it, they'd send justiciars after me."

"That doesn't seem fair."

She snorted. "Welcome to Pyrite." She stirred a liquid with a long, metal tube until it changed color from white to murky brown.

"The guild plays favorites. Bismuth is a liar and a thief, and she keeps her position." Imogen's eyes darkened like an oncoming storm. "Yet I make a mistake, and I'm thrown to the wolves."

"A thief?"

"The sentinels would never been possible without my research into spirit!" she snapped hotly, "if I had succeeded in my work in thwarting death, then I would have"— she tore her metal fingers through her short, greasy hair — "I would have what Bismuth has now. Respect. Praise." Something sharp and hurt fractured across Imogen's expression. "A place among them."

Maeve frowned. *Imogen wants to be among the people who killed Gregor. Why?*

"I don't understand. Why—"

Imogen cut in, "No, you wouldn't." Her glossy eyes sliced toward Maeve before she shoved her dark goggles back on.

"The guild was my home for five years, and that may seem like nothing," she said while working, "but for those years, I had colleagues who understood me, a place to sleep I didn't share with twelve other girls, and pride in what I did.

"You asked if what the guild does bothers me. I'll speak plainly, sweet Maeve. It doesn't because I see beyond the materials used. We cannot change the world by playing it safe." She extended her metal arm. The tiny flames of candlelight gleamed across her arm's delicate golden pieces.

"To construct this, I followed the pillar of comprehension. I dissected cadavers. I studied bones. It's one of a kind because I wanted something special. I went beyond the creations the others made." Imogen clenched her fist. "They'll never have this." Her lips flared white at the corners. "Never."

Maeve's curiosity was piqued. *She built her prosthetic, studied spirit to save lives, and dedicated her life to understanding Calorum.*

"Imogen, do you think you could study this?" Maeve placed the sunstone on the table. At first, Maeve thought it needed a priestess. But the stone wasn't attuned despite her daily meditations. "It should react to Juno's light, but it doesn't."

"Hold that thought." Imogen yanked a book from the shelves and rapidly thumbed through the pages. She dropped it open-faced onto the table and pointed to a drawing of two stones. One was gold and bright, and the other was pale and luminescent. *I was right.* Maeve leaned closer. *Hagken was wearing a moonstone.*

"How did you know Vivindale had this book?" She scanned the page. It detailed the known mythology of the stones and their theorized magical abilities. The book said the stones were pieces of the goddesses themselves and proof of their awe-inspiring power that extended beyond Calorum.

"Because I've read most of his collection." She held the sunstone near the candlelight. "I need the moonstone to study this. You can't understand one without the other."

"What do you mean?" Maeve searched the shelves and found three that covered Estoria's history. *One of these books should include*

Pyrite and, hopefully, the guilds. She clutched the books to her chest.

"The theory is that every sunstone that exists must have a sister moonstone," explained Imogen, "they're destined to be a pair. If your sunstone isn't attuning, it may need the moonstone nearby." Imogen wrote something down and brushed her blonde hair away from her face. *Well, I don't have the moonstone. Hagken does.* Maybe she could somehow still connect to it. *I'll keep trying.*

"Thanks, Imogen." Maeve smiled. Imogen wanted respect, praise, and a place alongside people like her. She could have that outside the guild.

Maeve cleared her throat, and Imogen looked up from her notes.

"If you ever want to leave Pyrite..." Her voice wavered, and nervousness skittered across her skin as the fear of rejection weighed on her mind. "There's a place for you in Ferne."

Imogen stared at her from behind her reflective goggles. The moment stretched silent and agonizing, and Maeve's scalp prickled. She thought to run, but her feet were glued to the hardwood floor. *I shouldn't have said anything!* Imogen's lips twitched upward. *Maybe I can appeal to her sense of pride?*

"You'd be the only alchemist in Ferne."

"Would I stay with you?" asked Imogen.

Maeve's flush deepened. "I suppose so." She thought of the empty rooms in her cottage and imagined Imogen setting up a worktable, and her heart rate quickened.

"A tempting offer," she said, "I'll sleep on it."

Maeve clutched her books tighter to her chest and smiled.

* * *

She found a comfortable place to read in the light-soaked sitting room. She ate fish and noodle soup without tasting it. Her eyes devoured the text for any insight on the guilds. There was little written about the merchant guild. Unlike the mages and alchemists, there was no central figure or guild master in charge. The majority ruled inside the merchant guild. *This means I'll need to convince as many merchants as possible if I want their help.* She stopped reading when the words blurred together. She held Juno's pendant in her palm and lulled herself into peace with sunlight burning red and hot on her thin eyelids.

She repeated her prayers, "Praise Juno, mother of the sunlit path, sister to darkness, who rises and falls eternal, as we rise and fall with Her."

An eternity passed between the morning she healed Archie's arm and today. *I've eaten, I've meditated and repeated my prayers.* She hoped her time of solitude would warrant an actual vision from Juno. A solution to all her problems. It was a childish thing to wish for. Juno gave visions to her sunseers, and she wasn't one of the blessed eight who lived in Everdawn, wearing golden blindfolds and sweltering in the oppressive heat of the desert for hours upon hours. She pressed the pointed tip of the amulet into the fleshy pad of her thumb. It wasn't enough pressure to make her bleed, but enough that tiny pins of discomfort shot along her finger. *Why can't I feel her?* The burning ember of Juno's power in her diaphragm was painfully absent.

"There you are!"

She startled at the sound of Alistair's voice.

Maeve asked, "Where have you been?" They disappeared after she entered Vivindale's study.

They draped themselves on the couch like a big, black cat.

"Prowling the streets and keeping my ear to the cobblestones," they said with a lackadaisical wave of their gloved hand. "Everyone is tied into knots over tomorrow's Pallanos celebration." *The holy day of*

Juno and Janis.

"That's what they're worried about?"

Maeve wanted to tug her hair from the roots. It was as if she was screaming underwater. No one beyond her few friends wanted to listen to her. Her last hope remained in the trade-focused merchant's guild, which Hagken had belonged to before he became king. She lamented over this knowledge and the impossibility of her task. She couldn't stop him alone, and Pyrite stonewalled her at every turn.

Alistair bit the tip of their thumb, and their brow crinkled. Their pensive expression piqued Maeve's curiosity. *They've been helping me on this journey since our first day together. There's a chance they've thought of something.*

"Coin for your thoughts?" she asked.

"I've got an idea." They sat up. "Pallanos will gorge the city with travelers. A few well-placed conversations should be enough to spread the word about Hagken's army."

"And they'll listen to us?" Maeve joined them on the couch.

"Don't look at me like that, Maeve." They chuckled. "It's not a perfect solution. We run the risk of the town guard or the justiciars learning of our rumors, and they might get the wrong idea and assume we're trying to encourage Hagken's claim. But, if we spread the word, there's a chance it'll dig its roots into the city's web and beyond. Some citizens may leave before his arrival, or they might enlist in Pyrite's militia."

Her fingers twisted. "Could you reach out to your contacts? The people you used to work with when you were the shadow general? I imagine they'd be good at spreading rumors."

All levity in Alistair's expression vanished.

"I'd rather not." They grimaced. "King Hagken will learn I'm in the city soon enough after our break-in at the alchemists' guild."

"Are you in danger?" She scooted closer to Alistair's outstretched legs.

"Always."

"Be serious."

"I'm being perfectly serious." They folded their arms behind their head. "My existence remains a threat to King Hagken. As long as he's alive and wishing to rule, my life will be in danger."

"Then shouldn't you be in hiding and not helping me?" A worm of fear crawled through the cavities of her heart. *What will I do without Alistair's help and insight?* They've been her guiding star to navigate through Pyrite's unfamiliar waters. *I don't want to face the merchant guild without them.*

"I'd never give him the satisfaction." Alistair flashed a grin. "I recognize that furrow in your brow, Maeve. Don't worry about me. I'm comfortable with a healthy amount of danger in my life."

Alistair was as stubborn as Pyrite. *I'll have to hope Hagken doesn't reach them.* She would trust Alistair to handle themselves if things went awry. *They've done a decent job staying alive so far.* She steered the conversation to calmer waters.

"Tomorrow's celebration, what shall we do?"

"We'll meet in the three spires district and work outward toward the silver gates and the docks. That'll be where most of the visiting merchants set up." Alistair's gaze drifted to the ceiling. "It'll be easy. We mention the rotten, deposed King Hagken here and there and then find time to enjoy ourselves."

"The simple fact that you can even think of pleasure is a mystery to me," said Maeve.

"Pyrite isn't good for much, but we throw excellent parties." They arched their eyebrow. "Even a priestess of Juno can afford to enjoy herself, can't she?"

"Maybe." She nudged their leg with her elbow, smiling. She brought the book back into her lap and leaned against Alistair. The muscled, warm length of their thigh pressed snugly against her spine, and silence fell over her like a blanket. *Juno's power will return tomorrow. I know it.*

19

The Pallanos Equinox bloated the city with travelers, vendors, and musicians. The air was rich with the scents of yeast from freshly baked bread, and thin trails of smoke billowed from beneath canopied stalls where merchants roasted fish on sticks, vegetables wrapped in seaweed, and whole-belly clams. The scent of char and smoke was a warm, earthy undercurrent to the perfumed air of various wildflowers. On every corner, there were performances. They read palms, sang, blessed pregnancies, and gave each other small pouches of grain for luck and bountiful harvests. The drummers danced with exposed bellies, their flowing silks wrapped around their chime-adorned limbs. A woman in a wheelchair whizzed past Maeve, and the wheels jingled from the bells attached. Bells and chimes were believed to bless the air and favor sailors with high winds.

Maeve shimmied past citizens, pouring handfuls of saltwater on their foreheads to cleanse and purify their spirits. They painted their foreheads with orange and red sunbursts or crescent moons on their cheeks. Today was Juno and Janis' holiday. Juno's celebration was held from dawn until her light sank from the sky. Then, Janis would begin and proceed until tomorrow's dawn. The windows were propped open, ribbons waving in the breeze, as strangers tossed flowers for fortune and fertility on doorsteps. Maeve lightly touched her sternum. *My connection to Juno hasn't returned yet.* Her divine magic never took longer than a day to replenish, but she remained hopeful. *My dedication to Juno is unshakable.* She set her worries aside.

Alistair was a shadow in the vivid crowd of dyed silk and chugging machinery. They slipped through groups without jostling a single shoulder or upsetting anyone's tankard of alcohol. Maeve noticed a few others wearing black or dark gray, with masks of foxes, owls, or mice. *All animals that are sacred to Janis.*

Alistair plucked a wineskin from a table and offered it to Maeve. She declined. Alistair tilted their head back, and their tanned throat shifted as they swallowed. They wore all black, and their makeup extended from the inner corners of their eyes toward their temples in broad, dark strokes of purple and gray. Their baggy shirt exposed their clavicle, and their high-waisted, voluminous skirt was embroidered with dancing gray foxes. *Their daggers are well-hidden.* Alistair wiped wine from their lips, and Maeve looked away, a fluttering sensation in her breastbone.

"Maeve, over here!" Imogen waved. Her sheer orange dress draped loose around her body as if enchanted by the wind. Her legs were long and slender and adorned with golden ankle bracelets. Maeve swallowed against her dry throat. *She's beautiful.* Her blonde hair was damp. She hugged Maeve and smelled like saltwater and feminine sweat.

Alistair snatched a crown of white and blue flowers from a

passing cart and dropped it onto Maeve's head, their smile charming and teasing. *Always a thief.* Imogen laughed, and her fingertip gently caressed a petal near Maeve's temple. Alistair plucked a smaller crown of yellow buds for themselves and a dreamy bouquet of giant vermilion blossoms for Imogen. They placed it on her head like they were crowning her into royalty. Imogen's cheeks were dusky pink, and she looped arms with Maeve and Alistair.

"Let's find a dance circle."

"What about talking to the merchants about Hagken?" protested Maeve.

Imogen pursed her lips together and trilled them. "Oh, *psh.*"

"We have plenty of time," said Alistair.

The drums vibrated beneath her feet and the scent of roses and grilled fish flooded her nostrils. Imogen skipped into the dance circle and twirled with her arms open. Her face turned toward the light, and a swirl of pink petals trailed behind her. She looked half wild, half-divine. Maeve's heart clenched. She hesitated at the edge of the circle. The sights and smells of Pyrite were dizzying and claustrophobic. *All these people. All this life.* She couldn't let King Hagken destroy it. Her eyes tore from Imogen and lingered on the merchant stalls. *Can I talk to them? Are they local or visiting?* She couldn't see their wares due to the shifting crowd moving through her line of sight.

"They don't have parties in Ferne?" Alistair asked.

"They do." Maeve flushed. "Not with this many people."

"Naturally." Alistair took Maeve by the shoulders and pulled her into the throes of bodies moving in euphoric delight. Her blood fizzed, her heartbeat fierce and heady in her chest. She turned to look back at the merchant stall.

Alistair spun her. Her view was muddled. Pyrite wouldn't

collapse if she danced with her friends. She'd talk to city visitors and warn them, and maybe with enough traction, the influential players within Pyrite would listen to her. Especially once she had the merchant guild with her. *Tomorrow*, she rationalized, *I'll find fresh leads.* This wasn't giving up. She would allow herself a few moments of respite and celebration as Juno would wish. She breezed into Alistair's arms like one of the many ribbons shimmering through the sky.

They grinned, white teeth and sparkling blue eyes. "You're radiant!"

"You're biased."

Alistair said, "I'm not lying, though, am I?" They looked at Imogen, blissfully dancing. She blossomed beneath the Pallanos banners, and her cheeks glowed rosy.

"Maeve looks radiant, doesn't she?" they yelled.

"Always."

Imogen smiled at her. Maeve's blush burned across her neck, and another shower of petals rained down their heads. They danced alone and with each other, trading partners between songs. A warm trickle of sweat pooled at the middle of her back. She stumbled often, but Imogen compensated for it, guiding her and pulling her into the rhythms of the drums and high-pitched flutes.

"You're a natural," Imogen sounded breathless.

"Hardly." Her friends were generous with their compliments today.

"Stop thinking so hard."

"How am I supposed to do that?" she said as her left foot awkwardly crossed over her right.

"Let go, Maeve." Imogen's golden head shone under the sunlight. She slipped from Imogen's grasp into Alistair's as fluid as water moving between two stones. The music, the sunlight, and her companions wove a tapestry of joy and tender longing. The drumbeats and tambourines continued in a cyclical rhythm. They were like the ocean kissing the shoreline, an endless rise and fall, never-ending. Alistair sidled to a merchant selling dangling pearls, and Maeve caught their half-smile before the crowd obfuscated them.

When Alistair returned, they said, "The first stone has been tossed."

"You told them about King Hagken?"

"Not exactly." They twirled Maeve between their arms. "I mentioned the safety of the roads and asked how their journey was."

She bit back an impatient groan, and Alistair laughed low and husky.

"Subtly is our ally, sunshine," said Alistair, "we'll keep tossing stones and see where the ripples take us."

* * *

The afternoon of music, fragrant smoke-cooked meals, and fruity wine blended into a dusky purple evening. The citizens of Pyrite adjusted accordingly. They traded flutes for low-toned string instruments sacred to Janis. Maeve watched the subtle change as people whispered secrets into each other's ears. She leaned into Imogen. They were drunk from dancing together and sharing plum wine and stolen glances. They jostled into each other, giggling as if Janis' strings of fate were tangled up.

"We should get some moon cakes." Imogen's smile stretched from ear to ear. "I wish they made them year-round." She pointed to a shop at the corner. A cluster of people huddled around its entrance. "I bet that one has moon cakes."

"On what authority?" Alistair snorted. "Have you cased the place?"

"Not all of us are thieves." Imogen snickered. "I'm an alchemist, and that's what we call an educated guess. What do you think, Maeve?"

Her head swam. She blinked, then laughed. "I can't remember your question."

"Wonderful." Alistair laughed with her. "We've got a drunk priestess, tarnished royalty, and I use that term lightly, and a degenerate alchemist. Someone should write a ballad about us."

"I'll commission it." Imogen tugged them both by hand.

"Do you have enough coin?" asked Alistair.

Imogen rolled her eyes. "It's one song, Alistair. What could it cost? Ten gold?"

A fine sugar powder drifted through the air. *It's like snow.* She reached up to try and catch the dust and smiled at nothing and everything. Her footsteps were light, and her body was pleasantly floaty. Alistair's gloved hand settled at the back of her neck and gently massaged while they waited for Imogen.

"Janis' celebration calls for a sharing of secrets." They smirked. "We've followed all the other celebratory traditions. We shouldn't miss this one."

Maeve scrunched her nose and said, "I don't know if I can trust you with my secrets."

"Straight for the heart as always, sunshine." They winced and rubbed a hand over their chest.

She laughed. "It's not my fault the truth easily wounds you."

"Fair. Although I do think you derive some pleasure by insulting me." Alistair's eyes danced with amusement.

"Perhaps."

"I can give you my secret if you'll have me," said Alistair.

Her heartbeat thundered like an echoing festival drum. The

dripping and twinkling hanging lights blurred at the corners of her vision. They gripped her face between their hands, their leather gloves warm and sweet smelling. *It's like a dream.* Alistair's blue eyes softened, and she cherished this private moment of closeness. *Oh, Juno above. I think they might kiss me.* Her smile widened, and she touched Alistair's lean chest. *I want them to kiss me.*

Alistair dropped their lips onto hers. They tasted like honey wine. The sweetness of it trickled down her throat and pooled into her belly. Their kiss was golden, and her overjoyed heart pulsed into her fingertips—an unspoken secret molded into the shape of her lips.

Her fingers twisted the front of their shirt, pulling them close before she relaxed into their embrace. She giggled—*because of the wine*—and rested her forehead on Alistair's cheek. Her skin fizzled as if imbued with Juno's divine light.

"Maeve." Alistair's breath tickled the top of her head. "I'll follow you anywhere."

Imogen carried three flat pastries, and the surface glistened with clear glaze and powdered sugar. They embodied Janis's cold, brilliant surface and light. She passed them with sticky fingers and an excited smile.

"You bought only three?" Alistair asked.

"Don't be dumb." She pointed to a new pouch tied at her belt. "I got myself extras for later."

They returned to the calm streets and gentle strum of guitars. Maeve bit into the soft, sugary pastry with a delighted gasp. It melted in her mouth. She closed her eyes. In Ferne, they never made anything like this. They celebrated the equinox, but the celebration for Janis was subdued. They gathered at the village center, built a bonfire, swapped stories, and listened to the wisdom of the elders. Although folks agreed that sharing a secret with a friend or loved one on this day was good luck, it had yet to be a tradition Ferne followed.

Besides, Maeve didn't have loved ones within the village anymore. She cared for everyone as was expected of her. She knew their names, stories, and families, but distance was necessary except for the children. It was difficult for Maeve to create a wall between herself and the children. Maeve stared at her moon cake with wistful yearning. She wished they could be here. The children of Ferne would scream with joy at these little cakes.

"Maeve?" Imogen gave a little nudge to her shoulder. "You alright?"

"Hm? Oh, yes. Yes." She blinked. "I was thinking about home."

Alistair and Imogen shared an indecipherable glance.

"Do you want to talk about it?" Alistair offered, "I'd be willing to count it as your secret."

"No." Maeve's smile wobbled around the edges. *I don't want to ruin their good time. We were having such fun before I went and turned melancholy.* There was nothing to be done tonight. She might not have any friends in Ferne, but she had two friends before her with powdered sugar on their lips and a worried tightness around their eyes.

"I can give you a different secret, though," she said around another bite of moon cake, "if you're interested."

Imogen brightened, and Alistair raised a single eyebrow. Maeve looked down. The sugar coated her fingertips. Her heartbeat was uneasy with the weight of her confession. It was no simple thing to lay yourself out, even on an enchanted night like this.

"I'm incredibly grateful to have met you," she said softly, "and now I cannot imagine my life without you."

A dozen flecks of copper gleamed inside Imogen's dark amber

eyes, and a constellation of freckles traveled across her nose and between her thin eyebrows. Her nose bumped into Maeve's. It wasn't the music or heat that made Calorum tilt off its equilibrium. It was them. Imogen was as brilliant as a new star. Alistair was as electrifying as lightning. She considered herself sensitive to magical energy, but this was something else; something raw and primal flowed between them. She felt Alistair and Imogen inside her bones, her blood, her spirit.

Maeve trembled, sweat cooling, damp, and sticky on her face. She wondered if it was possible to burn from the inside out. Her face was on fire, and her heart burned like a comet. She didn't want this moment to end. She wanted to pull it like saltwater taffy between her teeth and stretch it into eternity.

She tilted toward Imogen and admired her molten eyes and the firework of freckles across her nose. Her eyes fell. Imogen's lower lip was chapped and tinged dark purple from the plum wine. *Tonight is ours. Tomorrow can wait.* She leaned in, and Imogen's pale eyelashes fluttered against her freckled cheekbone. *A secret can be unspoken. A secret can be a gesture.* Maeve's lips met hers. Her soft mouth tasted of wine and sugar and shared promises. Imogen breathed raggedly, and her tongue delved between Maeve's lips. She pulled a soft keen from the back of Maeve's throat. *How embarrassing,* Maeve thought once Imogen pulled away.

The festival-goers went by in their animal masks, trading keys tied with ribbons, humming, and singing. Imogen smiled and angled her face toward Alistair. Alistair cupped Imogen's jaw between their fingers and kissed her. The kiss spoke to familiarity and practice, and Maeve was entranced by it. *They've kissed before.* Her blush traveled from the tips of her ears down to her toes. Her gaze went heavenward toward the serene, dark, and brilliant sky. Enveloped between Imogen and Alistair, Maeve melted like candle wax and forgot her stress and looming terror. She was at a festival in a beautiful city with two beautiful people, where moonlight beamed across the stones in dreamy white slices.

When she returned to Estoria, Imogen's eyes darkened, and she leaned her forehead on Maeve's shoulder. Her chest swelled with an emotion too big and too terrifying to identify. Alistair pressed a sugary kiss to Maeve's cheek.

"Do you think it's extra good luck if we have the same secret?" Imogen whispered. Maeve laughed and blinked away the tears blurring her vision.

She closed her eyes, surrounded by their warmth and the cool metal of Imogen's arm touching her bare skin. She chuckled. She wanted to blame the wine for pulling vulnerability and levity from her. Yet she knew that would be untrue. Tonight was enchanted. The secret-keeping goddess blessed them. And if she could trust Juno with her life, then she could trust Janis with her heart. *And maybe I can trust Alistair and Imogen with my heart, too.*

20

Alistair went to find a room and metaphorically dropped more stones into the water. Imogen swirled her skirts around her slender legs and rambled while Maeve listened and tried to keep up, figuratively and physically. Her face ached with the permanency of her smile. It was pleasurable to listen to Imogen. She was passionate and animated when she spoke about alchemy. Her entire face brightened as if empowered by Juno's light.

"It's fascinating, actually," Imogen said, "you know that bracelet Bismuth made?"

"The shackle," Maeve corrected.

"Mhm. Yes. The shackle." Imogen twirled with a broad, satisfied smile on her face. "Could I have it? I want to find out what else it can do."

Maeve recalled the intense secrecy of the guilds, the marker on Bismuth's work, and her stomach twisted. She didn't want the guild to start pursuing Imogen after their narrow escape. *Our luck shines* *tonight, but tomorrow...*Maeve resisted the urge to hold her pendant out of fear of thieves. *Tomorrow, I'll meet with the merchant guild; our future is unknown. I don't want to lose her.*

"Won't that get you into trouble?"

Imogen slid her arm around Maeve's waist. "Oh, my sweet Maeve." She shook her head. "Studying in the privacy of Alistair's home is different. I promise I won't try to sell Bismuth's work or pass it off as my own. I'm curious about the mineral and how it might benefit us. Hagken has mages on his side, remember?"

Maeve frowned. She removed the dampeners from her pouch and passed them to Imogen.

"I don't like the idea of using this against Hagken..." Her words faded, and she couldn't organize her thoughts into neat boxes. Hagken had a capable, ruthless spirit mage on his side, and the alchemist guild created this at the cost of Gregor's life. The answer was obvious if her choices came between saving an innocent life by using the dampener or doing nothing. *And if Hagken had this, I know he'd use it on us.*

Maeve said, "We have to use every resource if we're going to have a chance against him." Imogen's grip tightened, and she pressed her face into the side of Maeve's head.

"Maeve, Imogen!" Alistair's voice rang out from the intersection of the street. Their dark skirt billowed around their legs as they ran. "You'll never guess where we're staying," they didn't wait for a response before announcing, "The Pearl!" with a dramatic flourish and deep bow.

"The Pearl, Alistair, really?" Imogen teased, "I haven't been there since I was a teenager."

"Is it nice?" asked Maeve.

"It's stellar!" Imogen smiled. "They've got giant beds, and you can watch the ships come into port."

"I booked us the best room."Alistair interlocked their fingers with Maeve's and Imogen's. "We'll drown in decadence until dawn."

Maeve smiled. Her worries about Hagken and Imogen's future experiments with the dampener ebbed into a quiet corner of her mind. "Sounds lovely."

"It will be." Alistair squeezed her hand. They walked together with Alistair between them, and Imogen began a heartfelt seminar about a flower that grows upside down on stalagmites. The longer Maeve listened, the less terrifying the future felt. *How can I be afraid of anything when I have these two beside me? Imogen is brilliant, and Alistair is resourceful.* Maeve glanced at her companions as silver glitter rained from the walkways above. *Tonight, we have Janis' blessing, too.*

The Pearl glimmered. The balconies were covered in twinkling lights, and the roof tiles shone like the insides of an oyster. Unlike the other taverns they passed, the patrons within the Pearl were quiet, their conversations intimate and hushed, while a musician lightly plucked a harp on stage. They followed Alistair upstairs, earning passing and knowing looks from the patrons, and neither she nor Imogen could contain their giddy laughter. The room was splendid in colors of cream and teal, and a beaded curtain of pearls laid across the windows.

Imogen flopped onto the giant plush bed and pulled Maeve alongside her. "Let's order some wine, but I need to eat first."

"Don't you have leftover moon cakes?" Maeve propped her chin into her hand. Alistair chuckled and shot Imogen a heated look.

"I want something sweeter than moon cakes," Imogen said boldly before rolling her body on Maeve's, and her mind fell silent for a *long* time.

* * *

Maeve kicked the silver tray teetering at the corner of the bed and knocked over the bowl of grapes and two leftover figs. However, her companions didn't wake. The latticed windows dripped with morning mist. She smiled and tilted her head to see Alistair sprawled across the mattress, their head near her ankle, their mouth open in a soft, whistling snore. They were lean, dangerous sinew and corded muscle; their defined abs peeked out beneath their cropped top. More than a few scars decorated their midsection, but Alistair gleefully and proudly informed her that no one managed to get a lethal strike on them. Alistair snorted and smacked their lips. A wave of fondness crashed over her and doused her heart in sentimentality. She shifted her shoulder as a new tingling sensation ran through it.

Imogen muttered in dissent, nuzzled closer, her arms were a vice around Maeve's stomach.

"Sorry." She trailed her fingers across Imogen's freckled nose. Her short blonde hair stuck out in every direction. Maeve's cheeks tingled as she remembered the intensity of Imogen's affection last night. Imogen's desire to understand and repeat actions to obtain a similar result was...effective. Her fingertips trailed to Imogen's shoulder, where a faint impression of Alistair's teeth was embedded onto her shoulder. *She's as fierce as she is beautiful and brilliant.*

"I'm awake," Imogen replied. Maeve found she didn't want to separate in the tangled sweat of limbs. Her arm prickled with numbness. She propped her back with lush feathered pillows, and Imogen settled like a lazy cat in her lap. She heard the stirrings of life outside, wagons moving down the road led by horses, snippets of conversation, and inn patrons walking down the hall.

"I've got somethin' for you," said Imogen. She reached for her discarded belt pouch and offered Maeve something small in her palm. The band was silver; a pearl was mounted into the apex, surrounded by two opalescent fish chasing one another. Maeve's heart and eyes burned with gratitude.

"You deserve more jewelry," she explained before settling into Maeve's lap. Maeve slid the ring onto her finger. It fit perfectly.

"I don't know what to say."

"A thank you kiss would be appreciated." Imogen chased Maeve's lips with a soft nibble and smiled.

Her new ring plunged through Imogen's fine, short hair like salmon swimming upstream as she carded her fingers through it. The scar at the base of Imogen's skull stood like a ridged crescent, and Maeve traced it with her thumb.

"How'd it happen?"

"Sharing war stories, are we?" She smiled into Maeve's soft stomach.

"You don't have to tell me," Maeve said in concession. Some stories were not hers to know or hear. She resumed her ministrations, and Imogen huffed a lofty sigh like a giant beast.

"After the orphanage, but before I was old enough to apply for the guild, I was on my own for a while," she said, "people love to claim Pyrite was safer when we had the council. It wasn't. The heart of Pyrite will never change.

"I was on my own. It was a blitz attack. They hit me from behind, stole whatever meager coin I might've had, and left me bleeding in an alley. No one found me or saved me. I woke up and carried on." Imogen watched Maeve's reaction with magnified focus.

Maeve asked, "Did you see a healer?" *She must've been young.*

"No." She gently scraped a metal fingertip across Maeve's lower lip. "I went to my room in the inn, wrapped my head, and got to work on a tincture for headaches. Which all worked out in the end since the tincture earned me a place in the guild."

"No one helped you? No one checked on you?" She grimaced at the idea of a young Imogen, fair and delicate, her inquisitive eyes too big for her finely boned face and left to heal alone with bloody bandages around her brilliant mind. *How heartless can this city be?* In her village, they would rush together to help someone, even if they were a stranger, especially a child.

"In their eyes, I was someone else's problem." Imogen must've noticed Maeve's growing horror on her face because she said, "Don't judge them too harshly, darling. Everyone acts in their own best interests."

Maeve dropped a kiss on Imogen's forehead.

"I'm sorry."

"Whatever for?"

"You shouldn't have experienced that..." she said with difficulty, "and you shouldn't have been alone..."

Imogen traced the arch of Maeve's nose with her fingertip. "I have you now, don't I? You'll patch me up if anyone tries to crack open my skull."

Despite the grim topic, Maeve found herself laughing.

"That's better," Imogen said with deep and genuine warmth.

Alistair poked Maeve's calf and grumbled, "How are you both awake and coherent at this hour?"

Maeve and Imogen shared a look toward their sleep-mussed rogue with early gray light spooling across their tan and scarred skin. Their shared laughter bounced off the walls, and they ate breakfast, drank, and traded citrus-tasting kisses. *This morning is more peaceful and delightful than any others I spent in Ferne.* Maeve stroked the nape of Alistair's neck as they pillowed their cheek on her thigh. The air danced across their sweaty skin and rapidly cooled them with a touch of salt from the bay outside.

"We could get on a ship today," Alistair said, kissing Maeve's inner thigh with a chaste kiss. "We could leave it all behind. The war, my stepfather, the shitty general who left his city to the dogs." Imogen sat cross-legged by the fruit platter and shook her head.

"I can't." Maeve tugged at the root of Alistair's thick, curly hair to force them to look at her. "I won't abandon them, Alistair."

"Is it abandonment?"

"Yes. I promised them I would return. I promised with my entire heart and soul."

"And what of *my* heart and soul?" they asked, nuzzling their face into her soft stomach, "you said yourself I might be put on trial for my part in his reign. We could run away before I lose my pretty head."

"Alistair, is this breakfast conversation?" Imogen squished a fat purple grape between her fingers. "You know how tenacious our Maeve is."

"I'd stand witness for you in the trial," said Maeve.

Alistair isn't without blame. But they acted under King Hagken's orders. They were controlled from early adolescence to obey and prove their worth through violence and deception. It didn't excuse their history, and Alistair would have to face justice for what they did, but perhaps their sentence could be lessened.

Alistair said, "You've thought of everything, have you?"

"Not everything, I'm sure, but I've thought about our futures–I mean–" Maeve pressed her palms against her flushed cheeks. "I've thought about my future and how I'd like you both to be in it."

"Are you asking me to live with you again?" Imogen grinned.

"I...." Maeve blushed. "I was thinking we could return to Ferne together."

"I've always wanted to raise horses," said Alistair.

"That makes sense." Imogen nudged Alistair's leg with her foot. "You're about as temperamental as a stallion."

Alistair caught Imogen's ankle and tugged until she shook free. Maeve smiled. If Alistair remained free, then they could return to Ferne together. She could show Imogen her garden, and Alistair could raise horses, and they'd fill her cabin with joy and light. But first, she needed to convince the merchants to support their cause. Once the merchants joined them, the other guilds would follow. Fenris' ruling advisers would have no choice but to listen! Maeve, well-rested and well-loved, closed her eyes to summon Juno's lights. *Juno?* A hot, prickly sense of frustration grew spikes inside her chest. *You've always known your limits and stopped before it became too late. Now, she isn't answering. Did she break our bond?* Maeve's shoulders trembled. *No, no!* Maeve rejected the idea. *That's impossible. Juno doesn't abandon her priestesses. I have to try harder.* Her tether wasn't gone. It couldn't be.

"Maeve?" Imogen's cool hand encircled her calf. "Are you alright, love?"

"I don't..." She struggled to untangle her words. "Ever since the guild, I haven't been able to connect with Juno." She told them about Bismuth's experiments and her theories about how divine magic functioned. *She said it was tied to my life force. If I'm alive, then I should be connected to Juno.*

"Has this happened before?"

"No, she's always come back."

Alistair said, "Then it'll return."

"Alistair's right." Imogen rubbed Maeve's shin. "And as much as I dislike her, Bismuth is a good alchemist; well, she's not as good as me, but..." Maeve laughed despite the cavern of fear collapsing within her stomach.

"You think Bismuth's theories are correct?"

"I do," Imogen said, "I also think she's too arrogant to stomach being wrong, so she wouldn't have said anything to you if she wasn't certain."

Alistair raised their eyebrow. "Imogen, how'd you manage to give a backhanded compliment, reassure Maeve, and insult your ex-girlfriend all in one conversation?"

"I have a gift." Imogen shrugged. "We could try praying with you if you think that'll help."

Maeve forced her spine to relax into the pillows. Imogen's suggestion was thoughtful.

"It's worth trying." Maeve used to pray with her family in their small, cozy homestead. They formed a circle on the bed, heads bowed, hands interlinked, and Maeve's spirit softened and glowed. *How lucky I am to have found them.* She led their morning prayers with careful and practiced ease. *I must follow my mother's wisdom. No matter what happens as long as I remain calm, positive, and grateful then Juno's light will return.* She was a third-generation priestess. How many others could claim the same level of dedication? Her connection would return, and she refused to entertain any alternatives. She would accomplish the goals she set for herself when she fled Hollyhock, and Juno would reward her stalwart faith. *There is no other path for me beyond this one.*

Maeve finished the prayer, "Beneath the light of the Dawn Mother, we are blessed, we are purified, and we claim the day in her honor."

21

The doors opened. The boisterous conversation hit Maeve's face like a waft of hot air. The central atrium swirled with color and sound, servers carrying trays of bubbly amber drinks and tables laden with food, their legs nearly buckling under the weight. Maeve sighed, and Alistair touched the middle of her back. *Thank Juno, I had the foresight to make that tea for our hangovers before we got here...*

"Chin up, sunshine," they muttered warmly and close to her ear. Her skin flushed with goosebumps. She pushed her shoulders back and strode into the room. Every set of eyes was on her—some curious, others leering, and many suspicious. The merchants were dressed in fine suits of every color—a rainbow of dark plum, mustard yellow, charcoal, and evergreen. If someone wasn't wearing a suit, they wore jewel-toned silk blouses and draping, elegant floor-length skirts. In her dusty trousers and mud-speckled boots, Maeve tried to ignore how much she and Alistair stood out in this crowd of lavish haughtiness. She stifled a yawn in the back of her throat. *I've not done myself any favors by staying up all night with Imogen and Alistair.* Instead of sleeping late and taking advantage of their room, she and Alistair strolled the walkways and discreetly mentioned Hagken and rumors of conflict on the roads. Meanwhile, Imogen returned to the burned district to study the dampener.

Maeve and Alistair walked under a twirling acrobat. *I wonder if any merchants have caught the gossip we've been spreading.* She sensed people were making deals and changing the fabric of Pyrite with their conversation. They circled the room, and Maeve plucked a pastry from a plate of desserts. She ate while walking, cupping her hand to catch the crumbs beneath her chin. *These aren't as tasty as the moon cakes we shared last night, but they'll do.* Alistair watched her with a small, secretive smile.

"There's Terrayn," they said, tilting their chin toward a gilded balcony decorated with golden glittering ribbons and strings of abalone shells. Terrayn stood next to several large potted leafy fauna with orange and yellow flowers bursting from their stems. She looked as if she would bite off someone's head if they dared to approach her. She wore a blue ensemble with the first brass buttons undone to expose her clavicle and show off the pearl necklaces wrapped around her throat.

Maeve met Terra's eyes. *I promised Terrayn I'd do everything in my power to ensure she comes out of this arrangement with more gold than she can carry and have her revenge against Hagken. Her motives are personal. I have to remember that.* The merchants sat in glossy halls with feathered hats and pink-dusted cheeks. They exchanged coins as if it were as easy as breathing. Her stomach grumbled. She tried not to despise them—it had been a long morning. They were her potential allies. If she allied with the merchants, she influenced the docks and the meager town guard. If she could conscript the mages to her cause, she would unite Pyrite, keep everyone safe, and eventually return to Ferne alongside Alistair and Imogen.

Terrayn took Maeve's fingers and kissed the back of her knuckles in greeting.

Maeve blushed, and her word stumbled between her teeth, "When will it start?"

"Oh, not until after midnight, I'm afraid. This is the carousing part of our little get-together. We drink, we eat, and we make private deals. The more official things happen behind this door." She jerked her thumb over her broad shoulder. "For now, I suggest you introduce yourself and see who might be open to listening before we start properly. You never know who you might find."

Maeve asked, "Anyone you recommend?"

"A few." Terrayn plucked the strawberry slice from the rim of her glass flute. "Over there is Lady Ilmar Cove. She's a devout follower of Juno. I think Maeve would get along with her. She's got a sharp eye for liars, though, so watch your tongue."

Lady Ilmar Cove fixed her large brimmed, feathered hat. Her cream-and-honey dress ran like liquid across her bony shoulders in swaths of shimmery silk. Terrayn gestured to a stocky individual wearing a long skirt and wrapped fabric headpiece.

"That's Lemrel. They're shrewd. They're also a tad ruthless. But, if you appeal to their sense of pride for Pyrite, then you might find a friend." Terrayn grabbed a passing glass from a server's tray and passed the drink to Alistair. Alistair's clear eyes scanned the room, their face inscrutable. Maeve rubbed her forehead. *It's going to be another long night. How will I possibly make it to midnight? And will my connection to Juno return by then?*

Terra said, "I'll see who else I can find."

"I suggest we split up," Alistair said after Terra walked away, "you speak to Lady Cove, dazzle her with your charm, and I'll speak to Lemrel. I lived in Pyrite for more than half my life. I should be able to woo them."

"Meet back here?" Maeve suggested.

"We can do better than that." Alistair produced two curved metal apparatuses from their pocket. "Imogen made them to help us stay connected." They brushed Maeve's hair away from her ear and slid the device into place. *Oh, Imogen.* She rubbed her thumb against the ring Imogen gave her. *I'll have to thank her properly.*

"When you touch the side here, it should allow you to communicate with me as long as we aren't *too* far apart."

"That's incredible," she exclaimed, "she's incredible."

Alistair cupped Maeve's chin. "As are you, sunshine. If anyone can impress the merchants with passion and resolve—it's you."

They captured Maeve's lips. Her skin tingled from head to toe, and her breath quickened. Their affection set her heart ablaze with overwhelming ferocity. No wine nor moon cake tasted as sweet as the pressure of their lips upon hers. *They're a shadow no longer. They're the light burning at the center of the Estoria.* Alistair's elongated, sharp makeup crinkled around their blue eyes.

"Juno, guide you." Maeve's buoyant heart threatened to float away into the performing acrobats above.

"May Janis watch your steps." They disappeared like a black viper striking into a field of wildflowers. Maeve touched her lips with her fingertips and smiled. *May all the gods watch over us tonight.*

She awkwardly stepped into the crowd of jostling elbows and fast-paced conversation. Lady Cove lifted her shrewd, dark eyes at Maeve in her approach. Her lips stretched into a thin, bloodless smile.

"It is so lovely to see fresh faces in the guild." She extended a thin, ring-adorned hand toward Maeve. "Who do you work with?"

"I'm acquaintances with Terrayn. You can call me Maeve."

"Ah." She clicked her tongue. "She's as willful as the wind. Not many would've returned to the guild after what happened."

"She suggested I introduce myself to you. We share something in common."

Her thin, dark eyebrows raised. Everything about this woman reminded Maeve of a sharp instrument. Her rose-dusted cheekbones were high in her moon-pale face, narrowed dark eyes, straight nose, and pointed chin. Her mouth was thin and finely wrinkled. It was a mouth that suggested she pursed her lips more than she smiled.

"Did she?"

Maeve's stomach flipped. She was blood in the water, and this woman was a shark. She recalled the pressure of Alistair's hand on her back to encourage her forward. She thought of Bertha's sweet face, of reckless Archie, of the elders and little babies. *I'll survive this.* It was a simple conversation. She didn't come this far to be scared by conversation.

"We share the same faith. I'm a priestess of Juno." Maeve lifted her necklace from inside her shirt. The heavy golden pendant dropped between her breasts and settled warmly near her heart. *I hope I haven't given myself away too soon. Calom and Bismuth desired Juno's power for their own gain.* Ilmar's eyes widened. *I hope Ilmar is different.*

"You'd be surprised how few merchants follow the sunlit path," Ilmar said with an air of superiority and a scoff of distaste. "They live and die by Theadora and her blinded justice."

"I..." Maeve licked her lips and aimed for honesty. "I was surprised to discover the tallest spire in Pyrite belonged to Theadora."

Ilmar clutched Maeve's shoulder with tight, bony fingers. "Oh! I've petitioned a dozen times to have Theodora's tower moved and give the worshipers of Juno the sandstone tower. But, they turn it down each time."

"That sounds frustrating." Maeve was grateful Ilmar actively petitioned for change, but she needed more than building petitions to understand her point of view and how the city functioned. "Is it difficult to hold an audience with Fenris' council?"

"No. Not for me." The feather atop Ilmar's hat quivered as she tilted her head. "Pilgrims don't typically cross paths with the merchant's guild. What brings you here, Lady Maeve?"

"It's an unhappy story."

"I am certain I can stomach it."

Maeve rubbed the surface of Juno's pendant. *I wanted to wait until I was in front of everyone, but it wouldn't hurt to gain support before the meeting. Terrayn selected Ilmar because she suspected the woman would be sympathetic to my cause.* The story was a woven groove at the center of her heart. She replayed it in her mind often. She avoided the detail of King Hagken's burning and the truth of Alistair's connection to him.

Ilmar's smile sharpened like a knife. *Has she noticed something about my story?* Maeve shifted her weight. *Terrayn said Ilmar recognized liars, but I didn't lie. I omitted details.*

"Oh, you poor thing," she crooned, "how did you escape that wretched man?"

"One of his guards distracted him."

"He didn't notice you leave the room? He didn't chase you?"

Maeve's stomach bottomed out into her shoes.

"No."

"And you happened to stumble across Alistair?" Her nails

clinked against her glass. "What fortunate timing. Our Lady Juno must be watching over you."

"I am very lucky," Maeve said, "that's why I'm trying to find support within the guild. I want to present a united front before King Hagken arrives and bring him to justice."

Ilmar took a slow sip of wine. "It is unfortunate General Fenris is busy within the hematite mountains. Maeve, did you ever visit the city while King Hagken ruled?"

Maeve said no.

"Then you have no idea the bounty we've been gifted. You see, with General Fenris away, the guilds have stepped into power. We have more freedom than ever. We manage ourselves. It's been a greatly auspicious time. However, it has its dangers. Why, last week, a colleague of mine had his entire shipment destroyed. All his livelihood gone in a flash!" She snapped her bony, long-nailed fingers.

"Now, *that* never would have happened if King Hagken was here."

Hagken isn't the lesser of two evils here.

"Hagken is a tyrant."

Ilmar appeared unperturbed and shrugged. "All ambitious men are tyrants."

"If Hagken is held accountable for his crimes and arrested, then General Fenris would return. You'll have order and peace."

Ilmar laughed a high-pitched and grating sound.

"General Fenris is a hunter, my dear. He is content to let the city rule itself."

Maeve's mouth twisted. Everyone she spoke to in Pyrite was convinced nothing could change. *I thought Ilmar would be different. I thought she wanted change.* The ambitious, greedy people ruled and used others as pawns in their games. *There can be peace here and stability and empathy. Ferne is proof of it.*

"You would support Hagken's return?"

"I support rulers who allow me to run my business without interruption," Ilmar said, "my connections to Everdawn make it possible for priestesses like yourself to reach the eternal flame."

Her lungs shriveled. The eternal flame was the final pilgrimage made by a priestess. At the precipice of death, a devout priestess abandoned their worldly comforts and connections and attempted a journey to dawnbreak priory. It was seen as the final act of faith to Juno. Those who succeeded were honored by the sunburst prioress, cremated by the sacred flame, and had their ashes scattered into the desert. Maeve disliked this ritual. She couldn't understand why Juno would ask her followers to leave their families, friends, and responsibilities to die alone in the priory.

"I have a suggestion for you, Lady Maeve," said Ilmar in response to Maeve's awkward silence. "Rather than worrying about who sits upon the throne, you should focus on your own ambitions." She conspicuously leaned toward Maeve. "If you were to replace High Matriarch Allustera." Her brown eyes twinkled. "You would have my support."

Maeve twisted her ring around her finger. A chorus of laughter erupted. A smattering of applause beside the twirling acrobats. She thought of Allustera sitting on the tree roots surrounded by light. *That dream of mine has been laid to rest.* She belonged to Ferne.

"I have no desire to be a high matriarch."

"A pity." Ilmar's lips thinned.

Out of the corner of her vision, Maeve caught Alistair watching her, no longer conversing with other guild members. She cringed at continuing to discuss politics or faith with Ilmar Cove.

Maeve bowed, "Lady Cove, I must continue to introduce myself.

I appreciate the wisdom you have shared."

Ilmar smiled without moving the muscles around her eyes. "Be well, Lady Maeve. May Juno's light guide your steps."

She escaped into the crowd of greasy palms and stiff smiles, but Alistair was lost to another conversation before she could reach them. She leaned against the wall and tried to melt into the shadows of a potted plant. Ilmar's words rankled her. It was becoming repetitive. *How can Pyrite's people believe so little in each other? Or in the idea of justice?* Lady Cove must be an oddity. She can't represent the entire guild. She touched the copper apparatus curved around her ear.

"Alistair, I hope you're having better luck than I am." She rubbed a knuckle between her eyebrows. "Lady Cove would rather see me as high matriarch than stop Hagken."

Alistair's voice crackled in her ear, "You'd make a beautiful high matriarch."

Maeve rolled her eyes in exasperated fondness. She took another pastry and dove back into the crowd. She found a tall, gaunt merchant standing alone and made her introductions. The merchant, Theobald, slicked back his gray hair beneath the harsh gravelight. She tried a subtle approach to warn of Hagken's threat.

"Have you heard any news from the south?" she asked.

Theobald's green eyes glimmered behind his spectacles. "I have." He adjusted his eyeball-shaped cuff links. "Whispers and rumors but enough to make me prepare my ship to leave at dawn."

"Really?" Her heart lightened. *Have the seeds of our gossip finally taken root?*

"They say Hagken is returning with an army of ten thousand necrotic beasts at his back."

"Ten thousand?"

"Oh yes." His exhale shuddered. "I expect the number is much higher, considering they never arrested Duskryn."

Duskryn? The fine hairs on her forearms lifted. *How does he know Cara or Calom? How infamous are they?* Her fingers twitched. She wanted to cling to her mother's pendant for comfort but kept her hands at her side. Theobald leaned away and shook his head.

"I suggest you bargain and bribe whoever you need to and leave the city before sunrise, Lady Priestess," he said solemnly, "spirit magic is unparalleled. Not even your divine magic can overpower it."

Maeve bristled. *Juno's magic can heal and help hundreds of people. There is no possible way that spirit magic is more powerful than the goddess's light. Theobald is mistaken.*

"I'm inclined to disagree. Juno's light protects us all."

"I've spent my entire life in Amethneas," he said. "The academy may have officially banned spirit magic, but that doesn't stop the students from exploring it on their own time. The horrors I've seen..." His eyes glossed over.

The pastries in her stomach soured at the memory of Cara's bone chimera thundering through the dark woods with murderous intent. *Alistair said Cara was the only capable necromancer within Hagken's retinue. She couldn't create an army of ten thousand beasts.* Theobald nervously cleaned the lenses of his spectacles. *Could she?*

"Sunshine," Alistair's voice in her ear startled her. "Meet Terrayn and myself in the third private room next to the chocolate fountain."

"Theobald," Maeve said quickly, "do you believe the city could prepare before Hagken's arrival?"

"No." His voice was flat, though his green eyes regarded her with sympathy. Maeve's shoulders sank. *At least Theobald is afraid of Hagken. That's better than Lady Coves' banal acceptance of the state of affairs.* She excused herself and left Theobald to find her friends in the private rooms. The rooms were small and contained hanging lamps of gravelight, silver fish hook ornaments, and paintings of massive merchant vessels. Alistair lounged on one of the brown couches with a silver platter of cheeses on their chest. Terrayn stood in the middle of the room with her arms crossed and her hip cocked to the side.

Maeve shut the door. "Any good news?"

"Unfortunately, Lemrel supports Hagken's return," Alistair said. "They appreciated Hagken's loyalty to the guild."

She sat near Alistair's legs. "Lady Cove doesn't care who rules as long as her business remains profitable, and Theobald fears Hagken and plans to leave Pyrite at dawn."

"We need to change our approach." Terrayn paced the room. "We can't feed into the fear, and we can't downplay the seriousness of the situation." Maeve rested her elbows on her knees and interlaced her fingers. *How many obstacles must I run into before making progress?*

"What do we do?"

"We appeal to their greed," Terrayn said, "you promised me wealth and revenge as payment for my help. How do you plan to uphold your side of that bargain?"

Alistair said, "You can have everything within Hagken's coffers. I'll make sure of it."

The nacreous beads in Terrayns' locs clicked together when she nodded. "That settles our debt, but we need something to offer the guild members."

A poignant and thoughtful silence fell across the trio. Maeve clenched her interlaced fingers and felt strangely exposed without Juno's light. *What can I give them when I have barely any coin?* She blinked. *Wait. Pyrite is ruled by commerce, bartering, and exchanging. It's my duty to heal others, but what if that's untrue for the priestesses in Pyrite? Juno's powers were coveted enough that Bismuth betrayed our deal for it.*

"Terrayn, how expensive is it to visit the temple of Juno?"

"Depends on the service."

Her heart skipped. A solution coalesced within the murky waters of her mind. *This might just work.*

"Merchants don't have priestesses working for them independently?"

Terrayn barked a laugh. "Gods, no! Any priestess hoping to settle in Pyrite is bound by Theadora's law to work for the temple." Her gaze sharpened. "But you're not planning to remain here..."

"Yes!" Maeve stood abruptly, and Alistair's cheese plate clattered to the floor. "For any merchant willing to use their influence to gain us an audience with Fenris' council, I will offer my healing services without charge to their crew."

Alistair plucked a piece of cheese off the floor with the tip of their dagger. "Appealing to their frugality. I like it."

"It could work," Terrayn said.

Maeve smiled. *I don't like bargaining Juno's gift like this, but we don't have a choice. I can't convince the merchants with coin I don't have. This is all I can offer. They don't have to know that I'm still recovering. And besides...*She squeezed her pendant. *One of Juno's pillars of faith is to eradicate sickness and disease. I am acting in service to Juno. I'm not betraying her. This act might even help our connection return!* Yes, yes. This would work.

Alistair swung their legs over the side of the couch and stretched their lithe arms overhead. "Alright, let's continue to bump elbows with Pyrite's finest." They winked, and Maeve hid her flustered expression by tucking her chin into her shoulder.

* * *

The merchants filed into a meeting room that reeked of smoked herbs. Maeve sidled beside Terrayn. Alistair stood behind her. *Buh-bump. Buh-bump.* Her heart lived in her eardrums. *Buh-bump.* She had a plan. She had her friends. She would survive this night. After introductions were made, the floor opened to the crowd. Terrayn nudged Maeve, and she stepped into the center.

"I am Maeve Theywnn, a priestess of Juno. I've enjoyed speaking to a few of you this evening, and I bring concerning news from the south." She squeezed her shaking fists together. "King Hagken plans to return and take the city."

They muttered like a flood of angry bees.

"I know your livelihoods are tied to the safety of the city. However, I'm offering my services as a priestess to anyone willing to help. We need to convince Pyrite's council to prepare for this attack. We need to organize the city militia and alert the citizens."

Several voices rang out at once: "This doesn't concern us!" and another, "I liked Hagken!" and Terrayn's voice was louder than the rest. "What's the cost healer?"

"I'm offering my services for free," Maeve said, "General Fenris remains in the hematite mountains. We must take this news to his council immediately."

"No, he isn't! I heard he went home to Lunesca."

"Free? There's always a catch."

Someone yelled, "Fenris is as good as dead."

"I bet she's not even a priestess."

"I'll not have my ships burned for this."

"Your ships? What about my inn?"

"Blast your inn! Your ale tastes like dog piss."

They argued and tossed scraps of gossip and flaunted their petty disagreements. The room unraveled from Maeve's control. *I'm losing them.* She looked at Terrayn for help, and the merchant grimaced.

"I heard Hagken has an army of ten thousand necrotic beasts," Theobald shouted into the fray, "we must flee before it's too late."

Someone yelled, "Lay off the honey wine, Theobald." Their laughter boomed like cannon fire off the walls. Maeve tried to speak above them and scanned the crowd for support. No one was listening.

"Please," Maeve shouted, "we are wasting time."

A feminine and haughty voice said, "You ought to listen to her."

Maeve's spine chilled. She knew that voice. She knew it among the blackened trees hunted by a monster made of bone and flesh. The doors flew open, a torrent of guards poured in, their swords alive with flashing steel, and the merchants screeched with indignation. A man wearing resplendent crimson and bronze armor stepped forward, bringing his blade directly to Alistair's throat. *A justiciar.*

Maeve's heart stopped. Cara Duskryn stepped out from behind the shadow of the justiciar. The veins in her face shimmered lilac. Her green eyes snapped to Maeve like a lioness, closing her jaws upon the flank of a gazelle. *How is she here?* Maeve pinched her own thigh. *Okay, I'm not dreaming.* Cara's smile was slow and taunting.

The justiciar announced, "Alistair Jas'dune, you are under arrest for conspiring to take the throne from its noble protector, King Hagken."

"What?" cried Maeve.

"Our true king has returned," Cara said, "and as far as I'm concerned, this entire guild is complicit and wishes for Hagken's demise." She snapped her fingers, her eyes bright and triumphant. "Arrest them."

The justiciar grabbed Alistair. The room swelled with shoving bodies and voices. Maeve backed into someone and wine-filled crystal goblets shattered to the floor. The guards grappled the merchants with loud declarations of Theadora's laws as the merchants screamed for their innocence. Chaos. Her mouth dried. The knot in the middle of her gut tightened. *No, no. It's all wrong.*

A flash of steel whistled through the air as Terrayn drew the rapier at her hip.

"Maeve," Alistair shouted above the din, "run!"

She elbowed through the colorful and aromatic bodies. She pushed a door open and ran mindlessly into a darkened hallway. She reached for Juno, for a light to guide her, but no divine magic answered her call. She stumbled left, raised voices following her, and ran downstairs. *Terrayn,* she thought with a bitter frown. *Did she betray us to Hagken?* But she drew her blade on the justiciars. They wouldn't arrest her if she were involved. *Was Cara controlling the guards?* It sounded impossible. Hagken's army couldn't be that close. Maybe Hagken sent Cara on her own. Her stomach curdled. *What if I was wrong, and he never meant an outright siege attack? And what about Imogen? Did the justiciars come for her? Or do they only want Alistair?*

The cool night air kissed her face. She ran thoughtlessly and frantic and didn't slow her step until she was lost in the flow of citizens spilling from taverns and homesteads. The docks were familiar, but she didn't feel safe. She passed beneath the three spires and paused before Juno's temple. She touched her amulet and thought of Allustera and the comforting sight of the oak tree. *Would she help? Or would she barter for the sunstone?* She glanced at Theadora's temple. *Ollie?* But Ollie was a clerk to Theadora. She couldn't trust him, especially considering he accepted bribes. *Hagken has enough coin to bribe all the clerks of Theadora.* And she couldn't trust the alchemists' guild after her escape and the death of Gregor.

Maeve bit her lip, and indecision coiled around her heart. *If I'm going to help Alistair, then there's only one person I can trust.* She turned in a circle, seeking familiar landmarks to guide her, and ran toward the burned district. *Imogen...I hope you're safe.*

22

The burned district hummed with idle chatter thickened with clouds of earthy pipe smoke. The citizens loitered in hollowed-out doorways like black moths as low-lit lanterns swung above their heads. They played dice and cards in shadowed alleyways and drank from flasks. She averted her gaze from someone exchanging coins with a hooded seller. The wind stirred, and two barefoot children ran past. *I shouldn't draw attention to myself.* She tucked her trembling hands into her pockets. The device wrapped around her ear and hummed with constant static. *Alistair is too far from me.*

A congealing terror lived inside her lungs. It expanded and contracted them in hiccuped, stuttered gasps. Every cursory look stuck to her clammy skin. *Is Imogen among the sellers? She said she'd be home tonight. Janis below, I hope she's okay.* Once the crowd thinned, she cupped her hands together and begged Juno to lead her to Imogen. *Please, Juno. I need you now more than ever.* The echo of silence rang through her spirit like a funeral dirge. *Please. I don't know where*

Imogen is. I need her help, Maeve prayed desperately. Her frustration clawed her throat with nails as sharp and long as Lady Coves'. She blinked the tears from her eyes. *Stay calm, stay calm,* she reminded herself; *I am a priestess like my mother before me.* Her shoulders bunched to her ears, and the wind funneled through the hollowed-out buildings and pushed against her back, urging her forward. The burned district sprawled like the long black legs of a great spider. Her pace quickened. And despite her fervent prayers, Imogen didn't manifest before her, and Juno's light remained vacant. *Maybe I should return to the temple district and see if Allustera will help.*

The low, humming static in her ear stopped, and in her haste, she nearly knocked the device from her ear.

"Alistair?"

"Gods above!" Imogen yelped, "You nearly stopped my heart."

"Where are you? I'm in the burned district and"—her vision blurred with tears. *Thank the Gods that the justiciars didn't arrest her too* — "Alistair's in trouble."

"When aren't they?" she laughed.

"No, no." She paced in a circle. "Serious trouble. The justiciars grabbed Alistair and dragged them away. Maybe Terrayn betrayed us?" Her forehead wrinkled. "I'm not sure. And Cara is here. I saw her. She led the justiciars. She arrested merchants. Hagken can't be here, can he?" A nervous warble entered her voice.

"Okay, okay, my love, I'm listening." She instructed Maeve to wait. She said the burned district wasn't large, but if Maeve stayed near the city wall, then she would find her. Maeve sank into a squat and covered her head with her arms. This night was surreal. *It wasn't supposed to be like this.* She reached for Juno, and the chasm of desperation in her chest doubled in size. *How am I going to help Alistair?* She couldn't save them without Juno's divine help. She watched herself from a bird's eye. She was hunched over, small, and helpless, surrounded by the spirits of a forgotten district. *Who am I if I don't have Juno?*

"Maeve!"

She stood in time for Imogen to collide with her. For a fleeting moment, Maeve's nerves calmed. She lacked her connection to Juno, but she had Imogen. After arriving at Imogen's home, the alchemist unrolled a map onto the table, and Maeve leaned over her shoulder. She expected a map of Pyrite, but no, Imogen had a map of General Fenris' castle located in Thorduun's quarter.

"My theory is Hagken used the influx of travelers to sneak his forces in." Imogen tapped the castle's front gate. "We should've planned for spies within the merchant guild. Someone must've tipped Cara off that Alistair was there. We're going to need to enter Fenris' castle through the front."

"You think Hagken is there already?"

"If Cara has justiciars under her thumb, then yes, I'm confident he'd go straight for the throne and ambush Fenris' council."

"How do we get in? Scale the walls?"

"They'll cover us in arrows. No. The only reason they'd open the gate is if Thorduun's quarter was in danger."

Maeve's eyes lingered on the venomous, dark-colored potions scattered around Imogen's workplace. Would the danger of innocents be a balanced price to pay for Alistair's freedom? She raked her fingers through her dark hair.

"There has to be another way."

"There isn't." Imogen shoved several metal containers into her bag. "Hagken will kill them if we don't rescue them tonight."

"Maybe Hagken isn't at the castle yet. Maybe we can talk to the council, and I'll explain everything."

Imogen held Maeve's face, and cold metal kissed her cheek. "Maeve! There's no *time* for explanations. Either we do this and save Alistair, or we leave them to their fate. Not everything can be solved over tea and rice crackers. Are we going or not?"

Maeve followed Imogen to the crest of Thorduun's quarter. The arcane barrier shimmered like oil upon water beneath the eerie, green gravelight. *How are we supposed to get past this? Alistair and I entered through the sewers last time.* Imogen reached into the alchemical pouches strapped across her chest. She took several paces back and gestured for Maeve to do the same. A thread of nervousness strained around Maeve's heart, and she tugged her hood closer to her face.

"It's something I've been working on since you gave me Bismuth's dampener," Imogen explained. *It's been less than a day, and she's already made something?* Maeve's eyebrows raised, impressed despite the severity of their situation.

Imogen underhand tossed a vial toward the barrier where it shattered upon impact. The splash radius dissolved a section of the barrier like spun sugar in water. They ran forward, and the arcane wall shivered, but the entryway Imogen had created didn't dissipate. Maeve clutched Imogen's cool, damp hand. Her last journey into the alchemists' guild resulted in death and awful, blood-soaked injuries. She prayed this excursion would end differently and for Janis to hide their movements through the night.

"No turning back now," Imogen whispered, "we've gotta save our shadow-slinger."

Maeve's breath struggled through her lungs. *We should be careful. I doubt the alchemists will welcome us.* A crew of laughing alchemists passed, and their bright hair glowed beneath the moonlight. Maeve turned her face away. Imogen said they needed to gain entry into the guild's basement, and the experiments within would create a disturbance so severe that the guards would have no choice but to open the keep. She trusted Imogen but couldn't shake the feeling something terrible was about to happen. Vox was slouched, arms crossed, and snoring at the bottom step. On his wrist, a dark watch displayed the moon's cycle, full and bright. *We aren't going through the front door, are we?* She met Imogen's tawny eyes.

"This way." Imogen circled to the side of the guild. "Give me a boost."

Maeve pressed her back against the wall and cupped her hands together. The tall lamps of gravelight at the ends of the alleyway watched her like two flickering green eyes. A slow, creeping sense of dread crawled down her spine. Imogen planted her foot into Maeve's waiting hands, and Maeve grunted as she boosted her toward the window. A faint hissing noise cut through the silence, and Imogen hoisted herself into the opened window. She dangled one leg out, her hood blown back, and grinned triumphantly at Maeve. Maeve's smile was tight against her mouth. Her thoughts lingered on Alistair's safety. *They always joked they were hard to kill. Juno above, I hope they're right.* Imogen helped Maeve inside.

The room was dark and overcrowded with wooden crates. Her chest rattled with a soft, unsteady sight of relief. *Nearly halfway there.* Imogen adjusted the scarf around Maeve's face.

"Keep your eyes forward and look annoyed," she said, "most of the guild will be asleep or sleep-deprived and working on their projects. They shouldn't spare us a second glance, but if they do, we have to act like we belong here."

Maeve asked, "Is that what you did when you rescued me?"

"Yes." Imogen smiled. "And it worked."

A thin, wispy smoke overhead glittered blue motes. They stopped before a copper door flanked by two imposing iron sentinels. *We can't fight them.* The magical rotating cube at the center of their chests crackled with contained electricity. *If we can't access it —then what will we do?* There hadn't been time to create multiple plans with Alistair's life at stake.

"Now what?"

"Gregor gave us a key."

"What?"

Imogen removed Bismuth's dampener from her bag and held it against the door. Bismuth's mark appeared on the shiny copper surface. The door slid open. The guardians remained inert. *Alistair was right,* Maeve thought; *their protection isn't as good as they believe it is.* Could she have changed his fate if she had known of Gregor's disappearance sooner?

"I need you to do something while I go down there." Imogen rummaged through her backpack and pulled a helmet over her head. It covered her face and had a strange apparatus at the front like a dog's muzzle. She held out a dark leather pouch with a long string attached.

"Go up the stairs, take a left, and that'll lead you to a balcony overlooking the dining hall. See the end of this string? Ignite it and throw the pouch into the center of the room."

"What does it do?" Her fingers curled around the pouch.

"Covers the place in smoke for a bit. Shouldn't kill anyone. Afterward, I'll meet you outside."

Her mind whirled. She kept repeating Alistair's desperate and feral expression, yelling for her to run. *I won't leave them behind. Not after everything we've been through together. But what if I'm too late? What if Hagken had already killed them?* Maeve blinked. She couldn't entertain hopeless thoughts. She needed to stay somehow positive. Alistair wasn't helpless. They were clever. They were resourceful.

She ascended the carpeted steps, went left, and overlooked the dining hall. Roughly twenty alchemists sat below. The candelabras chained overhead flickered with candlelight. Her fingertips dug into a fine, grainy texture inside the leather pouch. She removed a match from her healer's pouch and struck it against the railing. The flame sparked and hissed as it caught on the end of the thread. Maeve waited, debating if another path might be taken, and then tossed it from the balcony.

The pouch landed on the floor—*Whoosh!* — a miasma of black vapor flooded the room. The alchemists shouted with surprise as smoke engulfed the ceiling and extinguished the candles. She clamped her hand over her mouth and nose. Her eyes watered. Her lungs burned, and she had a desperate and aching desire to cough and release the toxins she had ingested. She ran down the stairs, stumbling and blinking back tears. The smoke rapidly consumed the hallways, and a chorus of horrified, high-pitched shrieks and echoing wails followed her. Their screams dug into her mind, and guilt took hold of her heart.

*What have **we** done? What have I done?*

She coughed wetly and stared at her blood-speckled palm. She doubled over, and a steady, low throb started at the base of her skull. She instinctively called to Juno to ease the headache before it could induce white spots in her vision. Yet Juno remained absent. She looked up to see Imogen standing beside an overturned workbench. Several body-shaped shadows moved within the smoke, coughing, screaming, and pushing toward the front doors. Imogen ripped off her mask and stood with smoke curling in obsidian wisps around her. Her bright eyes scanned the destruction, and her cheeks flushed.

"Come on!" She beckoned Maeve. "We don't have much time."

Maeve forced herself upright and stumbled toward her. With

each step, her breath rattled inside her rib cage. Her vision warbled. She clung to Imogen's arm, wheezing, her throat burning. Her blood-coated tongue slithered behind her teeth. She mouthed Imogen's name.

Imogen said, "I've got you."

She pinched Maeve's jaw, her thumb pressed into her skin, and pried her mouth open without ceremony or comment. A crowd of vague, human shapes rushed past them. Imogen yanked the stopper of a vial with her teeth and shoved it between Maeve's lips. Maeve flailed. An icy sensation spread throughout her chest.

"I'm sorry, my love." Her thumb caressed beneath Maeve's eye. "I thought Juno's magic would've fought it off."

"It hasn't returned." Maeve flinched. Her admission was an open wound flushed with salt water. She tore her gaze from Imogen's bewildered expression. Her breath lodged in her throat. *Has Cara attacked the guild?* A horde of a hundred or more shambling, gaunt creatures spilled from the guild hall's broken windows.

"Don't worry," Imogen said, "they won't hurt you."

Their empty eye sockets radiated an eerie purple light, and it moved like mist when they turned their heads. A grey creature reached and grabbed a fleeing alchemist by their hood. It pulled with wiry strength and threw the screaming alchemist onto the ground.

"No. No!" The alchemist thrashed before the creature's boot stamped onto their chest. Maeve jolted forward, but Imogen seized her forearm with her hand. The creature sank its teeth into the alchemist's shoulder. A viscous spray of blood soaked the cobblestones and over the creature's ashen face.

"Imogen!" Maeve pulled. "We have to help!"

"No." Her voice was flat and hard. "We have to go to the castle. We have to save Alistair."

A rumbling explosion trembled the stones beneath her feet. *This is the price to save Alistair?* The creatures funneled into the streets, climbing, smashing windows, and grabbing those who tried to flee. A cacophony of minor explosions vibrated through the screaming night, and flecks of ash and sparks drifted into the air. *I have to help. I'm a priestess.* Imogen's grip tightened.

"Hollows," Imogen said, her voice light as smoke, "I called them hollows. They were my patients."

Her patients? Maeve stared at Imogen, and the chaos and terror flickered in and out of her peripheral.

"I tried to pull their sickness out, but I took something else," she said, "and this is what's left." Her lips twitched downward, her hair pallid and colorless in the moonlight.

"Maeve." Her dark pupils reflected the firelight, and her grip slowly released. "Go. Save Alistair."

A beast of revulsion churned in her stomach, and she couldn't bring herself to run. *How many hollows are in Thorduun's quarter? How many are injured?* All the teachings of her grandmother and mother told her to stay. Juno's touch was needed. Juno was the herald of light and life. Even if she didn't have her power, she had herbs, knew the remedies, and could bind a wound. But, if she didn't find Alistair, then all this would be for nothing. She dug her fingers into her palms. *Who am I becoming?*

"You're staying here?" she asked.

Imogen said, "I need to, or they'll get into the rest of the city. I'll try to join you when I can."

"You control them?"

She scrunched her face. "Not all of them, no. Some recognize me, and they follow my orders." She tapped her temple with one finger. "It's like we have a bond like the mushrooms in the forests. I don't know how else to explain it."

"Then make them stop," Maeve yelled, "they're killing people."

A resonant bell pealed through the smoke-filled air.

"I'll try." She nudged Maeve. "Go! Before they close the castle gates."

The horrible, deafening chaos echoed in her skull. She ran. The hollows didn't stop her. They barely looked at her with their empty, glowing eye sockets. She couldn't tell which ones listened to Imogen and which didn't. The gates of the castle were open, and guardsmen flooded Thorduun's quarter with their drawn weapons. Everything bubbled over. Steel swords, the massive guardians, and hollows. It was a nightmare. Her shoulder collided with someone. The castle guard surged like desperate ocean waves and fought against soldiers wearing black and gold armor. *Hagken's soldiers?* Her horror grew like a festering infection. *Hagken's soldiers are here fighting Fenris'. The gates were already open.* She shoved through the bodies with tears drying on her cheeks. A red flame launched into the smoky sky, and she glanced at the crimson-hued battle.

A hollow looked at her with its jaw unhinged from its skull. The cold, purple light glowing from its eye sockets seemed to blink. The hollow lifted its bony, thin arm toward her. A sword cut through its arm, and it lay twitching on the cobblestones. Her blood iced over. *Horrors upon horrors, I've done this. This is my fault. I released them into this world. Juno, forgive me. Please, please forgive me.*

She sucked in a harsh breath, turned, and ran.

23

General Fenris' navy and silver banner snapped in the hazy wind. The meager castle guard spilled like an upset inkwell. She drew her hood over her head and pushed through the mayhem. *How many are loyal to Hagken? And how many are following the orders of General Fenris' council?* She bit the inside of her cheek and removed Imogen's map from her belt. The dungeons were below the keep. *Hagken won't execute Alistair outright, will he? Alistair is technically his heir.* She refolded the map and adjusted her scarf. Tonight, she was a thief. She would steal Alistair from Hagken and make amends for the hollows—and everything else.

The city of Pyrite devoured itself in darkened entropy. She jogged by terrified servants and panicked soldiers and empty rooms with half-eaten dinners. No one cared to stop her. The servants' pockets jingled with each step as they bolted across the carpeted floors. She stopped short and peered around the corner where two guards stood outside the dungeon stairwell. A murky wash of gravelight scintillated over their dark armor and glinted off Hagken's golden crest on their breastplates. They held halberds at a cross over the door. She clenched her fists. She didn't want to harm them, but they needed to leave their post or let her through. Imogen's words came to mind. *Act like you belong.* Maeve lowered her hood. She smothered the panic simmering in her stomach and marched forward.

She recalled Cara's imperious tone. "Move."

"Eh?" The guard on the right tilted their head. "Who're you?"

"I'm here on Cara's request, and you are wasting my time." She lifted her chin. "I need to speak to one of the prisoners."

"No entry," The left one said.

She folded her arms, and her pulse fluttered.

"Very well. I'll return to Cara and inform her that the imbeciles at the door refused me." She pulled at the memory of her first meeting with Alistair. Their confidence and ability to sharpen their smiles like a knife. She hoped her expression contained a modicum of Alistair's confidence. The guards didn't budge, but they looked warily at one another.

She turned on her heel. *Cara is the only worthwhile necromancer in Hagken's army.*

"Perhaps Cara will come to collect your bones," she said over her shoulder. Her panic bubbled into her throat. *Am I going to have to wait for Imogen?*

"Wait. You can come through," the right one said, moving his halberd aside. "Tell Mistress Duskryn that we cooperated."

Her nerves rattled against her vocal cords, and she pressed her lips into a line and hoped she looked disapproving. Her shoulders sagged after the door closed behind her. *I'm not sure what Alistair and I will do when it's time to leave. Maybe it's dark enough for them to manipulate the shadows?*

The dungeon smelled like moss and stale air. She carried one of the gravelight lanterns by the door into the chilly prison. Her queasy stomach dragged behind her like a ball and chain. Her worst fear of seeing Alistair dead on the ground flashed at the forefront of her mind each time she looked. Although several forlorn faces peered through the bars at her, none belonged to her Alistair. She followed each twist and turn until stopping at a dead-end. She pressed her palms against the stone, hoping for a secret door. Nothing gave way. *What if Imogen was wrong? What if Alistair is dead already?* She closed her eyes and pressed her forehead into the damp stone. *No.* Alistair wasn't dead. They couldn't be.

The doors above opened, and heavy metallic footfalls thumped down the stairs. Maeve extinguished the gravelight and ducked into the corner. *Janis, don't let them come this way.* The muffled voices cleared.

A smooth, charismatic voice said, "I can make you rich."

"No thanks."

"Wait. I have a daughter," the familiar voice said, "you wouldn't make her an orphan, would you? A girl needs her mother."

Two people laughed—a faint jingle of keys.

"You should've thought of that before you conspired for the crown, Brysk." The surname tugged at Maeve's mind.

"Can't blame a gal for trying, can you?" Someone grunted, and the cell door slammed shut. Maeve waited until she no longer heard footsteps before she crept through the darkness. She re-ignited her lantern, and Terrayn's surprised face greeted her behind the cold iron bars.

"High winds be praised," she said, laughing. "I never thought you'd be the one to rescue me."

"Where's Alistair?"

"Hagken's boys brought them to the throne room." Her expression darkened. "After you escaped, Cara ordered the justiciars to bring Alistair straight to Hagken. And they— well —they listened to her. It was like they were puppets on a string."

"I'm familiar with Cara's magic." Maeve's neck prickled. *And I never want to endure it again.*

She stared at the residual dirt lingering on the stones. She and Imogen could flee to Alistair's house and hope by morning that Fenris would be in the city. But to what end? Hagken infiltrated Pyrite. He was in the castle. The merchants supported him. The alchemists' were scattered. The mages were cloistered within their academy. She believed Hagken would attack Pyrite head-on, and instead, he snuck into the city like a snake and pumped venom through the streets. A nebulous plan shaped in the back of her mind. *What does Hagken want more than Pyrite?* Before the thought could expand, Terrayn cut her from her reverie.

"Are you gonna break me out or not?" The shadows of the cell cut lines onto Terra's sweaty face.

"Right, sorry." The tips of her ears burned. "Terra, this fight against Hagken isn't over. We can stop him. Where can I find you after?" *Once Alistair is safe, we'll find a way to stop him. We can force Hagken to step down.*

"Amethneas," she said, "we tried, Maeve, but we failed. Let's cut our losses and run while we still have our heads."

Maeve's anger was a wild beast running rampant through her chest.

"You didn't give up after Hagken burned your ship," Maeve said fiercely, "why are you giving up now? Isn't Pyrite your home? Don't you care about these people?"

She pressed her face against the cell door, and the metal kissed her forehead. She couldn't reign her words in. Alistair's life was at stake.

"I swore to you that I'd do everything in my power to uphold my end of our deal. If you won't stay with us..." she faltered. Alistair could flee on Terrayn's ship. They could escape. Then, she would stay in Pyrite and handle everything alongside Imogen.

"Then I have no reason to free you, Terra," she said and dropped her hands away from the bars. Terrayn stared her mouth agape with incredulity. The gravelight lantern shifted her wide violet eyes into a muddled dark gray.

"That's how Pyrite functions," Maeve continued, "it's a constant game of bartering. If you want your freedom, I require your loyalty."

"I never thought I'd live to see the day I was bribed by a Priestess of Juno." Terrayn snorted. "I thought your order believed life was sacred?"

"At this moment, Alistair's life is more precious to me." Her declaration hung in the air like a ribbon from the equinox. Terrayn regarded her with a raised eyebrow. *I don't want to lose Terrayn, but I have to be practical.* She would add it to her list of transgressions.

"I am at your service, Lady Maeve." She opened her arms and gave a dramatic and flourished bow.

"Swear it," Maeve said, "on something that matters. Swear it."

Terra's lower lip pouted, and Maeve was grateful that she was taking her threat seriously.

"I swear on *Solace* and her crew."

"Good." Her heart pounded. "Stand back." She never thought herself capable of being coldly pragmatic. Yet, she had no other choice. Alistair needed her. She removed a milk-white vial from her pouch. 'In case we run into any locked doors,' Imogen had said. She poured it onto the lock, and Terrayn's shackles, and the metal melted in cloying driblets with a sickly sweet smell. *Imogen ought to give warnings alongside her concoctions.*

"Neat trick." Terrayn cracked her knuckles. "Got anything that'll make our exit easier?"

"I think so."

They crept to the dungeon stairwell. Maeve asked what happened to the other merchants, and Terrayn explained that Cara convinced the justiciars that they weren't involved. The merchants returned to their comfy homes or extravagant ships. *How many will flee the city, and how many will stay for Hagken?* Her palms dampened. Alistair's safety came first, and everything else could wait. She stuffed the curled dark plum leaves of nighthood into the gravelight. *I hope this works.* She had never ignited nighthood with gravelight before. She set the lantern on the floor, and she and Terrayn wafted the smoke through the gap under the door.

Terrayn pinched her nostrils and asked, "How long will this take?"

"Not long." Nighthood, when smoked and inhaled, gave the recipient sluggish movements and mild drowsiness. It worked more effectively when brewed into tea, but she doubted the guards would accept a cup from her. The door swung open.

"What the—" Terrayn kicked the guard in his chest and yanked his halberd from his clumsy grasp. Maeve twisted the key on the lantern and extinguished the gravelight. Terrayn knocked the guard in the jaw with the butt of the halberd. He clattered to the floor in a tangle of limbs and black armor.

Maeve tucked further into the dungeon entryway. The second guard swung his halberd towards Terrayn. She blocked. The ring of metal vibrated through the hall. Terrayn's white teeth bared in a snarl, and her arm muscles strained as she fought with the halberd. Maeve crouched beside the unconscious guard and checked his pulse. *Alive. Good.*

"Toss me the blade at his hip," shouted Terrayn.

Maeve struggled to pull the heavy longsword free. She disliked touching it, but she wasn't going to deny Terrayn her request. She slid the blade across the floor and toward Terrayn.

Terrayn stepped on the hilt, blocked an attack, and grabbed the sword. She moved into a sideways stance. Her violet eyes brightened with exertion. She struck. The guard trapped Terrayn's longsword in the halberd's curve. He pulled forward. Terrayn's boots squeaked against marbled tiles. He rotated his halberd, but the action released her blade from his axe. Maeve's heart jumped. Terrayn's sword sliced clean through the bridge of the guard's nose.

He howled in pain. She lifted her sword overhead and smashed her pommel into his forehead. Maeve flinched when his body hit the floor. Terrayn's dark skin shone with sweat, and her dreadlocks fell in front of her face. She took the sheath and second longsword from the guard.

"Are you okay?" asked Maeve.

Terrayn brushed her locs out of her face. "Never better." She strapped both swords to her back, and their leather fastening belts criss-crossed over her heaving chest.

"Be careful, Terra." Maeve said, "Imogen—" *with my help,* "—released creatures from the guild. I don't know if they'll be hostile toward you."

"They'll meet the exciting edge of my blade if they are." She extended her hand toward Maeve. "*Solace* will be at the docks if you need her."

"Before you go, I want you to have this." Maeve removed

Imogen's device from her ear and explained how it worked. *It'll be better if Terrayn keeps it, especially if we need to use her ship to get Alistair out of Pyrite.* Terrayn curled her fingers around the invention.

"May the winds be in your favor, Lady Maeve."

The tumultuous interior had calmed since Maeve's arrival. It was eerily empty, devoid of movement and life, but she looked out a narrow window and saw torchlight in the courtyard. *They're still fighting the hollows and Hagken's forces. How many of them are from Ferne?* As much as she wished to know if the darkened shapes were her friends and neighbors, she couldn't tell. *Did we need to release the hollows? Could we have used Hagken as a distraction instead?* Maeve twisted her fingers.

What does King Hagken want more than Pyrite? A single name came to mind. *Maren.* He held onto the crazed belief that Maren's spirit was trapped inside Maeve. Her nebulous plan took shape like smoke filling a vase. She would be the bartering chip. She would barter for the safety of Pyrite, Alistair, and the release of Ferne's people. She prayed to Juno and Theadora that Hagken desired Maren more than he desired dominance over Estoria.

24

Maeve wove through the dead like Janis' thread of fate. The halls of the castle were bereft of staff, but many guards lay slain on the floor. *I wonder if any of Fenris' council survived? It seems unlikely.* Hagken slaughtered anyone who disagreed or defied him. She quelled the impulse to check if anyone was breathing. Her pace slowed when she reached the twin ivory doors that barred the throne room.

A tall silver-haired man stood with a greatsword clasped between his hands. His dark armor glistened in shiny patches of wet blood.

"Ah, there's a face I'd never forget." Calom smirked. "It's good to see you, my healer."

Her surprise waned. *Cara and Calom are never far from one another. I should be grateful that he's guarding the door and it's not his sister.* She tamed her wild heart and injected as much confidence as she could into her voice.

"I've come to speak to Hagken." There was a chance that Hagken imprisoned Alistair elsewhere. *Or he executed them.* Maeve shoved the morbid thought from her mind.

"King Hagken." He tutted, and his lips remained in a taunting half-smile. "But I know he'll be overjoyed to see you. Come along." He pushed the doors open with both hands. Maeve glanced over her shoulder toward the dead guards. *I hope Imogen is safe.*

The throne room bled dark blue, shimmering silver, and pearl white. Heavy and oversized iron sconces hung chained from the ceiling and cast shifting shadows across the massive room. The throne rested above a dais and beheld a fist-sized sapphire at the apex. A cool chill danced along Maeve's spine despite the lit braziers and sconces. She searched the room for Alistair. *They're not here.* The impassive full moonlight leaked through the stained-glass windows and painted mottled mosaics onto the marble floor. A handful of skeletal warriors surrounded Cara. Her warriors were covered in blood, and five individuals wearing extravagant clothing—Maeve assumed they were Fenris' council—were bound and gagged at Cara's feet. Hagken stood above everyone next to the throne, and the light shone against the stretched, rubbery scar on his face. This was in a hall of monsters, a place of nightmares.

"My king!" Calom dropped to his knee and laid his sword over his lap. "Maeve Theywnn has returned to us. She wishes to speak to you."

Hagken's dark eyes gleamed. "My heart yearned to see your face ever since we parted, Maeve." He gestured to the room. "As you can see, Pyrite has welcomed us with open gates and open arms. The council has agreed to relinquish the throne as long as I spare their lives."

Maeve stepped past Calom's knelt form and drew her shoulders back.

"Where's Alistair?" she asked. *Once I know Alistair is safe, I will convince Hagken to end this.*

Hagken clapped his once. "Bring them in!"

The marble floor vibrated, and several layers of the foundation withdrew like peeling layers off an onion. Maeve steadied her hands on her knees. The hole in the floor groaned with a metallic screech. Alistair's bowed head appeared as the platform raised several inches above the floor. Their dark, flamboyant makeup was smeared down their face. Their wrists and ankles were clasped in shackles and chained to the platform. Maeve stifled her gasp with her hand, and emotion strangled her throat. Momentarily, her terror and guilt faded, and relief and longing took over. She wouldn't have known what to do if she was too late.

"Alistair Jas'dune," Hagken's voice boomed, "you stand accused of treason and conspiracy. You are a child cut from my own cloth even though you aren't born from me."

"That's it?" Alistair grinned and glanced slyly at Maeve. "No charges for theft?"

Hagken scoffed. His contempt thickened the chilly air with malice and disdain. *Oh, Alistair, for once in your life, could you take something seriously?* Maeve turned to the platform. Her shoulder and wrist jerked back. *Wha—* She met Calom's wintry, silver eyes. He shook his head and held her wrist in his hand.

"I was a fool," Hagken said, "I should've killed you after Maren died."

"Those are bold words, considering you couldn't manage to arrest or kill any of the others conspiring against you," said Alistair.

One of Cara's skeletal warriors drew their short bow from their back and aimed it at Alistair. Hagken raised his hand. Cara didn't look up from cleaning her nails, but the warrior lowered its bow. *I need to do something before this escalates.* Alistair remained faithful and loyal to her since the beginning. They could've fled, but they chose to stay. They had no ties to Ferne, and yet they were willing to face an executioner for them. For *her.*

Hagken said, "Do you deny it? Did you come here to claim for Pyrite yourself?"

"I'm sure I'd make a better ruler than you." Alistair shrugged, and their chains clinked together.

The ringing *'shrrk'* of naked steel resonated as Cara's warriors and Hagken's guard drew their swords. Maeve studied the chains. She couldn't melt their shackles using Imogen's vial without drawing attention to herself. *Diplomacy it is.*

"They didn't come here for the throne," Maeve interjected, "they came here because I asked them to."

Hagken stepped from the raised dais, and his guard drew closer.

He said "I will give you the throne, Maeve. I will give you Pyrite and every other city and hovel in Estoria. We will finish our legacy."

"Second time's the charm," Alistair said, pulling forward, "Maren never wanted this. And you never could save her, Marcus. My mother was dead years before the void whisperers performed her final rites. Spirit magic won't bring her back, and even if she did return"— Alistair's blue eyes shone bright—"she would throw herself from the cliffs before she allowed herself to be tied to **you** again."

"Enough," Hagken shouted. *Alistair is goading him! What in Juno's name are they doing!?* She recalled Hagken's temper nearly killing Calom. *I need to stop this.* She pulled against Calom's relentless hold.

"Alistair, stop!" Calom's hand clamped over her mouth.

"This is not Theadora's temple, my healer," he whispered. "There are no objections."

"You were chased out of Pyrite. Overthrown. No one wants you as king. Maren didn't want you as her husband," Alistair said sharply. They opened their arms as wide as the chains would allow. "I am the consequence of your incompetence, Marcus."

Hagken's scarred upper lip curled. "You are a threat to my reign."

"Aww." Alistair placed their hand over their heart. "That's cute. But anyone with a modicum of sense is a threat to your reign. I could kill your warriors and Cara's pets with one hand tied behind my back."

Hagken's guard standing behind Cara's skeletons stepped backward. Calom released Maeve and pulled his greatsword free. The massive blade rippled in the pale light. He approached Alistair and widened his stance. Maeve scrambled onto the platform and wrapped her arms around Alistair's midsection. *I should be able to melt the chains, but it's going to take time.* Alistair didn't look at her. They stared down Calom and Hagken with their expression as sharp and cold as granite.

"What is your command, my king?" Calom asked.

"They are guilty of all charges. As Ruler of the Gilded Kingdom and Sworn Protector of Pyrite, you leave me no choice." Maeve's heart lurched into her throat.

"I demand a warrior's death by combat." Alistair lifted their chin.

Hagken laughed. An abrasive sound. "You are no warrior, shadow general." He nodded to Calom. "Strike true, my boy."

Hagken's gaze slithered to Maeve. *He won't hurt me. Alistair is safe as long as I hold onto them.* Her knees wobbled. *Juno, protect us!* Her goddess didn't reply, and Maeve clung to Alistair. *Fine. I'll defend them with my body. I'll give my life if I must.*

"Hello sunshine," Alistair whispered, "Janis is waiting for me, but my heart soars to see your face beforehand."

"Don't say that." Her eyes prickled with tears. "You're not going to die."

They pressed their cheek to the top of Maeve's head. "You're resilient as always, darling."

"Cara." Hagken tapped his ring-adorned finger against his chin. "Please help Maeve to safety."

Cara stepped onto the platform. Maeve's body stiffened, and her arms tightened around Alistair. She desperately wished she had Juno's light to protect them. *What is she going to do?* Cara removed her fingerless gloves and tucked them into her pocket. Her green eyes fell upon Maeve and studied her like an insect beneath one of Imogen's apparatuses. *She's a spirit mage. She's more dangerous than her brother with a blade.* Cara removed a needle-thin blade disguised as a hairpin from behind her ear and pricked her fingertip. She wiped the blood across the platform in an intricate and angular shape. Maeve shivered. Cara's magic was a painful, sharp frost that burrowed into her bone marrow and numbed her skin. Cara bled and drew the symbol over and over again before approaching Maeve.

"Don't touch her," Alistair said.

Cara clenched her jaw. "You aren't in a position to threaten me."

Cara's fingertips stroked Maeve's jaw, and Maeve jerked her head away.

"Hagken, I'll join you. I'll help you bring Maren back." Maeve's voice trembled. Her attention remained on Cara, but Hagken shifted from the corner of her eyes.

"I know you will. It is our destiny to be reunited."

Cara's fingertips glistened with Maeve's sweat. "This'll do."

Maeve barely heard her over the drumbeat of her racing heart. Cara brought her fingertips to her lips, her eyes flashed lilac, and she blew a puff of air onto her index and middle fingers. A thunderous force knocked Maeve's arms away from Alistair. She screamed. Her spine and hips slammed onto the hard marble floor, and the pain launched stars into her vision.

"Cara!" Hagken scolded.

"You said 'to safety'. Should I have laid a few pillows down beforehand?"

Maeve pushed herself onto her hands and knees. *At least that proved my theory that Hagken needs me alive.* Cara kicked Alistair's legs out from beneath them and forced them to kneel. Calom lifted his sword. *Alistair!* Everything narrowed into this singular, terrifying second. *Hagken needs me alive...he needs me alive.* She ran forward and threw herself between Calom's blade and Alistair's body. Calom cursed and stopped his downward swing. She held her arms open and met Hagken's enraged expression.

"If you execute Alistair, I will burn my body and spirit before you ever have the chance to reunite with Maren," she said, "I will ruin your destiny. I will melt your crown and throne. I swear it as a divine priestess of Juno." A deafening silence fell over the throne room.

"My king," Cara said, "the ritual will fail if we don't have a body."

I don't like the sound of that.

"I know." Hagken paced between the dais stairs and the raised platform. Calom's blade remained level at Maeve's heart, and his stormy eyes glared at Alistair.

"Release Alistair," Maeve demanded, "as well as anyone else in your army who you bribed or bullied into fighting for you."

"No." Hagken whirled on her. "You ask far, far too much." He shook his head like a beast shaking water from its fur. "No. No. No.

We do the ritual now. Now!"

Calom lowered his sword. Cara's skeletons, who carried the prone and bound council members, formed a half-circle around her. Cara brought her palms together, her voice low and undulating, and her eyes rolled back into her skull. The council members thrashed and convulsed. Their skin sloughed from their bones in slimy chunks. The veins within the marble floor emanated lavender light, and a multi-layered glyph expanded from Cara's feet. Maeve's courage faltered in response to the low, throbbing fear bubbling inside her stomach.

"Let Alistair go," Maeve shouted, "or I'll burn this palace to the ground." She wouldn't – couldn't. The people of Ferne could be within these walls, and she would never sacrifice them.

"I carry her ashes with me. We have bodies." Hagken muttered while rubbing his hands with gray ash. "The moon is full. We have all we need."

He pressed his ash-covered palms onto the floor, and the magical lines erupted in black flames and encircled Alistair, Maeve, and Hagken. He lifted his eyes from the floor and stared wetly at Maeve.

"Together, Maren. Together at last."

Squelch. The organs fell out of the council members' open chest cavities and landed like wet red slugs onto the floor and were consumed by the black flames. Maeve backpedaled onto the raised platform. Her palms slipped against the heavy chains.

"I can melt them. Imogen gave me..." she said around a choked sob, "hold on."

A shackle fell to the floor with a resonant thud. Maeve's hands dropped from the second shackle as Cara's spirit magic grabbed her upper limbs. Her shoulders spasmed. *Juno above and Janis below; this can't be how it ends.* She pressed her forehead into Alistair's shoulder and inhaled. They smelled like leather and old books and salt. *Three more shackles. I can do this.* Her twitching fingers curled around the second vial, and the liquid hissed through the metal. Her vision doubled. *Two more, two more.* Her rapid breath drowned out the sound of Hagken and Cara muttering incantations behind her.

The doors blew apart and launched ivory and debris into the throne room. Maeve's head jerked toward the sound and beheld the glorious sight of Imogen leading her shambling and terrifying hollows. Alistair inhaled sharply, and Maeve wanted to weep in relief. *She's here. Thank the light.* Maeve dropped to her knees to release Alistair's ankles from the platform.

Imogen made a face as if she tasted something sour. "It smells like something died in here."

"To arms," Calom roared, "don't let them disrupt the ritual!"

The hollows clashed with the living. They snarled. Their rotten fingers scrambled for purchase on the guard's sleek dark armor. Calom swung his greatsword, and it rendered flesh from bone with a sickening, dry, and crunchy sound. Imogen box-jumped onto the platform and gripped Maeve's shoulder. The hollows encircled them. *I never thought I'd feel safe surrounded by a hoard of strange creatures.*

"Imogen, we have to stop Hagken and Cara," said Maeve.

Maeve's fingers wouldn't bend. A hollow on the ground was separated by its spine, and it rolled onto its stomach and crawled toward its lower half. The hollow reattached itself with a heaving gasp. Its bones and skin snapped and fused back together. *They can't die? Maybe they'll be powerful enough to stop Cara's personal guard.* Alistair crouched and held Maeve steady. *We're together. The three of us can do anything together.* A hollow lunged at Cara. Her skeletal guard's blade sliced through the hollows' wrist. Its hand clattered to the marble like dice knocking together in a gambler's cup. Imogen poured the white liquid onto the final chain and passed Alistair one of their throwing daggers.

"Gods above and below." Alistair breathed. "I always feel much safer with steel in hand."

We did it. Imogen smiled at Maeve. A thing of beauty amidst the carnage. Her hollows advanced upon Hagken, who shielded himself behind Calom. Cara stood her ground and met Maeve's eyes over the unruly thrash and pull of bodies and swords. The pulsing, painful paralysis of Cara's magic started to fade, and Maeve's limbs tingled. *She can't focus on the ritual when her life is in danger.* Maeve looked behind her. Another handful of Imogen's hollows crossed the destroyed threshold with bloodied jaws. Alistair moved like liquid smoke surrounded by shadow. Their strikes were lethal and precise. They could win. Three of Imogen's hollows dog-piled onto one of Hagken's guards. Together, they could push Hagken back and force him to surrender.

Thwump.

"Imogen!" Alistair's panic sliced through Maeve's hopeful heart. She spun. Imogen made a strange gurgling sound. A crossbow bolt protruded from her freckled chest. Her white shirt blossomed violent crimson. Her hollows screeched and buzzed like a kicked hornet's nest, and their attacks grew furious and wild. Imogen fell backward onto the platform. *No, no, no!* Maeve placed her hands over the wound. Imogen's blood seeped through the gaps between Maeve's fingers and streamlined down her wrists. Alistair manifested within a plume of shadows beside her and held their bloodied dagger at the ready.

"No, no, no, no. P-please." She wrapped her blood-slick fingers around the crossbow bolt. Once it was removed, then she could heal it. She would save her. *You won't die, Imogen. I promise.* She yanked the bolt free. A spurt of blood erupted from Imogen's chest. *Please. Please, Juno, I need a miracle.* If there were ever a time for her goddess to return, it would be at this moment, with Imogen's hot blood oozing through her fingers. She applied pressure to the wound. *I'm not letting you die.* Her vision of her future alongside Alistair and Imogen was slipping from her grasp, and she was powerless to stop it. To stop any of it. Hagken would win. He'd take the city, take her, and complete his ritual. How did it all go wrong so quickly?

"Don't go, don't go, don't leave me," Maeve babbled, "please." The blood gushed from the wound, and Maeve's vision turned fuzzy and gray. Their time together was too short. She wanted more. More dances, more of Imogen's rambles, more of her brilliance, and her humor and creativity. She wanted a lifetime. Imogen's warm eyes stared listless and empty at the high ceiling above.

"She's with Janis now," Cara said, "even divine magic can't heal a fatal blow. Everyone knows that." Her tone was insufferably mocking.

"No!" Maeve screamed. She pulled at the empty wellspring of power inside her. Juno's familiar and comforting light was as cold and absent as an unlit hearth. A strand of blonde hair stuck to Imogen's oil-smudged cheek, and Maeve wanted to brush it aside. *If I stop the bleeding, then I save her.* Imogen's hollows formed a shambling and lopsided circle around the platform. Maeve hoped that meant her spirit hadn't joined Janis' web. *She said she had a connection to the hollows. She's here. She has to be.* Calom cleaved a break in the chain of hollows, and Hagken stepped closer.

"Don't try it," Alistair snarled, "if you come near her, I'll slit your throat and enjoy it."

"We must complete the ritual," Hagken said, "step aside, my

child."

"No." Alistair's tone was corrosive.

Juno. Maeve prayed fiercely, *you are the Goddess of Life. Please.* Imogen's wound wept into her hands. *I cannot endure a life without Imogen. I won't.* Juno would help her. Juno would save Imogen. Her connection must return. It had to. It needed to. Juno wouldn't abandon her at a time like this. Maeve's wailing cries were carved from her chest. Her shaking, bloodied fingers reached into her pocket and pulled the sunstone free. *I never attuned to it.*

She pressed the sunstone against Imogen's wound. *Imogen told me the stones functioned as a pair. They need one another.* And the textbook said the stones were pieces of the goddesses themselves. *And now, this is the only piece of Juno I have left.* She bowed her head to Imogen's ashen face and pressed her lips to hers. *Juno, if you're listening, then please bring her back. Return her to me. It's all I'll ever ask of you. Please. I'll give* anything *to have her back.*

The sunstone pulsed. Her throat seized. A golden light scintillated beneath her hands. Maeve was used to feeling Juno's presence through her veins, but she hadn't been an observer of Juno's light in many years. Her sense of awe opened like a flower in her chest. The sunstone sparkled with flashes of red and white gold and grew hot beneath her hands. The hollows screeched, and the frequency shattered the windows and propelled shards of glass across the room.

"What is she doing?" Hagken yelled, "Stop her!"

A dome of protective light surrounded them and fluttered like the dying heart of a rabbit. Her hope swelled. The room burned with iridescent light. Imogen's pupils dilated into pinpricks of blackness within a field of gold. The light raptured. It wrapped them in a radiant embrace. Her tears evaporated to steam on her cheeks. The fires swelled in gusts of hot air and leviathan flame but didn't burn them. The sunstone burned, and Maeve was forced to pull her hands away. *I think it's working.* She tenderly held Imogen's face between her hands.

"Come back, my love. Alistair and I are waiting for you," she whispered.

The sunstone embedded into Imogen's wound pulsed before shattering and releasing a storm of radiant light.

Imogen gasped, choking, and arched her back. Her cool metal fingers clenched around Maeve's nape in reverent desperation. She kissed Maeve and laughed wetly against her lips. *I did it. She's alive.* Maeve leaned back. The hollows crowded Cara. Their papery skin rustled as they advanced with renewed vigor. Calom barreled forward and blocked an oncoming attack meant for his sister. *We're going to fight endlessly if I don't end this.*

"Hagken." Maeve's knees shook when she stood. "You need me for your ritual, but I need them. You've witnessed the depth of Juno's divine power. If you don't let us go, then I will destroy everything you've built."

Another empty threat. *Solace is at the docks waiting for us. I can buy them time to reach Terrayn. Then, I'll negotiate for the release of Ferne and everyone else. Hagken was a merchant before he was king.* The flaw in her plan was how she might overpower Hagken before he completed the ritual and destroyed her. *Alistair said he couldn't be killed.* She locked eyes with Cara. *If anyone knows about death-defying magic, it's her.*

"Maeve." He looked disappointed. The moonstone around his throat glowed in pale blue light. *I wonder if using the sunstone affected his moonstone.* "I don't need your compliance to complete the ritual."

His fists dripped with black ooze. A terrifying, sickening scent of rot and wet clay filled her nostrils. The lights in the room vanished, and Maeve shoved her partners from the platform.

"Run," she said, and her weak knees crumpled beneath her. A shock wave of pain pulsed across her joints. Alistair pulled her upright. The putrid vapor rolled toward them in plumes of greenish, gray clouds.

"The docks, Terrayn'll be—" she wheezed. "Take Imogen."

Alistair grabbed Imogen's arm and vanished in a swirling mist of shadows. The hollows were unaffected by the vapors swirling into their mouths and eye sockets and dutifully followed their maker. Her throat burned. Her eyes watered. Imogen and Alistair reappeared at the threshold of the throne room. *We'll make it.* As she ran, she reached for Juno to heal the corruption burning through her lungs. *I don't have her. The sunstone brought Imogen back, but it didn't reconnect me to Juno.* She stumbled. An interlocked web of glyphs manifested in front of Maeve, and her body slammed into it. The painful electric sensation traveled from the tips of her fingers to her toes. *Caught like a fish in a net.* Alistair and Imogen stood on the opposite side of the net. Imogen cried her name, and she reached out to Maeve, but Alistair grabbed her around the waist.

"We have to go, Imogen." They disappeared together in a twisting warp of shadow, and Maeve's world plunged into darkness like a knife between her ribs.

25

Maeve jolted upright, surrounded by evergreen bed sheets. Her vision swam, and her dry, crusty lips smacked together. She threw her wobbly legs over the side of the bed and stumbled to the mirror above the washing basin. *Juno above, I've seen better days, haven't I?* She splashed cold water over her face and nape. *Hagken captured me again, but at least Imogen and Alistair are safe*; she swallowed. *I hope.* Her tears pricked at the back of her eyelids like a thousand tiny needles. She couldn't allow herself the luxury of tears.

The people of Pyrite were in danger. Her partners were in danger. She gripped the edge of the water basin. Her vision snagged onto the opalescent ring from Imogen. *Gods above, please be safe.* She shattered the sunstone to return Imogen from Janis' grasp. Could she have used it to reconnect with Juno? Maybe. But she'd rather have Imogen. She rinsed her mouth before focusing on the room. *I need to figure out an escape plan.* She wasn't surprised to discover her supplies were taken alongside the map of the castle. *Great.* She'd have to find another way to escape. She wouldn't be able to use nighthood to sedate guards or heimenta for a bolster of strength.

A chandelier filled with glittering diamonds hung from the exposed wooden beams and bathed the room in tiny, swaying rainbows. The window locks jiggled beneath her hand, and it was too high to consider leaping. Her eyes tracked the columns of smoke pluming from the city into the night sky. How much destruction would Hagken cultivate? Would he ever be satisfied? Or was he content to govern a city of ashes? She paced. The absence of Imogen and Alistair was profound. She was trapped in a cycle of saving them and losing them, and it wrung her heart dry. Her isolation was acute and torturous and compounded by her lack of knowledge. She searched the room. No blank paper for messages. No sharp objects. Nothing she could use. She tried digging at the window latch with her amulet, but her efforts were wasted.

The door creaked, and Cara slipped inside, flanked by two soldiers. She cocked her hip against the empty writing desk.

"Have a nice nap?" asked Cara, and Maeve looked away. *Is she here to gloat?* "Okay, maybe I deserve the silent treatment after our little spat, but we could be friends, Maeve." She moved into Maeve's line of sight.

Maeve replied, "I don't think you know the meaning of the word. You—"

"Fine," she interrupted, "not friends. But you are special, Maeve. We need you."

"I'm not a vessel for Maren's spirit."

"I disagree." Cara flipped her braid over her shoulder. "The ritual text said the spirit of the deceased would return in a vessel of light and reunite with its maker during the sickle moon."

I won't convince Cara or Hagken—they're both deranged. She thought Cara was more sensible than the king, but this conversation proved otherwise. *And after everything I've done, I'm hardly a vessel of light.*

"Hagken is empowered by ancient magic. Juno had her champions of the past, and the scorned gods have their champions today." Cara said, a line forming between her thin eyebrows. "Save yourself some pain, priestess, and follow his orders."

Ancient magic? Scorned gods? She can't mean the betrayers, can she? When the gods walked Calorum, two other gods ruled alongside Juno, Janis, and Theadora. They were known as Ophelia, the goddess of wilderness, and Oberon, the first god of magic. But when they attempted to overthrow the pantheon, they were banished. *If Hagken worships the betrayers, then he'll never stop.* He would kill or curse whoever he needed to continue his conquest. She didn't know the betrayers could grant magic. *There is so much of this world I don't know.*

"And what are his orders? Take part in his ritual and sacrifice myself for his selfish and impossible goal?"

"Not tonight, no." Cara made a frustrated noise at the back of her throat. "We missed our cosmic alignment. We have to wait for the next full moon."

Sorry for the inconvenience, thought Maeve while crossing her arms.

"Besides, you have to get ready for dinner."

"Half the city is on fire, and he's worried about dinner?" she balked.

Wasn't Hagken worried about traitors? He killed Fenris' council in an elaborate spirit magic ritual and slaughtered the town guard. *How arrogant can one man be? Does he honestly believe he's untouchable?* This could be her chance to escape. She glanced at the guards at the door. *I could run. I'll reunite with Imogen and Alistair. We'll come up with another plan.*

"I assume you want Ferne's population alive." Cara took a swath of vermilion fabric from a guard and laid it on the bed. The dress was embroidered with teardrop rubies, golden accents and trim, and brown lace adorned the bodice. Maeve didn't want to ask where Hagken got it from. "So that means you'll join him and play nice."

"I'm sorry?"

Her smile lifted one corner of her mouth. "Did you think we left everyone at Hollyhock?"

Maeve stepped into Cara's personal space. "Where are they?" What had Hagken done with them? Were they safe? Her shoulders shook. *The children. He can't have children fighting for him, right?*

"All over. Kitchens, guard towers, although we probably lost a few — I don't know — dozen? A hundred?" Cara pursed her lips. "It's so hard to remember. They're so insignificant in the grand scheme of —"

Maeve's open palm trembled in the air next to Cara's reddened cheek, and her rapid breath stuttered in her throat. Cara's eyes slowly cut to Maeve's face, and her haughty expression sharpened. *Goddess above, what have I done?* Maeve withdrew her hand and clenched it against her chest. *I'm a sworn priestess of Juno. I shouldn't harm anyone.* Maeve tore her gaze away from Cara, ashamed.

"Hagken wants you there." Cara grabbed Maeve's chin and forced her to make eye contact. "You're his guest of honor."

Maeve's cheeks burned.

"A dead body is a resource to me, Maeve," she seethed. "Behave, or I'll send the corpses of children to come and collect you."

* * *

It took an hour before anyone came to collect Maeve for dinner. She refused to wear the dress on principal. Hagken would have to content himself with her bloodied clothes and gnarled hair, for she would never indulge his fantasies. She expected a large dining hall, like the one at Hollyhock, but Maeve was escorted into a private dining room. The room was washed out with neutral colors of beige and gray. Even the small portraits of Pyrite's docks were subdued and understated. *I don't like how small this is. It feels too...cozy.* The rectangular table sat four chairs, though only two spots were set. Hagken smiled when she entered, and she reluctantly sat in the chair opposite him. The candlelight wavered. Maeve glanced at the cutlery while laying the cloth napkin on her lap. *Could I sneak a knife out of here?* She would never use it on anyone, but she was starting to understand why Alistair felt safer with something sharp nearby.

"Do you not like the color red?" Hagken asked, "I thought it would suit you."

"I like my own clothes." Maeve said, "Thanks."

Hagken's nostrils flared. *He seems more in control than he was in the throne room.* She twisted her ring. *But that doesn't make him any less dangerous.* She didn't know if his magic granted to him by the betrayer gods drained him as Juno's magic did to her. He looked healthy enough, she supposed. His eyes were clear. His ring-adorned hands didn't tremble when he lifted the stem of his glass and took a reserved sip of wine. A server placed a bowl of fish head soup in front of Maeve, and its glassy eye stared up at her. *What am I doing?* She swirled her spoon through the pale broth.

"Where's everyone from Ferne?"

"Here and there." Hagken dabbed his lips with his napkin. "We have time until the cosmos align; you may run into an old friend or two."

Her heart galloped at the idea of seeing anyone from home, but she quieted her excitement. She'd rather see them free, safe in Silvercliff, or back at Ferne than trapped behind the castle walls with her.

"I've spent quite a bit of time with your people," he said, surprising her, "oh, the tales they wove about your generosity and kindness. They could hardly believe you did this." He pointed to his burned face, and Maeve's shoulders tensed.

She opened her mouth to apologize, but the words wouldn't come. She shoved soup into her mouth. She was sorry she abused Juno's power and used it for violence, but she wasn't remorseful about burning him. He manipulated Alistair. He worshiped the betrayers. He tried to kill Imogen.

"We both want something from one another," said Maeve. "You want me for your ritual, and I want my people freed. You've got Pyrite. You can let them go."

"I want my empire, Maeve, and for that, I'm going to need bodies." Hagken's dark eyes glimmered.

Not soldiers. Bodies. Maeve's spoon clattered against her bowl. *A dead body is a resource to Cara. Is the true same for Hagken?* She tried to quell the rushing sensation in her stomach before she lost its contents.

"Release the children."

He laughed. Her unfinished bowl of soup was removed and replaced with a pile of steaming crab legs and garnished with herbs.

"Why should I?" Hagken noisily sucked the meat from the crab leg. "Children are an excellent resource in war. They're small and quick, and their minds are so...malleable."

"You need me alive, Hagken." She glanced at the candles. "I'll use Juno's light to burn myself alive before the full moon."

She didn't want to die. She wanted more than anything to live and experience a life with Imogen and Alistair. But her life compared to the several hundred from Ferne? There was no question. She would die for them if she must. Hagken tossed the empty crab leg onto the floor and wiped the juice from his lips. His silence gnawed at Maeve's nerves. She willed her hands not to shake as she reached across the table to grab a piece of warm bread.

"You are as stubborn as my Maren." He leaned back and interlaced his fingers, his head tilted slightly to the side as he peered at her. "I will give you one for each day of good behavior leading up to the full moon."

"No." She shook her head. "That's too few." Ferne's populace had more than thirty children.

"I am being generous." His dark eyes narrowed. "And you seem to forget who I am. I have alchemists who could put you into a living sleep. I could command Cara to trap you, curse you. Gods below, she could sever your connection to Juno if I willed it." His voice raised, and Maeve's spine pushed into the stiff wooden back of her chair.

"I am indulging your pathetic demands because it amuses me." He cracked a crab leg between his hands, and Maeve flinched at the sound. "It amuses me to see you pretend like you're more than a healer from a village no one cares about, and no one will remember when I rewrite the maps of Estoria."

She clenched her fists beneath the table. Her mother told her anger wasn't helpful, and it had no place in her life as a priestess. *Stay calm, Maeve. Stay calm.* She didn't want him to know how his words affected her. Her calmness was her strength. No matter what happened, whether it was broken bones or head injuries, she was as unshakable as a great tree sprawling through the forest. *Mother said our emotions are tied to our relationship with Juno. I can't lose sight of that either. If I'm going to have any hope of Juno's light returning, then I need to be more dedicated than ever.*

"In a few days, we're going to have a celebration." He acted as if his outburst never occurred. "I expect you to wear what I give you."

She whispered, "And if I don't?"

"Then I'll be upset." He laid his hands flat on the table and said, "And I cannot imagine what fate might befall some of the children of Ferne if I'm upset."

Thirty. She would save thirty of Ferne's youngest and most vulnerable if she behaved. She had less than thirty days to stop Hagken and his ritual to kill her or escape and reunite with her partners. *There is a chance,* she thought, *as small and stupid as it may be, that Alistair and Imogen didn't flee on Terrayn's ship.* But Maeve didn't want them to risk themselves to save her. She would do as Hagken asked of her. She would save thirty of Ferne's children. And she would pray that Juno would offer salvation from this darkness.

26

Maeve rubbed her sore, tired eyes with her fists. She woke at dawn to pray to Juno, but it was nearly midday now, and her connection hadn't returned. *What am I doing?* She pinched the bridge of her nose. *Did using the sunstone sever my connection to Juno?* That sounded unlikely but not impossible. *I can realign to it. I have to try harder and focus on the positives.* She hadn't seen Hagken. He didn't visit her room or force her to eat breakfast with him. But she didn't know when he'd release a child. In the evening? Every dawn? She stared out the window of her comfortable prison. She wished she had a view of the courtyard or the stables. She would have a better understanding of the climate of Pyrite and Hagken's occupation. Unfortunately, her window faced the walls and gifted her a slice of the sea. *Positives,* she reminded herself. She lifted her amulet from inside her bodice and watched the play of light across the shiny surface.

Hagken's guard came to collect her. They informed her that

Mistress Duskryn demanded her presence but said nothing more. Maeve ascended the tight circular steps of a tower and tucked her hands under her arms. The air sank cold fingers beneath the fabric of her green dress. *It shouldn't be this cold.* Maeve found herself in Cara's study. The small windows and hardwood floors glowed with painted angular shapes. A chained sconce of gravelight hung from the ceiling and cast long shadows over piles of books and shelves lined with jars of red and white liquids.

Cara dug through an open wooden crate and lifted a femur bone from the pile within. She said, "How do you feel about taking part in a little experiment, Maeve?"

"Bad."

"Well." She opened her spell book. "I'm afraid you don't have a choice in the matter. Sit down."

Maeve comforted herself with the knowledge that Cara couldn't kill her. Hagken threatened her last night, but the truth remained. They needed her alive and her body whole to complete their ritual.

"What're we doing?"

"Your body is a vessel for Maren's spirit." Cara laid out several bones in front of her. "I want to see if we can pull Maren's spirit out and place it in another vessel." She placed a palm-sized urn etched with runic markings onto the floor. "And then you're no longer a part of the problem."

Maeve asked, "And what happens to me afterward?"

"Don't know and don't care." She shrugged.

"Does Hagken know you're doing this?" If Cara's experiment failed and killed her, then Hagken wouldn't be happy, and Maeve's chance at freeing Ferne would evaporate into dust and ash. She wiped her damp palms on her skirt.

"He knows." Cara's emerald eyes were as sharp as glass. "No need to look so worried, Lady Maeve." She waved her shapely, pale fingers across the bones. The gravelight flickered above their heads.

"I am the best spirit mage in Calorum."

Cara's magic was unlike Hagken's rotten magic. Her magic was biting cold and serrated. Its sharpness dug into the meat of Maeve's bones. A lavender tint overtook the whites of Cara's eyes. Maeve thought of bolting and running down the stairs. But to what end? Hagken knew about the experiment. *He'll punish Ferne's children if I run.* The veins under Cara's skin glowed white and sprawled across her face and throat like roots seeking water. Maeve flinched as the laid-out bones started to disintegrate. *Her magic is an aberration against Juno.* The chips of bone rotated and swirled around them. A foreboding sense of anticipation clawed into Maeve's skull. *Maybe her spell isn't working.* Maeve didn't feel any different. *It's not working because I'm not carrying Maren's spirit.* She squeezed her chilly fingers together.

"Maren Hagken," Cara said, "arise." The swirling bone chips congealed into a shape reminiscent of arrows. Maeve looked around the room and half-expected Maren's spirit to manifest before her. Cara lifted her hand. Her unfocused eyes were on Maeve. The chains groaned overhead as the gravelight swung back and forth.

"Cara, it's not working."

Cara smiled. "Oh, it is." The light overwhelmed Cara's irises, and Maeve thought of Imogen's hollows. Her breath misted in front of her face. Her limbs wouldn't move. The clawing sharpness of Cara's magic dug into her skin, her muscles, and organs. Maeve would've cried out if her vocal cords weren't frozen to her throat. *Juno! Juno! Juno!* Maeve screamed in her head, desperate. *Juno, please!* She called to her, her goddess, full of warmth and light and peace. The golden light of magic remained desolate and empty with a lingering painful and sharp realization of abandonment. The magic pushed into her ears and her nostrils and latched into her mind. *No, no, no, no!*

An inky void of darkness closed like a steel trap around her.

* * *

There was no light within the void. She rolled her shoulders and tried to relax her quivering, anxious muscles. *Did Cara's experiment fail? Am I dead?* She didn't *feel* dead. Although, she didn't know what death felt like. She tilted her head and tried to ascertain her surroundings. *Nothing, nothing, and more, nothing.* Her under-stimulated mind pulled from the present and flashed memories of Alistair and Imogen like fireworks. She pulled herself back and inhaled. *You don't breathe when you're dead.*

"Dark womb. A place of entropy and transcendence." The voices flooded from each direction as if they stood around Maeve at every angle. "You were a priestess of Juno."

"I am a priestess," Maeve corrected, proud. Even if Juno wasn't responding, she remained a priestess of life and light. *Okay. I'm not dead, and there's a voice talking to me.* It couldn't be Maren, could it?

"Call to Juno."

She searched for the warm, bubbly energy contained in her stomach or at the base of her spine. It was like trying to pull water from misty air. Insubstantial. Frustrating. She bit down, her teeth digging into the fleshy meat of her lower lip. *Juno answer me!* But this was a place of shadow and ice, the air musty, a blurred line between life and decay. *This isn't Juno's realm. I don't even know if this is Janis'.* She dug around her chest cavity like a novice healer and wanted to scream at the emptiness she found between her ribs.

"You have rage," the voice sprawled akin to lichen.

"I don't," Maeve said. "I'm not angry."

A tingling heat flushed along the back of her neck. *I'm not angry.*

Frustrated, maybe. But like a valve, she could tamper it, close it, and bury it. *Mother said anger wasn't becoming of a priestess of Juno. We're the lighthouse in the storm; we're beacons of hope and tranquility within our communities.* She frowned, remembering her conversation with Cara. How was this part of Cara's ritual? She scrambled across the twisted and gnarled roots of her spine for a golden echo of Juno's magic, and her forehead moistened with sweat.

"Why do you reject parts of yourself? Doesn't anger burn like Juno's light?" The voice sounded like a key sliding into a lock. "Did Juno not rage when her sister was struck by the betrayer Ophelia?"

"I know the myths," Maeve hissed between her teeth.

"You've read the myths. There is a difference between reading and knowing."

"I'm not angry." It sounded hollow to her ears. "I'm fine."

She shouldered the weight of her responsibilities and smiled because that's who she was—who she was raised to be. *Is this Cara?* It didn't sound like her. It lacked the haughtiness in Cara's tone. *Then who is talking riddles and insinuating they know my feelings?*

"Janis sees all, Maeve. She keeps our secrets. We know what happened within the walls of Pyrite, the walls of Hollyhock, the walls of your cabin." A cold breath tickled the side of her sweaty cheek. "Imogen used you to release her hollows."

Was she somewhere in Janis' domain? Not dead, but not fully alive either?

Maeve stiffened. "She didn't use me." *Alistair's life was in danger.*

"You do not regret releasing those creatures into Pyrite."

"Of course I regret it," she shouted, her voice echoing, "people were hurt." Her skin flared with warmth, and she strangled it back. She wouldn't give in. She wouldn't let this disembodied voice in the darkness goad her. "Imogen could've been more forthcoming, yes, but she was doing what she thought was right. We both were. We had to save Alistair."

"Do you forgive her?"

"I —it's complicated." Did she forgive Imogen? She hardly had time to think about it, and they didn't have time for a conversation before Hagken tried to kill them. "How is this relevant?"

"Who left you before Juno did?" A set of bony fingers dug into her shoulder, but the sensation disappeared when Maeve jerked away. "Who was the first?"

"No one." The words clung to her throat. She recalled her grandmother's wrinkled, knotted hands chopping herbs. Her mother, her mother...Maeve thrashed her head to the side, tucking her face into her shoulder, and her face crumpled. *No. No.* She did what she had to. She chose the faithful path. She didn't weep for her then, and she wouldn't weep for her now.

"Where did she go?"

"What?"

"You told Alistair," the trio of voices merged into one, "we will hear it now."

It had been a lifetime ago when she mentioned her mother's pilgrimage. '*You are old enough to look after the village,*' her mother said after Maeve's twenty-first birthday. Cait draped her amulet of Juno over Maeve's head, said she loved her and left. *It's been six years.* She hated this memory. She hated it. Her thundering heart pounded; rage, grief, and fear crackled like lightning across her skin.

"Cait," she rasped, "my mother. She went on a pilgrimage six years ago to help the nearby towns and never came back."

A thick silence permeated the air. She strained to hear footsteps or breathing, but her heartbeat roared and blocked out all sound.

"She abandoned you."

"She didn't. She was a devout priestess of Juno. She committed her life to helping others."

"Was, was, was," the voice mocked, "you know the truth, don't you, Maeve?" Maeve outstretched her arms and tried to follow the voice. "Cait Theywnn was dying, dying, dying."

Maeve stumbled against the memory of her mother coughing blood into linen and then hiding it away in her apron.

"No," she argued, "she was getting better. That's why she went on her pilgrimage. She's going to come back someday. I know it."

"She walked the path to the eternal flame. She chose Juno over you."

"You're wrong. You don't know what you're talking about."

She tried calling for Juno and found oblivion instead. She was alone. No magic, no friends or allies, with a mocking voice hellbent on warping Juno's teachings. Her stomach twisted like a snake in her gut.

"You're afraid."

"I'm not." A hysteric giggle slipped free.

A whisper grazed across her cheek, "How long will you deny it? How long will you live your life as a shadow of a woman?"

Maeve clenched her jaw. "You're the shadows. Why don't you show yourselves, and we can talk like civilized people?"

"We will reveal ourselves to you once you reveal yourself to us."

"What do you want from me?" she screamed into the impassive darkness. She was a second away from breaking down and crying the way a child does, all red-faced and snotty and gripping her knees. *Why did Cara do this? This isn't bringing Maren's spirit back. I'm taking to shadows and going mad.*

"Truth."

"Fine." She threw her hands in the air. "I'm scared! Is that what you want to hear? No matter what I do, no matter how hard I try, I can't seem to get it right." Her words echoed back at her, "You'd be scared too if you were here."

Empty silence and impenetrable darkness stared at her. Her eyes sought shapes, colors, or outlines within the darkness. Yet, the darkness embraced her, ensnaring each sense and depriving her of most of them.

"And I" —her molars clacked together in a painful clench— "I miss my partners." Her lip quivered, and this time, in the dark, Maeve didn't try to stop it. A hot tear slid from the corners of her eyes and burned down her face. "I understand why Juno's left me for good. The things I've done. I've hurt people, I couldn't save Gregor, and I used her gift frivolously to show off to my friends."

Her words choked around a sob. She was a bird with a broken wing, a ship capsizing into the rocky cliffs. Her grief and fear slammed into the blackened, slick, obsidian walls of hopelessness and disappointment. She sank to the floor, and her palms flattened against the rough, textured stone. She hit her fists against it. It was immovable, but there was something cathartic about hitting her hands against the moist rock and feeling sharp pinpricks jolt across her skin, down her wrists, and ricocheting into her elbows.

"The one infallible presence in my life rightfully decided I wasn't worthy and took her gift away, and why wouldn't she?" She wiped the snot collected in the divot above her upper lip. "I'm sacrilegious and damned, made an orphan by two mothers, and left to rot. I ask again: what more do you want from me? I have nothing to give."

"Call your power."

Maeve whipped toward the voice without a body.

"Aren't you listening? I have no power. I have nothing. I am nothing."

"Flowers can grow from rot. Call your power, Maeve."

Her anger, her sadness, it was a maelstrom of swirling energy throughout her entire body from head to toe. *Juno's light is gone. It's gone.* If she tried to locate it, she'd burn herself from the inside out and turn into a black hole of pyrotechnic energy. She needed to find calm, find her center. Yet all she could feel was Imogen's head in her lap; all she could see was Alistair's blue eyes narrowed in amusement, and at the end of it all—her mother's brown braid swaying as her horse clopped toward the forest. *Please.* The act of wrestling her emotions was wrestling smoke. She was destined to crash.

"Call your power."

"I can't!" Her scream reverberated through the cavernous darkness.

"Try."

It'll kill me. Cara wants to kill me. That's all this is. Maeve's diaphragm spasmed, and she hiccuped. She braced her hands on her knees. Her tears dropped salty gifts into her open mouth. *I don't want this. I don't want it. I'm afraid.* Her heart bundled and twisted like a sailor's knot inside her throat. *Juno left me. I can't save anyone. I can't save Ferne. They're all going to die because of me.*

"Only in darkness can we find ourselves, Maeve," the voices said like ocean waves lapping along the shoreline.

"I want Juno back," she admitted, "I'm scared to be powerless." A frosty slush of cold crept along her throat and into her skull. Maeve saw herself from the outside, a scared, lonely, and powerless woman in the dark.

"Powerless? You've done plenty without Juno's blessing." The voice 'tsked' before continuing, "You are as blind as an old dog, and now you attempt to shun my gifts."

"I'm not worthy to receive anyone's gifts." She would ruin it like she ruined her connection with Juno through her selfishness.

"Irrelevant." The voice said, "Do you want it?"

The gears and tumblers clicked into place like a key finding its home. All her anger, her sadness, her grief, and painful longing rushed forward. *Juno chose me after years of study and dedication. Now, whatever this is — whether it's a connection to Janis or a hallucination from Cara's magic— wants to give me a gift without anything in return?* She swallowed.

Maeve turned her fish and pearl ring around her finger. "Will it help me save my friends or Ferne? Will it help me keep people safe?"

"That is up to you."

What if this was an elaborate trap? What if she was accepting a gift from a betrayer god? She had too many questions and no answers. All that remained was faith in herself to make the right choice. The choice that would save others rather than harm. Her instincts told her that she was between worlds, a place between life and death, but closer to death and Janis with the influence of Cara's spirit magic.

"Then I accept."

The living darkness concaved into Maeve's chest. She gaped at the shadows as they coalesced and surged into her and twisted around her wrists. *This is the gift?* She checked within herself. She couldn't feel Juno's warmth, but an icy pinprick needled the nape of her neck. She scrubbed her hands over her damp face. *Is this Janis?* She frowned, remembering the words in the darkness. *Why did it choose me?* Maeve wouldn't fool herself into thinking she understood anyone's divine plans. *There must be more to this. It can't be this simple.* Her emotions swirled inside her chest. *Can this magic be taken away like my connection to Juno?*

A tiny, nebulous prick of light appeared in the darkness. Maeve walked toward it. It doubled in size. The chilled air inside her lungs thawed. Her fingertips tingled. A sense of urgency entered Maeve's gut. She needed to reach that light before it vanished. Her pace quickened into a brisk run. *Wait!* Maeve reached for the light.

* * *

Maeve awoke to a set of piercing gray eyes framed by snowy lashes. The pliant bed sank beneath her, and the warm room glowed from the roaring hearth. She flailed. Panicked.

"Easy." Calom caught her wrist and drew his palm away from her forehead. "You've broken your fever." An incense burner hung from her bedpost, and a sharp forestry smell wafted through it. *Caezinnia.* The thorny plant was a common remedy in Maeve's home to combat infections and sickness.

"F-fever?" Her tongue stuck to the roof of her dry mouth. "What happened?"

The last thing she recalled was Cara's magic worming into her brain and the voices that followed. She didn't know what bargain she struck or if it was real. She didn't know what it was capable of. With Juno, she had her mother and grandmother to guide her. *What if what I accepted is dangerous?* She wanted to believe it was Janis' influence. She wanted to trust that the goddess of death came to her and offered her a gift. Yet, Maeve sensed a locked door inside of her. *Where did the magic go? Was it all a dream? A hallucination?* Every moment within that void felt real.

"You collapsed in Cara's study and have been bedridden for days," he said, his tone flat and clinical. "King Hagken asked me to guard you." He handed her a cup of water. She imagined it irked him to watch over her when he was a lieutenant within Hagken's army. He was a warrior, not a healer.

"He'll expect you to attend his coronation tonight."

"What?"

"You should rest in the meantime," he said, ignoring her question. "There will be guards outside your door."

"The children." Maeve sat up. "Has Hagken released any? The children from Ferne?"

She searched Calom's face. His expression was carved marble, and his eyes hardened like iron. He stood straight with his hands clasped behind his back. She missed the expressive nature of Alistair's dimpled smile and Imogen's focused and pinched brow.

"To my knowledge," he said, "King Hagken has not removed anyone from Hollyhock." The shadows danced across his stern face.

Her heart dropped. Why did she expect Hagken would keep his word? He didn't respect her. He didn't care about Ferne or anyone else. She called to Calom before he reached the door.

"Did you say Hollyhock?" She fisted the damp sheets between her hands. "Are the children not in Pyrite?" Gods above and below, she hoped the children weren't here. She assumed Hagken would've taken everyone with him to reclaim his throne. *Cara and Hagken could've been lying to intimidate me.*

"I train and lead soldiers, Lady Maeve," he said, "not children."

He slammed the door shut as if her words offended him. Maeve tried to look at the situation objectively. Hagken marched from Hollyhock to Pyrite with soldiers, equipment, and supplies and snuck his forces into the city. She wasn't an expert on war or deception, but she knew how difficult it was to herd children into the town square for celebrations.

What if Hagken kept the children at Hollyhock for leverage? A soldier wouldn't run away if he knew his family would be punished. *If the children aren't here,* Maeve thought, *then it will take time for Hagken to release them from Hollyhock.* Her eyes ached.

Two individuals wearing black veils entered her room to prepare her for the coronation. Their crimson robes bore Hagken's crest. Maeve sat silent as they braided her dark hair into two large buns on top of her head. They spritzed her with perfumes and covered her tawny skin in glimmering lotion. *This could be my night of escape. But, if I do, Hagken will punish the children wherever they are.* They brushed gold and glittery powder onto her eyelids and wrapped delicate golden chains through her hair. Eyes closed, Maeve called to Janis to understand her visions, but the goddess of secrets and moonlight didn't reply.

27

Hagken's held his celebration in the ballroom and within several sitting rooms. She flexed her fingers at her side as she peered through the narrow slits of her mask. Her stomach turned inside out at the revelry. The guests' faces were half-covered or entirely obscured by animal masks, and people laughed, drank, and shook hands as if it was expected to have a masquerade while the city suffered. Maeve lifted her white skirt and slipped through the perfumed crowd like oil.

The crimson ladies had curled pieces of her hair over her shoulders to contrast her pearl embroidered gown and gold-leaf feathered mask. She would've preferred to attend in her bloody, dirt-covered clothes. She searched the crowd for familiar faces, but it was impossible to recognize anyone among the myriad of masks and costumes.

She played with Imogen's ring on her finger.

Calom was a shark. A silver stripe ran along the side of his dark-tailored pants, and it matched the cuffs on his long black jacket. He carded his fingers through his short, pale hair as he stalked toward her. *Why isn't he wearing a mask?* He bowed and peered at Maeve beneath his heavyset brow.

"Hagken requested that I look after you."

One Duskryn almost killed me, and the other is my eternal silver shadow. Maeve frowned. *I'm not sure which one is worse.* If the stars designed her fate, then neither option boded well. *If I run, Ferne will be punished, but if I stay, then Hagken will kill me.*

"Shall we?" He offered his arm.

"I don't feel like dancing."

"This is the beginning of a beautiful era, Maeve."

"Isn't the city falling apart?"

"Thorduun's quarter was damaged, yes, but our impressive military and magical force has it under control." He leaned closer. "I ensured the spires were unharmed," his voice lowered, "because of you."

Maeve stepped back. "What?" *Why does he care about the spires?*

"You've renewed my faith, Maeve. I didn't want to see Juno's tree burned."

"But you'll burn other trees and other villages?" she argued, "you'll spare Theadora's temple and enact your own justice in the throne room? You'll save Juno's spire, but stand idle and let me die in the name of Hagken's delusions?"

"It's complicated."

"It's not." Maeve tore her mask off and stared up at Calom's strong features. "Your loyalty to Hagken blinds you. We share a life debt, Calom, and you refuse to honor it. You're not a man of faith, you're not a man of honor, you're a—" she stumbled through her words, "—a dog following its master."

"Are you trying to wound my pride?"

"I'm sharing my perspective." Her nostrils flared, her spirit and willpower worn thin. She wouldn't stand here and listen to Calom try to paint himself a hero. She didn't regret saving his life at Hollyhock, but she wished he'd take accountability rather than continue to follow Hagken blindly. *He hasn't changed. He's the same man who sent the elders out in the dead of night.* A claw of tension raked through her aching shoulders. *He's cut from the same cloth as his sister.*

"Then allow me to share mine, Lady Maeve." He jutted his chin toward the carousers. "Pyrite welcomed King Hagken. They embrace and celebrate his return because they see his vision. They see that we're stronger when we fight together under one banner. King Hagken is going to unite Estoria. He'll become our emperor for the peace and safety of all."

Maeve inhaled. *The siege weapons in his camp weren't for Pyrite.* She tried to recall the map from Hollyhock and the conversation they shared at dinner. *The Lupine Forests are close to Hollyhock. Maybe that's his next target.* Although, she'd give herself a headache trying to understand Hagken's machinations. *He wants all of Estoria. Not just Pyrite.*

"You're a part of that vision," said Calom, "even if you refuse to acknowledge it."

"If this is so important, then why isn't Hagken here?" Maeve raised her eyebrows. "Shouldn't he be among his loyal subjects?" She remembered Hagken's rise to power. *He poisoned the council and made himself a crown.* A server passed carrying a tray of wine, and Maeve recoiled.

"That"— Calom jabbed a finger into her face— "is not your concern."

They were interrupted by guests who descended upon Calom

like a hoard of vultures. She caught snippets of their praise and their questions about Calom's family in Amethneas. A hand settled on the middle of Maeve's back. She jolted. The stranger's impish mask covered their face, but a pair of clear blue eyes stared at her.

"Juno rises to meet you, Lady Maeve." *It can't be.* She gasped, then smothered the sound with an unsteady laugh. *How did they get here?* Calom's eyes burned into her cheek. She shifted her weight and wrangled her overjoyed grin into a polite smile.

"I was hoping I might have this dance?" Alistair asked.

Calom cut in, "She's unavailable."

"I'd be honored." She took Alistair's gloved hand. "King Hagken wanted me here, Lieutenant Duskryn, but he doesn't control who I dance with."

Their arm slipped comfortably around Maeve's waist and pulled her into their side.

"One dance," Alistair promised before gently guiding her away. Maeve's heart kicked like a spooked horse. *If Alistair is here, then does that mean Imogen is too? Is everyone safe? Did they find Terrayn?* She didn't know which questions to ask first. Calom's steely gaze remained on her, but he didn't move from his spot surrounded by diplomats and merchants. Alistair took her hand and led her through a simple box step.

"It's funny." They began, "When we met, I traveled with you because I wanted a backup if Hagken caught me. You were my bargaining chip. I'd trade your life for mine if necessary." Maeve resisted the urge to smile to herself. She had the same idea, but hers was nobler.

"But everything changed after the alchemists' guild. I wanted–I want–you to succeed." Their eyes softened. "I meant what I said during the equinox."

"Why are you telling me this now?"

"Because it might be my last chance to say it."

Maeve's grip tightened on Alistair's fingers. "Why?"

"Because I'm getting you out of here. Tonight." Rivers of golden glitter ran through Alistair's dark curls. "And I'm staying behind."

"You can't smuggle me out." She glanced to Calom on the sidelines. "Someone will notice. And what do you mean by staying? You can't stay here. It's not safe."

"You have such faith in gods and none in me."

"I have faith in you," she said, "I do."

The music swelled. Maeve foolishly wished she could remove the mask from Alistair's face. *They can't stay. They have to come with me.* Beneath the cover of violins and cellos, Maeve explained her conversations with Hagken and Calom and the experiment she endured. Alistair's eyes squinted through the mask.

"The Duskryns are charmers, aren't they?" Alistair said sarcastically.

"They're something."

She scanned the room over Alistair's shoulder for any sign of Imogen.

"She's not here," they said, "she's got a different job tonight."

Maeve inched closer. "All the more reason for you to come with me."

"I'm releasing the captives, Maeve." They explained, "I'll find Ferne's people before Cara or Hagken does. I promise."

They adjusted the dance step, and Calom's glowering expression disappeared from her peripheral vision. Her heart doubled. *They're going to save Ferne.* If anyone could reach Bertha and the others—it was Alistair. They knew the castle and how their stepfather operated. *I don't like the idea of leaving them behind.* But she'd sacrifice her comfort for the sake of Ferne's safety and liberation.

"Here." Alistair slipped a dagger into her hand, and Maeve recognized the twin-viper hilt. *This belonged to Terra.* She tucked it away into the billowy sleeves of her white dress.

"What's this for?"

"It's our backup plan."

"I'm not stabbing anyone."

"Stab doesn't always mean to kill. Just avoid the vital points. I assume you know where those are."

"What's the real plan?"

"We wait for Imogen's cue." Alistair's eyes crinkled. "My contacts within the Janis conclave are going to get you out."

"That sounds detailed," Maeve teased. Then, somberly, she added, "don't die. I can't bring you back if you do." *Without knowing how to access the gift I was given, I am powerless to save anyone.*

"Don't worry, sunshine. I plan to live forever." Alistair's laughter was hot and bright.

Calom's large hand clapped onto Alistair's shoulder and sliced their laughter short, and Maeve retracted her hands. Calom glanced between them, unamused. Her heart skipped. *What if Calom recognizes them?* She stepped closer before he could examine Alistair any further.

"Sir Duskryn." She touched his forearm. "Could you escort me to the washroom? It's so stuffy in here." *And I have a dagger to hide.*

"Of course, Lady Maeve." He bowed his head toward Alistair. "Excuse us."

Maeve resisted the urge to look behind her as Calom led her out of the crowd of swaying, extravagantly dressed guests. *Be safe, Alistair. We will see each other again. I swear it.*

Maeve barely registered the passage of time. The band resumed after a brief respite, and the sharp, flowing vibration of strings swallowed the buzz of conversation, and Maeve longed for the wild, erotic drumbeats of the equinox festival. She and Calom moved to one of the arched doorways, and Maeve tilted her neck to see the domed glass ceiling. If the sky hadn't been polluted with smoke, then it would've been a marvelous and enchanting view.

King Hagken made his appearance alongside Cara and his council. He wore an elaborately stitched suit of gold and black that gleamed and shimmered beneath the lights, and a golden mask covered the burned half of his face. *The masked theme of the party was an excuse to hide his injury,* Maeve guessed. Cara strode into the ballroom, her chin high and her moon-white hair fashioned into a braided up-do. She wore the same uniform as Calom, but her shoulders to her wrists were wrapped in intricate patterns of bones. Plenty of merchants and diplomats approached Hagken, but none approached Cara.

Calom said, "He'll want to see you." *And I don't want to see him.* Maeve squeezed her mask between her fingers.

"I need a moment," lied Maeve. She searched the room for Alistair's familiar imp mask. *Did they already leave to look for the others?* If she could slip away from Calom, then she could search for Bertha. *Does Hagken have someone looking after her?* Her lips thinned at the idea of Cara helping someone through childbirth. *Maybe she stayed at Hollyhock.* She hoped Bertha's daughter, Lenora, was safe from the horrors of the city.

"Nervous?"

"Merely overwhelmed." The dagger secured on her thigh by scraps of linen itched her skin. The walls of the ballroom threatened to squeeze her like a vice. It was easier to look above than at the shifting, colorful crowd.

A small comet whizzed across the canopy of blue-gray smoke and popped into a burst of light. Calom grabbed her elbow.

"What was that?" Maeve asked.

Calom's eyes were stormy despite the perfect neutrality of the rest of his face. *I bet that was Imogen's signal.* A sense of trepidation bubbled through her veins. Another firework lit up the sky and erupted in red light. A hazy and blood-hued flash bathed the guests. A quick succession of two more fireworks exploded, their colors blue and green. The show elicited a mummer of awe and polite clapping. Calom released her elbow and pushed his long coat aside to reveal his sword at his hip.

Calom said, "I'll escort you to your room, Maeve."

A resonant boom vibrated through the floor. A shower of broken glass rained like deadly snowflakes to the choir of screams. A burly man wearing a purple mask grabbed Cara by the throat. The room erupted into motion as figures in black rappelled down from the ceiling. Calom shouldered into the crowd, his intention clear as he barreled toward his sister. *Calom always follows orders,* Maeve thought, *except when Cara is in danger.* She supposed she ought to be grateful for their loyalty to one another.

She searched the writhing mass of strangers for Alistair. She couldn't find them. The bones on Cara's sleeves separated and congealed. A series of purple nodules melded the bones into barbed armor. The surge of bodies moved around Cara like frightened cattle. Calom's blade sank into the assailant's neck, squirting blood onto Cara's face and over Calom's jacket. The screams muffled and turned to cotton in her ears. *I have to find Alistair's contact.* Adrenaline and fear forced her limbs to function.

She stopped at the end of a corridor with her hand on the knob. *What if I stay? Alistair might need me.* The thoughts fluttered through her mind like sparrows. The doorknob vanished beneath her grasp as someone opened it from the other side. An abrupt gust of wind snuffed out the candelabras on the wall and doused them in darkness.

Maeve choked on her gasp.

A veiled, all-black figure stood before her.

"Come with me, lost daughter of Juno."

Alistair said she'd meet someone from Janis' secret conclave. *Is this who I'm meant to meet? What if they belong to Hagken?* She might be able to claw her way through a fight, but she doubted it would last long.

"Who are you?"

"A daughter of Janis." She replied flatly and motioned with an urgent, impatient gesture. Maeve looked into the yawning, black hallway, and her mind swelled with doubt. It was now or never. *I know what fate awaits me if I stay. I have to trust that Alistair will reach the captives in time.* Maeve pressed her hand to her burning throat and dashed through the threshold.

* * *

Maeve followed the veiled woman through a winding staircase. She coaxed the shadows to bend and coalesce around them and beckoned Maeve forward like a blade in the dark. Whey they were finally free of the claustrophobic keep and its divine horrors, Maeve looked at the stars peeking through the haze.

"Juno, be with me," she mouthed, "Lady Janis guide our steps." She lost her connection to Juno, but that didn't mean she lost her faith.

"Goddess above," the shadow said with horror and awe. The domed membrane of arcane magic shifted like a half-finished glass sculpture. A spark ricocheted across the dome. *Something is destroying it?* Maeve pressed her hand over her mouth. *It's Imogen. She must've found a way to make her solution stronger.*

The arcane energy dissolved from the top down. It shimmered in waves of purple and melted like candle wax. The hollows within the city released a cacophony of excited yips like a pack of wild dogs. A new sense of urgency entered her bones. The banishment of the arcane protection meant anything from the quarter was free. *Hagken will have to send out his forces.* The hollows, the guardians, alchemists, and mages now moved across the board without resistance. *Janis, if anyone from Ferne is fighting, please look after them.*

The ground vibrated beneath their feet with a distant explosion.

The veiled woman said, "The mages and alchemists will need to set aside their differences to restore the magic, but I doubt they will."

They moved from the keep. The woman manipulated shadows and guided Maeve to dodge Hagken's guard.

"Wait. A guardian of Thorduun's quarter." The woman inclined her head, and her black lace quivered after her breath. The impervious guardian stomped, and the dodecahedron in its chest pulsed with blue and white lightning. Its attention pivoted onto someone else across the street. A pimply-faced soldier of Hagken stood with their sword trembling in their arms. A hollow dragged its limbs toward the soldier.

"St-stop, beast!" he said with as much bravado as a wet dog. Maeve launched from the mouth of the alleyway as a hollow lunged at the young, terrified soldier.

Her fingers met the hollow's bony, gray-skinned shoulders. She used her momentum to throw the creature off balance. But, it bucked her away with surprising strength. Her dress tore when she fell onto the cobblestones. She clenched her teeth against the shock wave of pain in her knees and shins. The hollow looked down at her. A chunk of its face had disintegrated to reveal smooth, white bone.

The empty sockets of two twin purple flames flared. The hollow opened its mouth to reveal a few rotted, yellow teeth.

"Ahhh!" The soldier yelled. His sword cleaved into its collarbone. Its papery skin emitted a fine gray dust with each impassioned blow. Maeve slid her dagger free from her makeshift holster. She hesitated. *Do the hollows feel pain?* As a priestess, she was proud of her pacifism and dedication to protecting life. *Can I kill it?* A group of soldiers rounded the corner, rushed toward them, and saved Maeve from her moral dilemma.

"That was foolish," the sister said.

"You could've helped."

She scoffed. "I could not."

"Why not?" *Everyone in this city is so eager to turn away from people in trouble!* Her anger flared like a firework singing across the sky.

"It would've given away our connection. Alistair said your disappearance must be confusing and difficult to track." The taste of brine was in the air. They were near the docks, though Maeve couldn't see them. The sister stopped, inhaled sharply, and touched her chest.

"Are you alright?" Maeve placed her hand on the woman's shoulder.

"One of our own has fallen." The black lace trembled. "I felt his echo through Janis' web."

I didn't know someone could feel the web.

"I'm sorry..."

"It is the cycle of all things." The sister said, "We are almost there. I must blindfold and deafen you."

This was a temporary solution. She would reunite with Alistair and Imogen. *Although, I don't know what we'll do after that. I don't know how we're going to stop Hagken.* In her eyes, Hagken would gorge himself on the deaths of innocents to get what he desired. It didn't matter who got caught in the crossfire. A sense of hopelessness and dread pulled at the strings of her heart.

The magic bit Maeve's exposed skin. The air compressed inside her lungs, squeezing and tightening until she shook from it. A sour smell filled her nostrils and hit the back of her throat. Alongside the blindfold, the world became a disorientating and deafening absolute black.

28

Maeve inhaled sharply as her blindfold was removed. A dancing arrangement of bright spots swam before her vision, and her ears rang. She screwed her face and blocked the onslaught with her arm. A figure stood and moved. She watched through the spaces between her fingers. She couldn't tell if the person standing before her was real or an illusion from stress and heartache. The darkness carried her between worlds like a womb. *Is this the conclave?* Maeve rubbed her eyes. *Where is the veiled woman from earlier?*

The cloaked figure gestured to a stone wall and small keys strewn together with tiny glass beads dangling from their wrist like a prayer chain.

"Where is–" Maeve's words broke off.

The cloaked person walked through the wall as if it were made of gossamer. Maeve followed without a second thought, for there was no turning back for her. The corridor was dim, deathly still, and silent as a tomb. Maeve scuffed her boot against the dirt and felt the texture, but the movement was soundless. *I don't understand this place.* They led her to a lush room covered in hanging plants and subdued gravelight. A cluster of bleached white tables and chairs cluttered around the room like barnacles. Two black-clad, veiled figures sat at a circular table, mending black fabrics, and a veiled woman approached Maeve. Her voice was familiar.

"Welcome to the conclave of Janis." She traced a circle with two fingers in the air toward the dirt by Maeve's feet. "May our shadowed Lady guide your steps."

She's the one who brought me here.

She continued, "Her web is rather disorientating for those not blessed. I hope you do not feel too ill."

"I – we – went through the web of fate?" *That's impossible. Only spirits move through the web.*

"I carried you through a piece of it, yes." She said, "My name is Nora, and I am one of the secret keepers of this sanctuary."

In the muddled green gravelight, Maeve noticed her robes were stitched with crescent moons along her black sleeves. A belt of heavy, rusted iron keys wrapped around her waist and miraculously didn't make a sound when she moved. A silent cloaked figure set a tray in front of Maeve with dried jerky, coin-sized crackers, and a smear of plum jam. *I can't believe I'm here. I walked my entire life in Juno's light. I never thought I'd see the shadows of Janis too.* A tall individual with fabric around the lower half of their face watered one of the hanging, leafy plants above her head. Beyond the gravelight, no other light sources existed, but the plants continued to thrive. *What would Imogen say if she saw these plants?*

"You have questions," said Nora.

"How is traversing through Janis' web possible? Where's Alistair?" The edge of the table dug into her sternum. "What about

Imogen? Do you know her? Is she alright?"

Nora folded her gloved hands into her lap. "Priestesses of Juno are given the power to heal. Is it so impossible that those who earn Janis' blessing also have gifts? As for your friends, I believe the void has answers, but I am not at liberty to share them."

The piece of jerky scraped down Maeve's throat. *No answers. Only more questions.*

"Could someone send word to Alistair or Imogen to tell them I'm safe and ready to fulfill my promises?" *For Ferne, for Pyrite, for Alistair and Imogen.*

"Not all promises can be kept, Maeve, and all promises are burdens." Nora turned to the individual watering plants and said, "Vi, escort Maeve to Inera." *She's wrong,* Maeve thought as she stood; *my promises motivate me. They keep my hope alive. I will fulfill them.*

Vi had sleek, braided dark hair, and their brown eyes crinkled with warmth above the fabric covering their nose and mouth. The conclave was a labyrinth of gray stoned corridors. Maeve tried to track their movements but gave up after they walked through several walls. *I don't know why I bother trying when shadow-slingers surround me.*

"It is good to meet you," they said, their voice husky, "Alistair spoke fondly of you. I can tell you are precious to them."

Maeve flushed with the pleasure of being called precious.

"And Alistair is precious to me." She grabbed Vi's elbow and stopped their long gait. "I'm grateful the conclave helped me escape Hagken, but I need to return to my partners." She prayed Vi would be more receptive. *I can't stay here. I can't hide while everything crumbles.* Vi's notched eyebrow raised.

"Not yet," said Vi, "Alistair was explicit in their instructions about your care."

Maeve chewed the inside of her cheek. Perhaps Nora or another sanctuary member could take her back through the web. She could appeal to their sense of logic and sensibility.

"Nora, the secret keeper—is she in charge? Do I need to impress her?"

"No." Vi chuckled. "I think she would find it funny if you told her that." Their eyes crinkled in a smile reminiscent of Alistair's.

"I can't stay here," she said, though Vi continued walking and expected her to follow.

"Perhaps the void will speak to you tonight when you rest."

"You keep referring to the void like it's alive." She knew of void whisperers who performed Estoria's death rites and wondered if the two were connected.

Vi's brown eyes crowded with laugh lines. "I cannot reveal all our secrets."

She passed conclave members wearing dark gray leather armor with silver sickles strapped to their backs or hips, but their faces were covered or half-concealed. *A place of secrets.* She tried to imagine Alistair stalking through this hall. *I would never wish to hide their smile from the world.* Vi stopped before a stone arched doorway inlaid with pale runic carvings. The space inside the archway pulsed and undulated like a slab of black gelatin.

"Can you promise me something?" Maeve held her hand close to her chest.

"I am not a creature of oaths," Vi said, "but for the sake of Alistair, I will hear you."

"If you hear anything, and I mean anything, about Alistair or Imogen, will you please tell me? Or have someone else tell me." Her time here would be more bearable if she knew the fate of her partners or Ferne's people.

They said, "I will try."

Before entering to meet Inera, Maeve muttered, "I give my heart to dawn. I give my spirit to the zenith. I give my sorrow to the dusk."

Inera wore a featureless white mask and layered black makeup around their rich brown eyes. Inera was a void whisperer. They performed death rites, oversaw burials, and acted as guides into Janis' web. They were trained herbalists and administered tinctures and salves to ease the pain of the dying. They often weren't tied to one city or town and moved freely throughout Estoria. However, the sight of a void whisperer caused a ripple of discomfort in the air as their presence meant the presence of an unavoidable death. Maeve felt that same level of discomfort now. *Why would Nora send me here? Or is she acting on Alistair's behalf?*

"Janis is death, and she is the veil between life and death," Inera said.

"Which means?" Maeve set down her teacup.

"We can reach beyond and avoid what should be a death blow. I will show you." Inera approached Vi, and Vi drew their blade. A wordless exchange passed between them. Maeve didn't recall blinking, but in one moment, the blade drew back and was going to pierce the whisperer's heart, and in the next moment, Inera stood in front of Maeve—safe and sound.

Inera picked up their teacup with a trembling hand. "It's exhaustive but useful. Alistair has asked us to teach you this skill before you leave."

"And you're going to teach me?" She wasn't one of Janis' chosen, but maybe she didn't need to be to learn the conclave's skills. *I wonder if Inera knows about the locked magic inside of me. Can they sense it?*

"No." There was a smile in Inera's voice. "The reverent shadow will.”

“Who’s that?”

“It is the highest order of our conclave. A chosen vessel for Janis to exert her will and wisdom through.”

Vessel? Maeve frowned. *If the Janis conclave can have a vessel holding the essence of a god, then does that mean—?* She twisted her ring. *No. No way. I’m not a vessel for a dead woman’s spirit.* There was no world in which Hagken’s conspiracy was true.

“This way, Maeve.” Vi held the door open for her.

The second journey was as confusing as the first. Although Vi led her, they didn’t enter the darkened room alongside her. She resisted the desire to try and summon her lights of Juno. Juno’s light no longer lived inside of her. Something else did, something unknown and unreachable. *The reverent shadow will have the answers.*

“Hello?” Maeve called out to the darkness, “I’m Maeve. I’m here to speak with the reverent shadow.”

Bony fingers wrapped around her throat. She flailed, white spots flared to life in sharp bursts of cold light behind her eyelids, and her windpipe was released. Her body keyed into hyper-awareness, and she gripped her sore throat. *What in Juno’s name was that?* She strained to peer through the absolute darkness. *Where is the reverent shadow?*

“Focus on your breath,” someone said straight into her mind, their voice unsubstantial and empty. “Become your body. Your blood. Your heart. Do you feel it?”

Maeve pulled her attention inward like a stone being dropped into a well. Her nails pressed her neck, her blood sang in her veins, and a strand of hair tickled her jaw.

“This is life. But each space between breath and heartbeat is death.” The voice said, “You will learn to move inside the vacuum and the vacancy. Do not panic.”

The pressure snatched her throat, and Maeve strained to stay calm. She focused on her heart, the wild, loud throbbing pulse in her neck, and the trapped air burning inside her lungs. Her hands twitched a primal wish to claw away the pressure and release the danger. *I could die. Right here, right now.* A myriad of colored lights danced before her blackened vision. Yet, moments before her legs buckled, the pressure released, and Maeve braced herself on her knees with rapid, painful gasps.

"You can do better than that."

Maeve wrangled her self-control and took deep, intentional breaths. She didn't know how much time passed in the chilly, echoing chamber, though her instructor didn't relent until Maeve's throat was raw and her eyes watered. *This isn't so bad,* Maeve thought. *Mother taught me to stay calm.* She blinked away a fresh wave of tears. *I miss her, but I'll forever carry her wisdom.*

Time stretched like an elastic band before snapping back into her skin.

"Better," the voice said, "you have taken the first step and embraced Janis' cold touch, but there is more for you to learn."

"Oh." Maeve wheezed, "Good."

"We will resume tomorrow."

"I can't." She rubbed her throat. "My partners need my help, and my people are trapped under Hagken's control. We have to keep going."

The silence was deafening.

"Very well. I will not save you if you die pursuing this knowledge."

"I'm not going to die," Maeve replied stubbornly.

I'll survive this. The reverent shadow, formless and unseen, created a brutal and bloody regime. It asked her to move without her sense of sight. It asked her to fight with bruises singing on her skin. It asked her to lay on the cold floor until she went numb like a corpse. In the silence, Maeve listened to the blood in her ears and summoned the memories of her loved ones. *I'm doing this for them.* She thought of Imogen. *What will she do with her hollows when this is over? What will happen to the alchemist guild?* She thought of Alistair. *Did they free anyone from Ferne? Why haven't they come to the conclave?* She thought of Bertha. *Did she have her child? Is Lenora safe?* Maeve's lower lip quivered. Usually, she'd refrain from crying in front of others and force herself into calm tranquility. But Maeve let the tears fall.

Her limbs ached with a tingling sensation from a lack of blood flow. She prodded around the skin of her eye, *and I think I have a black eye.* She tried to heal, and nothing happened. Her heart sank. *I don't know why I'm surprised.* Much like her own mother, Juno wasn't coming back. Her heart would heal faster if she learned to accept it.

29

The blackness around Maeve coalesced. She reached out. *Can I touch it? Is it real?* A swooping sense of vertigo made her ears pop. And Maeve found herself standing in an open tundra with her arm outstretched. Sharp and spindly dark purple vegetation clustered around her feet. The night sky shone with unusual brightness as three moons hung in the air. *Where am I?* Maeve turned in a circle and saw the starlight horizon stretch endlessly.

"You've found me again," a feminine voice said, laughing.

Maeve spun toward the voice, and every hair on her skin was electrified. The woman's head was shaved, but her features were unmistakable. She and Maeve shared the same sloped nose and rounded face.

"M-mother?" *It can't be! How is she here? How is she within the conclave of Janis? Is she the reverent shadow?* The questions chaffed against Maeve's recent acceptance that her mother walked the path of the eternal flame. *This can't be real. She's gone.*

"Not exactly." Her eyes softened, and Maeve blinked away her surprised tears.

"I chose this form. I can choose something else. I have as many faces as those who have walked through my web." Her face flickered to the lined warmth of Maeve's grandmother. Her white hair was pulled into a severe topknot, and the folded crinkles around her mouth and eyes were reminiscent of an oak tree. Maeve's throat prickled. *I can't talk to the faces of people I've lost.* She was terrified Imogen or Alistair's face might appear.

"I choose to see you as you are," said Maeve.

The stranger's face shifted into a featureless white mask. Two plumes of black smoke unfurled from the eye slits. A billowing dress the color of sea foam and storm clouds curved over her hips and chest. Her skin mirrored the slate rocks of the tundra and pulsed with blue-white runic markings across her limbs and chest. An aura of cold power radiated from her as she towered over Maeve.

A massive, silver cat's cradle twisted and wove between her fingers. Maeve watched tiny motes of light move along the web. *It's the web...Janis' web.*

"You're..." Maeve stared, "Lady Janis..." Her shock ebbed. *The sunseers within Everdawn sit blindfolded for hours with the hope of a visit from Juno, and here I am— neither a priestess to Juno nor a member of Janis' conclave —and I'm talking to a god.*

"You have journeyed far." Janis' voice was everywhere and within everything. "A journey that not many would have survived. It is a good thing you have my sister's favor."

"I don't," Maeve said painfully, "I'm no longer connected to Juno."

She could hardly call herself a luminary. She was something else. Undefined. She spent her entire life as a priestess, and her heart still ached with longing.

"Ah." Janis wove a thread through her fingers. "You used the sunstone."

"Yes?" Maeve shifted her weight. *Am I in trouble?* She would defend her decision if Janis asked her to. *I wasn't going to let Imogen die.*

"Juno would not have let you use the sunstone if she did not deem you worthy."

Janis' words triggered her memory. "Was that you during Cara's ritual?"

"Yes."

"What gift did you give me?"

"A gift to change the woven patterns of fate," Janis explained, "Hagken made a pact with Oberon – the wretched betrayer—and now my moonstone is an abomination. You must destroy it. Destroy the stone, and I will finally have Hagken's spirit."

Her mask fractured, and her eyes flared with brilliant, thunderous light. The sparse vegetation twitched from a strong gust of wind, and snowflakes churned through the air. The cat's cradle vanished from her hands. Janis lifted two sickles above her head. Maeve didn't flinch. She recalled the pale, luminous moonstone worn around Hagken's neck. *I'll never get close enough to Hagken to reach the moonstone.*

"I don't know how to do that," Maeve stammered, "you've given me a gift, but I can't reach it despite your conclave's best efforts to teach me. I'm not a shadow weaver or void whisperer or anything else." She said, "I'm not anything. I'm nothing."

A sun and moon circled Janis' head. The two celestial bodies collided, and the sun turned black. The cold air nipped at the back of Maeve's neck. Janis remained silent, and moonlight glinted off her twin blades.

"Destroy the moonstone," her voice was as deep as the dark ocean.

"How?" A note of petulant frustration entered Maeve's tone. "I don't have Juno's blessing. I don't even know if I have your blessing." She shouldn't argue with the goddess of death, but her patience was razor-thin. *I'm tired. I want to go home. I want to lay my head in Imogen's lap. I want this to be over.*

Janis resumed weaving the great web of fate through her fingers.

"You have the key, Maeve," she said, "and I find your lack of creative thinking...disappointing."

The sparse yet beautiful tundra shifted as if viewed through mottled glass and blended like a watercolor painting.

"If she's dead, I'm blowing this place up," a honey-warm voice, "and I don't care if you're a sacred place to Janis. You're inside a cavern, and gods can't stop rocks from exploding."

Maeve's mind pieced the fragments together, the faint smell of oil, the pressure of cold metal on her cheek, and her blonde hair washed out from swaying gravelight. She moved. The hanging, lush plant leaves caressed her face.

"Imogen?" She sat up from Imogen's lap. "You're here!"

"Nearly didn't make it." She kissed Maeve's cheek. "One of the shadow-slingers helped me get out of the city. Did you know they can walk through Janis' web?"

Maeve clung to Imogen and kissed her. Her motions were desperate and frantic, a single word repeated in her mind: *Alive, alive, alive.* Her fear for Imogen's and Alistair's safety never ceased between everything that happened. She trusted their resourcefulness and brilliance, but Hagken's ambition and cruelty knew no limit. Maeve was aware of others in the room but paid them no mind. She had

Imogen in her arms, half her heart, and wouldn't let go.

"I have so much to tell you." Maeve's vision blurred with tears.

"Me too." Imogen smiled. "and I have surprises."

Imogen gestured to her hollows within the main chamber. "I lost a lot of them, but these few haven't left my side."

"You should have told me about them," Maeve said.

She understood why Imogen released them. The hollows existed somewhere between life and death. Their bodies were decaying, but they had enough sentience to follow Imogen's requests. They shouldn't have been locked away under the guild, and someone should've brought them to Juno's temple for a chance at recovery. However, that knowledge didn't change the fact that Imogen kept a secret from her.

Imogen's cheeks flushed. "I know." She took Maeve's hand and kissed each knuckle. "You're right. I should've. But, I was afraid you'd reject the idea, and we wouldn't be able to save Alistair in time." She held Maeve's hand to her lips. "I'm sorry."

Redemption was a stone-by-stone built temple. They would need to talk about repairing the damages the unbound hollows caused, but not today. To save Pyrite, they needed to eradicate Hagken before he stretched outward and corrupted Estoria like an infection. *He won't stop until he's claimed the country for himself.*

Imogen asked, "Vi, would you mind taking us through the web again?"

"You've only just arrived," said Vi.

"Maeve." Imogen squeezed her fingers. "Do you feel up to it?"

"We're going back into Pyrite?"

"Yes." Her face brightened. "I have something to show you. And we'll need your help to stop Hagken's ceremony outside Theadora's temple."

Juno above, Hagken loves his ceremonies, doesn't he? Maeve considered staying within the conclave. She endured the trials with the reverent shadow but hadn't learned anything. She couldn't outmaneuver a deathblow or manipulate shadows, and her magic remained blocked. *If I go,* she thought, *I'll be useless.*

"I don't know how much help I'll be," she admitted, "I should stay here and keep training." She couldn't face Hagken or destroy his moonstone without magic.

"My love." Imogen touched her forehead to Maeve's. "You've never hidden yourself in the shadows before," she said, "so why now?"

"My connection to Juno is gone, Imogen." *And it's not going to return.* She wished Imogen's presence could assuage her fears about her future.

"I don't need Juno's light," she said, "I need yours."

Maeve smiled softly. *But will I be enough?*

* * *

Vi trotted through the caverns with practiced ease. The new tunnel's walls hummed with magic and faint, glowing runes. *Some of these look familiar.* She traced her fingertips against the stone. *Janis' skin was covered in runes like these.* A tingling sweat pooled on her lower back and within the hollow dip of her armpits.

"Not again." Imogen cursed while holding the detached arm of her hollow. The runes pulsed blue and white, and phosphorus smoke clung to the hollow's skin. She pressed the shoulder bone into the socket, and the hollow groaned as it re-attached with a wet, suckling sound.

"The web and my hollows don't mesh," she explained, "because my hollows are half-spirit and half-something else. It's like the web wants to eat them."

Maeve said, "Maybe they want to return to the web of fate." She couldn't imagine living a half-life and shambling through the world as your body decayed and your remnant spirit withered.

"Maybe." Imogen shrugged. *When this is over, Imogen can bring her hollows here and let them rest,* Maeve thought; *they were trapped under the guild. They deserve to return to Janis and be born again someday.*

"If you hear anyone call to you," said Vi, "don't answer and don't look back."

The air tasted metallic, and she touched her lips out of fear she had chewed them bloody. A far-off, sorrowful voice vibrated through the tunnel.

"Come home," it said, "Virmaer."

It repeated itself in varied throes of emotion, from sadness to rage to disbelief and confusion. Maeve couldn't determine the tone. At times, it was high like a flute; other times, it echoed low and gravelly.

"Imogen..." A sorrowful voice rang out. Imogen clutched Maeve's arm. Her lips turned into a tight frown, and her brown eyes shone.

"False voices of the dead," Imogen said, "that's my guess. It happened last time."

"You're right. They're echoes." Vi sounded impressed. "Merely impressions of those who walked with Janis through her web."

"Maeve," the voice cried from the ceiling. A clammy sweat broke out across her skin. The cadence reminded Maeve of her grandmother. The carved runes brightened, and the taste of blood thickened and grew nauseating.

The voices started screaming and begging. *I wish I had been blindfolded and deafened like before.* She grabbed Vi's elbow and squeezed her eyes shut. She was tempted to ask Vi how much longer but was afraid to open her mouth. The hollows dragged their feet and moaned in low throes of agony. Her stomach flipped. *It can't be much longer...*

A tremendous pressure popped inside her eardrums. The harsh crimson color behind her eyes faded to mottled, buzzing darkness.

"We're here."

Damp, cobblestone walls surrounded them, and rushing water echoed through the chamber. *Are we in the sewers?* A lantern of gravelight flickered. The individuals in the room were dressed in a motley of colors—from dark grays to flushed reds. Terrayn stood with her muscular arms crossed beside guild master Irryn, and two luminaries of Juno healed an injured man lying on a table. Theobald pushed his glasses up as he hunched over a map as a shadow slinger pointed at something. Theobald nodded.

"Surprise!" Imogen said, "You touched more hearts than you thought."

She scanned the room. She knew how to find Alistair. She knew which shadowy corners they preferred. She knew which chairs and window ledges they favored. They were undeniably good at not being unseen, and Maeve felt immense privilege and joy when they locked eyes.

"Alistair." Her heart sparked like one of her old spells to Juno.

Alistair's left cheek was swollen, and a freckle of blood swam in the whites of their eye. Their lean, muscled arms encased her like amber trapping an insect. She pressed her face into their familiar dark leather. *They're both safe and alive.*

"You truly must have the purest heart in all of Estoria to be crying over a bastard like me," Alistair said, catching Maeve's tear with their thumb.

"Stop it," admonished Maeve, "give yourself more credit."

She wanted to ask Alistair about the captives and Hagken's activities and how this rebellion came to sequester beneath the city.

She wanted to tell her partners about her fever dream and communion with Janis. *There are so many stories to tell, and we're running on borrowed time.* She doubted Hagken was ignorant about his citizens hiding in the sewers. *Unless above ground is more chaotic than I imagine.*

"We have a lot to catch up on," Imogen said, "but first, has anyone seen a left hand?" She held up her hollow's stumped wrist. "Because otherwise, I'm gonna need some materials to make a new one."

30

The sewers expanded and stretched like veins throughout a body. The rebellion built their workstations around copper tanks and pipes. She cracked her knuckles before continuing to grind blood-wormwood into the mortar. The herb released a temporary paralyzing effect when it entered the bloodstream. *I never imagined using my knowledge of herbs to prepare for a fight.* She declined to help the alchemists engineer poisons. *My people from Ferne are going to be among Hagken's soldiers. I don't want to hurt them.* Alistair rescued twenty of her neighbors and brought them to Silvercliff, and she was grateful that a small percentage of Ferne was safe. The alchemists worked in a line, their prosthetics shining in the light, mixing powder and liquid into fragile glass jars. The sealed jars were passed to the shadow-slingers. She asked Imogen what the alchemists were creating.

"Liquid shadow." Imogen picked through the scattered metal pieces on her worktable.

Alistair said, "Shadow-slingers can't summon shadows." They coated an arrowhead in the paste of blood-wormwood and set it alongside the others. "We can only manipulate existing shadows. A vial of liquid shadow allows for more..." Alistair twisted the arrowhead between their fingers. "Creativity."

Creativity. The pink paste scraped along the sides of a wooden bowl.

"Alistair, do you call to Janis when manipulating shadows?"

"No." They frowned. "Why?"

"Janis gave me something, but I can't reach it." Maeve massaged her cramped fingers.

"There's plenty of shadows down here," said Imogen, pointing at them with her screwdriver.

"It doesn't work like that," Maeve said. She needed to establish a relationship with Janis. That's how it worked with Juno. Why wouldn't it work the same with her sister? Devotion and servitude were intrinsic to divine connections.

"Says who?" Imogen snorted.

"Imogen," Maeve said gently, "you don't understand. The members within the conclave trained hard to earn Janis' blessing. They went through trials to understand her gifts. I worked with the reverent shadow, the highest member of the conclave, and I couldn't learn anything. I can't stop death or move through shadows like Alistair. There must be a reason this gift is locked inside of me. Janis must want me to prove myself, or she needs me to sacrifice something." She looked at Alistair. "Right?"

"Stop relying on what you think the gods want you to do," Imogen interjected before Alistair could reply, "and try something."

Try something? The shadows flickered on the wet walls. She wanted to call Janis and ask the goddess of secrets and moonlight for answers but refrained. *She said I had the key.* Imogen's words rang inside her skull. *Remember the warding stone? Alistair triggered it without niceties or prayers of devotion.* Janis gave Maeve this gift because she wanted it. *And maybe wanting is enough.* Her desires were neglected seeds beneath the soil. All her dreams of traveling the world were laid to rest long before her mother walked the eternal flame. But this power could make a difference. It could change fate.

She stretched her calloused hands and pressed against the locked door within. Her doubts threatened to devour like termites against her hopeful foundation. There were no indoctrination rituals or thousands of nightly trials. *Janis is unlike her sister.* A shadow jumped across her knuckles. *I have to stop treating them as the same.* The lock twisted, tumblers and gears clicking into place, metal teeth grinding against metal teeth. *This power belongs to me. It's mine.*

To the surprise of Maeve and her companions, a dome of shadow ruptured over Imogen's workbench.

"Maeve!" Alistair grabbed her shoulder. "Is this you? This is you, isn't it?"

"It's me." Maeve waited for fatigue or nausea to consume her, but the sensation never arose. *Bismuth theorized that Juno's power came from my life force. Where does this magic come from?* She examined the unchanged lines on her palm. Whose fate could be changed? Hers? Hagken's? Or was it grander than that? The commotion brought two unknown alchemists and guild master Irryn to their table.

"Huh." Irryn probed the shifting darkness and said, "A conjured darkness. Can you create it at will?"

"I think so."

Maeve couldn't say what else the powers were capable of. She could use these powers as she pleased. She never had freedom before and wasn't allowed to dream of a life bigger than the fences surrounding Ferne. She was untethered from Juno and her divine tenants, but the lack of title and connection no longer terrified her. Maeve was free to do what she wanted for the first time in her life. *I'm going to destroy the moonstone and save Pyrite and Ferne.* She slid her hand over Alistair's, *and afterward, I will see the world alongside them.* Her promises and goals hadn't changed, but the future had. Maeve had no control over whether or not her connection to Juno returned. And she couldn't sit idly by and wait for Juno. This was her new path.

"Good." Irryn said, "Hagken won't know what hit 'em."

Everyone gathered in the central cistern beneath a complicated maze of pipes. Alistair stood at the head of the table, and a glowing lantern painted their curls ruddy, flickering orange and copper, like blood and dark water.

Alistair circled an entry point on the map and said, "We'll enter the three spires district from here."

The three spires were at the center of Pyrite, surrounded by homes. Maeve disliked fighting Hagken within a residential area, but her objections were overruled. The argument was that they needed to strike Hagken before a clerk of Theadora officially swore him in. 'He'll petition that Pyrite needs a strong ruler since the council is gone. He's got the support of the merchant guild, plenty of coin, an army, and Cara's influence,' Alistair had said. Maeve thought the politics of the situation were backward. She couldn't understand how Pyrite would accept Hagken for a second time without input from its people. But Hagken never played by the rules. He slaughtered General Fenris' council and established his army within the city. And if General Fenris returned from the mountains someday, then Hagken would have him arrested and executed without trial, as he planned to do with Alistair. The longer they waited to stop him, the further his claws would dig into the city.

"I'll go this way." Irryn rapped her knuckle against another marking. "It's where I have the sentinels waiting. But it will take us some time to reach the three spires from Thorduun's quarter, so plan for that."

Maeve said, "Sentinels?"

Irryn's dark eyes pinned her like a spider, sinking its fangs into prey. "Bismuth called the deal off, but it was you and I who shook hands."

"Even after what we did to your guild?" Her guilt gnawed at the bones of her throat.

"Which time?" She smirked, and Maeve's scalp prickled. She tossed a toxic chemical into the dining hall, Imogen released her hollows, and Alistair killed several alchemists to save her. Her guilt chewed deeper. She wrapped herself in the injustice of Gregor's death without taking accountability for the others. Yet, Irryn agreed to hold up her end of the bargain. *Set in stone, set in bone.* A deal witnessed by Calorum, crafted by stone and salt, and the words held together like the bones within the body. If deals held such immense power within Pyrite, then it was no wonder Hagken managed to keep his allies.

"Settle your bad blood after the snake's dead," Terrayn interrupted, "how do we reach Hagken? I'm not discrediting the ability of our shadow-slingers, but we have merely a handful, and Hagken will arrive at Theadora's temple with his entourage."

"I've thought of that," Alistair said, "we're going to have to move in groups. Imogen, you'll need to take your hollows through the north end. Cara tends to fight on Hagken's left side. Your hollows are a match for her spirit magic. Vi, you'll take your archers through the south, and Maeve can help you remain unseen."

Vi, standing beside Alistair, winked at Maeve, and Imogen snickered.

"We'll need another force sent to the castle," Theobald said timidly, "to dissuade reinforcements."

Alistair shook their head. "We don't have the strength for that."

"Block the castle." Everyone's eyes snapped to her, and she tucked her hands into her pockets. She was out of her element, but she wanted to protect people. Thorduun's quarter used arcane magic to keep the city safe, and she used to summon shields using Juno's light. Why use people like living shields when they had other alternatives?

"Instead of sending the guardians to the spires, send them to the castle and have them block the gates." She shrugged. "I don't know. It's an idea."

"And it's a decent one," Irryn said, "the castle is closer to me than Theodora's temple."

"Then let's do it," Alistair said and returned to outlining and shifting pieces across the map, their expression focused and humorless. Maeve sank into the background noise, and her eyes unfocused. The lantern light reflected off the copper tubing, creating a blurred, distorted circle around Alistair's dark head. *A heavy crown upon your head.* Maeve twisted her ring. Was this the prophecy the Crone spoke of during her first night in Pyrite? Did she see Alistair, surrounded by unlikely allies, leading a charge to stop their adopted father? *What else does your future hold, Alistair Jas'dune?*

"What happens after we stop him?" Maeve asked, "Because we can't leave the guilds in charge. No offense, Irryn."

Everyone turned to Alistair. Alistair held their hands up as if to stop their questioning stares.

"We'll hold the city until we can reach General Fenris and a new council can be chosen and sworn in."

She touched Alistair's wrist. "You're staying in Pyrite?"

She couldn't imagine it. Alistair didn't love this city, not in the way she loved Ferne. They didn't want a crown or the burden of leadership. What changed? *They were supposed to come to Ferne with me, raise horses, and travel the world.*

Their eyes closed as if her words pained them.

"Maeve," they said her name like a prayer. It brimmed with worship and adoration. It burned with love, and her heart skipped like a stone across the water to hear it. "I can't leave Pyrite vulnerable to another ambitious madman. I trust the people at this table, and I trust that we have Pyrite's best interests at heart—"

"You don't need to explain it," said Maeve, "I understand."

She knew better than anyone the sense of responsibility that came with worrying for an entire population. And she knew of Alistair's life before their meeting. They lost their father and then spent years at Hagken's beck and call while watching Maren die. They hid in shadows and became a weapon, a tool. They could've left her side but chose to stay. They risked their life for her. They killed for her. She loved Alistair as profoundly and reverently as she loved Imogen. She wouldn't try to stop them if they wished to stay in Pyrite. Pyrite would benefit from Alistair's generous and gentle heart.

"Theobald and I could take refugees to Galena." Terrayn slid a small wooden ship to a nearby coastal town north of Silvercliff in the same bay as Pyrite. "We can't rely on the shadow-slingers to take everyone through the web."

Alistair looked relieved by the change in topic. "But we already have refugees from Ferne in Silvercliff."

"Galena is closer."

Imogen's cold metal fingers slid through Maeve's. Alistair would stay in Pyrite, but Imogen could return with her to Ferne. She wanted to see her people settled and safe before she left. *Everdawn,* she thought of the shifting red sands from her storybooks. *We'll go to Everdawn first.* And she would pay respects to her mother's spirit at dawnbreak priory. Hagken wouldn't take this future from her. She wouldn't allow it.

* * *

Their meeting ended, and Alistair pulled her and Imogen aside. Since Maeve's arrival, their private moments had been few and far between, and she relished the quiet intimacy they shared as they huddled together in the low light. Alistair kissed Imogen's brow and held Maeve's cheek with their hand.

"It's temporary," Alistair said urgently, "I'll rejoin you as soon as the city is stable."

"That could take years," said Imogen, "you'd make us wait so long?"

"Would you hate me if I did?" A rogue curl fell against Alistair's brow.

"Never." Maeve unfastened her amulet of Juno. A gift from her mother, her anchor in times of stress, a memento to the women and healers of her life. She couldn't claim to be a priestess of Juno anymore, but Juno's light guided her, and Alistair would need a little light to traverse the dark unknowns of Pyrite's future. Their path wouldn't be easy even if they located General Fenris within the hematite mountains and established a new council within the year.

"Hold onto this for me," her voice was thick with emotion, "I want it back when we see each other again."

"Only if you name a foal after me." The amulet dangled from their gloved fingers, and its golden surface bounced with light like a dying sun.

She extended her hand, and Alistair shook it. She promised herself that it wouldn't take years to see Alistair again. She wanted to see Everdawn first, but that didn't mean she couldn't travel north to Pyrite afterward.

Imogen said, "Set in stone, set in bone."

They crashed into each other in an embrace of tight limbs and shuddered breaths. Maeve squished between Imogen and Alistair, like during the equinox when they offered her secrets and their hearts. Maeve knew sleep wouldn't come easily to any of them tonight. Tomorrow, they would end this, and Pyrite's fate would irrevocably change.

31

She walked through the dirty, ribbon-scattered street alongside Vi's troop through the merchant's quarter and toward the three spires. A frowning elderly woman swept up shards of glass outside her home and told her neighbor that she felt a storm in the air and the repetitive clang of hammers rang out as two men repaired their merchant stall. *I hadn't realized this much damage bled out from Thorduun's quarter.* Maeve missed the familiar acidic, smoky taste in the air from roasted fish and baked clam shells and missed the children running and weaving through adults' legs.

Pyrite was subdued. The rambunctious energy bowed and bent at the whims of Hagken and his forces. The gold and white streamers fluttered in tatters in the stale wind, and her heart ached. How many citizens fled? And how many happily supported Hagken? She wished his celebration hadn't been a masquerade; she could've seen and remembered their faces after the tides had turned. She manipulated the shadows as Vi instructed her to keep their group hidden from the guards and the citizens. Anyone not within their inner circle was seen as a danger or a risk.

"This way," Vi said.

The buildings and houses in this district weren't as vertically stacked as those closer to the wall and within the merchant quarter but were higher than those near the docks. Her fingers cramped as she climbed the hemp rope and scrambled onto the slanted rooftop. Pyrite sprawled below, and Theadora's sandstone tower peered judgmentally down at her beneath a painfully blue sky. *Don't look at me like that. We're doing this to save Pyrite.* A collective murmur of voices buzzed like a kicked hornet's nest.

Vi passed her a pair of goggles that allowed her to see in the distance, and Maeve sought Imogen's hollows moving in from the north. *There's Imogen;* Maeve sighed, relieved, and angled the goggles downward to check for Alistair's signal. The concentric space between the three spires crowded with Hagken's soldiers to block the citizens from entering Theadora's temple. *So many innocent people.* She glanced warily at Vi as they drew their short bow from their back.

"Vi." She swallowed. "I have an idea."

Her allies spent their morning dissecting each piece of the plan until Maeve memorized it. But failure loomed like a dark cloud on the horizon, promising cold rain and chained shackles. *Hagken will execute all of us if he can, except for me. I can't stay here safe with the archers and let others die.*

Vi quipped, "Rather last minute."

"I have to confront him," she said, "the moonstone can only be destroyed by me."

An abrupt burst of inky, liquid darkness saturated the area outside Theadora's temple. Alistair's signal. Her heart froze. She teetered at the edge of the rooftop. It was time for her to conjure her shadows to provide cover and flexibility for the shadow-slingers, but she needed to get down. Hagken stepped from the temple wearing ceremonial robes of burgundy and black.

Vi gripped her shoulder. "Use the shadows."

"What?"

"Use them. Go!"

A slight nudge and Maeve lost her balance. She toppled. Her head flipped over her heels. The wind whistled through her ears. Her scream stuck in her throat. A wintry panic seeped into her bones, and the shadows coalesced around her limbs. She didn't want to hit the cobblestones below. It would kill her. *Gods, how do the shadow-slingers avoid death?* She had never learned the technique. The shadows latched onto something—the building? Another shadow? She couldn't be certain, but her body abruptly righted itself, and her feet slammed onto the stones outside the temple, and the shadows wafted off her in waves of black smoke.

A pair of gray eyes impaled Maeve through the lawless rush of bodies. The afternoon sunlight glinted off his silver armor and dark green gauntlets. Though his expression was grim and tired, he held the same steely determination, a leader's calm and pragmatic energy.

"My king." He drew his great sword from behind his back and stood at Hagken's side with both hands on the pommel. "I will handle this. Please, get to safety."

Maeve clenched her jaw. He was the same man, the same soldier, loyal to a king who would destroy him if necessary. *But he isn't heartless. He chose to save Cara instead of following his orders to protect me.*

"Would you let Hagken kill Cara?" she called out to him, "if the ritual called for her spirit instead of mine?"

Calom paused.

"I would never hurt Cara." Hagken drew his sleeves up to his elbows and revealed badly scarred arms.

Yes, you would. Her anger bubbled inside her chest. Before, she would've stifled that anger and let it corrode her. Today was different. She was different. She wasn't bound by the same laws or lies as before. Her righteous anger propelled her forward.

Calom stepped in front of Hagken.

"I would have preferred if you returned to the temple, sire," Calom said conversationally.

"I would never miss this." Hagken steepled his fingers together. "Remember, I need her alive."

Calom looked annoyed but then schooled his features back into flat concentration. He thrust his sword into the ground, and Maeve pressed her tongue against her teeth. She planted her feet. She knew she was unmatched, but all she needed to do was to keep Calom preoccupied until Imogen's hollows or Alistair's team breached the guards.

Calom rushed her. His speed surprised her, but she could protect herself. A wall of inky darkness manifested between herself and Calom.

He lifted his fist. Hagken laughed. His dark gauntlet shattered through her shield. *What? How?* His blow connected with her nose in a sickening, powerful crunch, and her nose gushed with blood. She stumbled backward, her eyes watering and stinging, and choked around the metallic taste at the back of her throat. Calom's face radiated triumph. *The gauntlets,* Maeve pinched her nose; *they're made of the same mineral that Bismuth used on her shackles.* Hagken's forces must've raided the alchemist guild after Irryn went underground.

Calom said, "I knew I saw a spark of rebellion in you."

He lunged. He outclassed her in weight, height, and experience.

She needed to do her earlier technique from the rooftop. She had to. She randomly picked a shifting shadow from a fighting guardsman. Her body latched into it, pulling her through a momentary vortex of darkness before she landed where she wanted to. Calom spun, snarling, and stalked toward her.

His maroon cloak snapped behind him in the breeze. Calom underestimated her. He believed she was weak. Her blood-covered lips twitched. *Be creative, be creative;* she scanned the crowd. *And try something.* She outstretched her hand, and a hazy swirl of darkness wrapped around Calom's head, creating a nebulous black halo.

"I don't need my sight to stop you, healer." Calom dropped to one knee and pressed his fingertips against the stone.

What is he doing? Maeve used the moment of respite to look around. A column of smoke rose from the northern end of the street. *Imogen,* Maeve touched her ring. *I hope she's giving Cara a hard time.* A volley of arrows crested overhead like a swarm of blackbirds flying through the air.

Hagken shouted, "Pathetic!" The arrows were veered off-course by a gust of swirling magic.

Calom launched from his crouched form and rushed her. She scrambled, planning to use a shadow step to escape, when Calom's hand snatched her wrist. They grappled, elbows twisting, the pain radiating through Maeve's limbs and joints. She had forgotten Alistair said Hagken's closest could fight blindfolded.

"Surrender," he spat, "Hagken wants you alive. Make it easy for yourself."

"No!" She wrestled against him. "He wants me alive because I'm useful. What happens to you when you're not useful to him anymore?"

Calom threw her to the ground. She gasped as the wind was

knocked from her lungs. He straddled her. His weight crushed her stomach. He locked his hands around her throat, and a swarm of spots danced in front of her vision as she gasped for air. Her fingers slid on the shiny surface of his armor. His face doubled in her vision, and she reached for him. *I made it this far. I can't let them take me.* The dark halo around Calom's head faded, and his quicksilver eyes narrowed. Her palm pressed his cheek, and her fingertips slid against his abrasive stubble.

Something warm and wet splashed onto Maeve's face. His grip weakened. The shaft of an arrowhead protruded from Calom's neck. His body slumped and fell forward onto her. She wiggled her hand from his face to his neck and checked his pulse. *Alive but paralyzed.* It wouldn't last long. She couldn't say Calom was a good person, but he wasn't as corrupted as Hagken.

"I forgive you for not honoring our life debt," she whispered, "I will give you that small comfort before Janis claims your spirit."

She slid out from beneath him and quelled her ingrained healer instincts to bind his wound. Her skin prickled with cooling sweat, and she faced Hagken with her hands fisted at her sides. *I will end this one way or another. I will see the people of Ferne freed from you. I will see Alistair freed from you.*

"Your magic has changed," Hagken noted, "but you are no match for the champion of the betrayers."

A surge of dark, maelstrom energy slithered toward her, and she dodged it with the shadow step. Hagken's spell split into two, forking like a snake's tongue, and careened off toward other targets. He hit two of his soldiers. Their armor was paper against this cursed magic. Their skin withered and decayed, and their bodies dissolved to ash. Hagken's eyes were strangely reptile in the sunlight. She dug her heels into the vibrating ground. *Irryn must've released another sentinel.*

She noticed a hollow running past from the corner of her eye. *And Imogen is closer, too.* Hagken was losing this fight. He just didn't know it yet. She pulled the twin-head viper from her belt and exhaled slowly.

"A dagger?" He laughed. "Neither steel nor iron can pierce my skin. Don't you understand, Maeve? I am chosen. I am your emperor! I will unite Estoria to the far reaches of the citrine deserts, and you"—he pointed at her—"you will return my Maren's spirit to me, and we will ascend to godhood."

Maeve clutched the blade's hilt. *I wish Alistair were here. They'd have better luck at this.* But Alistair was fighting their own battle. She manifested a shadow in front of Hagken and stepped into it. She sank the blade into his shoulder, piercing his ceremonial dark red robes, and grabbed the moonstone with her free hand. She yanked it from its chain and stepped into a different manifested shadow. *I just stabbed someone.* Her knees shook.

Hagken cackled and tore the blade free, unconcerned by the blood saturating his robes.

"You cannot kill me!" Terra's dagger clattered noisily onto the stones.

Maeve filled her palm with cloying, curling shadows. *Come on.* The moonstone was cold in her grasp and yet remained unchanged. *Why isn't it working?* The sunstone shattered when it filled with Juno's light. She assumed the moonstone would break once it was consumed with Janis' shadows.

"Foolish," Hagken proclaimed. Suddenly, two onyx bolts shot out from beneath the cobblestones, speared through the meat of Maeve's thigh, and sank into the left shoulder, impaling her and pinning her. Hot agony burned bright through her veins, blood gushing from the entry points and running sticky and wet down her limbs. The moonstone bounced onto the stones, unchanged and unbroken.

"Did you think you could beat me? You and your paltry rebellion?" An arrow whizzed past his head.

His magic sank its fangs into her skin, penetrating her muscles, and Maeve choked on blood dribbling from her mouth. She didn't call to the gods. She didn't need to. *I can get out of this.* His magic crawled over her legs like an infestation of spiders.

"I won't kill you, Maeve," he said, "not until the full moon."

She tried to cling to a shadow and twist out from Hagken's grasp. Yet, his bolts kept her in place. She trembled, recalling the bolt impaled in Imogen's fair skin. An explosion in the distance rumbled beneath her feet. One of Hagken's rings was fashioned into a talon point, and he used the sharp tip to carve a line into his wrist. His blood dripped onto the stones, and his magic slithered through the air. An intricate webbing of crimson bubbled and grew around herself, Hagken, and Calom's prone body. The next arrow bounced off of his blood-borne shield.

"You will sleep," Hagken said, "until I need you."

Maeve gnashed her teeth. "Stay away from me!"

A shadow encircled her and repelled Hagken from approaching. He snarled, his teeth yellow and sharp. Her pulse throbbed in her neck, and without prompting or conscious thought, a myriad of cosmic threads manifested before her. She gasped, but Hagken didn't react. *He can't see them.*

It was a complicated and fibrous network of shifting and spinning iridescent colors. A thread connected to Calom's spine pulsed with a nodule of light. *His spirit?* The light burned red and thrashed against the call to enmesh deeper into the network. She thought Janis collected spirits without resistance, but Calom's spirit refused to detach from his body. *He doesn't want to die.* She nudged the light closer to Calom's spine, and it vanished.

He coughed. *He's alive!* Calom pushed himself up onto his feet with one hand clutching his injured neck. She saved him and pushed his spirit back into his body, but to what end? *I'm meant to change Hagken's fate, not Calom's.* She saved Calom's life twice now, but she knew better than to assume he'd honor the debt and save her life in return.

"Duskryn," Hagken snapped, "fetch the moonstone for me. I require it." The skin around his face drooped. The fibrous threads wavered but couldn't touch Hagken; it was as if he had an invisible arcane shield. *Janis said she couldn't collect his spirit.*

Calom struggled. He pressed his gauntlet against Maeve's weak shield and shattered it without resistance. His pale face gleamed, and his hair hung limp. Her throat tightened and prickled. *Hagken can't win. I have to destroy the moonstone and save everyone.* She clutched the shaft, impaling her leg. It wouldn't break. It wouldn't break.

"Don't do this," she said desperately, "the moonstone must be destroyed."

"Don't listen to her. She's a vessel for Maren. That's all she is. Now, bring me the moonstone, Duskryn."

A layer of blood congealed around Calom's neck and seeped through the gaps in his gauntlet. A hollow screeched and slammed itself against Hagken's blood-woven webbing, and Maeve searched the thrashing bodies for Imogen's blonde head. There were more shadow-slingers and alchemists than Hagken's soldiers, but Maeve couldn't see her allies or partners. The pain stabbed sharp fins through the gummy tissue of her lungs.

"This wound will kill me," he rasped, "Gods, Cara is going to be unbearable."

That's the difference between Hagken and Calom, Maeve thought; *Calom has someone who loves him.* Hagken's magic twisted like a knife in her stomach. Her chest spasmed, but something cold and bright burning in the back of her skull stopped her from collapsing, and the interwoven threads pulsated in time with her heartbeat.

"The stone, Calom! I need the stone," yelled Hagken.

Maeve asked, "Did he punish you after I escaped?"

Calom knelt before Maeve with his head bowed. His labored breath chafed over his lips and a fraught line of tension buried itself between his eyebrows. The threads of fate converged around him, and Maeve witnessed innumerable lifetimes that Calom might've lived. *A painter, a father, an explorer,* her heart anxiously tripped at the sight of Cara, *and he's looking after his sister within every lifetime.*

"If Cara's ritual fails to reunite Maren with Hagken," Maeve said urgently, "what will happen to her? What will her punishment be? Are you willing to risk her life?"

Hagken's cruelty wasn't reserved for his enemies. The wind tousled Calom's pallid hair, and he lifted his exhausted, bloodless face to meet her eyes. A thunderous storm brewed within him.

"You can't save yourself Calom, but you can save her," she whispered.

The crimson nodule of light writhed across his pale throat. She sensed his energy weakening. The goddess of death was beckoning Calom's stubborn spirit to enter her web.

"Consider our debt paid, Maeve Theywnn." The moonstone crushed between Calom's fist, and sparkling, white dust drifted from his palm into the wind.

Maeve prevented Calom's spirit from leaving his body. He slumped forward, unconscious. *Hang on a little longer, Calom.* She didn't know if she could thwart Janis from collecting his spirit, but she would try for his sake. His good deed shouldn't go unrewarded. *He turned the tides back in our favor.*

"No! No!" Hagken stumbled, screaming, as viscous black ooze poured from between his lips. "Duskryn, I curse you!" His eyes bulged from within his skull.

There was a sudden, loud, suckling sound. At the junction of Hagken's neck, something wet and black oozed from his skin like a speared egg yoke. The ooze dribbled out and congealed. He screamed louder. His shoulder tore open. His hands curled into claws. Something crawled and pushed its way out from Hagken's body and formed a second, grotesque head. The pulsing, black pimple peeled back to reveal layered rows of sharp teeth. His screams sweetened to uproarious, triumphant laughter. His crimson barrier disintegrated, and a shower of blood-red ash rained onto them. The bolts impaling Maeve sank into the upset ground and slithered to Hagken. She adjusted her weight off her injured leg and clutched her throbbing shoulder.

The hollows surged toward Hagken. The creature inside Hagken gorged into a hollow's shoulder with its teeth, and a scream of pain vibrated Maeve's eardrums. A flicker of shadow emerged at the corner of Maeve's vision.

"Hello, sunshine."

Alistair's dagger spun through the air, but Hagken's claw swiped it aside. He slammed his claw into the ground and fractured the stones, upsetting the hollows and knocking them off-balance. His eyes were wild. His head lolled strangely to the side as pieces of floppy, pink skin hung from the exit point of the abomination's head.

"The moonstone?" asked Alistair while using one of Maeve's shadows to side-step an attack.

"Gone."

The dark abomination writhed and whipped its bulbous head before it lunged for Alistair. Hagken's power was weakened. She sensed it in the fibrous threads that now clung to his skin and threatened to pull him in. *A spiderweb finally catching its prey.* Maeve conjured a pool of shadow around Hagken. His claw slashed at Alistair, cutting through the air.

"I should've bargained for your spirit instead of mine to save Maren," Hagken said.

Alistair smirked at him. "My spirit is certainly worth more."

Their daggers plunged into Hagken's eye socket and through the top of the abomination's head. Hagken released an astonished, wet, and red laugh. Alistair withdrew their blades with a clean, precise movement, and Hagken fell to his knees, reaching for Maeve and mumbling Maren's name. The thing attempting to crawl out of Hagken squirmed for a few seconds and then went still. It lay like a puddle of slick, dark oil around his corpse.

She thought she would feel guilt or relief standing over Hagken's dead body. She didn't. A sense of pity filled her heart.

"It's over." Maeve breathed, gratefully leaning into Alistair's side. "Where's Imogen?"

"She took her group to Juno's temple to protect the healers."

Maeve scooped her hands beneath Calom's armpits and ignored the pain that ran down her leg. "Help me carry him."

32

A scream cut through the soft cries of misery reverberating throughout Juno's somber temple. Cara barreled past the priestesses and luminaries and latched her hands around Maeve's throat, squeezing air from her lungs. Her jade eyes shone with tears, and her face contorted.

"What have you done?" she snarled, "you killed him, didn't you? I saw you fighting!"

Imogen pulled at Cara's wrist. "We're helping him, you bonehead!"

"Unhand her!" Allustera stood from Calom's side, and the blood running from her nostrils smeared her golden makeup. "Otherwise, the man will die."

Cara's gaze hardened.

"I'm not a priestess anymore, Cara," Maeve choked out, "I couldn't heal him."

Calom's red spirit wavered, and Maeve clutched it tighter.

Calom saved them, saved her. She wouldn't release him. Janis would have to come and collect this spirit herself if she wanted it. She was tired of losing and tired of hitting obstacles. Calom would live. She would save him as she saved Imogen.

"I don't rely on gods." Her eyes glowed with misty, lilac light and obscured her pupils. She released Maeve and fell to her knees beside her brother. She gripped his pale face between her hands and whispered to him.

"We go together or not at all."

Alistair shook Cara's shoulder. "Cara, think rationally."

What is she doing? The web of fate, with its hundreds of light nodules, twisted and writhed like a fishnet caught within the churning depths of a storm. Cara's eyes curdled to a milky white. Her head snapped backward, her arms spread, and her voice resonated in lilting incantations. A hundred rivers of lilac light poured from her skin and filled the temple. Cara's light and the threads converged and intersected in a helix of radiance. The injured citizens and soldiers within the temple groaned, and their spirits surged toward Cara. Maeve gripped Imogen and Alistair's hands. *Is she sacrificing their spirits to save him?* His crimson spirit darkened to garnet and doubled in size. It quivered, and Maeve held it steady.

"Cara," Maeve shouted, "you don't have to do this. Allustera can heal him."

"I don't know if I can," Allustera said quietly, "unless you have the sunstone."

A voice drifted into Maeve's mind like cold snow. "If you wish to keep my gift and save the dying within the temple, then you must release Calom's spirit," Janis said, "let him return to the web."

She frowned. *How alike are Calom and Alistair?* Alistair followed orders from their stepfather, and Maeve vouched for their redemption. She wanted Calom to have the same opportunity. He should face trial and judgment like anyone else. His last act had been an act of love and protection for his sister. She would have done the same for Alistair, Imogen, Bertha, or any children in Ferne. *No, he should live. I'm not letting anyone die. He has to face retribution for everything he's done.*

"Take it back then."

She didn't want to be at the whim of the gods anymore. *My grandmother, my mother, and I gave everything to Juno.* She didn't want the cycle to repeat with Janis. She lived most of her life in service to others. It was time for something else, something new—a life on her terms. A searing white-hot pain exploded within Maeve's skull. She writhed, clutching her head, and was vaguely aware of her partner's shouts of alarm and concern. Someone drove a hot poker through her ears. It lasted hours. It lasted seconds.

Cara finished her chant, and the following silence was deafening.

"What did you do?" Allustera said, horrified.

"The spirits of others to save my brother," Cara said, "death has its uses." Her left eye was milk-white and blind. Calom's chest steadily rose and fell. Maeve scanned the shocked and terrified faces of priestesses and luminaries. One of Hagken's soldiers sat up in his bedroll and promptly vomited.

"I should ban you from my temple," Allustera's voice sharpened, "spirit magic is outlawed."

"Go ahead and arrest me then." She smirked and snapped her fingers. "Oh wait, you can't. Half of the justiciars are in prison, and the other half are dead."

Allustera glared. "Leave us, spirit mage. Immediately." Her blood-covered hands flickered orange and red.

Cara reached into her silver-trimmed coat and tossed a handful of bones onto the ground. The three priestesses assisting Allustera backed away, nearly tripping over each other. Cara scoffed. The bones congealed into misshapen skeletons that looked half-animal, half-human. The creatures lifted Calom into their arms at Cara's vague beckoning.

"I know it's blasphemy," Imogen whispered to Maeve, "but it's kind of neat."

Maeve bit her tongue. Cara's magic was terrifying, not fascinating. But Imogen's mind worked differently. *I hope Bismuth never gets her hands on a spirit mage.* She feared to know what the world might look like with such a combination.

Alistair cleared their throat. "Cara, you and your brother will need to stand trial for your part in Hagken's crimes against Estoria."

Cara tossed her braid over her shoulder. "Alongside you?" Surrounded by an unconscious Calom and her necrotic creatures, Cara relaxed into the term 'grotesque' like a queen relaxing into her throne.

Alistair shared a look with Maeve and nodded.

"I'm looking forward to it, shadow general."

* * *

Maeve squeezed the top of her oak cane as she walked with freshly cut linens draped over her arm. The late afternoon light poured into Juno's temple like liquid gold, spilling over the oak tree branches and reflecting off the hanging trinkets. Maeve winced while lowering herself beside an injured shadow slinger and began the slow, careful task of unwinding the wrappings around his wrist.

"Lady Maeve." A young, boyish priestess approached her. "I can heal your injuries."

"Leave it be," she said, "I'll be okay."

Let the wounds heal naturally; I'll carry their scars as a reminder of my journey through the dark. Besides, she preferred Juno's light to be used on those in dire need rather than herself, especially after Cara's ritual. The priestess looked uncertain but bowed their head in acknowledgment, and her heart swelled with sympathy. She knew from experience how difficult it was to walk away from someone who was hurt. She rinsed her hands, letting the cool water stroke across her knuckles and mounds of her palm, ignoring the twinge of pain in her shoulder. Her motions were methodical and well-practiced. *This is who I am now—a once-priestess forgotten by her goddess. A woman no longer hunted by a mad king and his delusions. A partner to a disgraced alchemist and deposed royalty.*

Allustera joined her. "You know, when you arrived at my temple carrying the sunstone, I thought perhaps Juno found her next champion." She helped Maeve dress the wound. "Do you know the tragedy of Lueltala?"

"Tragedy?" Maeve echoed.

Lueltala, the first champion, and priestess of Juno, traveled across Estoria for decades. She healed blighted lands and the sick and taught the first herbalists the power of flora, fauna, and fungi. She built the city of Everdawn with help from Theadora's champion, Ul'gaar. When Lueltala reached the end of her exceptionally long mortal life, Juno created the sacred flame at the precipice of her temple. It was written that Lueltala walked into that flame and ascended to her resting place. Some scholars believed she lived among the divine after she served Juno. But Maeve couldn't understand how it was a tragedy. She changed the world.

"Lueltala's near immortality came with a price."

"Ah." Maeve sucked her teeth. "Of course it did." She wondered if Estoria's love for bargaining came from the gods or if the gods designed themselves to mirror Estoria's culture.

"It was said that she forgot everything before her championship, including her name." She dabbed at the beading sweat on the shadow-slinger's neck. "I'm relieved to know that you aren't her champion after all."

"As am I."

She would rather have a handful of years with those she loved than a thousand years without them. Juno's championship would've reduced her life to devotion without the joys of love, community, and friendship. Her feelings towards her lack of divine connection to Juno constricted and flowed like the pulse of her heart. In some moments, she missed the connection. She missed how it bonded her to her mother and grandmother after their deaths. She missed the usefulness she felt when she healed. In other moments, she was grateful to be freed of the responsibility. She could heal without divine light. Her usefulness wasn't tied to her self-worth. She was more than a healer. *Moving forward, what new tapestries of my life will be woven with the threads of fate?*

"Hi, my love." Imogen dropped a warm loaf of bread into her lap. "You should eat something."

"She's right." Alistair's mouth was half-full.

"I honestly cannot believe you let her leave," Imogen said, referring to Cara, "do you think she'll turn up to stand trial?"

Maeve interjected, "We have to travel to Hollyhock and release Hagken's captives first."

"And we should contact your elders in Silvercliff," said Imogen.

"By the storms and the sea." Alistair sighed. "It never ends, does it?"

She cupped Alistair's cheek. Pyrite would heal. It would recover. But the path towards healing would be arduous. There would be power struggles, unrest, and various factions trying to fill the void of the council and the vacuum Hagken left behind. She couldn't ask any of the goddesses to swoop in and fix it all. No, no. The days of asking the divine for help were behind her. Pyrite's recovery would be like setting a broken bone into a plaster cast. Her remedies for this task were time, patience, and wisdom.

A bright voice interrupted her reverie, "Lady Maeve!"

Her hand slapped over her mouth in a silent, pained gasp. It was Archie—little, precious Archie, whose arm she healed an eon ago. By the time she got to her feet, Archie was throwing his arms around her midsection and burying his face into her chest. She clung to him. He smelled like freshly turned hay and wheat. The scent reminded her of home, and her tears burned hot.

"Archie! Why? How are you here?"

"I was supposed to be with the horses at the stables," his words came out in a rush, "but I slipped away 'cause I wanted to see the ceremony. I've never seen a crowning ceremony before. But then everything got so scary and..." His face crumpled with anguish. "I really miss father. I thought maybe he'd be out here. You know, protecting the king and stuff."

She hadn't seen Archie's father, but knowing another member of Ferne was somewhere within the city lessened the burden on her heart. She held Archie until his shoulders stopped trembling. He wiped away his snot on the sleeve of his shirt.

"Bertha and Maven are gonna be so excited to see you."

"Maven?"

"She pushed him out before I left from Hollyhock." His smile widened. "I helped. It was gross."

She could've fainted with relief. Not only did Bertha have her child, but she wasn't alone. *They look after one another even without me there.* She was painfully proud of him.

"I'm sure you did amazing. Bertha was lucky to have you nearby." She lightly pinched his cheek. "Archie, this is Imogen, she's an alchemist."

"Wow!"

"And this is Alistair."

"I'm honored to meet you," Alistair said shaking Archie's hand.

Archie's brown eyes widened in awe and Imogen laughed warmly. Maeve sank onto one of the pillows on the floor and ripped her bread into pieces to share with Archie. Archie recounted his experience with Hagken's ceremony. The guards had blocked his way, and he had to scale buildings and market stalls to reach the three spires. *Of course, he went climbing.* She closed her eyes and leaned into Imogen's side, listening and smiling wistfully.

They would travel to Hollyhock, and she'd reunite with Bertha and meet Maven. They'd all go home. *Home.* Her small cottage with its wondrous garden and the sounds of baying sheep. She'd watch the fireflies in the fields with Imogen and drink tea by the hearth. She'd race the children through the pastures. *Home.* Alistair showed Archie the sleight-of-hand trick of a coin flipping along their knuckles. Archie laughed and shyly asked if they could do it again. Maeve's heart flipped.

"I'd like to return to Pyrite after Ferne is settled," she whispered to Imogen.

"You've changed your mind about Everdawn?"

"Everdawn isn't going anywhere," she said, "and neither is the rest of Estoria. I'd rather see Calorum with both of you."

Imogen placed a light, gentle kiss on Maeve's temple. *Home,* Maeve thought, *isn't a place anymore.* She would always love Ferne and see it as a safe place to return to, but her heart belonged to Alistair and Imogen. Her future, her fate, was intrinsically twined together with theirs. The leaves overhead rustled, and twinkling chimes sang a quiet song.

Her fingers played through the motes of divine light. *I've been blessed by two goddesses, one of dawn and one of dusk;* the light circled her wrist, *life and death, love and loss, fate and free will.* Her chest smoldered with tender warmth. It wasn't divine. It belonged to her. And she imagined if she could see her spirit as she saw Calom's, it would burn as bright and hot as a surging bonfire and be as gentle and serene as the moon's reflection on flat water.

Her future rolled and stretched and stretched like the beams of light cutting through the verdant leaves.

Acknowledgments

This book would not have been possible without the generous help of my editor, Terayn. Fun fact: Terrayn, the character, existed long before Terayn, the editor, and I teamed up! I truly believe that she helped me create the absolute best version of Maeve's story as possible and I am so glad that fate decided to intertwine our pathway. Additionally, I want to thank my beta readers, for their comments at 3:00 AM, bringing me to delirious tears.

My friends, for their endless support, kindness, and inspiring me day-in and day-out to be brave and share this piece of myself to the world. My writing buddies – I don't know how I functioned without you.

A massive thank you to Xeninda for helping bring Maeve to life with her gorgeous cover and typography work. I know you shouldn't judge a book by its cover, but this cover is pretty sick, right?

To my readers, this story has lived inside of me for years and writing it has been a life-changing and life-affirming experience. I'm so grateful to have shared this story with you.